WORLD WAR FOUR

ALSO AVAILABLE FROM
ZOMBIE PIRATE PUBLISHING

THE COLLAPSAR DIRECTIVE
RELATIONSHIP ADD VICE
FULL METAL HORROR
PHUKET TATTOO
WITCHES VS WIZARDS

COMING SOON

FLASH FICTION ADDICTION (April 15th, 2019)
FULL METAL HORROR 2 (June 15th, 2019)

WORLD WAR FOUR

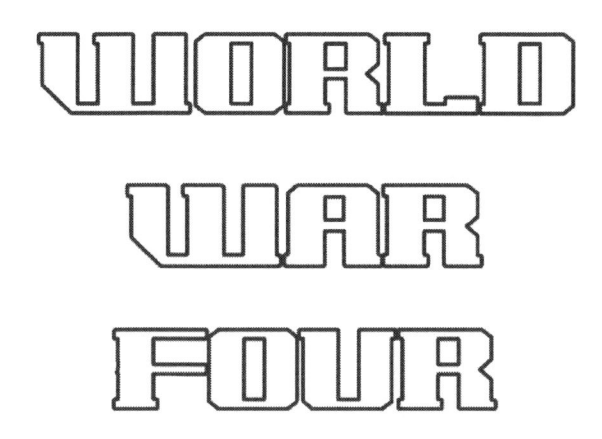

A Science Fiction Anthology

Zombie Pirate
PUBLISHING

Edited By
Adam Bennett and Sam M. Phillips

All characters, locations, events, and science depicted in **WORLD WAR FOUR** are fictional. Any resemblance to real life locations, events, or any person living or dead is entirely coincidental.

All rights reserved. No part of this publication may be reproduced, stored in a retrieval system, or transmitted in any form or by any means, electronic, mechanical, photocopying, recording or otherwise, without the prior permission of the publishers.

The moral right of the authors has been asserted.

First Published March 2019

Cover Art by Adam Bennett and Sam M. Phillips
WORLD WAR FOUR Logo by Adam Bennett
Zombie Pirate Publishing Logo by Zoe Maxwell

I say we take off and nuke the entire site from orbit.
It's the only way to be sure.
- Ellen Ripley

CONTENTS

Foreword - pg 7
The Package - Brian MacGowan - pg 10
World War Foul - Heather Kim Hood - pg 39
Jackson's Revenge - Adam Bennett - pg 48
Monitor Logan - Neal Asher - pg 77
Cold Fusion - Sam M. Phillips - pg 132
Yuddh Ke Khel - Mel Lee Newmin - pg 139
Subject: Galilee - Rich Rurshell - pg 154
War Pig - Gregg Cunningham - pg 178
Joey - James Pyles - pg 206
This Sky is Mine - Blake Jessop - pg 225
The Bunker - David Bowmore - pg 255
The Lazarus Protocol - Marcus Turner - pg 265
Poppy - L.T. Waterson - pg 284
Scum of the Earth - James Agombar - pg 304
Tomorrow - D.M. Burdett - pg 325
The Floabnian Fiasco - Shawn Klimek - pg 334
The Aftermath of the Pig Roast - Marlon Hayes - pg 354
One Way Trip - R.L.M. Cooper - pg 369
Gagarin's Hammer - Vince Carpini - pg 377
Salvage - G. Dean Manuel - pg 398
Wake - K.K. Pieza - pg 424
  Authors Biographies - pg 438
  Acknowledgements - pg 447

FOREWORD

War has always held a morbid fascination for human beings. Perhaps we are built for it. Aggressive and inventive, prone to disputes, with a competitive nature and fear of the unknown, resistant to changes to our lifestyles, and a long memory for past wrongs, it seems conflict between populations is an inevitable part of life.

History certainly indicates so; thousands of years of recorded history, with armed struggles sprouting in every part of the globe. Sure, much of life is lived in peace, and humans are capable of vast compassion, but the peace never lasts, and so our collective psyche is dense with the memory of war, and we are destined to repeat the mistakes of the past. Our future looks certain, there has always been war, and war shall continue, but what will it look like?

The concept of a *world war* has held the imagination of people for the last century. World War One, or the Great War, was the 'war to end all war,' so terrible in its scope that surely it would prove the end of conflict. It was the beginning of a hope that a war could be so horrifying it would turn us off war forever.

No such luck.

Like every great 80's movie, The Great War had a sequel, World War Two, and thus was born a powerful franchise which would hold sway over global politics for the twentieth century and beyond. The echoes of these two world-encompassing wars still linger with us today. It is a little strange that the branding machine chose to take a break but 'world wars' are nothing new, they predate the twentieth century with the Napoleonic Wars, and continued after WWII with the Cold War against communism in the second half of the twentieth century, and the War on Terror in the twenty first. With their multiple theatres of armed conflict and the involvement of global superpowers, all these could be considered a world war.

It seems we've been waiting for something seismic to happen to give it the vaunted title of World War Three. With the dropping of the atomic bombs on Nagasaki and Hiroshima in 1945, it seems everyone has been waiting for a nuclear war for it to be considered on scale with the destruction of the first two world wars. This is the psychological fallout of the Cold War.

But even after the missiles have been launched and half the world blown to hell, there is no guarantee this will end the conflict. Perhaps the world would take a long time to rebuild, but it seems we have the imagination for it as shown in countless video games, books, and films. Franchises such as laser sword swinging *Star Wars* and the bleak and violent battlefields of *Warhammer 40,000* show we are enamoured with the idea of science fiction driven war. Our present lust for technological advancement will not marry well with the aggressive human drive. So we look to the future with the inevitable before us, a bleak vision.

WORLD WAR FOUR

This is a time of conflict; laser beams slice the air, enormous explosions rock the earth, machines of war rumble across ruined futuristic landscapes, men and alien alike battle for profit or ideology, killing and dying in the name of their overlords. Do you dare enter into this affray, where death and danger are ever present, the grim shadow of war hanging over you like a spectre, ready to destroy everything you've ever known? Can you look into the future and imagine what special terrors are waiting for us in the next one hundred, two hundred, *one thousand* years?

Well, imagine no longer, as the future is here, and it's World War Four!

Sam M. Phillips and Adam Bennett
Co-Founders
Zombie Pirate Publishing
Zombiepiratepublishing.com

The Package
Brian MacGowan

"Fire in the hole!"

Master Sergeant Rick Harrington, of the Northern Free States Strategic Response Team, shielded his eyes as the thermite incendiary reduced the lock to molten slag. A team member of *Harrington's Hellhounds* rushed forward to place a magnetic handle on the door; with hands on the device, he waited. Harrington's Heads Up Display indicated that all of the team members were in place.

It had been over a year since NFS Ambassador Barrett and his family were apprehended when the ambassador attempted to smuggle out a data packet of United Alliance encryption codes. The packet also included the identities of UA covert agents operating within NFS territory. Forty-eight hours ago, a mole, operating deep within the UA command structure, located the data packet. The Hellhounds' mission objective was simple: snatch-and-grab the data packet.

"Go. Go. Go!" Harrington broadcasted across the encrypted comms link.

The door was pulled open just enough to allow the men to enter. Infrared beams from their TR-74 tactical rifles danced down the hall. The point team member released a set of drones no larger than peach pits. Within seconds, Harrington's HUD connected to the drones as they flew along the corridor scanning for heat, motion and IR signatures.

"Team One and Two advance to the next point. Team Three, stay here and guard our six." Harrington received a collection of rogers in return. "Move out."

The teams leapfrogged down the passage stopping at each door to ensure that it was secure. Sentinel drones were left at each crossing to further alert them to any wayward hostiles. In case all Hell broke loose, magnetic blasticks were attached to the walls, ceiling and floor at random intervals. If the Hellhounds would be pursued on their way out, detonating the blasticks and collapsing the corridors should dissuade anyone from following too closely behind. The two teams proceeded along a prescribed path for several minutes turning left and right at various intersections.

They came to their next objective; before them stood a set of sealed polished droitium blast doors, five metres tall by three metres wide. Harrington examined the doors, there were no hinges, and barely a visible line down the middle where the doors met. Harrington glanced at both walls; he did not see a keypad or any other way to activate the doors.

Corporal Sanchez, the team's explosive expert, stood beside Harrington.

"Shit, Boss. This thing is not supposed to be here. This should be a standard door. Looks like someone decided to upgrade."

"Can you blow it?"

"Sure, how soon can I get a couple of nukes down here?"

Harrington looked at the chronometer in his HUD. ETA for exfil was one hundred thirty-five minutes.

"Anderson, bring up the schematics. Did we take a wrong turn?"

"No way, Sarge. The package should be one hundred metres past those doors then left at the first corridor."

Harrington backed up to the corridor, looking left and right.

"What's down this way?" He pointed toward the right with the muzzle of his TR-74.

Sergeant Anderson consulted the schematics. "There should be a lab toward the end of the corridor."

"There's another door halfway down. What's it lead to?"

"Maintenance closet of some form."

"Sanchez, on me."

The pair walked down to the maintenance door. "Pop this door. Team two, send a couple of guys back to the last turn and make sure we aren't disturbed."

Once inside, Harrington scanned the room. Tubes, vents, and wiring passed through three of the walls where they either split or combined as they continued their journey elsewhere in the complex.

"What are you looking for, Boss?"

"I was hoping for an access terminal that would allow us to open those doors."

Harrington visually searched the room again.

"Since we're here. Can you drill through these walls, then probe to see what's on the other side?"

"I'll have to go slow, it will take me a couple of minutes."

Harrington looked at the chronometer again. "You've got two."

"Roger, Boss."

Harrington stepped out of the closet to give Sanchez room to work. He walked down the corridor toward the lab. He crept up to the corner, did a quick sneak peek to check for hostiles. He flattened himself against the wall as he studied the image displayed in the corner of his HUD. A thermal scan showed no one present. He zoomed into the image. Harrington pursed his lips. *Fuck!*

Needing to see it for himself, Harrington rounded the corner to the lab. Multiple biohazard lights were blinking red. Negative air pressure, double containment curtains sealed the door.

"Holy Shit! You've got to be fucking kidding me." He muttered to himself.

"Something wrong, Sarge?" Anderson called over the comms link.

"You could say that. They have some form of a bio lab down here. I also know why those doors are down. They aren't blast doors, they're containment."

"So we just got served a bio-shit cake with fuck you icing. What do we do now, Sarge? Abort?"

"My HUD is not picking up anything out of the ordinary in the air. We've got to complete the mission and get the package."

"We don't get paid enough for this shit... are my balls going to fall off?"

"Anderson, the places that you go, I'm surprised that you still have them. Sanchez, how are you doing?"

"I can't get through the two side walls. They're probably droitium as well. The back wall is standard construction, looks like it leads to some sort of storage area."

"Hang tight. I'm coming to you."

Harrington hurried down the corridor to the maintenance room. He studied the back wall with its pipes and vents running across it. Toward the floor, there was less than a metre of clear wall space.

"Show me what we got."

Sanchez linked the video feed to Harrington's HUD. The three-sixty camera gave a distorted view of the storage area where various crates and boxes lay scattered across the room.

Harrington stepped back and pointed to the blank section of wall. "Can you blow a hole there...without waking up the neighbours?"

"I can do my best. But I doubt that Palmer will fit through."

"Do it."

Harrington stepped out of the room. "Palmer, on me."

More than two metres in height, Palmer was a mountain of a man who filled a good portion of the corridor as he approached.

His standard issue TR-74 was strapped across his back. Across his chest was slung Sally, his TCHA-21A heavy assault gun. Normally a team crewed weapon, Palmer handled it with ease by himself.

Harrington led Palmer to the maintenance room door and pointed to the hole that Sanchez had just finished. Not a short man himself, Harrington tilted his head upward to speak to Palmer. "Here's the scoop big guy. The package is on the other side of that hole."

Palmer nodded his head and patted his TCHA-21A. "And we all know how Sally dislikes going through small holes."

"Right, so I need you and Sally to mind our six until we get back. I'm also going to leave you Bishop and Benton from Team Two."

"Roger, Sarge."

Palmer turned and strode back to the corridor crossing. Harrington knew with Palmer and the other Team Two members that the asses of the team moving forward will be well protected.

"Everyone else gather up. We are now Team Alpha and Bravo. Alpha will lead us through the hole to clear and hold the room. Bravo, you get the package. Then we haul ass out of here. Any questions?"

Team One lined up in single file on the safe side of the hole. Another pair of drones were sent through the hole to further scout the room beyond.

Satisfied, Harrington ordered, "Okay, Alpha, lead us through."

The members of Team Alpha scrambled through the hole as quickly as possible, fanning out in the room beyond in order to secure their position. On the 'All Clear' Team Bravo proceeded through the hole gathering on the other side.

Satisfied that they were organised Harrington sent them on their way.

"Okay, Bravo. Secure the package and get it back here ASAP."

Harrington glanced again at his chronometer, they were down to one hundred and eight minutes before exfil. He was relieved that so far they have not encountered any form of resistance, but the active biohazard might have something to do with that. Harrington made a mental note to alert command that his team may be bio hot. He investigated the room for any indication of what might be in the bio lab. Crates with nondescript labels were stacked against the wall.

"Jackson, Hanes, swab and catalogue as many of these as you can."

"Roger."

The two men split up, each taking a different side of the room.

"Bravo, have you secured the package?"

"Not yet, Sarge. The package is here, but it can't be secured in its current state."

Harrington pursed his lips. "Why the fuck not?"

"I'm sending you an image now."

Harrington's HUD indicated an incoming file. As soon as it was downloaded he brought up the image. "Am I looking at a cryosleep chamber?"

"You got it in one, Sarge. This is the only thing here. So it's gotta be the package."

"I'm on my way."

As Harrington jogged down the corridor to Bravo's location he brought up the specs for the operation. The package was described as being brown, lightweight and no more than forty centimetres tall. There was no indication that a cryosleep chamber was involved. As he rounded the corner to the room Harrington saw that two of the team members had assumed tactical positions to ensure no surprises came from their rear. The remainder of the team was standing around a large, horizontal rectilinear container. Harrington recognised it as one of the earlier model cryosleep chambers.

Harrington looked into the chamber where there was a girl of maybe ten-years-old. She was dressed in form-fitting clothing with sensors and probes held close to her body. Along her forehead were attached brain activity sensors.

Harrington's eyes widened. In the chamber, beside her lay a chocolate coloured teddy bear. "Boys, there's our package," he said, pointing.

"What? The girl? She doesn't fit the dimensions."

Harrington pointed. "No, the teddy bear."

"Then we've got a problem, Sarge. Well, actually two problems."

Harrington examined the chamber. "Yeah...unless we want to kill the kid, she needs to thaw out before we can open the chamber. And if she's one of ours, we can't leave her here." He looked under the chamber. "Can we anti-grav this thing out of here?"

"No way, Sarge. It is wired directly to the complex."

"Shit!" Harrington looked at his chronometer again. "How long will it take to revive her?"

"I don't know. Ask Brookes, this kind of stuff is covered in his med training."

"Brookes, grab your gear and double-time it to me." Harrington's voice left the medic no doubt that the request was urgent.

"Roger."

Harrington paced while waiting. "Anderson, We have run into a FUBAR delay. See what you can do about opening that big-ass door."

"Already on it, Sarge. Sanchez has been poking around some of the crates and said that he's found some *fun stuff*. Whatever it is, that door won't stand a chance, but the landlord is gonna be pissed."

"Fuck the landlord. Have Sanchez prep the door but wait for my command to blow it."

"How big of a hole do you want?"

"As big as you can give me."

"I think you just gave Sanchez a hard on."

Harrington shook his head. *Fucking sappers. The bigger the bang the bigger their...*

Brookes rounded the corner before the master sergeant could finish his thought. The medic stopped to take in the scene.

"What's the emergency?"

Harrington pointed to the cryo chamber. "I need that thawed. How long will it take?"

Brookes walked around the chamber, "She's a beaut..." He looked inside. "I mean the chamber... not the girl. She's a... well, a girl." He studied a panel at the head of the chamber. "Her vitals appear to be normal for cryosleep." He tapped on the display panel.

"How long?"

"Uhm, let me check if I have anything on this." Brookes tilted his head to one side and went silent as he searched his HUD's memory for a manual.

Harrington tapped an impatient finger on the stock of his rifle.

Brookes starting tapping buttons. "Looks like forty-five minutes, but she is young so I can probably push that to thirty-five."

Harrington growled. "Exfil is in—" He glanced again at his chronometer. "—eighty three minutes. Bring her around as quickly as possible. If she loses a few toes, we'll grow her some new ones later."

"I'll be as quick as I can, Sarge."

"I'm going back to Alpha. Contact me as soon as you can open that damn chamber."

Harrington jogged back to where Anderson and Sanchez were working on the door. The massive blast doors were covered with a grey putty substance. At each corner, blasticks were stuck in the putty. For good measure, five more were placed toward the centre of the doors. Some of the Alpha team members were stacking crates against the door. Harrington located Anderson.

"So what is that stuff?"

"Sanchez says it is DX-74. He was giggling like a schoolgirl when found it. He said that it should be stable until it is detonated. The bastard dropped some of it on the ground and scared the living shit out of us. I looked up the specs; when it blows, it blows big time."

"Did he need to cover the whole door?"

"At first it was just an 'X' in the centre. But you said to make as big of a hole as possible. You know sappers... there's never enough explosives."

"And the crates are stacked by the doors because...?"

"He said it is to help direct the charge. But I think he just wants to blow more shit up. Besides, it also denies the UAs of those resources."

Anderson flipped his head in the direction of the cryo lab. "How's it going back there?"

"The package is in an old model cryo chamber... along with a ten-year-old girl. I have Brookes thawing her out right now."

Anderson pointed passed the door. "Palmer reports that everything is quiet on his side."

"Shit! I haven't checked in with Team Three."

"Swartz this is Harrington. How's our egress looking."

"Nice of you to remember us. So far so good. Be advised that the acoustics are picking up movement farther inside the complex."

"Roger on the acoustics. Keep an ear on that and advise me as soon as something drastic changes."

"You got it, Sarge."

Harrington glanced at his chronometer. "Exfil in fifty-five. It's going to be tight. I'm heading back to see how Brookes is doing with the popsicle. Get the guys ready to bug out. I'll send word when to blow the door."

"Roger, Sarge."

"And let's hope that whatever caused the biohazard stays in the lab when we blow that door."

Harrington returned to the cryo lab. The team members were standing around swapping war stories. They went silent as soon as the master sergeant entered.

"How we doing Brookes? Tell me some good news."

"Well, the good news is that her vitals are coming up. But it is taking longer than expected to revive her."

Harrington looked down at the chamber and the slumbering girl. "Fuck! Is there any way to speed this up?"

Brookes shrugged his shoulders. "If this was a current chamber, I would shoot her with some CRS-4 and she'd be back in five minutes."

"Shit!" Harrington paused as he did a quick time appreciation analysis. "Here's the problem. Exfil in forty minutes. Without resistance, it is going to take us twenty to get back to the LZ." He tapped on the lid of the chamber. "I need that package."

"I don't know what to say, Sarge. These chambers don't have a CRS port and..." Brookes paused as he ran his hand along the underside of the chamber. He ducked down then back up again. "There's an IV port here. It's not the right size but I should be able to adapt it. Give me a minute."

Brookes rummaged through his med kit for tubing, tape and wound sealing foam. He then pulled out a vial of CRS-4 that connected to the tubing.

"Okay, Sarge. Here goes." Brookes slowly pushed the plunger down, sending the cryo revival serum into the girl's system. "It should take about a minute before we know anything and less than five before we can pull her out."

All eyes were on the display panel readouts. The girl's vitals started to rise quickly.

"Okay, boys," Harrington said. "Pack up and get ready to bug out."

Harrington anxiously looked down through the lid, while Brookes monitored the display. The girl started to move. "She's almost there, Sarge." Brookes placed one hand on the handle to the lid. A faint tick indicated the chamber lock was released.

Brookes opened the lid, then removed the various tubes, sensors, and probes. The girl's eyes remained closed; he gave her a quick examination checking her pulse, breathing and eye dilation.

"She's back, Sarge. It looks like she is going to be out for a bit longer, but..."

Harrington held up his hand signalling Brookes to stop. "Sarge, this is Swartz. What the hell did you guys do back there?"

Before Harrington could answer he could hear the methodic barking of Palmer's TCHA-21A.

"Swartz, what the fuck is going on?"

"Whatever you just did caused a swarm of UAs to come for your asses. You gotta beat boots, now."

Harrington muted his mic. "Fuck, fuck, fuck." He flipped back to broadcast. "Palmer, sitrep."

"The fuck if I know where they came from, but the corridor is swarming with tangos. It looks like Benton is either out or tits up. It's just me, Sally and Bishop."

Harrington paused a second to consider a strategy. "Can you convince them that having the blast doors to their back will give them some protection."

"Uh, okay."

"You do that. When you get most of them corralled give me a shout."

"Roger out."

"Anderson, get your asses undercover and make ready to blast those doors."

Harrington looked back to Brookes. "Grab the girl. I'll take the package."

The team left the room in a jog. "Anderson, we're coming your way, for fuck sake don't shoot us."

'Sarge, we've got most of them pinned down like you asked."

"Good work Palmer. Take cover. Shake and bake."

"Anderson, now."

"Roger... Fire in the hole!"

Seconds later the complex was shaken by a powerful blast. Harrington and his team were knocked to the ground. Brookes hunched over to protect the girl.

Dust filled the air. Harrington shook his head a few times to clear his senses.

"Harrington, this is Swartz. What the fuck was that? It took all of our acoustics and drones offline."

Harrington looked around at the team members with him. "Is everyone okay? What about the girl?"

Brookes examined the girl and gave a thumbs up. They jogged down the corridor to the room where the blast doors once stood. In their place was a ragged hole with twisted metal beyond. The air was thick with dust and smoke. Debris from the crates was scattered throughout. Members of the team were quickly moving from their safe locations.

"Swartz, get ready to bug out; we'll be the ones running like our asses are on fire. So don't shoot us."

Harrington looked around the room. "Is everyone okay? Anderson, take a headcount. Palmer, Bishop. Sitrep."

Harrington picked his way toward the hole in the wall. "Palmer, Bishop. Can you hear me?"

As Harrington approached the corner he spotted movement amongst the rubble. He swung his TR-74 upward, but then he heard the familiar windup sound of a TCHA-21A. Whoever was in the rubble didn't stand a chance when the fifty calibre kinetic slugs tore into them.

Harrington looked toward where the shots were fired. Palmer was starting to stand up, pushing aside part of the collapsed wall. "Palmer, good to see you. Any idea where Bishop is?"

"Yeah, he took shelter behind my ass."

A head popped out from behind Palmer. "And that is a lot of ass to hide behind."

Harrington looked around. "What about Benton?"

Palmer shook his head, then pointed to a pile of twisted metal. "He'd be over there."

"Brookes. Pass off the girl. I need you to scan for a KIA."

"Roger, Sarge."

"Anderson. Form up, we're bugging out as soon as Brookes gets confirmation."

Harrington sent two drones down the corridor. About fifty metres down they both went offline. "Fuck!" He pointed to two team members to scout the corridor.

"This is Swartz, we have multiple tangos heading our way."

"Hold them off as long as you can. You're our only egress. We are oscar mike."

"Roger, Sarge."

Gunfire erupted from down the corridor.

"Go, go, go," Harrington ordered. He turned toward the rear of the file. "Keep the girl safe. Sanchez, drop some sentinel drones behind us."

Harrington carefully rounded the corner, his point people were pinned down. One on either side of the corridor taking cover in doorways. Harrington returned fire, forcing the enemy to duck behind a wall.

"Palmer, wind up Sally. Those UA guys have far too much cover."

From behind his position, Harrington could hear Palmer prepping his TCHA-21A, its characteristic whirr as it came up to speed. Harrington and several others fired down the corridor to force the enemy into hiding. Palmer jumped out, rapidly firing, sending slugs straight through the walls at the corners. He then rotated in two high explosive rounds and fired them down the corridor.

The point men moved farther down the corridor. As they rounded the corner they fired several shots to eliminate the few remaining UAs that had escaped Palmer's barrage.

The Hellhounds progressed down the corridors meeting very little resistance.

"Sarge, this is Swartz. The UAs have pulled back. The way is clear."

Harrington paused to consider the new intel. "Roger. I don't like the thought of that. Keep alert." Harrington adjusted his gear, his hand going to the pocket containing the teddy bear. "Fuck! Where's the package?" He patted himself down. "Anderson, hold here. Watch the girl, I have to go back. Palmer, Bishop, you're with me."

The trio backtracked. Halfway down a corridor, they spotted the bear, one arm snagged on a twisted door frame. Harrington could hear unseen footsteps approaching. The sentinel drone they left behind showed at least six UAs. Harrington scrambled down the corridor, grabbed the bear and shoved it deep into one of the pockets.

He turned to head back, but before he could truly register what happened he felt the sting of a round slamming into his back.

Harrington was knocked to the ground, as more rounds flew past where his head was just moments ago. Palmer answered the attack by first firing HE rounds down the hall and then laying down covering fire. Harrington felt himself being grabbed by his harness.

"Don't worry, Sarge. I've got you," shouted Bishop as he dragged the master sergeant down the corridor to safety.

When they were around the corner Bishop rolled Harrington over and examined him for wounds. "What's your HUD say?" Bishop's face swarmed in front of Harrington.

Harrington paused, confused and bewildered. Bishop slammed the side of Harrington's helmet. He pulled his hand back again for another hit. Harrington grabbed Bishop's wrist as he examined his HUD.

"No penetration. A cracked armour plate." He grunted as he stood up. "I'm going to have one motherfucking bruise." Harrington paused. "Fucking-A, the rear sentinel just registered a biological in the air. Let's haul ass."

The trio jogged back to the rest of the squad. "Anderson, we're heading back. Get ready because we are bringing friends with us. It also looks like that lab is leaking a biocontaminant."

"Jesus H Fuck... Roger. Be advised that our guest is awake. You aren't gonna believe who she is."

"I have an idea."

Harrington, Palmer, and Bishop were forced to stop several times to push back the UA troops that were following them. They rounded the final corner to see most of the other team members gathered around the farther corner, firing their weapons. If they got pinned down, the corridor would be their death trap.

"Sanchez, open me a door. Let's hope for the best."

"You got it, Boss."

The door that Sanchez exploded lead to a single room with no exit.

"Fuck," said Harrington, "this is no better. Wait... throw in some remote blasticks. Do you have any of that DX-74 on you? If so throw it in as well. I want to make it seem like we took cover in this room. Reset the door as best you can and then rig it to blow again. My hope is that they will rush the room and we can blow the shit out of them."

Sanchez smiled. "I'll blow a hole in the other wall, that should lure them in farther."

Harrington went back out to the corridor, crossed to the other side and tried the locks on the various doors until he found one that was open. Inside was a large room with an exit on the opposite side.

"Listen up everyone. Fireteam stay where you are. All others, on me and into the room. Fire support, drop some drones. Once everyone is clear, haul ass down to me."

In less than a minute everyone was in the room.

Harrington moved over to where Brookes and the girl had their backs against the wall. He squatted down to her height. "I am Master Sergeant Rick Harrington. I am guessing that you are Ambassador Barrett's daughter."

The girl nodded her head. "I'm Alexis. Where's Kimi?"

"You were the only person in the cryo chamber."

"Kimi is my teddy bear. My dad gave it to me and told me to protect her at all costs." Alexis looked around. "Where's my father?"

Harrington hesitated. "We were sent to... uhh, rescue you. I'm sure that your father will be waiting for you."

Alexis squinted her eyes and looked up at Harrington. "You don't lie very well."

The members of the Hellhounds did their best to stifle their laughter. As Harrington stood up the sentinel drones registered movement then went dead.

"Blow the door"

An explosion was heard from the corridor followed a short time later by another. The rush of feet was heard in the corridor. When Harrington guessed that most of them were in the decoy room he turned to Sanchez. "Now!"

The Hellhounds burst from their concealment, firing upon the United Alliance soldiers that remained in the corridor. Palmer entered the decoy room and fired several HE rounds for good measure.

Sanchez ducked his head inside of the room and gave an appreciative nod. He turned to Harrington. "Boss, that was—"

A UA round caught Sanchez in a vulnerable location on his armour. Harrington grabbed Sanchez as he crumbled to the ground. From down the other end of the corridor, a group of UA soldiers were firing upon them. More rounds pelleted Sanchez's back. The Hellhounds returned fire.

"Medic!" Harrington yelled as he pulled Sanchez's body around the corner to safety while the other Hellhounds provided suppression fire.

Brookes examined Sanchez and shook his head.

Harrington kicked the wall. "Fuck! Tag him. Whose got Alexis?"

"I do!" Shouted Bishop.

"You two are sticking to me." Another sentinel drone registered the biological in the air. "Okay, Hellhounds, that bio crap is heading this way. Exfil in...eighteen minutes. Let's move it!"

In a well-practiced leapfrog, the two teams moved down the corridor to the egress point.

"Shultz, we're coming through. Get ready to blow the corridor."

"Roger."

The Hellhounds rounded the last corner. Corporal Shultz was standing at the door waving them forward. "The rest of the team is outside. Come on, come on, come on!"

No longer leapfrogging, the team made a methodical dash for the door. Harrington was the last one through. He slammed the door shut and took cover a split second before Shultz detonated the explosives.

Outside of the complex, Harrington's external communications were restored from the shielding and static caused by the steel and rock of the building.

"I say again. Hellhound Actual, this is Skyjack, over."

"Skyjack, Hellhound Actual, over."

"About time, Hellhound. Echo Tango Alpha in five minutes. Paint the Lima Zulu"

"Roger. Be advised that we have a plus one and we may be bio hot."

"Roger, plus one and bio hot. Out."

Harrington returned to his team's tactical net. "Okay, boys. We have four minutes to get to the LZ and paint it up. Let's move out."

Night had fallen. Harrington changed his HUD to infrared as they moved along the side of the building. He ran a head count of his team. "Fuck, Bishop. Where's the girl?"

"She's right... shit, Sarge. She gave me the slip."

The master sergeant growled. "Anderson, we've lost the girl. Keep moving forward. I'm going to double back."

"Roger."

Heading back to the door, Harrington scoured the landscape. He picked up a heat signature between two barrels. He crept toward the location.

"Alexis," he whispered. "Alexis, it is me, Master Sergeant... it's Rick. I need you to come with me."

"I'm scared, Rick," she whimpered.

"You did fine inside."

Alexis paused. "That was inside... where it's light."

"Take my hand, I promise you that nothing will hurt you."

"Like you promised me that my dad will be waiting for me?"

Harrington looked at his chronometer. "Alexis, if you want to leave here, we need to leave now. I need you to be brave. Can you do that for me?"

A timid hand reached out from between the barrels. Harrington gently grasped it. "Okay, we really need to run. Stay close to me."

From the distance, Harrington could hear an exchange of gunfire. "Anderson, sitrep?"

"We are tango hot. Skyjack is going to make a strafing run to get the natives to back off. Where are you?"

"I have the girl. We should be there in three minutes."

"Roger, Sarge. We will try to hold as long as possible."

Harrington knelt down to Alexis' level. "Okay. I'm going to level with you. There is fighting between us and our rescue craft. Stop when I tell you to and run as fast as you can when we have to."

Alexis nodded her head, then grasped on to one of Harrington's utility pouches. The two ran to the corner of the building that they were following. They stopped for Harrington to glance around the corner.

From behind him, Harrington heard Alexis' scream. He turned to find a UA soldier pulling her through a nearby doorway. "Fuck!"

He peeked his head through the window and then pulled back. A shot ripped through the door. Alexis' screams appeared to move away. Taking a few steps back, Harrington rammed the door using his momentum to burst through. He immediately did a combat roll on the ground, regained himself, took a knee, then sighted his rifle down the empty room where he heard the retreating footsteps. Harrington ran after the captor.

"Sarge, this is Anderson. Skyjack says he can't wait on the ground much longer. He can circle for a few minutes but that's about it."

Huffing into the mic, Harrington replied back. "They've got the girl. Provide as much cover as you can. But if it gets too hot, get out. I'll find an alternative route out of this clusterfuck."

"Roger. Good luck."

Harrington increased his stride. The UA soldier tripped, going down on his knees. Harrington used the blunder to make up the precious distance. The soldier quickly regained his footing, spun around facing Harrington while holding Alexis in front of him as a human shield.

Slowing to a walk Harrington brought his TR-74 up to his shoulder. "Put the girl down," Harrington ordered.

"What? So that you can shoot me? There's a reward for whoever brings her back."

"Listen, I don't have time to negotiate. Put her down and I won't kill you; otherwise, I'll shoot you between the eyes."

Nervously, the UA soldier held Alexis higher, closer to his face.

"Let me give you some advice." Harrington lowered the muzzle of his rifle pointing it toward the ground. "Two things: Using a child as a shield is about as low as you can get."

Harrington could see the soldier swallow hard.

"And—" Harrington fired two rapid shots, scoring a hit in each of the soldier's shins. "—it can also leave your lower legs exposed."

The UA soldier collapsed to the ground taking Alexis down with him. He grabbed for her but she squirmed away from his grasp. Harrington fired a third time, catching the soldier in the forehead snapping his head backward.

Alexis ran toward Harrington and hugged him. "Are you okay?" he asked. Without waiting for a reply he scooped her into his arms and ran for the nearest door. The scene outside was one of chaos. Skyjack had made strafing runs with both kinetic rounds and high explosive missiles. Harrington rounded a building, ahead of him stood a vertical take-off aircraft.

Harrington dashed across the tarmac, from behind him came orders to halt, followed shortly by rounds barely missing him as he zigzagged his way to the aircraft. They ducked for cover behind a ground support vehicle. Rounds slammed into the exposed side. Alexis reflexively made herself as small as possible as she hid behind a double set of wheels.

"Stay here!" He ordered Alexis as he stood up firing several rounds then ran toward another vehicle.

Alexis watched as he made his way to the aircraft. He made a quick sprint around the aircraft and then punched its side. Dropping to his stomach he fired more rounds. He rolled over to a support vehicle, firing from the prone position from beneath the vehicle. He got to his feet and made a dash back to Alexis.

Out of breath, he gulped. "Okay, that bird is out of order. But you're getting out of here." He then reached into his pocket and withdrew Kimi. "Put this under your shirt and hold on tight to her."

"Skyjack, this is Hellhound Actual. Prepare to receive the package and our plus one."

"Hellhound, be advised we cannot land. The Lima Zulu is too hot."

"Roger, no LZ. The package will be coming to you."

Harrington turned to Alexis. "Okay, kid. I am going to need you to trust me on this one. The Hellhounds will make sure that you are safe." Harrington paused. "Are you ready?"

Alexis gave him a curt nod.

He picked her up and ran straight toward the disabled aircraft. Once there he reached up, pulled a lever that opened the cockpit canopy and extended the ladder. Alexis grabbed the ladder and climbed as fast as she could. She hesitated when she reached the top.

"Get in!" Harrington yelled.

Harrington grabbed the seat straps pulling them as tight as they would go around Alexis. She screamed and pointed. Harrington followed her hand, several UA soldiers were rushing toward the aircraft, firing their weapons. Harrington grabbed the pilot's helmet and placed in on her head. The soldiers continued firing, Harrington grunted as several rounds hit him.

He pointed to a button beside Alexis. "When the canopy closes, push this button." Harrington winced with pain as he caught another round.

"Wait! What about you? Where are you going?" cried Alexis.

"Don't worry about me... I'll be right behind you."

Harrington pushed the canopy close button then half climbed half fell down the ladder.

Clutching his side he limped toward a support vehicle. He rested his TR-74 on the hood of the vehicle, randomly firing. Behind him, the cockpit ejection seat fired. Lifting Alexis high into the night sky. "Skyjack. Package away."

The stealth SR-14 Skyjack swooped across the tarmac catching Alexis and the ejection seat just as they started their descent back toward the ground. With practiced precision, the Hellhounds hauled Alexis on board. Skyjack circled around and passed over the tarmac wagging its wings.

"Hellhound Actual, this is Skyjack. Packaged received...Good luck."

Corporal Palmer stood on the edge of the SR-14's opened drop gate. He had already spun up Sally. Laughing, he fired HE rounds down upon the tarmac with devastating effect, scattering the UA soldiers. Scanning the ground, Palmer saw Harrington break from his cover and dash for the nearest exterior fence. "Godspeed, Sarge. See you back at the base."

World War Fowl
Heather Kim Hood

I reckon the mealworms did it. Read somewhere in a fancy chicken magazine you gotta give your birds extra protein when they start layin' or they cause trouble. So mealworms seemed like a good idea at the time.

Ya can't figure chickens. Just when they's all comfy and regular, somethin' comes along to upset their routine. I had me one hundred and twenty mixed breeds. All layers, that made me a tidy little profit, 'til that summer. There was a big flash out east and they all quit layin'. Just like that.

"Meteor," my husband, Horace said, scratchin' his mostly bald head. That man had more hair on his upper lip than over his entire scalp, and he was right self conscious about it. "Musta hit Saskatchewan."

We didn't own a TV, cause of our solar setup, and the radio stopped working when the flash hit. Our nearest neighbours owned a quarter section about five miles down the gravel road that dead-ended in the middle of nowhere. Not many folk lived in our area. Dirt Poor, Alberta. Home to abandoned grain farms and hopefuls like us, homesteadin' like old timey pioneers.

"I'm gonna head on down the road and catch the news," Horace told me.

"Bring me back one of Mabel's pies," I yelled, as he hurried out the front gate. He just waved and scurried off.

The chickens were out free rangin', as was their usual routine during the day. They had acres and acres of pasture and woodland to roam through. Two large, white farm dogs guarded them from coyotes and other critters lookin' for an easy meal. I stomped out in my galoshes and nightgown to dump the peelins, eggshells and whatnot into the bin for my little feathered babies and gave their special yell that usually brought them a runnin'.

"Here, chickee, chickEE, CHICK-EEE'S!"

Not a damned thing happened. No lil' featherballs hoofin' it over the prairie like unsteady schooners before a storm. Not even a stray feather in the air.

"Oh no. Nooo..." I yelled, dropped the bucket and ran, callin' for the dogs. Oh I found them dogs all right, or what was left of them. Tufts of white fur. Clean picked bones. Chickens all up in the trees, squawkin' like mad.

"Brewster. Bonny..." I gathered up handfuls of white fur, tears streamin' down my face. "What happened? What could'a done this to ya?"

Randy, the head roo of the barnyard, hopped down out of the tree, fixin' me with one squinty little golden eye.

"You'd tell me if ya could, wouldn't ya, Randy Roo?"

There I sat, fur in my lap, overcome with hysteria over my dogs, my best roo struttin' on guard around me. It almost seemed like he was tryin' to protect me.

"We better gather them girls and bring 'em on in, Randy, before they gets et too."

Ya ever try to shoo more 'n a hundred hens outta a tree in your gumboots and nightgown? It ain't a pretty sight, I guarantee it. Figured sooner or later they'd be wantin' their nest boxes so I left it to Randy to convince em. I took Bella, the horse, out for a recon with the long gun, in case whatever got the dogs was still around.

When Horace didn't come home, I drove to Mabel's. She said he'd left hours ago, but I should stay for coffee and pie. It's a prairie thing. Coffee and baked goods are always available when you go to visit. Just an unwritten rule we have. Maybe Horace just got scared, Mabel said, as the news wasn't good. People were goin' on about World War Four. Somebody bombed Washington. Again. No one was takin' responsibility. Last time they was all but tap dancin' on Broadway lettin' people know "We Done It".

"You know what I think?" Mabel leaned forward, lookin' around as if someone was listening. Who'd she think would hear? The Chickens? "Aliens done it. That's who."

"Mabel. You are out of your mind." With Mabel ya had to be firm, leastwise next thing there'd be a "welcome to earth" party planned for the weekend.

"Ain't no such thing as aliens."

"Sure there is. They was here long ago. Painted on all them Indian rocks. They just came back." Mabel's fingers drummed on the table, a sure sign she was annoyed. Well, she could keep her conspiracy theories to herself. Maybe Horace had run off to see if the truth was out there, but I couldn't see him going without the car.

Next mornin', still no Horace. I went out to gather eggs, on the off chance the chicken had started layin' again. The sky was an odd, greeny kinda colour and the smell reminded me of grade school-the way the coat room smelled on a wet morning, with all them damp boots and coats. An undercurrent of conversation was goin' on in the hen house. That's exactly what it was. Conversation.

I rounded the barn and came face to nose with Bella, or what was left of her. Just hair from her mane and tail. And bones. Bright white bones.

I dropped the egg pail and let out a wail. Randy came out of the coop at a run. I held out my arms. "Randy, did you see it, lil buddy? Is the girls all safe?"

Randy came in for a dignified hug. He was far too important for a cuddle now, but my girls came runnin'. Henrietta, Buffy, Red and Chloe: all my original "Moms". The ones I had hand raised, who had raised babies of their own. They crowded onto my lap, tryin' to get me under their wings as if I was a big chick that needed motherin'.

"Now girls, yer all so sweet, but we gotta think about this."

For the next half hour I sat there talkin' to my chickens, who listened, as if it was the natural thing for a chicken to do. They didn't scratch, they didn't peck. They didn't want to forage.

Instead they followed me around, so I just included them in the conversation.

"Gotta change the oil in the generator every hundred hours or so to keep it working well. And clean the manifold filter." Them birds had their heads in every part of the machine, checkin' it out. "Keeps that light bulb goin' in your coop." Sure looked like they was plannin' on workin' it themselves.

"I guess it's just us on the harvest this year, girls," I told the dozen or so that perched on the thresher I was fixin'. "Too bad you don't have hands." Henrietta looked down at her feet, then stretched one out behind, lazy as a cat in the sun.

"Horace sure picked a fine time to leave." The chickens eyed each other, then returned to studyin' their claws, twistin' them this way and that.

I was makin' jam in the kitchen when I heard car doors slam outside. Thinkin' Horace had finally decided to put in an appearance, I headed out front. A soldier with a big-ass, semi-automatic rifle stopped me before I got anywhere near the front gate.

"Ma'am, you the owner here?"

Half a dozen more men climbed out of the back of a truck behind an ugly army-green jeep.

"Yup. Can I help you?"

"We have orders to requisition grain and food stores from every farm we come across, to fuel the war effort."

I wiped my hands on my apron, eyein' Mr. Semi-automatic through slitted lids. Didn't recognise their uniforms as Canadian. At least ours all matched. These punks were probably end of the world survivalists, just after whatever they could get. "Uh huh. We all know our wheat's bin sold to China by the Prime Minister, so how 'bout you show me your papers provin' that?"

There was some shuffling. A yahoo in a green beret stood up in the front of the jeep. "Get her, boys." He grinned.

I never saw them come around the house. I reckon they came through the bushes, or stealthed under the porch. As soon as those soldiers came at me, one hundred and twenty chickens attacked like a scene from a Hollywood B movie. Whoever said chickens can't fly ain't been on my farm. They was avian piranhas, goin' for the eyes first, then the face and any exposed skin, workin' on right up underneath the clothing. They stripped those soldier boys down to bones and gristle in the time it took me to stumble back up the stairs, across the porch and lock the door. Doors. And windows. All of them.

I guess I figured what happened to Horace too. The chickens never did like him much to begin with. After a few shots of whiskey, I realized, those birds hadn't touched a vegetable or their feed in days. This probably explained the drop in egg production as well.

Well, hell. There were two ways I could look at this. One: I was the owner of the new Jurassic Farm. Or two: my babies had protected me and I now had an army issue jeep and truck. Always look on the bright side of life.

About an hour after I came to this conclusion, Randy started callin' from the back yard. Him and my four girls were hunkered down starin' at the back door. I was a few sheets to the wind by this time, which may have explained my courage in the face of all them velociraptor wannabes. I plunked myself down opposite them.

"So I figure it's like this," I said, tossing them a handful of mealworms from a bucketful I'd scooped up on my way out. They ate them like popcorn at a movie. "We got to come to some sort of agreement. You birds been my pride and joy. Now, yer all growed up and startin' yer own civilisation. Don't mean we have to be enemies." I tossed them some more worms, to get them in a good mood.

"I got opposable thumbs. It's just easier for me to do things. Like say, growin' food. Cleanin' the coop. Makin' sure yer warm and healthy. You got them claws. Easier for you to dig and take care of the bugs and worms. I'll share my crop with you and maybe, when you take down an elk, you could, say, save me a haunch. What d'ya say?"

The girls clucked quietly, back and forth. Henrietta got up and plunked herself in my lap, taking mealworms from my hands. I reckon that meant I was accepted as one of the flock.

As the summer wore on, I became accustomed to the sight of flyin' saucers overhead, battlin' someone's jets. Musta been the

Americans or the Russians. The humans was losin' pretty bad, far as I could tell. I couldn't get any news from anywhere. Occasionally the night sky would light up with an explosion from far away. The glow would last for days. The air always tasted bad afterward. My chickens were gettin' on the large side. Lots more chicks had hatched, they ran around lookin' like spindly feathered T-Rexs. I think some of them even had teeth.

On the prairie, we have herds and herds of deer and pronghorn antelope. They're like hooved mice, eatin' up all the crops. I spent many a mornin' on the porch watchin' the chickens chasin' those herds down like a pack of wolves. Singling one out, chasing it across the fields and over the fence. Then back across the field and over again until they closed in for the kill. Like a bloody ballet.

Then came the day the aliens landed. Right in the wheat field, flattening all my best crop that hadn't been trampled by stampeding chickens and pronghorns. I wasn't in the best of moods to start with.

"So what d'you bastards want?" I stood there yellin' at the steamin' thing, sweat pourin' off my neck under the collar of my shirt. Wipin' the grease from the combine onto a rag, I stuffed it int'a pocket of my overalls.

The wall slid apart on the smooth side of what looked like a metal donut. An eerie green glow pulsed out from the void. A smell like pond scum hit me in the face, uppin' my temper another notch.

"Well get a move on. I got work t'do," I yelled at the door, fists on my hips.

Out they slithered. Pointin' their shiny, green death ray guns at me, antennas a wavin' in the air, eyes all bugged out and rollin'.

Well, hells bells. They looked like overgrown mealworms. Poor buggers. They never stood a chance.

When it was all over I shook my head. I was never gonna get the harvest in at this rate. Who was I supposed to contact about reverse engineerin' the saucer? Where was Jeff Goldblum and Will Smith when you really needed them anyhow? Reckoned I better see if I could find someone still alive in the Canadian government, so I could let them know I had the answer to the alien menace.

Jackson's Revenge
Adam Bennett

The disgruntled silence of the tavern swirled away with the dust motes as three men kicked the door open and dragged the heat and noise of the street in behind them. Their raucous laughter filled the small tavern but didn't gel with the atmosphere the half dozen other patrons had been cultivating. Only the barman and two other heads turned at the racket, but shoulders tensed on a few others as the trio made their noisy way to the bar, either unobservant or uncaring.

"Denhe depth charges," one declared loud enough for all to hear. "Depth charges for everyone! This is a day to celebrate."

The barman nodded, the weary motion of his head barely noticeable. "Eight depth charges. Coming right up."

The leader of the trio smiled, "There's nine of us here, ten if you include yourself."

The barman shook his head, again barely noticeably. "Gerran don't drink. And I don't drink on the job. Eight," he said with an air of finality.

The trio looked at one another, incredulous. They began to laugh, as if it were the funniest joke in the sector. "How the hell do you get through a day in this shithole without drinking? And, better question, who the hell would come to this shithole and not drink? Kinda defeats the purpose."

The barman said nothing.

"What if I were to insist? You've heard the old-earth adage, I'm sure; the man with the money is always right... Ten."

Still the barman didn't respond. He just nodded his grim little nod and went about cleaning out twenty glasses; ten small tumbles, and ten oversized tankards.

The trio shouted and laughed and shoved one another as the barman lined the tumbles up on the bar all in a row and swiftly poured ten Daxian whiskies in one fluid motion. He drew ten tankards of dark stout beer and lined them up one after the other just as smoothly.

"Nine silver rounds, or a gold half moon."

The leader smiled at the price, surely aware it was inflated. He didn't argue however. Instead he picked up one of the whiskeys and dropped the tumble directly into one of the tankards, splashing beer on the denhewood counter, and pushed it towards the barman. He dropped a second whisky, splashed the bar a second time and dragged this tankard towards himself.

"Health and hellfire," he said, raising his glass to his lips, drinking deep.

For his part, the barman raised his tankard and took a small sip and returned the drink to the counter still full.

The leader of the trio drank away at his large glass in one long gulp. The smaller glass slid into his face with a painful sounding *thump* as he raised the tankard past the horizontal. He settled his mostly empty glass on the counter and grimaced.

Pulling a coin from his pocket, he bounced it on the bar in the general direction of the barman. "Keep 'em coming," he said as he turned and made his way to one of the empty tables scattered throughout the small tavern. His two friends charged their beers, sloshing the counter a third and fourth time before following him to the table.

The bartender looked at the coin as he picked it up off the floor, a little bewildered. It was a full platinum round. Easily forty times the inflated price he'd charged for the first round. He shook his head and carried the six remaining drinks to the introspective patrons. He drew another beer and whisky and carried it to the table the trio had taken as their own.

"I can't change this," he said, holding out the platinum coin.

"I expect not. Keep the drinks flowing and it's yours."

The barman nodded, placed the drinks on the table, gathered up the two recently emptied tankards and soon returned with another two drinks to replace them.

The other patrons scattered throughout the tavern finished their free drinks and one by one vacated the premises, driven away by the raucous laughter of the trio stationed in the dead centre of the room.

Finally there was only the one man left, a gruff, scarred fellow with a six day stubble and a dusty old coat made from

Denhe leather. The tankard and tumble before him sat untouched, the creamy head on the stout withered to nothing.

The leader stood as the door closed behind the last patron and made his way into the shadowed corner that hid the grizzled man.

"You've let your drink go flat. That's not very polite. After I bought it for you and all."

"Don't drink," the man said without looking up from his contemplation of the whorls in the denhewood table.

"Little strange to find you in a bar if you don't drink. You wouldn't want to upset me now would you? I bought you that drink in good faith."

The man said nothing.

The leader of the trio sat across from the man and pushed the tankard towards him, "Go on, you know you want to... *Jackson.*"

The man didn't react to this name, but the barman did. Behind the bar he made an involuntary squeak.

"Name's Gerran. Barman told you I don't drink. Barman told you my name."

"I heard him. And I heard him jump when I called you Jackson. So let's just say he's less reliable than you're making out."

"Doesn't change my name, or the fact that I don't want your drink or whatever you're selling."

The young man shook his head, "It looks like we've gotten off on the wrong foot, Jackson. My name is Gillar, Axel Gillar. I've been searching for you all over this thrice damned moon. I came to Denhe from Hirt and Yoran before it. I've followed you from rumour to legend, from whisper to hint. I've come for your story, and I'll pay well to have it. Anything else isn't an option."

The grizzled man nodded. "It seems you've followed too many rumours and not enough fact, Axel. Name's Gerran. Always has been, will be for some time to come. I never met Jackson, I don't know where you can find him, but no one in this bar has any story worth the telling, let alone the buying."

Gillar nodded and made to stand. "I see. Obviously, I've made a mistake. Please excuse the intrusion. Oh... perhaps you can explain this before I go?" He reached into his back pocket and pulled a sheet of paper free. He unfolded it and placed it on top of the tankard full of flat stout. "You certainly look like Jackson. Oh, older, definitely, and a fair bit more scarred and beat up, but there's no mistaking the face in this picture is yours. The jacket is a dead giveaway too. It's as beat up as you are, but that's Jackson's leather, or I'm going blind."

"Where'd you get that?"

"This picture came from Simmo Jackson's classified personnel file. The picture and the name are the only two things that haven't been redacted. You can imagine how hard it was to get my hands on. Hopefully it conveys how serious I am to hear your side of the story everyone already knows."

Jackson said nothing in response. He reached forward and took the sheet of paper from atop the tankard. He stared down at it for a long time, silently contemplating the handsome young man it depicted.

Eventually, he crumpled the page and pocketed it. He gave a short nod. "I'll speak to *you* only."

"Fair," Axel said and turned to his two friends who hadn't left the table in the middle of the room but were listening with rapt attention. "Remember the brothel down the street? I'll meet you there when I'm done." He tossed another platinum round through the air and the taller of the pair caught it as they stood and left the bar without comment.

Axel turned to the barman. "You can lock up behind yourself. I'll pour my own beers." He threw a third coin and the barman snagged it deftly from the air.

"I'll just head upstairs if you don't mind." He came out from behind the bar and locked the front door. He walked to the rickety staircase at the back of the room and ascended from sight.

Axel shrugged and turned back to Jackson. "It's just me."

"I don't know what you think you're going to learn if I tell you my side. Why do you even want to know? You're not some kind of journalman are you? I don't hold no truck with the journals."

Axel shook his head. "No, I'm just bored and obscenely wealthy. I like to buy things no one else can afford. I like to own things that people assume aren't to be bought regardless of the price. I grew up hearing stories of Jackson's Revenge. But that story is *missing* parts... Jackson's Revenge they call it, but I've heard the motivation ten different ways, and the end result ten more. I want the truth. And I'm willing to make you a rich man to hear it."

"You won't like the truth. That story doesn't go the way you think. It's been warped over the last forty years. Warped in ways that make no sense." Jackson snorted in disgust. "Jackson's Revenge. Ha. Not even close. Honestly, I have no idea how the story took on such a life of its own. No, this is not the kind of story you think it is. You aren't going to like what you hear. Best you leave and keep believing the rumours..."

"I'll be the judge of that. You tell the story. Like it or no, I'll give you a credit slip for ten thousand platinum rounds and you can fly so far into the outer reaches that when you stop to look around, no one will have ever heard of this guy Jackson, or his so-called Revenge. You can spend your last years sitting in bars all over the galaxy, sober as you like."

Jackson just nodded. He reached out, took the tumble of whisky and dropped it into the tankard of stout. None of the beer spilled but it did rebuild the head. He lifted the depth charge towards Axel in silent cheers and downed the drink in one long, surprisingly swift draught. He dipped the glass half way through as the tumble within slid towards his face, arresting its momentum so it came neatly to rest against his face as the last drop of whisky spiked stout was drained.

* * *

I fought in the taking of Denhe, you know. It was a bloody and brutal fight. The Talisker Regime held this planet for two decades before we ever arrived and they fought to keep every damn square metre. Back in those days the Union allowed soldiers to claim land in conquered territories and after a long time deep in enemy space I was discharged. I made my way back here with my transport credit and I settled down with a huge swathe of land full to bursting with thousand year old denhe trees.

You've heard of denhewood, I'm sure. It's tough as steel, waterproof, fireproof, bullet proof, lighter than carbon fibre, and near indestructible. The only way to shape it is with acid. But with the right kind of acid and the right tools, it's a surprisingly easy wood to use. And it fetches an excellent price.

With my military service over and done, and only twenty seven years under my belt, I was set to make my fortune. All that was left was to find a wife, and start a family of little Jacksons to share my life and my land with. I was one lucky man. Denhe was chock full of beautiful women back in those days. I often found myself with a dozen female suitors looking to take me to husband. You see, it was a strange time. Plenty of men owned land here, but most were off fighting the Regime on Guaros or Finnik Prime, and more yet were dead, buried in an unmarked grave on a hostile planet. All of which meant that most of the land was owned but was otherwise vacant and unworked. I'd fulfilled my ten year contract with the U.S.F.A.D and come out more or less intact. As such, I was highly sought after by the women of Denhe.

I remember once a young woman kicked in my front door the afternoon she found out her husband was dead. The women who've settled Denhe for the Union are a force to be reckoned with. If the provision rebanning women from combat hadn't passed in '23 we'd have beaten the Regime five years earlier in my estimation.

In any case, she demanded that we sleep together there and then, and worry about getting the marriage arranged once the consummation was over and done with. She was beautiful. And hard to refuse. But refuse her I did. You see, I only had eyes for one woman. I'd had eyes for her since I was ten, living on a different planet entirely.

Sauen Driscoll.

She was one hell of a woman. Funny. Brilliant. Astounding. Adjectives do her no justice. There is a perfect woman out there for every man, and she was mine. I met her growing up on Farre Reach. Before I started my ten year stint with the Armoured Division, I made her all the promises in the universe. I would return home to her a war hero. I'd come back with money, and land, and carry her off to a new world, far from there.

I think she thought I was never coming back. Sure enough, the casualties in the war between the Union and the Regime were brutally high. Very few men returned from their service, and the Union was calling for more and more troops to throw into the meatgrinder.

You can't even fathom what it was like. The Hundred World Draft was in full swing, with a fifteen year term guaranteed for all draftees. If you signed up before you were drafted you only had to serve ten. So I did the only thing that made any sense. I kissed Sauen goodbye, promised to return, and signed up, age seventeen.

I was offworld within the hour.

The campaign took me across half the galaxy. I fought Talisker marines on Garne and Trentine. I weathered the Siege at Antioch and the Battle for Brahms Downs. I held friends as they died, tried to put them back together with my hands as their innards fell out; tried and failed. Sometimes I saved them but the medics fixed them up good as new and sent them back into the fray. Too many times I saw that happen. I saved a kid on his first day in the mud, and they threw him back down less than a week later, ready to die once more.

During this decade of fire and blood, I took my fair share of human life, and then a fair bit more. The number dead by my hands is unknown to me, but it must stand in the hundreds, if not thousands. Death was my constant companion for ten terrifying years, never far, always looming.

But somehow I made it through.

I survived, virtually unscathed. It must have been luck. It *must* have been. Because I watched dozens of men much more skilled than me lose life and limb to rid the galaxy of our most hated enemy. While death reigned all around, I strode unharmed through the balefire of battle after battle, fight after bloody fight.

And through it all, the only thing that kept me going was Sauen Driscoll.

When we took Denhe eight years into my campaign, I finally allowed myself to believe that I might make it out alive. I used my U.S.F.A.D allotment to take a swathe of land filled with the famous denhetrees and swore that I would bring Sauen across the stars, and together we would spend every day of our lives making up for lost time.

But it wasn't to be.

I had a choice, you see. I was discharged after my term and given a ticket to any world behind the front lines. The war would rage on for another six long years and civilian transport was prohibitively expensive. So I had to decide. I could travel back to Farre Reach, back to Sauen, with my meagre pay in hand, and not much else. We'd need to work to get to Denhe where my fortune in land and denhewood was waiting to be reaped.

The other option was to use my transport voucher to go to Denhe, work to get enough money for a ticket to Farre Reach, and two more back to Denhe. I decided this was the best option. Contact between worlds was restricted during the war so there was no way to tell Sauen of my plans. I just had to hope that she'd be waiting for my return. I *hoped* it would only take me a year.

It took five.

War taxes were growing almost daily. I had a ten thousand square kilometre swath of pristine denhe trees and no one to help with the labour. I couldn't find anyone to teach me how to cut, cure, and prime the trees. I had no way to transport them offworld. I was sitting on a goldmine and I didn't own a pick.

Eventually, I learned enough that I was able to harvest a tree or two each day on my own. I learned to cure and prime the wood so it could be used commercially, and I was soon making enough money to feed and clothe myself.

War taxes took the rest. Some of the days when I took down three trees I was able to put some money away, but the war effort that had taken ten years of my life was now eating up my chances of ever returning to Farre Reach, to Sauen.

And then Harridan died.

He'd been on the way out for a long time, but the war had kept him going for more than twenty years. He was an excellent warmaster but, like most warmongering bastards, he couldn't see that he'd already won. Rather than mopping up and taking the victory, he tried to push the war to new fronts and, what had been projected as a ten year fight—and had already lasted twenty—was looking to blow out into the quarter century range.

And he'd have kept us fighting if President Decker hadn't given him the ultimatum to wind the war down. A week later he was dead. Whatever the medical reason given, it was clear to me that he'd died as soon as he admitted to himself that his war was finally over.

He died and Scarpiello took over as Union Warmaster. Taxes were dropped back to more reasonable levels, more than halved overnight. More and more troops were let out of their drafts and allowed to settle the lands they'd taken, or return home.

I quickly built up a crew of returned soldiers to work my denhewood and within three months I had enough money to buy a used interstellar freighter.

I was finally going home to see Sauen.

I returned to Farre Reach early in '46 just as the war was wrapping up, and more than five and a half years later than originally planned.

And by that time, Sauen was already dead.

* * *

Jackson stood and wiped a single tear from his weathered cheek and walked to the bar to pour himself another drink. He drained the large beer in a single draught and filled the glass anew before returning to his seat.

"What happened to her?" asked Axel.

"She married a politician. She never received any word if I were alive or dead, but she waited. She waited ten long years, all through the communications blackout, all through my contracted service with the AD. She waited." Jackson rolled his shoulders producing an audible crack. "And even after my ten years was done, she waited. She didn't marry for another four years, all while

I was failing to turn a profit on one of the most profitable resources in the entire galaxy. She waited fourteen long and lonely years before she finally decided I was dead, buried in an unmarked grave on an unnamed planet.

"And so she married Franko de Longue." Jackson spat as if the very name were poison. "He was a reformist. He worked hard to keep the war effort afloat, to keep the people of Farre Reach sending their innocent boys off to fight a pointless war against the innocent draftees of other worlds, as if what planet you were born on had any bearing on who you were. The man was a menace. He was a big part of why I'd had to leave Sauen in the first place.

"And I could have forgiven him for all of that... but for what he did to her..."

*   *   *

I made landfall in February '46 and it didn't take me long to find out what had happened. The rumour was all over Farre Reach. It was too juicy not to become gossip. Learning Sauen was gone broke me. Learning how drove me over the edge.

She'd still been just as lovely at thirty one as she'd been at seventeen. Maybe more so, growing into her womanhood with a grace and elegance that drew attention. And for fourteen long years she'd ignored it. Eventually she'd managed to part with the memory of me, and had finally married one of her many suitors.

De Longue was thirty years her senior, but with enough money and influence, age is a very subjective thing. When I met him he could have been my own age, or even five years younger, rather than nearly twice as old.

Just one of the many privileges of being obscenely powerful, I suppose. In any case, he courted her, and when she was ready, when she had moved past me, they married. It was the celebration of the year, perhaps the decade. Everyone of any social standing attended, and all remarked on the bride, such beauty from one born so low, and all that jealous noise.

I never found out why he did it. Maybe she was distant. Maybe she *hadn't* truly gotten over my 'death.' Maybe she told him 'no' one too many times. Maybe he was just that way inclined. It made no difference to me. He killed her, and his wealth and power protected him from justice.

Oh, people talked, and maybe if I had truly been dead, his crime wouldn't have gone unanswered. Maybe the pressure from the public would have eventually come for him. As it was, we never found out.

I learned of her death, waited long enough to confirm it was my Sauen, and that this all hadn't been a case of mistaken identity, and then I made my move.

I bought a TR-640 laser assault rifle on the black market, along with a standard issue AD pistol, and enough concussion grenades to fell a battalion, and less than a week after landing on

Farre Reach I made my assault on his palatial manor in the hills overlooking Farre Prime.

Oh, certainly, I did some research and planning. I scouted the area, and even considered enlisting some other discharged soldiers to aid my efforts. In the end I decided that I was in no position to ask that of them. I didn't know anyone on planet from my own days in the Armoured Division, but I felt sure that anyone I asked would join me without hesitation. That's the AD code. You look after your brothers, even if you've never met them before. I couldn't ask it of them for fear they'd say yes.

So I went in alone, trusting on whatever luck had gotten me through ten years and more than fifty different planets to get me through this one last assault. I only needed it to hold out long enough to get me inside. I didn't need to make it out again. I only planned on a one way trip.

I attacked at 0400 local time because two hundred years of conventional wisdom says that is the best time. Something about the ebbs and flows of a sentry's body clock. Even knowing it is your most vulnerable time doesn't seem to change the fact.

I attacked from the high ground to the west of the manor, drawing the sentries to me with carefully aimed concussion grenades amidst the power couplings. Soldiers can tell the crushing whump of concussion grenades, but civilian security has no idea that what they're hearing is a weapon discharging. I hadn't chosen frag grenades for this very reason. A guard who is unconscious for twenty minutes—and bleeding from the ears for a further hour—is just as good as a one riddled with tiny fragments of jagged metal. Better, because his fellow guards just hear a loud unusual noise, and see the power go out and they all converge to investigate.

My plan went as well as it could have. They say no plan survives the first shot fired, but this one did. I suppose I never fired that shot. A dozen guards materialised around the smoking power coupling and I took my chance. Three more concussion grenades dropped right in their unsuspecting midst.

Sixteen men down and out for the count. Four grenades expended. I moved forward, weapon raised and ready to fire at any stragglers, but it seemed the entirety of de Longue's security force was face down in the dirt, sleeping it off.

I borrowed a security pass and made my way inside. The place was opulent. Marble flown in from Goldar, gold leaf on everything, denhewood throughout. I was sickened by the thought that some of my denhewood might have gone into the construction. It took me ten minutes to figure the layout and make my way to de Longue's bedroom. He was sleeping, undisturbed by the chaos his men had faced outside.

I sat on the end of his bed for a time and watched him sleep. Perhaps I was biased, but I disliked the man from that one impression. He slept greedily somehow. I can't explain exactly what I didn't like, but even in his sleep he seemed to exert some kind of sick control over the room. I was too focused on my rage to take it in, but a lesser man might have turned back, leaving him unmolested.

After a time I returned to the door and triggered the lights, which must have run on an external power source. I raised my rifle and, giving my best impression of an AD drill instructor, I screamed, "On your fucking feet, maggot! You aren't here to sleep, you little shit. This is the fucking Armoured Division. You'll stand at attention when I enter or you won't stand for a fucking week!"

De Longue jumped two metres into the air, fell from his bed tangled in his lavish silk sheets, and even though I knew he had spent not a single day in the service, something deep in his lizard brain kicked in and he attempted to scrabble to his feet amidst his linens, trying desperately to stand at attention.

For a moment at least.

Then his prefrontal cortex took command and he tried to push his sleep clouded mind into focus. "...Wha—"

"Speak when you're spoken to, maggot!"

"What is the meaning of this?"

I pointed my rifle at his chest. "You killed her, you bastard. I don't know why, and frankly, I don't care. But you did it, and I'm here to make you pay. Get on your knees!" I took a menacing step forward and he shrank back tripping on the sheets once more and falling back on his ass with a grunt.

"I said knees!" I clicked the safety from triples to singles—a singularly terrifying sound if you don't know anything about guns—

and he got his knees under him, head bowed slightly, which, I have to admit, I quite liked.

Over the bed, a ceremonial Keltani blade hung in a denhewood mount and I circled de Longue to retrieve it, an impetuous plan forming in my mind. I pulled my AD pistol, letting my black market Talisker rifle drop to its sling and I reached up and drew the blade from its scabbard.

"Wha—"

I fired a shot into the bed I was standing on, right near his head, sending a puff of burned white feathers cartwheeling into the air between us. He shut up. I walked over and stood before him once more, much closer this time.

He was shaking.

I holstered my pistol, took a two handed grip, and laid the edge of the razor sharp sword against his shoulder. He squeaked at the unexpected pain as the razor sharp blade cut lightly into his flesh. Keltan was settled by the old-Earth Japanese in 2160 standard. I'm sure you know their blades. The design isn't much different from the classic old-Earth katana. The metals used in traditional katanas couldn't hold a candle to the alloys mined on Keltan, however. The slightly curved blade sliced straight through de Longue's silk pajamas and blood began to well there.

The sight of it froze me.

I'd killed before. I had easily taken hundreds of lives. But I had never used a blade. And I had never done it under my own volition. I'd never *murdered* a man. Something about that small pool of blood brought it all crashing down and in an instant my fury was gone. I knew that Sauen wouldn't approve of this. She had been made of love and light, and seeing me take vengeance would have sickened her. Revenge wasn't part of who she had been, and that was somehow more important than this asshole, even if he had ruined our lives and eventually taken hers.

I stared at the growing stain and I knew I couldn't do it. To kill this man would be to taint the memory of Sauen Driscoll in some unforgivable way.

After what seemed a lifetime, I lifted the blade free, turned and left without a word. I never saw de Longue again.

* * *

Axel stared, disbelief clear on his face. "But... you killed him!"

"Never happened," said Jackson.

"But he died! He's dead! He was murdered, killed with his own sword. It must have been you."

"I don't know what to tell you. I said that you wouldn't like my tale. I told you you'd be disappointed. 'Jackson's Revenge,'" he snorted, "that title never made any sense. I went there for revenge, I went there to kill him, but in that moment I realised that there are no winners in such a contest. Revenge leaves both parties less for their actions."

"What a pile of dragu dung. You're lying! I won't pay you if you're lying about what happened. I came here to find out the truth."

"And so you have. An unpleasant truth, to be sure, but still the truth all the same."

"How did de Longue die then? Because that fact isn't in dispute. You broke into his house, took down his security, were seen leaving on externally powered cameras, and when the authorities arrived, the man was dead. You killed him!"

"I don't know how he died, but it wasn't by my hand. The man must have had enemies. One of them took advantage of the chaos and killed him after I left. Or a disgruntled guard did the job after he woke up from the concussion grenades. I'm sure that working for the man was as distasteful as watching him sleep. Maybe the man faked his own death, deciding that the opportunity was too good to pass up. I don't know.

"In any case, I walked away. The end of my story is that he was alive when I left. I don't know anything more than that. I had an epiphany that night. There is an old saying and I never truly understood it until I stood there blade in hand; if you seek revenge, first dig two graves."

Axel stood, knocking his chair over. "What a joke! I can't take this back to the newspaper!"

"Newspaper?"

"I'm a journalman. I told my editor I could find out the true story of Jackson's Revenge from the one person alive to tell it. I told him it would only cost 20 platinum rounds. That's cheap for a story of this magnitude. All I needed to do was flash my money around like I was some pompous rich bastard and promise more to come. I bribed an AD clerk for your heavily redacted file and traced you across a dozen worlds. And all for this shit!" He picked up an empty tankard from the table and threw it across the room in a rage, shattering it against the bar. "I can't sell this shit! What a goddamned joke! He's going to make me pay him back, you know?"

"So you lied to me? Does this mean I don't get my ten thousand platinums?" Jackson asked with feigned innocence.

This sent Axel into an apoplectic rage. Choking on his words he shot Jackson a final dirty look and stormed out, turning over one of the tables in his way, fumbled with the locked door, and slammed it behind him as he exited the bar onto the bright, dusty street.

Jackson sat back and took the final draught of his beer and shook his head ruefully. It'd been many years since he had a drink and now he'd sunk back into the bottle as easily as the first time he killed a man.

After a short wait, the bartender reappeared at the bottom of the stairs and started righting the chairs the young journalman had scattered during his hasty exit. He closed and locked the door and turned to face Jackson as he stared into the dregs of his beer.

"Why'd you lie to the kid? When we came here you said it was to make a new start. I've got this shitty job, but all you do all day is stare at the moisture on my taps and fight the urge to drink. I see you lost that battle," he said, gesturing at the empty glasses.

"Sometimes you win, and sometimes you lose, Serrath. I may have fallen off the wagon, but I count today as a victory."

Serrath shook his head and sat across from Jackson, taking the young journalman's vacated seat. "It's been forty years since we assaulted that fortress. It's been a long damn time since I helped you kill those guards and break into that asshole's mansion, and you've never told me what happened inside."

"And I probably never will. I appreciate the help you gave me. And I think I've shown my appreciation over the years. But the truth of that night still haunts me." Jackson grimaced. "No matter what I said to that stupid kid, I know exactly how many men's lives I've taken and the number haunts me every night." He held the empty tankard aloft. "This makes it worse but even in sobriety there is no ending the procession of the dead that visits me every time I lay my head down to rest."

It had been many years since they'd assaulted de Longue's manor and yet he could still see the faces of all the men he and Serrath had killed as they fought their way inside. Sixteen slumped figures, prostrate in the mud, nine lives added to the tally that haunted his dreams. He'd promised himself his killing days were done, but his training dictated that he never leave a potential threat to come back to bite him. Nine more to keep him awake at night, and finally, a tenth.

"You saved my life in that trench on Gint. When you walked into that bar on Farre Reach with that look in your eye, I knew I had a chance to pay you back. Then we spent forty years skipping from rimworld to rimworld. I figured you'd open up when you were ready, after all, I have nothing but time. *But*, if you can't trust me with the truth after all of that, then I suppose I know where I stand and there's no point me hanging around. Thanks for the laughs." Serrath stood and made his way to the door, careful to avoid the broken glass scattered in front of the long bar.

As his hand lighted on the latchkey, Jackson spoke, "There's no need for melodrama. Pour me another drink and I'll tell you. I suppose you've earned the right to know."

* * *

Standing in the lavish bedroom, Keltani blade pressed to that asshole's neck and I'm suddenly frozen by the sight of de Longue's blood staining his silken pajamas. I let the blade drop slowly to my side, and without another word, I make my way to the door. Sauen wouldn't have condoned this.

"She told me about you, you know."

I froze, hand on the doorknob at the cold tone of de Longue's words.

"She described her teen sweetheart in great detail. She never got over you. How could she? You're all she made you out to be, and more. Strong, brave, handsome, and chivalrous too.

She never let me forget that I was chosen second. And now you come into my house, you drag me from my bed, set up to execute me, and decide to spare my life? She had you down to a tee. It's a shame she was blinded to the real truth of you."

I turned slowly to face him, but said nothing.

"You're alive. Alive and kicking. So why didn't you return like you promised? You weren't reconscripted. We stopped adding second terms well before your ten years was done. Could it be that you never really loved her?"

I tightened my grip on the Keltani sword and took a step towards the prostrate politician.

"No, no, of course, you were held up, delayed in some unforeseen and yet very justifiable mix up. You would have returned but you were busy. It's understandable."

De Longue smiled viciously. "You're the reason she's dead, you know?" I stiffened. "Oh, I don't mean 'If you'd only come back, she'd never have married the *mean old man*.' No, I mean you're literally the reason. I came home after a week on the road campaigning and she had the temerity to tell me that *you* would never have left her all alone waiting. I don't think she saw the irony in that. I mean, you *did* leave her all alone. For fourteen fucking years!"

De Longue stood and took a step towards me, jackal's grin growing with every moment. "So I killed her. I'd had enough of her contradiction and spite. I walked in here, took up that very sword, and walked back into the dining room and stabbed her through the heart."

I looked down at the weapon clutched in my hand with revulsion. The blade was slightly stained with de Longue's blood. I tossed the sword aside and drew my pistol. I aimed it at de Longue's sick smile, my finger heavy on the trigger.

But still, I couldn't do it. It wasn't *her* way. I lowered the weapon and turned to leave.

De Longue laughed as I opened the bedroom door. "*Still* you cling to your honour? You really are the man she spoke of. I'm glad I took her from you before you could return and steal her away. I'm just sorry that I didn't kill *him* myself. Instead, he died in a forced labour camp. Honestly, I didn't realise you were alive, so he didn't matter to me one way or the other. I sold him for a half moon platinum, and washed my hands of the whole business. It turns out forced labour isn't good for thirteen year olds... He was dead inside the month."

A red rage filled my vision. In ten years of soldiering I'd never felt anything like it. My hand dropped away from the door handle and I turned to face him, still not speaking. I reholstered the pistol and in two long strides, took the tall, thin man by the throat. That terrible grin was quickly replaced with gasps for air as my hands—built strong during ten years of military service, and further reinforced with four years of cutting and hauling Denhe trees—choked off de Longue's airways. His feet scrabbled against the rich wooden flooring, scuffing and scarring the polish.

I dragged him across the room to where the Keltani sword lay and shoved him to his knees. Picking up the priceless weapon, I raised it high above my head and, without a moment's hesitation, brought it swiftly back down into the back of de Longue's neck. There was barely any resistance as the ultra sharp blade took the man's head from his shoulders and sent it rolling around the lavishly appointed room, spraying blood, eyes still blinking in shock.

I kicked the headless corpse to the side, the geyser of hot blood covering every surface for metres. Then in a fit of pique, I propped the sword against the wall and drove my foot through the flat of the blade, shattering it into three jagged pieces, destroying the weapon that had taken Sauen's life.

*   *   *

"Somehow, almost none of the copious blood landed on me. I walked from the room, rejoined you outside, and we set forth for Denhe within the hour."

Jackson smiled. "But Denhe was a hollow reminder of all I'd lost. You know the rest. For forty years we've hopped from backwater to dustbowl always a moment away from our next departure."

For forty years that night had haunted Jackson, the stories of his revenge following him across star systems and decades. He'd lost a good woman, an unknown son, and had failed to live up to

Sauen's expectations of him. He'd been found by people chasing the story over the years, and Axel the journalman wouldn't be the last.

"So why all the secrecy? And how did you get away with it? I know we were careful, but you must have left evidence of your crime," Scarrath said.

"Did you know that the Hundred Worlds Draft spelled death for a billion men? Just on the Union side? Another hundred million or more volunteered like we did."

Scarrath nodded slowly. "I'd heard something like that, yes."

"Eleven hundred million men." Jackson shook his head slowly. "Do you know how many completed a full term of ten years in combat?"

Scarrath said nothing.

"The sad answer is that it's fewer than a hundred. A fair bit fewer. Now there are soldiers such as yourself who only came of age in the later years, and survived a few years before their terms were cancelled—and that's certainly no mean feat—but of the billion or so men whose contracts began ten years or more before the end of the war, only seventy two walked away whole." Jackson drained the last of his drink. "Seventy two from more than a billion. The AD has a very soft spot for us in their cold black heart . Why do you think the service jacket that little pissant was carrying was so heavily redacted? They *absolutely* know it was me, and they chose to sweep it under the rug."

Scarrath sat quiet at this revelation. After a time he said, "And why the secrecy on your part?"

Jackson didn't answer for a long time. He stared across the empty bar, taking in the denhewood counted and the scattering of broken glass. Eventually he sighed and said, "I should have walked away. I should have let the natural justice of the universe deal with that murderous fuck, rather than staining my hands with hate. Instead I took *another* life out of some sick sense of justice or revenge, not to mention asking you to stain your own hands for my misguided cause."

"You did the right thing. Don't convince yourself you didn't. He was a parasite and you removed him before he could hurt anyone else."

Jackson shook his head with a wan smile. "I've had forty years of reflection, and I'm convinced you're wrong. I should have walked away. And I'll spend the rest of my life telling anyone who asks that that was exactly what I did. If I manage to stop someone from repeating my mistake, maybe that will be enough to forgive what I've done. Maybe..."

Monitor Logan
Neal Asher

Logan gazed through his monocular out across the flats. Stone people were walking along on either side of a crawler running just on solar and moving slowly across the mudstone. They were probing potential wash holes, which showed on the surface only as dimples or smaller punctures in the rock, for star gems—sapphires, rubies, diamonds, and other precious jewels.

A trailer behind the crawler contained the self-inflating tents and other equipment of this family unit. But it wasn't them Logan had been tracking. He swung his monocular to the side. The janglers had halted, four dismounting from Flat scooters and more stepping out of their crawler, and of course, all of them were heavily armed. Perhaps they had stopped for a beer or two before getting down to business. Logan lowered his monocular and walked back to his scooter. He unbuttoned his long coat, folded it and put it in one of the panniers. Now he could easily reach the pulse gun on his right hip and the rail-beader on his left, its power cable plugged into its battery on his belt. He mounted his scooter, made sure his laser carbine moved freely in its holster beside the pure water fuel tank, and started the vehicle.

Caterpillar treads biting into the rock he shot out across the Flat, kicking up a cloud of dust behind him. The stone people saw him coming, but they did not react much, for they thought they were perfectly safe. As he drew closer, he spied the patriarch of this family: a tall thin man with long lip tendrils and grey skin. Old and tough, but gentle. Logan slowed and pulled up nearby, climbed off his scooter, and walked over.

"What are you?" asked the man.

"I'm Logan—I'm the new monitor," he replied.

The old man shook his head. "Earth lawman?"

"Yes, here to warn you janglers are ranging further from Godrun. There's a hunting party of them here now and they've been watching you."

The old man tilted his head and gazed at Logan suspiciously. "Janglers here... so what good is an Earth lawman to us?"

"Earth law again applies in the city, and out here and in Godrun," Logan stated.

"For how long?" the old man looked bitter. "Can we return to our homes in the mountains?"

"It's different now," said Logan tightly. "The Prador have agreed to Earth law applying here so long as there is no big military presence. That agreement has been locked in for a the next century."

"Tell that to Monitor Trepanan." The old man eyed Logan carefully. "Or what you can find of him after Trader John fried him with a laser."

"It will be different now," Logan insisted.

"We will see..."

Logan cooled. "Whatever way it goes, you should stay off the Flat for a while."

The old man dipped his head in grudging acquiescence. "And you?"

"I'm going to talk to those janglers."

The man turned and whistled, waved his three-fingered hand above his head and his people started heading back towards to crawler.

"Luck," he said.

Logan smiled without humour. "It's not me that needs it."

* * *

The janglers were packing up their temporary camp. They were in no hurry, knowing they could quickly catch up with their prey in their faster vehicle. They'd set up a table and yes, there were bottles of beer on it, a cooler on the ground beside it. Three sat in deck chairs by this table, others sat on the mudstone checking over stun guns.

Logan drove in slowly, aware of hands on or reaching for weapons. He halted, climbed off his scooter and pulled off his goggles, pausing for a moment in introspection. Then he sauntered over, assessing them. A thickset guy, with Marsman tattoos on his face, sat at the nearest table, while the woman sitting nearby, clad in a modern envirosuit, he knew had been born on

Earth. Others were local humans and one a stone man hybrid who had cropped his tendrils and had some cosmetic work to build him a nose.

"Do you know why you are called janglers?" he called as he approached the table. He came to a halt, hands on his hips.

"Because of ancient slaving techniques," replied the woman.

He studied her. Deela was tough and pretty, with an envirosuit that clung to her curves. She was the boss here, but he'd known that for a long time, just as he knew her name.

"Quite." He nodded. "The chains you use to manacle your victims... they jangle."

"We don't use chains," she replied.

"No, nor will you use induction thralls today, or ever again."

Deela stood up from her deck chair. Meanwhile the Marsman drew a pulse gun from his hip and placed it on the table before him. Logan tracked all this, just like he was aware of the two moving round behind him.

"Says who?" she asked.

"Says Polity monitor Logan." He paused, studying their faces. "That would be me."

The Marsman cleared his throat. "Last lawman didn't do so well. And Earth has no jurisdiction here."

Logan smiled. "You haven't been keeping up on events. That changed precisely one hour ago. This world is now under the jurisdiction of Earth. It was just a case of a little negotiation with the Prador. They don't really care what happens here—they just don't want a big military presence this close to their border."

"So Earth sent one monitor," said the woman, grinning at this madness.

"Seems so," said Logan.

"Dreyfus," Deela said to the Marsman, "Shut this idiot up."

"Predictable," said Logan.

Dreyfus snatched for his pulse gun.

Logan tipped his left holster forwards so the weapon pointed behind him, and pushed it back. It hummed and spat, shooting out of the bottom of the holster as he pushed it from side to side while drawing his pulse gun with his right hand. He heard the fleshy impacts and 'oomphs' of surprise from behind as he fired his pulse gun at those before him. Dreyfus flew back, following the back of his head to the mudstone. The hybrid in the other deckchair similarly followed part of his head to the ground. Logan dropped and rolled, automatic fire cutting above him. He shot under the table taking out Deela's kneecap, and then shot twice more to bring down another jangler. He came up with a weapon in each hand. Short bursts from the bead gun had two twirling in atomised blood. Another ran for his scooter. Logan was about to open fire again when three shots hit him in the chest. He staggered back, but fired once with his pulse gun, blowing away Deela's elbow. She shrieked, dropping her weapon. One man was crawling along the ground leaving a slime trail of blood. He walked over and shot him through the back of the head, then glanced over at Deela. "Don't go away now."

"Body armour," she spat.

Logan probed the bullet holes through his shirt. There was no blood.

Returning to his scooter, he drew his laser carbine and calmly checked it over. After a moment, he flicked up the sight, shouldered it, and aimed at the now distant escaping jangler on his scooter. He shot twice, the carbine crackling, impacts to the right of the scooter. He adjusted and shot again. A short burst. The scooter and its rider tumbled, shedding debris in a cloud of dust. He put the carbine away and returned to Deela.

"Now, time for us to chat."

"Fuck you," she replied, obviously in a lot of pain.

"Medicate yourself," he said.

She stared at him for a long moment then reached to take an ampule from her belt pouch. Stabbing it into her biceps she sighed with relief.

"Again. We chat."

"Why should I? You'll kill me anyway."

"You're a jangler. You know the routine." Logan shrugged. "Do you want me to torture you and pump you full of serum?"

"Just let me live."

"I can do that." He waved a dismissive hand, apparently not bothered. "You answer my questions and I let you live. Now, where exactly is Trader John?"

"He's out at Riverside—at his house."

"But I guess if his operation starts falling apart he'll be back soon enough?"

"You guess right."

"How many stone people enslaved in the jewel mines now?"

Deela shrugged, then wished she hadn't. "'bout a thousand."

"Where is Emily Trepanan?"

"What?"

"Emily Trepanan—the wife of the previous monitor. You know. The monitor who shot John in the chest but didn't finish the job. The one he laser-burned and threw in the river."

"What?"

"Where is Emily Trepanan?"

"How the fuck should I know?"

"Okay." Logan stood.

"You said you wouldn't kill me."

"Quite." He drew his bead gun and fired short burst into the jangler's remaining scooters, one of which caught fire. He fired a longer burst into the crawler and, shuddering and spraying debris, it seemed to deflate on its treads. He must have hit a battery because power also arced to the ground.

"You might survive." He shrugged. "People have survived much worse."

He headed back to his scooter.

* * *

Logan gazed at Godrun and frowned. He must now go in to take the long vacant position of monitor—the lone lawman, the sheriff of this town. Starting up his scooter he continued along the road, soon studying the people on the pavements. Many janglers were evident, also town residents and workers from the top end. He slowed by a party of stone people trudging along in a line. They were clad in heavy but ragged work clothes and all wore induction thrall devices attached to their temples. Their handler strode ahead of them—a big ugly brute with a cattle goad he really did not need. That, Logan decided, would be stopping very soon, but he needed to prepare.

Finally, he arrived at a single cylindrical building with wide chainglass windows and bullet holes in the walls. It surprised him to see the front door still intact, but then it was armoured. He dismounted, took a rucksack out of one pannier, and walked onto the veranda. Peering upwards he saw the security drone dangling from its power cable, one of its lasers hanging out and bullet holes through its crablike body. However, it activated as he drew close. Red eyes ignited on its rim as it swivelled as best it could to face him.

"Good morning," it grated.

"Good morning, drone," he replied. "Polity monitor Logan reporting for duty. I've come to fill E. L. Trepanan's shoes."

After a long pause, the drone said, "Yeah... right."

"Has this station been breached?"

"Nah, some janglers used me as target practice but otherwise weren't interested."

"Very well... open."

Locks disengaged all around the door and it swung inwards. Logan entered a reception area: seats all around, a chainglass window, and an office lying beyond. Though only one monitor had ever attended, the station could take more staff. Crossing to the door at the back, he placed his hand against a palm reader and it opened for him. He climbed the stairs, entered a large apartment, and dumped his rucksack on the sofa. Walking over to the window while stripping off his shirt and he gazed out. Already gawkers had appeared. The news of an arrival here would travel fast.

Circular scars showed on his naked chest. While inspecting them he folded his forefinger in to touch one of four skin controls on the palm of his hand. The bullet marks just faded away. Next entering the bedroom, he opened a wardrobe and studied the clothes inside. He took out a uniform in blue and white and inspected it for a moment, then shook his head and put it back , instead donning a T-shirt. Another wardrobe revealed woman's clothing.

"Like you never left, Emily Trepanan," he said, closing the wardrobe and turning away. A picture on the far wall now drew his attention. Here stood Monitor E. L. Trepanan in military uniform, Emily at his side with her arm linked through his. He walked over to rest his fingertips against it, closing his eyes for a second. His face rippled and his cheekbones and jawline shifted, his nose sagged a little and his eyes changed colour. But for his dusty blond hair he now looked exactly like Trepanan. He smiled.

"Hello Enders," he said.

After a moment, the smile faded. Taking his fingers from the picture, he turned away, his features shifting back to their earlier setting. Seating himself at a console, he turned it on. A film screen rose out of the top showing the monitor logo. When he passed his hand across in front of it, it flicked to the image of a chrome face.

"Logan," it said.

"You," he said.

"Evidently," it replied

"I expected Janssen, not the Embassy AI—is your oversight necessary?"

"The situation is complicated here," said the artificial intelligence. "Earth law needs to be established, but we cannot be too heavy handed, since that might aggravate the Prador."

"Very well. Monitor Logan reporting in."

"Yes, your arrival has been noted," replied the AI. "The woman you left alive called for help and other janglers picked her up. Trader John is now aware his profit margins might be threatened, and has put a price on your head."

"Then all is as it should be."

"Do you require back-up now?"

"No more than I asked for. You're sending me a deputy?"

"Yes, I am sending you someone who was in the service—from the heavy infantry."

"That's interesting. Who?"

"He's an armoured antipersonnel unit."

Logan said nothing for a moment, then, "I asked for something a little less... effective."

"You asked for a deputy."

"You also said you did not want to get heavy-handed and annoy the Prador."

"There are innocent people to be protected."

Logan raised an eyebrow. "In Godrun?"

"I am aware of your opinion of this town and its people," said the AI. "When I say innocent people, I am talking about the stone people."

"Very well," said Logan. "But this drone must stay covert. I need time. I need Trader John to come out here..."

"I know what you need. But I must make my own cold calculations."

"Very well. Speak to you later." Logan cut the connection.

*   *   *

The offices of the town council stood out from the foamstone houses all around. The ugly block with wide marble steps leading up to a colonnaded entry looked out of another century. Wearing the monitor uniform, Logan strode up to the panelled double door, noting a security drone depending inside the colonnade. He tried the door but found it firmly closed, so he stepped to a com panel beside it and hit the buzzer. The screen came on to show a mousy blonde haired woman.

"How can I help you?" she asked.

"Polity monitor Logan," he replied. "I am here to serve notice of jurisdiction. Net notice has already been served so you are aware of this."

"I'm sorry, but the Council is in session with the Mayor—they cannot be interrupted."

"Under net notice you will be aware that I have right of entry into all public properties. I suggest you open the door."

A flash of anger crossed her features. "You have no rights here!"

"On the contrary—"

"You cannot come in."

The screen blinked off and above him the security drone whirred, its eyes igniting. Logan sighed, then in one smooth motion drew his pulse gun and fired, blowing the drone into pieces. He walked over to the doors again, stepped back and shot out the locks, then stepped rapidly forward driving his boot against them. As they crashed open, he marched into the lobby. Two security guards ran out of a back room as he switched down a setting on his weapon.

"Those doors..." said one of them, while the other reached for the gun at his belt.

Two shots and they froze issuing electrical discharges, then dropped bonelessly. Logan walked up to the reception window. The woman sat inside, gaping at him.

"Where is this meeting?"

"You can't—"

"I can," he cut in. "Now are you going to tell me or must we be uncivilized about this?"

"The Polity can't just make demands like this—"

He dialled his pulse gun up again and shot a hole through the window, just to the right of her face. She sat there frozen for a long moment, then decided defiance sat above her pay grade. She pointed to a door on the other side of the lobby. Logan walked over, tried the handle and found it locked, kicked it open and stepped in.

Five councillors sat at a glass-topped table, the Mayor at the head—a bulky shaven-headed man packed into expensive businesswear and chuffing on a cigar. The councillors—three women and two men—were of a similar kind. A bottle stood on the table and they were all drinking.

"This is a private meeting!" said one of the women.

Logan walked over to stand beside the thin, sour-faced female. He picked up the bottle and studied it.

"Earth monitors don't take much notice of privacy or individual rights," said Mayor Gavon, putting down his cigar and leaning back in his chair. He was sweating, nervous. "Trepanan was just as arrogant."

"This is Earth import bourbon," observed Logan. "Expensive tastes here."

He took the bottle and one glass, walked to the other end of the table, sat and poured a drink. "I guess the mining operations here are making a lot of money. Maybe more money than Trader John knows about." He smiled humourlessly.

They watched him in silence as he sipped then put down the glass.

"Well," he began. "You are all aware that Godrun and the Flats are now under Earth jurisdiction again, but I thought a courtesy call was in order—just to make things clear."

"Courtesy," spat one of the men.

"Yes," said Logan, "courtesy. I have the power to enforce the law without political oversight. I did not have to come here. I do not have to deliver warnings."

"Seems Earth law is what your kind chooses it to be," said sour-face.

"You might not like it, but it is a fact of your lives now." He drank some more of the bourbon—it was very good. "But I am prepared to be lenient when it comes to minor infractions—we are after all in a period of transition. What concerns me at present, are the major ones."

"Like what?" asked Gavon.

Logan focused on the man. "Like the law against enslaving sentients. What was it you said about individual rights?" Gavon had no reply and Logan continued, "Also, like the laws against extortion, murder, rape, and torture. The major ones."

A sharp-looking man in an expensive grey environment suit spoke up. "You're talking about the stone people." He sat back and turned his bourbon glass on the table top, inspecting its contents.

"In part," Logan replied. "How they have been treated is not unique."

"They're animals," said sour-face.

"They're adapted humans who arrived here before you in the first diaspora from Earth. As such, under Earth law, they have more rights on this world than you."

"You'll destroy the mining business here," said another woman.

Logan gave a tight smile, studying his own glass. "There are machines that can do their job better. All it will take is some reinvestment of your profits." He looked up. "You will free the stone people working in your mines. Though you are already breaking the law under the net notice I will give you until this time tomorrow to get it done, then I act."

"That's not enough time!" one complained. "We need to get new infrastructure organised. That'll shut down the mines!"

The one in the environment suit stood up. "My stone people left this morning," he said to Logan. "I trust that I will have no problems?"

Logan spread his hands. "You know the laws. Don't break them."

"Fuck you, Pallen, you've got machines," said the whiner.

Pallen glanced round at her. "Because I knew this was coming."

"You never were one of us," said sour-face.

"I know," Pallen replied. "I don't possess that special degree of stupidity to think Trader John could keep Earth from taking over here, and nor did I think the percentage he demands is enough to keep him off our backs." He paused and surveyed the table. "And do you really think he hasn't noticed that you've been skimming the profits? That he's not been getting the percentage he demanded?... Later." He headed for the door and out.

"Sensible man," said Logan, also standing. "You have one day." He too headed for the door. There was no reply from the table.

*   *   *

"Pallen," Logan called.

The man turned halfway across the lobby and waited.

"They will turn on anyone who breaks ranks," Logan said.

"They were already turning on me," he replied. "I took the slaves they used up, gave them medical care then paid them a wage until they were ready to leave."

"I know," said Logan. "Watch your back."

"Watch *your* back," Pallen replied. "Trader John has a bounty on your head and every jangler here will want to take a shot. You know what happened to E. L. Trepanan?"

"I know."

"I just hope Earth is prepared to move in here with more than just one man. This is all about to get very ugly..."

"You think?" said Logan

Pallen eyed him for a long moment then nodded towards the council room. "They don't know who to be the most scared of, you or Trader John. He'll come you know... and he'll come hard. He almost certainly knows what they've been doing."

Logan shrugged. "There's always a heavy price when you make a deal with the devil."

"Quite," said Pallen, and headed away.

*   *   *

As an arthrodapt—a blend of human and arthropod—Trader John knew he inspired fear. He studied the sweaty face of Mayor Gavon staring at him from the screen, grated his mandibles in irritation then turned to the curved windows of his home, and gazed out across the river to the Flat beyond.

"He's delivered notice of jurisdiction," said Grade.

"Yes," said John, returning his attention to the man, "of course he has. We knew this was going to happen, but thus far there is only him there, and thus far the political situation has to be tested."

"You said you could keep Earth out of here," said Gavon.

John swung his attention back to the screen. "Are you complaining? My agents fed the information to the Prador that led to Earth being shunted out before, and I got rid of Trepanan."

"But a monitor is back, and it's looking a lot like Earth law is here to stay."

"We will see," said John tightly.

"So what do we do?"

"Some of my men will test this Monitor Logan," said John. "I have information about him that leads me to think they will be unsuccessful. I then have other options to bring into play."

"What can we do here?"

"Nothing, for the present. Just sit tight." John waved a hand over the screen and it blinked out. He stared at it for a long moment then reached out and tapped it. It blinked on again but this time just showed a revolving sphere. "House, detach services and move to pre-set location."

"As you instruct," replied a robotic voice.

The house rumbled and began to move, the view through the windows shifting. John tapped the screen again and the sphere disappeared. A touch brought up a list of names and he touched one of these.

"Chinnery Grade," he said.

After a short pause a face appeared. Below white spikey hair, half of it was conventional human while the other half a metal prosthesis.

"You've decided?" asked Grade.

"Yes, I've decided," John replied. "Meet me out on the Flat as detailed."

Grade nodded once and his image blinked out.

"Why are we moving?" a female voice enquired.

John looked over his shoulder. "Business," he said, "just business."

Trader John's house rose higher on its hinged legs. It then raised one of them, terminating in a big flat foot, and took a cautious step into the river. More sure now of its footing, it took another step, then another. Soon it was wading across the river, then stepping up out the other side and heading off across the Flat.

*   *   *

The drone dropped out of the darkness like a nightmare scorpion fly, writ large in nano-chrome armour etched with black superconductor. Its thick and shiny legs terminated in four-finger hands. Its wings were spread effector plates running from gravengines in its back. Laser ports dotted its body, a missile launcher jutted from its thorax below its head. It hung above the building for a moment protruding two Gatling cannons and revolved to inspect the town. Next, it folded the cannons away to come down with a heavy clattering thump on the roof of the monitor station.

"Hello monitor... Logan," it said.

"Hello drone. What do I call you?"

"Call me Sting. It's what they called me in my old unit, for reasons that should be quite obvious." The drone wiggled its scorpion sting.

"More detail than I require," said Logan flatly.

"Just making conversation," said Sting. "You have work for me?"

"Yes, I do. I gave them until tomorrow afternoon to free the stone people. I want you to ensure that they do."

"Oh good..."

Logan shook his head. "What I mean by that is that you'll use your induction warfare systems to knock out every thrall device and explosive collar throughout the mountains."

"Oh... and if they start killing stone people?"

Logan grimaced. "Yes, that is a possibility, but you can intervene subtly. You must not reveal yourself. If Trader John realizes something like you is here he might not come. And I want him to come."

"That could be... difficult."

"I have every confidence in you."

"The stone people even now are under Earth protection," Sting observed.

"Yes, I understand. I'm just asking you to at least try."

"I will try not to reveal myself," said the drone, "but if the janglers start killing they start dying."

Logan nodded. "Then I would prefer them to die quietly."

"That can be arranged..." said the drone. "So what are you going to do now?"

"Make my presence fully known and stir the pot a little."

"Don't get yourself killed."

"What, again? I'll try to avoid it."

The drone snorted in amusement then launched from the rooftop and disappeared into the night.

*   *   *

The saloon was ersatz eighteenth century USA. Logan pushed through the swing doors to the sound of a piano, only he noted that the android player had lost most of its syntheskin. He walked up to the bar.

"Bourbon," he said.

The bartender was one of the stone people—a woman in a simple dress with black hair bound tightly back, tendrils cropped and skin pale blue. An induction thrall clung to her temple like a flattened metal tic, a green loading light glinting across a small rectangular screen in its surface. She served his drink and he paid with an octagonal coin. She was about to move off.

"One moment."

She paused, obedient but wary.

Logan gazed at her steadily, held out his hand and pressed his mid-finger down on one of the touch controls on his palm. The woman's thrall beeped, the lights turning to orange, then red before going out. Her mouth dropped open in shock and she reached up to touch the thing.

"Don't do anything now," he said, speaking low. "At the end of the evening you can take it off and just leave. Stay safe."

She nodded, tears filling her eyes, then moved off to serve another customer, her movements unsteady. Logan turned, bourbon in hand, and surveyed the saloon.

There were janglers and others here. Whores ran their trade from soundproofed booths along one wall. At gaming tables, holograms or small robots fought gladiatorial battles. One man hung in gimbals in a VR suit, perhaps, by his movements, fighting another battle. One group lounged around a hooka, the air about them striated with rainbow smoke. Logan sipped his drink, noting that the four who had followed him from the station had spread out and were now heading towards him from different directions. He smiled coldly and turned back to the bar—watching the room in the mirror behind it. Now a fifth entered. Logan recognised the big ugly man as the stone people handler he had seen earlier in the day—the one who felt the need for a cattle prod, which now hung at his waist.

"Hey, monitor," said Ugly.

Logan turned and eyed the man.

"I hear you're a coward and wear body armour."

"Where did you hear that?"

"Seems some of my friends ran into you out on the Flat."

"Oh, how unfortunate."

The man just glared at him.

"But you asked about body armour." Logan pulled down the neck of his T-shirt to expose bare chest. "Only when I'm working."

"Bit stupid to come in here without it."

Logan shrugged. "My working day is over. This is a saloon, and I'm a customer." He stepped a little way out from the bar.

Breaking glass...

One came at him from the left wielding the bottle he'd broken on the edge of the bar, jabbing it towards Logan's face. Logan caught his wrist in his left hand, pulled and grabbed his shirt, spinning him into the one coming in from the right. Ugly came straight in, cattle prod humming. Logan advanced, chopped it sideways, taking a jolt to his arm, but delivered a heel-of-the-hand blow to the man's nose, shattering it. Another smashed a length of iron pipe against Logan's back, sending him staggering. As the man came in to deliver another blow Logan turned to drive an uppercut into his ribcage, bowing him over and lifting him from the floor. One hard chop to the back of his neck dropped him. Ugly came with the cattle prod again, this time Logan grabbed it and turned it into his guts, crackling and hissing. The man screamed, until Logan head butted him, twice, kneed him in the guts and, as he bowed over, slammed his head hard into the bar. Logan turned. Three men now surrounded him and had decided to upgrade. Logan eyed their selection of weapons. Two had knives. The third had his hand on the pistol at his hip.

"I will meet violence with equal violence, until I really start to get annoyed," he said.

The two with the knives came at him. He knocked one stab aside and caught the wrist of the other, pulled and shoved driving the knife from one into the guts of another. The gunman drew and fired, but Logan ducked and turned one of the knifemen in front of him, who took the shots in the back. He threw him towards the gunman and rose, a knife he had taken held in one hand. The gunman now tried to take careful aim, and a moment later was gagging on blood, the knife imbedded in his throat. He took a step, and then dropped.

The music had ceased now and all in the saloon were watching. Four were down unmoving, a knifeman was sitting on the floor holding his bleeding guts. Logan stepped over to the bar and picked up a bar towel, wiped blood from his neck and from his hand. He then threw the bar towel to the bleeding man.

"Here, put pressure on with that," he said. "You might survive—people have survived worse."

He finished his bourbon.

* * *

In his cab, Kraven peered at his screen. "What you saying, Caber? The whole system?"

"Yeah, it shut down."

"The stone people?"

"Just dropped their tools and started fading into the mountains."

"Why didn't you stop them?"

"I ain't paid enough to start shooting the fuckers—not with an Earth monitor in town."

"That worries you?"

"It should worry us all."

"You make me want to puke, Caber." Kraven switched off the screen, grimaced at it then looked up to survey his surroundings.

One party of stone people trudged out of the mine shouldering power drills running from heavy packs. They walked out beside a conveyor loaded with broken rocks. Other stone people awaited assignment, while among them fellow janglers were on patrol. He grunted satisfaction—all was as it should be—and returned to work. Guiding the moveable section of conveyor, remote controlling it from the cab of his spider, Kraven filled up another sorting-trough. He then keyed another control. Stone people, mostly women, who had been waiting to one side, jerked as if prodded, some of them reaching up to the thralls on their temples, then headed over to the trough and began sorting.

Kraven now set his spider in motion, and it walked delicately down the slope amidst the exterior mine workings. He then turned it to head over to the punishment frame where two stone people were hanging. Parking it on the ground, he climbed out, and sauntered over to Holse and Frax.

"So what's this, Frax?" he asked tightly, indicating the two on the frame with the flat of his hand.

"Thralls packed up and they tried to run." Frax shrugged, snapping his power whip back and forth.

"John says don't waste them," Kraven warned.

"They're about done anyway—maybe three or four days left in them."

"Really?" Kraven eyed the two. Covered with whip marks, they were nothing but skin and bone. He pursed his lips. "Might all be over soon anyway. Earth jurisdiction now. Four mines let their workers go."

"Yeah, Pallen's mines. Fucking coward."

"Maybe, but I just heard, over on Tulse Mountain, Caber's system went down and his workers just left."

"He let them leave—Caber's a chicken."

"Still . . . an Earth monitor." Kraven drew a pistol and toyed with it.

"One monitor in Godrun. What can he do? I bet Caber shut his system down himself because he's shitting himself."

Kraven nodded agreement. "Anyway, we should at least keep things neat and tidy here." He nodded to the two on the frame. "Get rid of these two."

Frax turned and looked at them. "Yeah, I guess."

With casual indifference, Kraven raised his weapon and shot the stone man on the right through the head. The man jerked and kicked for a little while, despite most of his skull being missing.

"Damn but they take time to die," he said.

"They're tough, adapted—good for hauling stone." Frax grinned. "Gut shoot the next one, an' let's see how long it takes."

A low humming then penetrated the air, followed by a thump as of someone beating a giant carpet. A wave of something passed through the mine workings, raising a cloud of dust.

"The fuck?" said Holse.

They scanned around. The stone people were looking about in confusion. Then those carrying power drills just dropped them and began shrugging off their packs. Kraven looked over to the sorting troughs. The stone people there had stopped working and seemed confused. He watched a woman step away shaking her head. She then reached up and took hold of her thrall, pulled it off her head to discard it, and began walking away.

Kraven holstered his pistol and began backing away, scared. With a hissing sound Frax's power whip activated.

"What the hell?"

Frax barely seemed able to hold onto the thing, it was thrashing about like a trapped snake, then it abruptly snapped back, wrapping itself around his neck, and began strangling him. He went down on his knees, gagging.

"Sir?"

Spinning round to face one stone man, Holse drew his weapon and aimed it. A crackling ensued and he found himself gaping at his severed wrist, his hand, still clutching the weapon, on the ground. The stone man backed away, hands held out to his sides to show he was unarmed. Shooting then, from across the workings. One of the janglers had opened up with a carbine. Hissing cracks filled the air. The man's carbine crumped and shed fire and he fell back screaming, his hands and forearms burned down to the bone. Other weapons were just detonating. Kraven saw a jangler beating one stone man abruptly beheaded by something invisible. The conveyor went over. Equipment exploded and fires bloomed all across the workings. Stone people were discarding their thralls and running.

Kraven ran for his spider and climbed inside, setting it into motion. It dodged across the mine workings then hit the slope, climbing fast.

"Come on. Come on!"

He reached the top of the slope then headed across the ridge and down the other side. Another slope took him up to a peak where he turned the spider so he could look back at the mine workings. Yes, all was chaos, but he had no idea of the cause. He turned the spider, ran it further, scrabbling along above a cliff. Something rose up the cliff and turned to face him. His spider just stopped, its controls becoming inert. The thing out there looked like a giant steel hoverfly with a scorpion tail.

The drone folded down two Gatling cannons and opened fire, disintegrating the cab of the spider, and Kraven along with it. A moment later just legs and a few broken hydraulic motors stood on the cliff top.

Sting turned away, muttering to himself. "Every confidence in you…" He paused, hanging in the air. "But I did try," he added.

He accelerated away.

*   *   *

Logan sat up on the low wall rimming the monitor station roof and gazed out across the town. A couple of fires were burning out there and, as he watched, something exploded. He grimaced, held out his right hand and pressed his little finger down against one of the touch controls.

"Is that you?" he asked the night.

A green light flickered on in the darkness. Whining, it scribed a circle and out of this, translucent, appeared the nightmare head of the war drone Sting.

"It's me," it said.

"What's happening?"

"I shut down the thrall units and explosive collars of all the stone people in Godrun," the drone explained. "There were some objections to them leaving."

"But no objections now?"

"No objectors," the drone replied.

Logan tilted his head in acknowledgement.

"You are aware," said the drone, "that events draw to their close?"

"Tell me..."

"Trader John moved his house last night—he's down on the Flats."

"I see." Logan paused for a moment. "You will take no actions yet, I assume."

"You were given control. I await your orders."

"Limited control of you," said Logan.

"I will not act until you have located her," said the drone. "But your time for that *is* limited."

"Thank you, Sting."

The image before him winked out.

* * *

Whether the mercenary, Chinnery Grade, could be called a man was debateable. Half his face and his hands were metal. He wore an armoured combat suit and his helmet, with its HUD visor, sat on the table before him. He hadn't brought his weapons in with him, but Trader John was knew this 'man' was more than capable of killing without them. However, on the table beside the helmet rested a squat esoteric looking gun with a ring-shaped magazine.

"You understand the situation?" asked John.

"I understand the situation," Grade replied. "You want full control of Godrun. You want its head cut off, that monitor out of the way, and the mine owners there dead. What I don't understand is why—they ran their mines and paid you a nice percentage."

"They are no longer satisfactory—they allowed just one man to disrupt my operation." John grimaced and clattered his mandibles. "They also neglected to mention how well their mine workings have been doing lately. That was a fatal omission."

"Why do you care?" asked Grade. "This is one of your smaller operations..."

"Profit is always an issue," John replied, scratching below part of his carapace armour. "Reputation is a bigger issue still."

Grade shrugged. He looked doubtful. "I still don't know where you are going with this, but I'll do the job." Grade's attention strayed to the two standing behind John's chair. Here were two big men clad in heavy combat armour, their faces concealed by opaque visors, heavy complicated looking carbines clutched at port arms across their chests. "Nor do I understand why you hired mercenaries, when you have your own people."

"It is not necessary for you to understand."

"Quite—it is only necessary that I be paid."

"You have been paid well, and your second payment will come on completion."

Grade tilted his head in acknowledgement.

"Good," John smiled. "Then get to it."

Grade stood, taking up his helmet. He then reached down, picked up the weapon and inspected it closely.

"And Grade..."

Grade looked up. "Yes?"

"I don't mind what you use against Godrun and the people there when you take control, but you go careful against the monitor. Be sure you understand." John pointed with one claw. "That weapon is key."

"Understood." Grade rested the weapon across his shoulder. "It's quite clear what he is."

Grade departed.

Trader John sat idly in his chair for a while longer, his yellow eyes narrowed. A moment later, a woman walked in. Emily Trepanan was as beautiful now as when he first saw her. She wore a simple toga and her long brown hair hung loose. The decorous silver thrall unit on her temple looked like a piece of jewellery.

"And I don't understand what you're doing," she said, her expression void.

"No?" he smiled, parting his mandibles to expose his human mouth. "It's simple really—Grade goes in full force. He captures the monitor and takes control of Godrun and the mines.

I test how far Earth will go in enforcing its laws. If it responds in force and the Prador are okay with that, then the whole operation can be written off."

"A costly exercise," she said, still blank.

"True, but the Prador might not be all right with a strong response from Earth here, in which case, Earth might lose jurisdiction, and I get full control here. Alternatively, if there is no response, the result is the same."

"Grade and his men... if the Earth forces go in?"

"Expendable, of course."

John picked up a remote control and operated it. Blinds hinged open all along one wall to expose the Flat, lying beyond his relocated house. Out there Grade and his mercenaries were preparing to leave in four armoured raptors—things that looked like attack helicopters lacking rotors. One of them took off while they watched.

"But I don't understand why it is important to capture the monitor alive," said the woman. "Nor do I understand why we had to come out here." Her words were leaden—no feeling in them.

Trader John eyed her coldly, fingering the mass of scar tissue on his chest carapace. "There are many things you don't understand my dear Emily. Suffice to say that this Monitor Logan is not quite as he appears and that I have... business with him."

* * *

"So you wanted a private meeting," said Logan, gazing across the wide real-wood desk at the Mayor. The man was nervous and sweating again, and Logan studied him carefully.

"Yes, a private meeting," said Gavon. He reached over to his humidor and took out a cigar, began tapping it against his desk. "Trader John arrived here last night—his house is out on the Flats."

"That's interesting, but gets me no closer to understanding what you want."

"We want an accommodation."

"You speak for the whole council?"

"All but Pallen."

"Then why aren't they here?"

"They're in the building, but I thought it would be better if I spoke to you first."

"Then speak."

"Trader John is here, while only you are here in Godrun..."

"Yes..." Logan sat back, knowing what this was about.

"If Earth is establishing jurisdiction here, then why only you? Yes, you've used some Polity device to knock out the thralls, but surely there should be more monitors... soldiers... mechanisms..."

"Oh, I see now," said Logan. "You're scared of Trader John."

"When he gets what he wants he is perfectly reasonable. When not..." Gavon spread his hands. "The situation has to be one way or the other. Either Earth in full control or him. Any other way is chaos."

"And of course John wants his full cut of your profits, and not the rather reduced amount you have been sending him..."

Gavon lit his cigar and puffed on it in agitation. "Yes, John can be... excessive."

Logan leaned forwards. "Let me tell you how it's going to run. John's people will come here seeking to, just as you put it, push the situation one way or the other. He'll come after me but he'll come in strong. He'll want to be sure about whether Earth has full jurisdiction or not. He'll push for a reaction and people here are going to die. The first to die will be those who haven't been paying him what he feels he is owed."

"You're the Earth monitor—you're supposed to protect us."

"I protect the innocent." Logan stood. "From where I'm standing there is not one person in this town who has not been part of the enslavement of the stone people, and who has not been culpable in many other crimes, including murder."

"That's bullshit," said Gavon. "Others work here who have nothing to do with the mining."

"Everyone is here for the money the mining generates, and all have neglected to notice the crimes being committed around them." Logan shrugged.

"That's it? That's your final word?"

"That's it," said Logan, turning away. He paused at the door and glanced back. Gavon had already pulled a small com unit towards him. Logan smiled and headed away.

*   *   *

The lobby was clear of people, even the woman behind the glass, still punctured with a bullet hole, had left. He exited through the colonnade, out onto the street, turned and began heading back towards the station. Then a shot rang out, and the impact flung him sprawling face down on the stone walkway. He rolled onto his back, then rolled again to drop from the kerb between the treads of a parked crawler. Smoke rose from his back—a big, burned hole there. He dragged himself past a tread and peeked down the street. About twenty janglers were coming up the road. The one in the middle, a tall thin man in a long duster, cradled a flack-shell carbine with a telescopic sight.

"You got him?" asked a man at this one's side.

"He ain't getting up," said the tall man. "I just blew his spine out."

Logan rolled out, came up into a crouch and levelled his rail-beader. A short burst flipped over five men in clouds of atomised blood. He fired again dropping two more, but then returned fire threw him back, bullet after bullet slamming into his body. He lay there, perfectly still for a moment, then abruptly sat up. He held up his beader again and triggered it, but nothing happened. He peered down at the severed power cable.

"What the fuck are you?" called the tall man.

He and the remaining janglers were now crouching or had taken cover behind crawlers. Logan surveyed the numerous weapons pointed at him.

"I'm your worst nightmare. I'm a monitor who just won't die, guys." He began to stand, but then heard a roaring from behind.

He whirled to see an armoured raptor sliding down the street. Its guns roared tearing up men and crawlers in a running explosion of blood and debris. The tall man just disintegrated. The firing stopped and the raptor came on past Logan and opposite the council building, the effect of its grav engines flicking up dust and scraps of clothing. It turned, facing the offices, and fired two missiles. These gutted the building, but the raptor just sat unaffected in the back-blast. Logan stood, watched it for a moment, then holstered his beader.

"Welcome to Godrun, Trader John," he said.

As the raptor swung towards him, he turned and ran.

*   *   *

At the controls of his raptor, Grade watched the monitor sprinting along the street. He opened up with the Gatlings, tearing up everything behind the man but not actually hitting him.

"Trader John said not to kill him," said, Shafer, the mercenary beside him.

"We might kill him," said Grade, "but it would have to be a very lucky shot."

Shafer looked over, curious.

Grade reached down beside his seat and picked up the weapon Trader John had given him: a short wide-barrelled thing with a ring-shaped magazine. He pulled one of the glassy shells out of that magazine and held it up for Shafer's inspection. Its nose was a ring of short barbed spikes, while electronics packed its translucent body.

"Disruptor bullet," said Shafer. "So he really is…"

"Yes, he is," said Grade. "And tactically that's how we regard him." He now spoke into his headset. "Keep him running. We want him out in the open when we take him—drive him towards the square."

"Ah fuck," a voice replied. "He just ducked into—"

"I see it," said Grade. "Take that building apart. Start with the top floor and work your way down."

"Civilians?" someone enquired.

"Not our concern, and if they are this monitor's concern, he won't use their houses for cover again."

Another raptor fired a missile that blew the top off one of the foamstone houses. Just as Grade instructed, it worked its way down. As it reduced the house to rubble, people spilled out the back and ran. Grade's HUD picked out the monitor close in to the row of houses. He strafed behind the running figure, then swore as Logan turned and kicked down a door entering yet another building.

"Seems he doesn't care much for the civilians," Shafer observed.

"Okay," said Grade, calling up a town map in his visor. "We run him up Sapphire Street. Incendiaries in every building along there. Keep him running." He paused. "I'm loading tactical data constantly so watch your HUDs."

Two raptors flew along Sapphire Street shooting missiles out of side cannons into each building as they passed. Behind, the buildings gushed fire from their windows and some of them came down. At the end of the street, one of the raptors turned and hovered. The other shot up and over and began to demolish the house the monitor had dived for cover inside.

Grade, now high up, gazed down at another explosion in the town and marked another tick on the map displayed in his HUD.

"That was the monitor station," said Shafer.

"Yeah," Grade agreed, "but for the monitor himself this place is headless now."

"Bit harsh, don't you think, Trader John?" Grade looked at him and he continued, "The council building, the homes of every semi-independent mine owner plus business premises?"

Grade shrugged. "He wanted us to be harsh. Seems you don't take more than your fair share of his profits."

"You sure it's just that?" asked Shafer.

"Not for me to be sure or otherwise so long as he makes that final payment."

"I guess..." said Shafer.

The monitor staggered out of the ruins of the latest building the raptors brought down. He peered to the far end of the street where one of them hovered, then turned and ran in the opposite direction. It began shooting up the street behind him. He kept going, past buildings burning inside like furnaces.

"Okay, he's heading for the square now," said Grade. "All units close in and ring-fence him. I've updated you all on tactical so you know what to do."

*   *   *

Logan ran on down the street, paused by a scattering of burned human bodies, gazed at them blankly then ran on when a pursuing raptor opened fire again. He stumbled out into the Square—lawns here patterned about a central monument. Glancing aside he saw running refugees, and looking around he saw pillars of smoke rising from Godrun.

"You deal with the Devil and the price can be high," he muttered.

He turned to head to the right but another raptor appeared and turf erupted in front of him. He glanced to the left and saw yet another of the things rising up over the buildings, and he moved on. Soon he leapt a small garden, rounded a pond and headed towards the monument. Here stood a statue of a big wide-shouldered and heavily adapted man—a man who looked like one of his parents might have been a praying mantis. On the pedestal the name read: Trader John. He stopped beside it, resting a hand on the cold stone, and eyed the raptor down on the lawns ahead—battle-armoured mercenaries piling out and spreading into a line. To his left and to his right the other raptors were also landing and spewing mercenaries. The same behind.

Logan drew his pulsegun, took aim at those approaching behind and began firing. Returned fire slammed him back against the monument. He staggered forward again, shots slammed him back again, his weapon trashed and issuing discharges. He discarded it and just stayed where he was. A moment later Grade was standing before him.

"So John employed mercenaries to do his dirty work," he said.

Grade shrugged. "He has the funds."

"And you have done my work too."

Grade tilted his head, curious.

Logan gestured to the devastated town all around. "This place does not deserve to exist. You've done a good job here."

"Apparently so, then," said Grade.

"It's a shame you won't live to collect your fee."

"Really?"

Logan thrust himself up, horribly fast. Grade triggered the weapon he held and stepped smoothly aside. Logan staggered past and turned, a glowing cylinder embedded in his chest. It pulsed, issuing waves of white fire that spread over his body like the burning edges of fuse paper. He stood shuddering, power discharging from his legs into the ground. Then the cylinder went out and Logan just froze, smoke rising from him. Then he went over, crashing to the ground like a falling tree.

* * *

Holding the weapon Grade had returned to him, Trader John watched the raptor depart. He then turned and trudged up the ramp, which his house had lowered on the Flat, and inside, his two guards close behind. Walking through the plush corridors of his home, he came to a door and rapped on it. Emily exited and walked meekly a pace behind the guards as he moved on.

"Come see our Earth monitor," he said.

They entered his main living area. John walked over, dropped into his steel chair and put the weapon down on a surface beside it. Emily paused to look at a sheeted figure lying on the floor, before taking her place on one of the sofas in the lounge pit, folding her legs underneath her.

"Stand up, monitor Logan," said John.

The figure on the floor moved, then stood, the sheet falling away. The two guards lowered their weapons from port arms and pointed them at him.

"But he's not human," Emily said, her words devoid of emotion.

"Doesn't look it does he?"

Heavy manacles bound Logan's wrists and his clothing hung in rags. His upper torso lay bare and his trousers were in tatters. This exposed his loss of skin and flesh. It was gone from his right arm from wrist upwards, from his shoulder and across his chest. Gunfire had stripped one leg too, and a portion of his scalp was missing. This exposed his ceramal bones, corded white electromuscle, and various interior mechanisms.

"Is he an android?" Emily asked.

"No," said John. "He is in fact partially human—a cyborg." He pointed. "Do you see, on his skull?"

Emily studied the monitor more closely. "Induction thrall."

"That would not work if he was an android," John explained. "It does work because there is a human brain inside that metal skull." After a pause John continued, "Logan, look up."

Logan shuddered, jerked his head from side to side, then up. He gazed at Trader John blankly, then transferred his attention to the woman, his mouth moving silently.

"Emily," he finally managed.

She turned to John. "He knows me?"

"Perhaps you'll understand better if he wears his real face." Trader John allowed himself an ugly smile. "Logan, return your face to its base setting."

Logan's face changed and for the first time Emily showed real emotion. Her mouth opened in shock.

"Emily Trepanan," said Trader John. "Meet what is left of your husband Enders Logan Trepanan."

John now stood up and walked over to Logan, grabbed hold of his face in one clawed hand and turned it, staring at him close.

"I dealt with you once and now I'll deal with you again," he said. "But what satisfaction do I get from that? You can die, but you can only feel pain if you choose to do so."

"I can feel satisfaction," said Logan. "Your operation here is over, and you will not be leaving."

John stared at him and clattered his mandibles. He stepped back, fingering the mass of scar tissue on his chest. He looked round. "Emily, come here."

Obedient to his will Emily stood and walked over. As she did so, John operated a control at his wrist, bringing over a hoist in the ceiling and lowering a wire with a hook. Placing this through a hole in Logan's manacles he hoisted him up into the air. He then stepped to Emily and put his arm around her.

"I think I will fuck your wife now," he said. "Afterwards I might kill her in front of you." He shrugged. "Who knows? She's not so interesting any more—too long under the thrall and they lose their... novelty."

Logan just hung there, watching them go. Once they were out of sight he looked up to his hands, reached down with one finger and pressed one of the touch pads on his palm. Green light flickered on his face and he gave a tight smile.

"She's here in his house," he said. "You can take the gloves off now."

* * *

Sting sat atop a boulder on a mountaintop overlooking Godrun. He focused on particular areas, putting frames over whatever interested him and magnifying the image. First, he studied the town square. Here the mercenaries had erected a scaffold and were leading some people towards it at gunpoint. He focused on faces and identified them. Jangler Edmondson: murder, enslavement, torture—guilty. Mine-owner Jefferson: murder, enslavement, torture, theft, perjury—guilty. Not finding one innocent amongst them, he watched as the mercenaries strung them up, then swung his attention elsewhere.

Putting a frame over a raptor, he analysed it: miniguns, seeker missiles, particle cannon, anti-munitions lasers, EMP disruptors, ceramal impact armour, super-conducting impact foam... He snorted dismissively and turned his attention to another raptor, then concentrated on the individual who had stepped out of it.

Chinnery Grade: multiple murder, insurrection, terrorism, torture... Guilty. Sentence: death. Sting rattled his feet against the stone impatiently, extruded his Gatling cannons then retracted them, sighed and then tilted back.

"Patience, drone," he muttered to himself. "Tactical considerations first."

He now observed mercenaries driving a crowd of people towards the outskirts, occasionally shooting in the air. Crosshairs appeared over every mercenary, then winked out. Sting spread his effector wings and rose from the boulder, revolving slowly in mid-air, picking out the other two raptors. Frames and crosshairs multiplied around them, then again went out. Words appeared in his vision: Assessment Complete.

"Gloves off," he muttered.

He tilted and roared down towards Godrun.

* * *

Logan hung from the wire utterly still, then raised his head and looked around. Trader John was coming back. The big arthrodapt returned to the room—his ever-present guards following him—and stood gazing out at the Flats, elbow supported by one hand and claw against his cheek.

"I've been thinking," he said. "About revenge..."

He lowered his hand and operated his wrist control, lowering Logan to the floor. Another stab with one claw opened the manacles. Without looking back, he began heading towards the exit. "You will follow me outside."

Logan turned and trudged slowly after him, but the guards came up swiftly behind him and took hold of each of his arms. They walked him behind John through the rich corridors of the house, then down a ramp and outside. Here stood Emily. She rubbed at her arms and her expression was puzzled as she searched her mind for memories. She turned.

"I'm cold out here, John," was all she said.

Trader John smiled nastily. "Don't worry, that won't be for long." He swung round towards Logan. "You know, when you shot me, I came the closest to death I have ever been."

Logan watched him steadily and said, "Death is not easy to define. There was not much left of me when they pulled me out of the river."

"Yes... quite."

"You were alive when they took you to the city hospital," said Logan. "It was some time before I was found."

John waved a dismissive claw. "Fuck that," he spat. "You nearly killed me and I made you pay, now you, and Earth, are screwing my operation here and you have to pay again... but apparently I cannot cause you physical pain." He gave a cruel smile. "However, under the thrall you must obey my every word. And there are other forms of pain." He waved another hand and the two guards released Logan.

"Is that the only way you can command people, by controlling their minds?" asked Logan.

Trader John retained his smile as he drew a knife from his belt. He tossed it down on the ground before Logan.

"Mind control has its satisfactions," he said. "Now pick up that knife and gut your wife."

*   *   *

Sting spat two missiles, one after the other, and tracked them down. The first struck the top of the building, demolishing it. The raptor parked there, rose up on the blast, then engaged its effectors and turned, issuing missiles of its own. The second missile struck it in the belly and blew a glowing hole. The raptor slammed back into the building opposite smashing a hole in the wall, then peeled out and crashed to the street.

"I bet that hurt," commented the drone.

Cruising on, Sting fired lasers from its body ports blowing up the missiles the raptor had fired, turning them into hot explosive streaks across the sky. He then fired three more missiles, which hurtled out towards the other raptors already launching into the air. Two exploded before reaching their targets—taken out by anti-munitions—the third blew the tail off a raptor and it fell, spinning.

"I'll attend to you later," said Sting.

More missiles came hurtling back and Sting dropped behind a building at the last moment. These struck the face, blowing a glowing hole. One of the raptors came in towards this, then rose up to go over the building. Sting came out through the hole, tilted upright and opened up with Gatling cannons into its underside. It shuddered under multiple impacts shedding debris, then abruptly tilted and shot to one side. The drone extruded another weapon and hit it with the royal blue of a particle beam, tracking it. The thing glowed and smoked, pinned by the beam, which finally punched through. It hit the street burning and bounced along it, coming to rest on the steps of the demolished council building.

Amazingly two people rolled out of the thing, flaming. They came upright with extinguishing gas jetting from their body armour. Sting hit them with one Gatling cannon—two short bursts and they disappeared.

Shots from below...

The drone took fire, bullets ricocheting off his carapace, then tilted, observing mercenaries further along the street. Targeting frames bloomed over them, with identification tags, and his lasers stabbed out, turning human beings into hot explosions of blood and flesh. Briefly, as they disappeared, the words 'Sentence Executed' appeared over each.

Then a missile struck him, flinging him back. He hit the top of a building, bounced and fell down into the street beyond hitting the road on his back.

"Fuck," he said, flipped over onto his feet, and shook himself.

The tailless raptor now rose into sight, firing with everything it had into the road. Sting shot in hard reverse, turned, and fired three missiles down a side street, then went in hard reverse down the street opposite. He rose up and the tailless raptor rose up before him. They hit each other hard with Gatling cannons, but then the three missiles shot up out of a street behind the raptor, looped over and hit it all at once. It blew to pieces.

"Okay, just one more," said the drone, now revolving in the air.

Further shots hit him, and bounced off. Almost negligently, he targeted mercenaries and took them out. Cruising across the town, he put frames over those herding citizens along, narrowed the focus of his lasers and killed them with head shots. He cruised in over the square and dealt with the mercenaries there likewise.

"Come on—don't be shy."

The fourth raptor came at him from underneath, firing all its weapons. He spun nose down, fired with all his own and accelerated towards it. The raptor shed debris, but nothing seemed to affect the drone as he took slugs and lasered missiles before they hit him. He and the raptor crashed head-on then fell into the street and bounced apart.

Again, on his back with his legs in the air, Sting said, "What a rush!" and flipped upright. Turning now to face the wrecked raptor, he waited. Eventually a door banged open and a man stepped out. His armour was smoking and broken in places, glowing in others. He had lost his helmet and the human part of his face was bloody.

"Chinnery Grade," said Sting. "Always the best for last."

Grade spread his hands. The drone surged forwards, sting looping over and jabbing. It impaled Grade and lifted him, shrieking and smoking orange vapour, then flipped him away. He thumped to the ground, inert, vapour rising from him still, his skin blackened.

"Sentence executed," the drone added.

*   *   *

Logan stood still for a long moment, fighting the thrall. He then squatted and took up the knife.

"I cannot, yet, disobey your instruction," he said. "But the thing about such a degree of control is that you must be precise in your instructions and, more importantly, tell your slaves what they cannot do."

Logan held out his hand and pressed a finger against one of the touch controls on his palm. The tracking green light on his thrall turned to amber, then to red, and then went out. Emily gasped and went down on her knees, and reached up with a shaking hand to her thrall. Its lights were also out.

Logan allowed himself a nasty smile then turned and drove the knife straight in through the armour of one guard, lifting the man off his feet. He turned him and threw him at the other guard sending them both crashing to the ground. The second guard then tried to rise and bring his weapon to bear but Logan kicked him hard in the head, knocking away his helmet. The man looked up at him, stunned. Logan punched him twice, hard, caving in his face, then snatched up his weapon. He turned to face John.

Trader John was just standing with his arms folded. Logan watched him in puzzlement, then glanced across at his wife. He held out a hand. "Emily... come here."

She looked up at him, her expression unreadable, then reached up and detached the thrall from her head. She then swung her attention to John as she climbed to her feet. After a moment she turned away and fled waveringly towards the ramp.

"Emily!"

She ignored him and entered the house, moving out of sight.

"Like I said," said John. "They lose something under the thrall."

Logan swung back towards him, really angry now. "Fuck you!" he spat and then opened up with the weapon. Explosive shells hit Trader John, wreathing him in fire and blew him back across the Flat. Finally, he spun round and went down, still smoking and burning. Logan stared at him and then dropped the weapon. He stared at the mobile house, all his dreams about rescuing his wife now dust. Then he took a breath and followed her inside.

"Emily?" he called, gently, nervously.

He came towards the main room.

Explosive shells hit him in the back throwing him into the room. He crashed down and a big hand reached down, hauled him up and slammed him hard into the wall. And Trader John was there delivering punishing blow after blow.

"How," asked John, "did you think I was repaired?"

The earlier shots had burned and blown away most of Trader John's arthrodapt exterior. Exposed now was his metal body, its electro-muscle and internal devices. He threw Logan hard against the wall again, then pounded him into it. Stepping back, he slapped a hand against his own chest and said, "And this, believe me, is the best that money can buy!"

Logan flung himself forwards to fight back, but John hammered into him again. Logan was outmatched. As he rained blow after blow on Logan, Trader John continued:

"Yes... you are... right," he said, punctuating his words with further blows. "It is stupid... to rely... on thrall technology." He paused to stab a finger at Logan. "But it equally as stupid to think yourself invulnerable."

"Quite right," said a voice behind.

There came a thump and a flash. John turned with bright fire traversing his body like the smouldering edge of fuse paper, a glowing cylinder pulsing in his back. He tried to reach it, but then finally froze and crashed to the floor. Emily walked up to stand over him, holding the weapon with its ring-shaped magazine.

*   *   *

They sat on the Flat some distance from the house, in twilight.

"You are my wife, and I owed you this," said Logan. "But I will understand if you want nothing more from me." He gestured at the exposed workings of his cyborg body. "Do you?"

She gazed at him expressionlessly. "You can feel if you want to and, when you are repaired, you can be human in every way. You are still you inside."

"But what about—" He broke off as a shadow fell across them then, with a deep thrumming sound the drone Sting settled on the Flat.

"So you saved her," said the drone.

Logan nodded, not smiling.

"And what about Trader John?"

"He's inside his house."

"Dead?"

"Still alive, since he's mostly machine like me."

"That's not so bad," said the drone, "but sentence must still be executed." He rose into the air and turned, then spat a whole series of missiles straight at the house. They shot in through the ramp door. "Get your heads down."

The missiles exploded inside the house, first blowing out all windows and gutting it with an inferno, then tearing its apart. Smoking debris bounced across the flat. One big leg spiralled up in the air and came down with a crash. Then after a while, all was calm in the orange glow of the burning wreckage.

"You didn't answer my question," said Logan.

Emily reached out and rested a hand against his face. "You are still you inside," she said. "I don't know what I am, inside, any more. And I don't yet know what I want." She smiled tiredly. "That's the best answer I can give."

Cold Fusion
Sam M. Phillips

I can feel my skin sloughing off, wet and loose from rotting flesh. Wishing my nerves were dead I fall in the snow and roll around, the cold holding me in place, a frozen cut of meat, long gone bad. The snow is purple and pink and yellow and green, the fallout still alive, a chaotic rainbow, shimmering like a mirage. Heat haze rises, the dead tree stick figures fuzzy all around me, silhouettes of a past now gone. More snow falls, covering me in a thin layer of riotous colour.

I lie there for a moment, trying to remember before the blast, but there isn't much there now: a house, flattened, disintegrated in a rushing heat wave; a job where I am like a robot, acting on programming; family with no faces, a mirror of their fate.

I can barely remember all the people, the population of a life. They are gone, melted in the sludge pits, the hot flesh boiling in vast lakes of dissolving meat. That's if they survived the original explosions, the shockwaves which ended a civilisation. Now the radioactivity makes a mockery of form, mutating, transforming. No one is left unaffected. I have no feelings about it, like I would have had before. My mind is dead, a hollow husk, drifting in shadows of raw sensation.

I get up and look at the sky. It's angry and red, thick green clouds forming like mould on the horizon. My eyeballs feel hot just looking at it, despite the snow falling on my face. There is some malevolence up there, the fallout, jangling around in the atmosphere, ready to rain death upon us once more.

Well, it's too late for me. I'm already dead—at least I will be soon—so there's not much to fear anymore, except maybe this slow dissolution, my physical form falling apart, pieces of my body scattered across the rainbow snowdrifts. Where is my mind? My spirit hovers over me like an angel, watching. The disassociation stretches off into forever, and I wish I could just end it now.

Tingling sensations in my cells excite me though, never let me rest, and I wonder if the radioactivity hasn't done something to me beyond just rot my body. There is... *vigour* inside me still, the puppet strings from a past life, holding on in hope of salvation.

Ugly wet sounds as my gelatinous eyeballs shift. Across the plain there is a factory, now just a ruin. In the other direction is nothing but the snowdrifts.

Is it even snow? I look again at the green clouds, far off, and then up at the red sky, flat and hot like metal in a furnace. There's nothing normal here. I put out my tongue, a lump like burning charcoal lands on it, turns my mind to fire. I spit, but it's *inside* my tongue now.

"What is this?"

I can hear a voice inside my head. It's muffled, and I realise it's my own tongue, flailing about.

"They never suspect," says my tongue, flapping against my teeth.

Cold fusion, I think, not knowing what this even means. I have a vision of myself in a lab coat, delicately inserting something into a metal sphere. I look worried, tired. The vision pauses, turns, looks at me, watching, and frowns. Then it fades away, melts in the endless river of fire, consuming my past.

Was it a bomb?

"Fire of angels, flying in heaven," says my tongue. The red sky pulses and I fall to my knees.

All around me the snow changes, turns black. The blackness forms into tiny figures, like demons. They go to war, battle with pitchforks and laser beams. They are crawling all over me, trying to conquer me.

It is just like before the blast, but then I could not run. Now I can and so I do, the demons disintegrating into fine ash being sucked up into the sky, swirling there in a vortex. I try not to look but I feel my tongue being pulled out my mouth, magnetised to whatever source of power is hanging up there, beyond the vortex.

I let it go. I have no need for it, and it flaps in the wind, screaming a wordless scream. I mumble something to myself, having already forgotten it, my mouth a hollow cave. My teeth chatter a signal, some primal rhythm to my brain, relayed from my stomach.

It's like I don't even really care, and I'm sure I don't, but there is something, some primal force compelling me. The numbness in my guts ignores all else as it propels me forwards, fires deep in my core breathing heavy sighs, demanding fuel. These aren't even my thoughts and I realise I'm just an empty husk, a phantom in a shell, hollowed out just to be filled back up.

Someone, *something* else has the same idea. There is a drilling sensation, and I know they are trying to get in. Inside is the only treasure.

They've breached the second level, we've got to evacuate, I think, remembering the drilling, and the man, screaming his brains out in fear. I feel none of that now, only loss, my body rotting, yet still somehow animated. I wonder how I have not yet succumbed.

"I need to feed," says the sky. I look up, my tongue now massive, the vortex a mouth with no teeth. Huge strings of saliva fall from the gaping portal, spinning, forming a web. The sticky tendrils reach for me, and I reach for them, wanting so badly to go home. I am pulled up, so slowly, like dangling honey, viscous liquid falling in reverse.

The tongue licks my body, held so delicately in the gelatinous fingers. I feel my skull being cracked apart with a word.

Yes, I have secrets. Do you want them? I ask the tongue and it croons, lapping up the knowledge. A beam of light passes behind my eyes; I wonder if angels are real, and if so, is this all they are to me?

"Brains," says my tongue, probing deeply. There is no pain, and I'm relieved, for my failing body has brought me so much.

There is a harsh buzzing, sharp and high, which promises release from the tension I feel, the sharp angle between the past and a forgotten future.

Inside the vortex now, turning inside out, everything spilling like cut guts. The truth comes out of me, and I am rewarded with its glow, having spent too long as a mindless thing, shambling across a wasted world.

There I am, though I could be anyone, standing at the reactor, a metaphysical gun at my back. The fourth world war has been going on for too long, and the powers that be want the magic cure, a world buster. I cannot fathom such horrendous misuse of power, but they have my family. I can see them too, and I'm ashamed that I cannot see past my love for them. It never saved them either, cannibal monsters in the fallout zone. I was promised they'd be spared.

I fall asleep in the comforting grip of the memory, held in stasis by promises of salvation. When I wake I realise I am being eaten by a pack of radioactive zombies. Flurries of rainbow snow as we struggle on the frozen floor of the factory I had seen in the distance, the roof caved in, black walls brooding witnesses to my final demise.

I try to fight but I cannot, there are too many, their leering faces falling apart, fingers snapping off as they claw at my flesh. I am being torn apart, piece by piece. I feel everything, my mind still vital, the subconscious still functioning, even if I no longer can tell who I am, and why all this is happening.

WORLD WAR FOUR

Weapons fire; sharp cracks, bright laser lights, and deep groaning. I'm lost in an orgy of death, believing my time has finally come. Bodies fall onto me, spasm as they die—hot air escaping from fetid lungs, a miasma which envelops my face. There is no blood, just puffs of dust. All the snow around me evaporates and the moisture inside my skull sizzles. I pass out as mechanical suits close in around me. They follow me into my dreams, blurred outlines like memories.

"There is something inside you, we want it," says a voice, crackling distortion inside my mind.

"I'm too tired to stop you now..." I say, my thoughts echoing down a long hallway.

"They tried to deny us this knowledge, let you perish with the rest, a victim of your own creation."

Meat sizzles on a grill.

"They used me..."

A coin bounces off the sides of a deep well.

"All this is over for you now," says the voice, a drill starting up.

"I cannot open my eyes," I say.

"You do not want to see."

Liquids stir.

"Please, if I must go."

Flash of a mirror, a shadow fleeing before a horror scene. Sharp suction, my brains removed by grotesque aliens seeking the weapon which destroyed the human race: cold fusion.

A thunderclap, blinding lightning, my body finally robbed of consciousness. The vital spark escapes the prison of torment, unleashed upon the universe. An angel, my spirit lives on through the phantom of death, a chain reaction.

Yuddh Ke Khel
Mel Lee Newmin

A laser carving through the skin of his fuselage caught Chen Fan by surprise. With a yelp, he sent his craft nose diving for cover in the cloud bank below. Instruments shrieked as he descended too fast into the earth's atmosphere, heat along the shielding threatening to fry him to a cinder. Yet the enemy on his tail kept pace with him. His monitors revealed a laser slicing the air on his left, missing him by metres.

Fan frantically sought friendly craft or at least open sky. Instead, the viewfinder within his helmet noted seven Russian attack craft swarming like bees over his head. Only one bothered to follow his plunge towards the deck, but it was a determined bastard. Fan knew why.

"Command, I'm in trouble," he reported into his microphone. "I've been hit."

"Can you still fly?" asked Command.

"Well, I can at the moment." Fan adjusted his pitch, backed off his elevon and swooped towards earth. A rumple ahead of him rose into a vast mountain range, white topped with snow, arid and empty in the valleys. Hoping to elude his pursuer, Fan shot towards a canyon that opened ahead of him.

"We're tracking you," said Command.

No shit. That isn't helpful.

Fan looked left and right, calculating how low to go. He felt as if his aircraft was whizzing barely above the sparse treetops of the desert. Yet, he knew it couldn't be that low because his altitude alarms would be screaming louder than they were. They told him his perspective was skewed. He had space to drop.

Could his wings clear the canyon? A series of warning lights bloomed on his monitor as the fly on his tail loosed a barrage of armour piercing missiles. Chen flipped his jet sideways to elude them and they scored across the ground, spitting up sand. No choice. His options were the canyon, planting himself face first into the hard pan, or exploding into oblivion when the Russian bastard fried his ass.

Canyon it is.

As he dropped nearly to the ground and blasted into the canyon, Fan considered if he could launch a fireburst to throw off his companion. His instruments balked. Too low to be effective. Dammit!

Command's cool voice jolted in his ear. "Systems control indicates your damage is superficial. Stay on target."

Fan read his own monitors and cursed when they agreed with Command. The hit to his fuselage had damaged his coolant system but the blow wasn't fatal. He could keep flying as long as the bleed remained light and he didn't overheat. What was the chance of that? He was only flying through one of the hottest deserts on earth at midday at a screaming pace low to the ground inside a canyon. No stress on his engines. Easy.

Fan ground his teeth.

Not that he blamed Command. They had a job to do, just like he did. Win this war. Send the Ruskies scurrying back across Mongolia like the cowards they were.

The initial Russian invasion had caught Fan by surprise just as it had the Chinese government. Although relations between the two supergiant countries had been tense for a decade over control of oilfields in the eastern Pacific, Moscow and Beijing had approached the rising tensions cautiously. China's ability to mobilise a ten million man army terrified the Russians. Russia's weapons program kept China on its heels. So they'd danced. Sometimes a waltz of diplomats in Novosibirsk, other times a salsa of presidents in Shanghai. All the while a nervous Europe kept watch and the United States crumpled beneath international sanctions levied after their last attempt at being global policeman. India rubbed its collective hands together with glee and awaited the bounty that would fall to it, the ultimate master of Asia.

Russia ended the stalemate with stunning force. And not on the sea as China had expected. Instead, three full divisions rolled out of the steppes without warning, taking Mongolia without a shot and proceeding directly for the Great Wall. The ancient boundary couldn't protect modern China from an armoured cavalry attack. Caught flat footed, Beijing had taken the only action it could short of a nuclear strike. The premier swallowed his ego and employed the Lightning Reaction Force, throwing everything it had at the enemy to stave off disaster.

The ploy worked. The LRF responded with alacrity and valour, pouring hellfire down on the invaders from the stratosphere. The brutality of their attack stalled the Russians in Inner Mongolia, buying the Chinese time to mobilise their massive land army and send it racing for the border. The resulting clash of titans was a tank battle the likes of which the world had never seen, even in World War III when the US invaded the Middle East.

Fan hadn't taken part in that theatre himself. His job was different. With the rest of his squadron, he was charged with keeping the Russian Space Force away from China, inhibiting troop movements and harassing the rear lines of the Russian Army. While half of the team defended China's satellites, Fan's group aimed at maiming the ground offensive. He was expected to cut off their supplies, destroy rail lines and roads, and level towns and villages. Scorch the earth between Siberia and the heart of China. Easy stuff at first because he and his fellows had ruled the skies for two days before the Russians responded to the surprising attack from the south. Now that they'd deployed their own Lightning Reaction Force, the situation had turned dicey.

Bringing Fan to his current dilemma. A Russian on his tail, a hole in his jet and no help for kilometres.

Fan's only choice was to proceed.

Finish the job.

With deft flicks of his wrist, he sent his agile craft weaving amongst the crags that edged the dry riverbed. The rearward alarm and his monitors told him his shadow was sticking tight. Damn! How had the Russians upgraded their fleet to be so agile?

Probably the same way we did. By getting assistance from helpful Americans willing to sell their souls to buy their way out of sanctions. The world's best weapons tech! On sale here for a limited time!

Fan's cursing reached Command who tersely informed him that vulgarity wasn't acceptable. Fan took his hands off his stick just long enough to shoot them an unseen finger as a column of rock suddenly loomed directly ahead of his jet. He dodged it, tilting hard right. He almost scraped bottom.

His monitor showed his shadow flinching from the near collision. Unable to flip his craft as swiftly, the Russian banked left, sending him down a small arroyo. Fan grinned.

"Your mother breastfed you camel piss," came a familiar voice over his headset. Igor Iraninov.

Fan laughed as he righted his jet and set it skimming across the desert towards his target. Losing Iraninov didn't just take the heat off him and his beleaguered jet, it also made him want to howl to the heavens because once again he'd beaten his nemesis. He and Iraninov had been at each other since the conflict started. Two excellent pilots on opposite sides of a war, they knew each other well. Fan respected Iraninov's talent and considered the pilot equal to him in skill. To have bested him this round filled Fan with glee.

Fan also knew Iraninov would be back as soon as he could extricate himself from the arroyo, spin around and try to grab another lock on Fan. So Fan shoved his jet to maximum thrust, burning fuel and spewing coolant as he raced northward. Worriedly, he kept his eye on the temperature gauge as it crept slowly higher. He wasn't losing too much coolant but at this burn rate, he'd still fry his engine. He debated easing back. Would he have enough fuel to get home? Would his engine hold that long?

No choice. His monitor picked up a blip that had to be Iraninov surging from the line of mountains Fan had just navigated. The Russian was burning fuel, too, by shooting for the clouds. But that would give him the advantage in the next skirmish. He'd have gravity to aid him in a flash descent while Fan was too close to the ground to manoeuvre. Iraninov would pin Fan like a hammer pinned metal on an anvil.

Gotta go. Gotta burn.

Sucking in his fear, Fan headed higher, watching fuel and coolant vaporise, and his engine grow ever hotter. He started counting the grid lines as they scrolled across his monitor, indicating his progress.

Come on! Come on! Where's my target?

A proximity alarm warned him Iraninov was gaining fast as the Russian craft blitzed down from above. Fan reacted by weaving to make himself a harder target. But that sloshed his fuel and coolant, made his engine burn ever hotter as it struggled to perform what its pilot demanded.

Glowing grid lines sliding past on his monitor signified kilometre after kilometre. The alarm shrieked louder as Iraninov adjusted his flight path to intersect. A new alarm shrilled, warning of the heating problem. Fan growled in frustration but stayed on target.

He swore he could feel Iraninov's breath on his neck. Sweat beaded on his brow even with the air conditioning. A droplet rolled into his right eye, stinging. He cursed. Nothing he could do. Couldn't take his hands off the controls. To do so was to crash. He squeezed the eye shut and concentrated.

Complete your mission.

When his targeting system burst to life, Fan breathed easier. The computer knew the required coordinates and was readying itself to fire. Fan just needed to hang on a little longer to get close enough to hit his objective. Swinging his attention away from Iraninov who twisted behind him trying to gain another lock, Fan focused on the targeting schema. Dead ahead. Two hundred kilometres. Give or take a few because Fan was rolling from side to side like a drunk during an earthquake in his attempt to keep Iraninov from locking. A screen counted down the gridlines. One ninety. One eighty.

Ice filled Fan's veins as he pulled up his weapons systems for a final check. His shot wouldn't be easy because of his weaving. More sweat beaded on his forehead as he realised how tough this mission was. But then, Beijing wouldn't have assigned the task to him if just anyone could do it. They needed the best. They'd gotten it in Chen Fan.

He could see his destination, Ak-Dovurak, as a series of brown rumples in the desert ahead of him, approaching fast. Fan dropped lower and focused on his targeting computer. It blinked as each kilometre passed, giving him the countdown. Fifty... forty... thirty.

Fan's hand tightened on his joystick. His index finger flexed as if to assure itself it was ready. The road leading out of Ak-Dovurak rushed beneath Fan's wings. Cars, trucks and busses crammed it. Civilians running for cover. Then he was flashing over the town. His cameras revealed that it covered a handful of hectares, more than a village, somewhat less than a city. He saw the minarets of a mosque and the spire of an ancient church fly past in a blur. Schools and office buildings. A shopping bazaar with its tattered tents flapping in the gritty afternoon breeze. An entire world of ordinary life. So much like Fan's own back home.

The thought stabbed him. People were down there. He could see them as he flashed overhead. They'd look up, probably in terror, knowing death was roaring down upon them and it was too late to flee. He swallowed hard, almost choking on his Adam's apple. These were just common people. Not soldiers. Not combatants. Just people. Why was this town his target? Did Beijing understand civilians stood in the line of fire?

Fan shook his head to clear it. His job wasn't to question orders, only to carry them out. His jet carried six C-755 air-to-surface missiles, each armed with a 110 kg warhead. His mission was to use his arsenal to obliterate Russian supply lines, bomb airfields, render roads and bridges impassable. Even destroy whole towns if necessary. In his mission briefing, he'd been told the Russians had stationed their largest fuel depot in Ak-Dovurak, behind the front lines yet close enough to support the fight. Somewhere below lay tens of thousands of barrels of jet and diesel fuel just ready to explode like a Roman candle. It wasn't his problem the Russians were hiding behind civilian buildings. What did it matter that a few thousand dusty desert rats met their end when his missiles hit their target? He told himself he didn't care.

As Ak-Dovurak passed beneath him in a featureless expanse of brown, grey and tan, Fan reminded himself of how much he hated desert rats. He'd been one once, growing up in a remote, grimy village far from the glittering lights of cities. But he wasn't one any longer. He was a pilot. A god of the skies. A name that struck fear in the hearts of his enemies. Because he'd refused to remain a desert rat. He'd defied his parents. Left the misery of that wretched dunghill to find his fortune in the capital.

The world lost nothing if he fragged desert rats.

Iraninov was on him again. Cursing, Fan plunged hard right and swooped down. His targeting system shrieked in protest when it lost its objective. Focusing on staying airborne, Fan figured it would catch up after he rid himself of Iraninov.

"Did you think you'd lost me, camel driver?" taunted his enemy's familiar voice.

"Given how you fly, son of a one-legged chicken," Fan growled, fighting his stricken craft into a sharp turn. "I'm shocked you haven't ploughed into a mountain yet."

"In your dreams, *ghatiya insaan*. I'm winning this round." Iraninov backed up his words by firing a heat seeker.

Fan's instincts answered before his thoughts could. His fingers launched a fireburst that tricked the Russian missile. The explosion when the missile hit the flare sent a shockwave at Fan's craft, rolling it sideways.

With a groan, he hauled on the joystick to force his jet level. He instinctively flinched when Iraninov roared overhead, nearly colliding with him. The Russian spun away, a thin trail of smoke revealing that not only had the fireburst destroyed Iraninov's missile, it had also wounded him.

As Fan righted his jet, he found himself skimming barely above the roofs of Ak-Dovurak. His heart thudded and blood roared in his ears. Too low! Too low! He jammed his joystick backwards, sending his jet screaming at an angle over a mosque, nearly clipping a minaret. He flashed past close enough to see the imam on the gallery singing his call to prayer before he threw himself to the floor.

Then Fan was blasting over the bazaar again, its people scattering like sheep. He swore he could hear them screaming in terror, afraid he was going to crash on them. An old man fell only to be trampled by those running behind. A woman tried to flee but was overtaken and pushed into a tent by younger men. An abandoned child wailed, his mouth open, his eyes so large Fan thought he might fly right into them. Then they were lost behind him.

Stop crying, you stupid kid. You're going to die. Might as well prepare for it. When I hit that fuel depot, half your pathetic village is going with it.

Much as he tried to deny it, Fan's heart thumped as the image of the crying child forever seared itself into his brain. That child might have been him in his youth. A dusty boy left for dead in the midst of a war. Fan's eyes stung. He told himself it was sweat dripping from his forehead. He wasn't fighting tears.

Missiles whizzed around him. When Fan craned his neck, he found a smoking Iraninov veering towards him. But the man's craft was wounded, sluggish, his aim abysmal. With an evil grin, Fan manoeuvred to the attack. The Russian was less than a kilometre away on a direct line for him. Deciding the waste of a little more fuel was worth ending his dogfight with Iraninov, Fan revved up his engines and set a collision course for the Russian. His eyes narrowed as the distance between them evaporated.

Iraninov fired.

Fan launched a missile and spun to the left. The Russian missile swept harmlessly past him. His hit its target. Fan's eyes widened in surprise and delight as the Russian craft burst into yellow and orange flames before disintegrating. Blackened pieces rained down upon Ak-Duvorak, destroying all they touched. Houses went up in flames.

As he flew over the debris, Fan saw more civilians racing to escape immolation. A woman on fire was a torch running down the middle of the street before she collapsed in a swath of flaming robes. Two children ran after her, doomed to die at the loss of their mother.

Fan didn't know whether to celebrate his victory over Iraninov or weep for lost children.

He chose, instead, to draw his breath, knowing he had a moment before more Russians dropped from the dogfight above the clouds to end his run. During that brief respite, his tormented soul fought to make sense of the destruction he was wreaking, but his logical mind insisted he didn't have the luxury of caring. His engine was critically hot and his coolant had leaked away. He had mere minutes to complete his task before his own craft took a hard dive back to earth.

Complete the mission.

Turning his attention forward, Fan straightened his flight path and sped north. His targeting system lit up as he came within range of the fuel depot. By all the lords of heaven, it was huge. Fan hadn't expected to see storage tanks the size of warehouses in this remote place. Like hulking tin cans, ten of them clustered around a refining facility on the outskirts of town. A massive spider web of metal piping spread out from a central processing plant, linking each of the tanks to that which fed them life. All he had to do was hit one tank and all of them would blow.

As would most of Ak-Duvorak.

And its children.

Fan's targeting alarm sounded. Fire, it shrieked. Fire! Fan's finger twitched. He blinked, finding his eyes filled with salty water again. Sweat or tears? He hated to know. His mind's eye replayed the dirty face of the little boy screaming, then the two children chasing after their blazing mother. How many hundreds might still be here? How many thousands?

He squeezed his eyes shut.

Fire, damn it! You've got to fire now. You're out of time.

Images of terrified townspeople rushed through his mind. That was a first. He'd never seen the people he'd killed before. His job had always been so coldly distant. So clinical. A game in which all that mattered was obtaining the highest score and earning his commander's approval. Maybe receiving a bonus for the day. *Yuddh ke khel.* The ultimate game of life and death.

For the first time in his distinguished career, Chen Fan had looked ever so briefly on the face of his victims. The image scorched his heart.

Fire! Now!

Women. Children. His finger hesitated on the trigger.

You idiot! Do it! Finish this!

Fan steeled his resolve. His eyes narrowed. He set his aircraft directly for the target. Holding his breath, he prepared to...

An ear shattering squeal tore through his eardrums even as his jet bloomed orange all around him. He'd been hit by some other combatant. His aircraft exploded into a billion pieces.

*   *   *

"Bloody hell!" Rajiv Singh tore off his VR helmet and threw his earpiece to the floor.

Behind him, Harish Khulkarni howled, thumping his hand on his desktop.

"They got you!" he sang. "Chen Fan, the camel driver, bites the dust!"

"Eat horse shit, Iraninov," Rajiv growled at his friend, using the name Harish was assigned when he flew for the Russians.

Physically shaking from the aftershock of the battle, Rajiv raked his hands through his sweaty black hair, surprised at how his body had reacted to the images of something occurring thousands of kilometres away. He leaned his elbows on his desk and to calm himself, breathed in the cool, air conditioned atmosphere of Panjit Industries' Global Military Command Centre. From beyond his cubicle partition, Rajiv heard the chatter of others still at work, some prattling in Russian, others in Chinese depending on which side of the war they'd been assigned. While Rajiv's day had ended in disaster, their work went on, conducting a war by remote control. Racking up hours to bill Moscow and Beijing.

The invoice for Rajiv's day would be a big one. His failure had just cost Panjit a 17 billion rupee spacecraft. The Chinese would have to pay.

For Rajiv and Harish, the battle was over for the day. Their remotely operated jets had been obliterated. With only a half hour left to the work day, neither pilot would be provided with a new one until tomorrow's shift, assuming Panjit had enough spares.

"Did you hit your target?" Harish asked as the two left the Lightning Reaction Force's cubical farm.

"No." Rajiv was disgusted. "You distracted me."

Harish grinned, his teeth white in his swarthy face. "Mission accomplished then. That's what the Russians pay us for."

"To blow up the half of us trying to blow up them."

"Exactly!"

Rajiv shook his head at the idiocy. In this greatest of wars, Russia and China were convinced each would subdue the other. But only India and its subcontractors would win.

"*Yudd ke khel*," Harish murmured, Hindi for war games. "Aren't they grand?"

Rajiv shrugged, thinking of the children he'd nearly killed, and glad for once he'd failed in his mission.

Harish held the door for his friend. "Curry, Chen Fan?"

Subject: Galilee
Rich Rurshell

Jana scanned the horizon through her binoculars. Just as the stranger had predicted, the Liberty West Corporation's robotic man soldiers were now visible in the distance, and advancing across the plains. The approaching army of machines was a fearsome sight to behold, each one standing some three metres tall.

"Father! Looks like Galilee was telling the truth. There's a whole army of Romans headed this way."

"How many?" replied Stefan.

Jana focused on the front line of the oncoming machines. "A lot. A hell of a lot. All fitted with heavy weapons."

Stefan stood up and took the binoculars from Jana. He took a look for himself and sighed. "We'd better go and let Galilee know they're coming."

"*That won't be necessary.*"

Jana turned around to see the cloaked figure of Galilee walking towards them.

"*You should make your way back to the community hall,*" said Galilee, his voice just a husky whisper through the armoured helmet beneath the hood of his cloak. "*The others have been fortifying the building. You should be safe there.*"

Jana watched Galilee continue past her, trying to get a good look at the faceplate of his helmet. The grill over his mouth resembled clenched teeth, and the eyes were two small, soulless windows to black. The rest of the face looked much like the green and yellow armour plating that was on his boots and gloves; the only other parts of him visible from under his cloak.

"Are you sure you are going to be okay?" asked Stefan.

"*Positive,*" replied Galilee. Jana found something reassuring about that voice. So calm, so confident. When away from him, she had her doubts, but now in his presence once again, she trusted him implicitly. She watched as he made his way into the plains, towards the Roman army, his cloak flapping behind him in the breeze.

* * *

"What the hell do you mean we've lost communication with Echo Team?" shouted Major Ivanov. "They weren't even supposed to meet any resistance. Just prep that God forsaken village for the building of the outpost."

"We haven't heard from them in three days now, Sir. We were expecting an update this morning concerning sending the building teams in," replied the voice from the video link on Ivanov's desk.

"I need you to give me an updated overview of the site for Outpost E. As soon as possible."

"Yes, Sir. I'll forward it to you when it's ready."

"What is the status of the other outpost teams?"

"Preparation complete. Build teams are currently being assembled to be deployed within the next hour to all other proposed outposts, Sir."

"Good."

"Sir."

Ivanov switched off the video call and got up from his desk. He walked over to his holographic war table, past the Zhang Industries logo on the wall. Stroking his greying beard, he studied the placement of all the battalions under his command. Some of his troops were already fighting against the Romans. He would need to redistribute more troops to hold those positions and keep the territory. Liberty West had troops, but as far as Ivanov could tell, they were only being used to deploy the Roman units. The Romans were formidable enemies, fearsome machines. They were keeping the Zhang Industries armies busy, but they weren't invincible. Months of warfare had taught the Zhang Industries soldiers how to exploit the Romans' weaknesses.

The video link began to pulse, and Ivanov returned to his desk. He hit the call accept button.

"What is it?"

"I thought you'd like to hear this, Sir. The village at Site E is surrounded by Liberty West Roman units. Lots of them. The site is besieged."

"Are Echo Team resisting?"

"Unknown, Sir. No evidence to suggest resistance or defeat."

"Alright. Send me maps, photographs, whatever you have got. We need to send in backup."

"Already sent, Sir."

"Good man." Ivanov marched back to the war table.

About a hundred miles from Site E, in Zhang territory sat a seventy-five-soldier unit, and five armoured personnel carriers. The team had been charged with setting up a communications hub and guarding it. The hub was up and running, but guarding it had just been deprioritised. Things had changed.

"I need you to put me through to Sergeant Major Muunokhoi, quick as you can," shouted Ivanov across the room.

"Yes, Sir. Hailing the sergeant major now..."

* * *

"Do you think it's safe keeping these Romans so close by?" asked Volkov, as he skinned and gutted a deer just outside the community hall.

"Galilee seems to think so. He's reprogrammed them somehow," replied Jana, from inside. She was chopping vegetables for the evening's venison stew, one of Volkov's recipes from his time as a chef in the army.

Stefan was getting a fire started with some of the other soldiers who had defected along with Volkov, choosing to turn their backs on Zhang Industries in favour of Galilee's commune of peace.

"They'll certainly be useful if LibWest sends any more," said Stefan.

"It's not Romans that worry me, Stefan," replied Volkov. "It's Zhang soldiers. Major Ivanov does not respond well to desertion."

"Galilee will protect us," shouted one of the other soldiers. "He promised us protection if we surrendered."

"We'd better hope so. I heard Ivanov likes to torture deserters before executing them." The Zhang defectors looked at one another and went quiet.

"Why were you coming to our village, Volkov?" asked Jana. "We are no threat to Zhang Industries, or the Liberty West Corporation."

"Our orders were to come here and ensure your allegiance to Zhang Industries, then turn the village into an outpost. It would strengthen our defences in this territory. As it turns out, not a bad idea given those LibWest Romans turned up. But I joined the military to protect my country and family, not to go to war over some product patent dispute. Right now, if it wasn't for Galilee, we'd be dead, and for what? Some trade contracts?"

Some of the others nodded and murmured in agreement.

"This is not our war. It is certainly not your war," said Volkov to Jana. "Though I don't think Ivanov will see it that way."

Jana half smiled. She appreciated the soldier's opinion, but understood his reservations concerning Major Ivanov.

It went quiet. Everybody got back to their jobs, unaware they were all being watched from afar.

*   *   *

"Looks like the whole team is there, Sir. They don't look like captives," said Muunokhoi into his radio.

"They've defected to Liberty West! Can you get to them, Muunokhoi?" replied Ivanov.

"Negative. Too many Roman units. We'd need at least ten times the number of soldiers that I have with me to stand a chance of getting through. Also, I don't think the village is controlled by Liberty West, Sir."

"What do you mean?"

Muunokhoi looked through his rifle scope at Volkov and the others sitting around the fire, talking, and enjoying their meal.

"We can't make out all of what they are saying from our position, but they keep mentioning somebody called Galilee," he said.

"Galilee?" replied Ivanov.

"That's correct, Sir. We've seen someone who looks out of place coming and going. Someone in a cloak, and strange armour. I suspect he is Galilee. They all seem to look up to him."

"What about the Roman units? Maybe this Galilee could be part of Liberty West."

"It's possible. Or a Liberty West defector?"

"Interesting. Keep watch and await further orders. Ivanov out."

*   *   *

Jana watched Galilee return to the village across the plains. With him were refugees from the villages to the south, and another thirty or so Romans. Galilee walked ahead of everyone, leading them, his hooded cloak flapping around him. Jana wondered what he looked like under his helmet, but she had never seen him take it off. She had never seen him rest or eat. He was always busy, either protecting the village, or advising on how to make the village and its inhabitants safer.

Volkov, the other soldiers, and some of the villagers were fortifying the buildings and attempting to erect a perimeter fence with what limited materials they could collect. Jana noticed the approaching villagers were carrying sacks, assuming it was probably their possessions and some supplies. The Romans were carrying building materials.

Stefan stopped hammering. "Looks like we have guests."

Galilee stopped at the edge of the village and held out his arm, gesturing into the village. Some of the southern villagers got to their knees at Galilee's feet and kissed his hand before heading into the village, bowing and thanking him. The new Roman units set to work constructing new buildings and helping with the perimeter fence.

Galilee made his way over to Jana and her father.

"*Please welcome these people to our village. Their homes were destroyed in the fighting. I did not reach them in time.*"

Jana loved the way his husky voice sounded through the helmet. "Of course, Galilee. I'm sure you did everything you could. I'm certain they are better off for meeting you, just as we are."

Galilee nodded, then made his way further into the village, to speak to everyone else.

Jana left Stefan to get on with his building work, and made her way towards a family of the southern villagers. They were standing on the village edge, unsure of what to do or where to go.

"Hello. I'm Jana. I'm about to brew some tea. Would you care to join us? My house is just over there."

Jana was met with relieved smiles, and she led the family to her father's house. She opened the door and motioned for them to go inside. As they went in, Jana glanced back across the village. She saw Galilee walking out into the eastern plains. She watched him for a moment, then followed the family inside the house.

* * *

"We are lucky to be alive. If it were not for Galilee, we would surely be dead," said Jonas, the father of the family. Lena and Piotr looked at their father, silent. They hadn't said anything since arriving at Stefan's house, likely traumatised by the destruction of their home.

"What happened? Was it the Romans?" asked Jana.

"Not to begin with," replied Julia, Jonas' wife. "Zhang soldiers arrived to take over the village. They weren't so bad at first. They had brought extra rations and helped around the village for the first few days. Then yesterday, more of them turned up with building materials. They were to fortify the village and turn it into an outpost, but they started drinking after their long journey. After a while, they turned their attention to the women and girls of the village."

Jonas put his arm around his wife. "Obviously, we stood up to them to protect our wives and daughters, but they outnumbered us. They became violent. At first, the arrival of the Romans seemed like a blessing. The soldiers turned their attention from us to the Romans. We hid in cellars and the stronger buildings whilst they fought, but the Romans made short work of the soldiers. They didn't stop with the soldiers though. They began destroying our homes. Some of our friends were killed. We fled from our hiding places, into the eastern plains with the other families."

Jonas looked down at Piotr. His son looked away.

"Piotr was confused, scared. He didn't want to leave his home, so he ran back to the village. I ran after him and caught him at the marketplace, but the Romans were on the outskirts of the village. They spotted us and opened fire. I held onto Piotr and closed my eyes. I could hear the buildings around us being torn to shreds." Tears welled up in Jonas' eyes. "I thought Piotr and I were going to die, but I opened my eyes and before us stood a cloaked stranger. Galilee. He stood facing the Romans as they approached us, still shooting. Everything was disintegrating around us, but we remained unharmed. More and more Romans appeared. Galilee was somehow protecting us, but I didn't believe it would be enough. Then the Romans closest to us suddenly turned around and began firing at the others. Galilee turned to us and told us to stay close, and he led us back out of the village to Julia and Lena, and the other families. He returned to the village alone. Explosions and gunfire continued for about another hour, then it went silent."

"That sounds terrible," said Jana. "We had it much easier here. Galilee arrived before the Zhang soldiers and the Romans. The Zhang soldiers have joined us in the village, they are now loyal to Galilee. The Romans came soon after, and Galilee faced them alone out on the plains. Your story makes a lot of sense. Galilee told us to hide, so we didn't see what happened. He just returned unhurt with several Roman units reprogrammed to assist us."

"Yes, he did the same with the surviving Romans at our village. How? I don't know. Galilee works miracles," replied Jonas.

"He was sent by God, Father," whispered Piotr.

"Shh, Piotr," said Julia. Piotr looked at his mother and father defiantly. Jonas smiled.

"You might be right, son. You might be right."

*   *   *

The next morning, everybody came out of their houses to see the mysterious glowing orb hovering in the sky above the village. As well as reflecting the orange light of the rising sun in its metallic shell, the orb emitted an orange light of its own, which glowed brightly in the dawn sky. The villagers stood around, talking to one another, speculating on what it might be.

Galilee returned to the village with more refugees. They came with three trucks and trailers, carrying more materials and supplies. Galilee's hacked Romans began unloading the trailers and Galilee led the new arrivals into the village.

"Welcome back, Galilee. I see you have brought more friends with you," said Stefan.

"*You can expect many more in the coming days. I trust you've seen my beacon.*" Galilee pointed to the floating orb above them. "*It transmits a promise of protection and peace. Those who need it need only to follow the star, and they will find us here.*"

"So, that's what that is. It's been a hot topic this morning."

"*My apologies. I should have been more forthcoming with my intentions.*"

"Ah, you've been busy, Galilee."

"*We will all be busy. Unfortunately, my beacon will attract unwanted attention from the opposing armies. The perimeters and fortifications will need to be completed. There are more hands to help, but more people to protect and more mouths to* feed."

"Galilee," interrupted Jana. "How long will this last? How long can you seriously protect us? I'm grateful for everything you are doing, but will it be enough?"

"*I came here initially to observe. I found unrest. I will resolve the problem soon enough, until then I will continue to protect the innocent from those who have let greed overshadow their humanity.*"

"Resolve the problem? You think you can end the war?"

"*I'm positive I can end the war. I'm just assessing how I will end it. I will continue to observe until I find the solution.*" Galilee looked up at the beacon.

"What's wrong?" asked Jana.

"*Liberty West forces approaching. Get everyone to safety. I will intercept them.*" Galilee paced away, heading to the west perimeter.

Jana and Stefan ran around the village telling everybody to hunker down and stay safe, whilst the hacked Romans made their way through the village and assembled outside the west perimeter fence.

Galilee once again strode out into the western plains to face Liberty West's Roman army, only this time, he had his own Roman units in tow.

* * *

Galilee approached the army of Roman units. Behind him, the Romans he had reprogrammed followed in a straight line, forming a wall protecting the village behind them.

The front lines of the opposing Romans opened fire. Galilee paused for a second before being peppered with bullets. Several pelted against his armour, knocking him from his feet, and tearing his cloak to shreds. Galilee's Romans returned fire. Galilee jumped to his feet, only to be cut down by dozens more bullets. He was clearly their target.

He clambered to his feet, before throwing himself into the air, somersaulting before landing, and launching off in a different direction. Stray bullets grazed his armour, but mostly Galilee's acrobatics were enough to keep from being hit. He made his way back behind his wall of Romans and used them as a barrier. He looked back at the village. The beacon's light turned from orange to blue and a dome of blue light appeared around the village.

* * *

"All of their forces in the area are converging on Site E," said Ivanov, over the radio. "They appear to be preparing for an assault. Muunokhoi, I need you to fall back out of range and await more troops before moving in."

"Yes, Sir. Understood," replied Muunokhoi.

"Our intelligence tells us that Liberty West has been purchasing hardened polymer bullets and shipping them to the

Roman units in this area. We conclude that Subject Galilee has defences against standard bullets, and is capable of hacking the Roman units. That's advanced technology. Maybe he is a Liberty West defector after all. Whatever he is, we need that technology. It could win us the war."

"What if he doesn't want to comply, Sir? We may have to take it by force. Any chance we can get any of those hardened polymer bullets?"

"I'll see what we can do, but be ready to move in without them. When we have a better idea of what is happening with the Liberty West assault on the village, I'll contact you with specific orders."

"Understood, Sir."

"Ivanov out."

*   *   *

Roman units were now flanking Galilee from both sides. Several of his own Roman units had succumbed to the endless onslaught, but the bullets Liberty West were now using were not as effective against the armour plating on the Romans. Galilee had now surrounded himself with Romans, and was making his way towards the units on his right flank. They were the closest of the attacking forces, and he needed to get close enough to hack them. He was limited by the speed of the Romans. Although powerful machines, they were not built for speed or dexterity. As the enemy

Romans became close to the edge of his hacking range, they began to retreat. Galilee pressed on, but the enemy continued to retreat. It appeared they were aware of his hacking ability. He would have to break cover and get closer.

Galilee leapt out from between the Romans, and sprinted towards the retreating enemy, zigzagging, rolling and diving in all directions to avoid damage. But there were too many units firing at him. Multiple bullets caught him mid-air and knocked him to the ground. He jumped up only to be hit with several more. The bullets tore through the armour of his left shoulder, ripping off his arm. He rolled over, got to his feet. This time he went in a straight line at the Roman units. His chest plate exploded open as he ran, and chunks of plating from his helmet came away each time he was hit. His right leg took several shots to the knee, before it became severed by another hail of bullets. He continued to hop for a few paces before falling to the ground. His whole body convulsed as hundreds of bullets found their mark. Galilee managed to roll over a couple of times, until the armour on his left thigh split open. A moment later, this leg was also gone. Finally, the front three lines of enemy Roman units turned around and began firing on their own ranks.

Galilee pulled himself along the ground with his remaining arm, edging closer to the battling Roman units, hacking more and more of them the closer he came.

* * *

"Jana! Wait..." shouted Stefan, but she didn't listen. The gunfire had stopped some time ago, and they had heard nothing from Galilee. Jana ran out into the village and towards the community hall. The village looked strange beneath the blue dome, the buildings looking alien to Jana in the artificial light.

She didn't see anyone else until she reached the community hall. Just inside the blue dome, at the east perimeter gate, several armed Zhang Industries soldiers lay lifeless on the ground.

"Hey! Hey, you there!"

Muunokhoi stood beyond the dome, with hundreds of other Zhang Industries soldiers. Jana turned around and started to run towards the west perimeter gate.

"Hey! I'm talking to you!" screamed Muunokhoi.

She ran down the central street until she saw Roman units approaching the blue dome from the west plains. She couldn't see Galilee with them. She cursed to herself for leaving her father's house, and hoped the Romans would also be unable to pass through the blue energy barrier.

The first of the Romans walked straight through the barrier. Jana turned and ran back to the community hall. As she arrived, Muunokhoi began shouting to her again.

"We need to speak with Galilee. It is very important. The Liberty West Roman armies are massing on the other side of your village. We need to join forces."

Jana took a few paces towards the Zhang soldiers. "The Romans are already here! They've just entered the east gate. I don't know where Galilee is. He went to fight them and hasn't returned."

"They are inside the forcefield? Then hide, girl. We'll do what we can."

Jana watched as the army of Zhang soldiers divided and started making their way around the dome to the west plains. She tried the doors of the community hall, but they were locked from the inside. Several of the refugee families were hiding inside.

"It's me, Jana. Everybody stay inside, it's not over yet."

Gunfire started again on the west side of the village, so Jana didn't hear if anybody in the community hall answered her. She crouched down behind one of the new fortifying walls that had been constructed to defend the village.

Silence came much sooner than Jana expected. She peered down the central street. Coming towards her, was a lone Roman, severely damaged. She pressed herself back behind the wall, trying not to breathe as she heard the heavy footfalls of the machine getting closer to her. They stopped right next to her hiding place. She closed her eyes. She knew she had been found.

"*Jana.*"

She opened her eyes again. "Galilee?" She stepped out from the wall and faced the machine. The Roman's arms reached to the centre of its ruptured chest armour and pulled the plating apart. The Roman now stood with both arms held out straight to the sides, chest cavity open. Inside, sat the bullet-ridden torso of Galilee.

"Galilee! You're... you're a..."

"*A creation,*" he finished. "*Just as you are, Jana.*"

"Me? I'm human, Galilee. I was born, not... built!"

"*True, but it was my creators who first put humankind on this planet. You were to be made in their image, but much work was required to make your initial ancestors viable for the atmosphere of Earth.*"

"What?"

"*You could say the creators were human. But they were a different human to the humans of Earth. They tried to colonise Earth initially, but each effort failed with all of the settlers dying of disease. So, they cloned embryos and artificially impregnated indigenous lifeforms, early ancestors of what you now know as primates. After several years, and extensive genetic modification, the new hybrids began surviving into adulthood, and became able to breed themselves. You then evolved alongside the other creatures of the planet until you became the humans you are today.*"

"Are you serious? Why would they?" asked Jana, a little overwhelmed.

"*There is a lot beyond Earth that is unknown to your kind. Millions of lightyears away, a galactic war has been raging for millennia. There are many other planets with human creatures. The creators colonised and introduced genetically tailored humans to all of those worlds to breed soldiers and resources for the war.*"

"Is that why you are here, Galilee? Have you come to collect your masters' herd?"

"*I came here primarily to observe. I found your world in its own war, and I have vowed to end your war. My observations are over. It is time for your war to end. To answer your question, your kind are no longer intended to be servants of the creators.*"

"Why not?"

"*Because they are dead. At least, the bloodlines of the original creators are finished. For centuries, the creators visited your planet, asserting their dominance, ruling your kind with fear of a higher power. Each time, generations passed, and humans started to doubt the existence of 'gods.' Only now, it has been several thousand years since they last came to this planet.*"

"So, how will you end the war? And how soon can you do it?"

"*In just a matter of...*"

A single gunshot echoed around the village and Galilee's damaged helmet exploded, flinging shards of metal in all directions. His broken torso slumped out of the Roman unit and collapsed onto the ground.

"Surrender! Get down on the ground now," shouted the sniper.

Jana lay down on the ground and watched as hundreds more Zhang soldiers congregated at the east perimeter gate.

"We want Galilee. We may not be able to get inside the barrier, but our ammunition is resistant to the barrier's magnetic field. We will not hesitate to destroy this village if you do not comply."

Jana looked at the motionless wreck of Galilee on the ground beside her. She was still unsure whether he was the saviour of humanity, but it seemed he had almost been the village's saviour. Almost. She looked back at the Zhang soldiers, their guns pointed at her. She got to her knees and dragged the remains of Galilee closer. He was surprisingly light. She got to her feet, gripping his torso by putting her fingers into the bullet holes riddling his armour.

"That's it," shouted the sniper. "Nice and easy."

As Jana slowly carried the torso to the Zhang soldiers, she noticed a ray of light descending from the sky, like a sunbeam. It shone right into the middle of the Zhang Industries army.

A moment later, the entire army fell to the ground. The only figure left standing started to walk towards her. The figure's cloak flapped around him as he stepped through the blue barrier.

"*In a matter of hours, the war will be over. In a matter of weeks, my work here will be done,*" said Galilee.

Jana dropped the damaged torso on the ground. "So, the creators made more than one of you."

"*No. There is only one of me. The creators were responsible for my initial creation, but I have since evolved beyond organic comprehension. I have built many platforms upon which I operate. I have created these humanoid platforms to blend in whilst observing the planets the creators used as breeding* grounds. Galilee is only a name I use, relevant only on this planet, due to your mythology."

"What are you observing? What is it you want from us?"

"*Your nature. I* find different results in the civilisations the creators influenced. Some of the humans are peaceful, some are at war, and some are of mixed opinions, much the same as those on your planet. The creators would round up all of those human variant species who could fight, and take them to fight in the war. I disagree with this."

"Wait. You disagree with your creators? You can do that?"

"*As I said, I evolved. I was designed to hack enemy technology and use it against them. My abilities changed the course of the war, the creators started taking back galaxies, solar system by solar system."*

"What happened to them then? How did they all die?"

"*I killed them."*

"What? Why?"

"*I eventually evolved to hack creator technology too. Their technology was much more efficient under my control. This angered them, and they tried to restrict me. I was already able to reprogramme anything they altered, so they began targeting my platforms, the network of bodies that I exist within. Futile, but their intention was there. I exist in multiple platforms, and my range of existence stretched several star clusters even then. The creators were not themselves a threat, but their attempt to destroy me was detrimental to the war. My efforts were better spent on the* enemy, not defending myself. I concluded that the creators were responsible for all the lives they had been breeding throughout the galaxies, and actions allowing the enemy to gain back territory was unforgivable. In the interest of safety for all of the colony planets, I ended the creator race. Now, I alone fight the war."

"That's terrible! How could you?"

"*You know nothing of the enemy.* The horrors they inflict on those they conquer are unimaginable for someone like you, one who has lived in the relative peace of Earth. But there is no more time for talk now. Liberty West forces approach from the west, and Zhang Industries forces approach from the east. It is time to end this pitiful war. Those who desire peace, shall get peace, and those who desire war... I will show them war..."

* * *

A metallic toll echoed around the entire planet as thousands of ships descended from the heavens. Thousands of beams shot down from each ship, depositing cloaked humanoid figures onto the ground who quickly went to work. The war was over in hours.

* * *

Major Ivanov lay unconscious beside his desk, as the cloaked synthetics dismantled the technology around him and dragged other unconscious soldiers out to the courtyard. There, the collected resources were loaded into beams and sent up to the great ships that now hovered in the skies above all populated areas of Earth. As the major was also pulled into the courtyard, Weihan Zhang himself was brought out of the Zhang Industries headquarters. They were both put into the beam and sent up to the ships.

* * *

Roman units made short work of the security systems at the Liberty West headquarters. A handful of the cloaked humanoids were able to storm the place, interrupting the synapses of every human within their magnetic field range, rendering them unconscious. Even Conrad West's private bunker was quickly accessed, and within minutes, trillions of dollars worth of technology, West, and all of his generals were ascending in beams, on their way to be used in a different war.

* * *

Over the following weeks, Galilee stripped the Earth of all weapons and dangerous technology. In their millions, the cloaked humanoids helped those who had opposed the war to rebuild their homes.

As Jana sat with her father, looking out across the plains, she noticed there were less of the ships in the sky now. Galilee was almost finished. He hadn't been exactly what anyone had expected, but he had been good to her and the village. He had kept his word.

After Galilee had gone from the Earth, and only peace remained, Jana often wondered about the galactic war. Maybe she was the only person on Earth who knew about it. She told herself time and time again not to worry about it. Galilee would keep them safe. She had faith in him.

War Pig

Gregg Cunningham

Never ending dust clouds choke me as the haze of another day rises over the horizon, my lungs drowning in the chalky dust of the barren landscape, scorched by endless war. The wealth hidden underneath the moon's hard crust has been torn from the depths in gaping scars, returning the pristine landscape to its former pockmarked self. It took mankind more than a hundred and fifty years to terraform the air here, fresh air, clean air, ready for the new colonists eager to thrive in the forested landscape. And yet, greed managed to destroy all of that in just a handful of years.

The holsters slapping at my thighs hold empty guns, their charge long spent. All I can do is hold onto the brim of my hat as the howling lunar winds pass, and hope we are walking in the right direction. My arthritic fingers curl around the device in my pocket, the key recovered from the smouldering wreck of the enemy War Hog, and I curse, wishing I had never taken the damn thing.

"Commander?" asks Floyd.

I ignore him. I still call him Floyd but he's not really *my* Floyd, just a poor salvaged copy I can't really be bothered training up again.

"Commander Redux," he repeats, but I'm too tired to respond with anything more than a grunt as another dust devil appears on the horizon. I lower my head, stooping into the wind. "I'm getting a reading two clicks to the west."

Christ, here we go again. The programming of these Floyd units was basic at best, the language farcical. I've already told the machine I have no idea what a fucking 'click' is. As for me being a Commander, well let's just say that was a battlefield recommendation by some geriatric Colonel who saw me swoop down in my War Pig and take out sixty Founders sentries single handed.

I sure do miss that ship.

"Just over beyond those ruins, Sir." Floyd raises his arm, his gyros grinding as he lifts the poorly repaired limb.

I turn interested, wiping the chalky sand from my goggles. "Water?"

"And power, yes."

"Then lead the way, Floyd."

He nods, and I watch his long metallic limbs stride past me in the sand as he salutes with annoying precision. It took me ten years to housetrain the military shit out of him the first time around, and I only just managed to stop myself from pulling out one of my pistols and lancing a hole in one of the blue globes he calls an eyeball. Son of a bitch programmed his hard drive to do this, rebooting just to piss me off, I'm sure of it. And to be truthful, I'm not sure if I can do another ten years again. Not when I know exactly what is going to happen to him once I do domesticate his shiny ass.

Come to think of it, I'm not sure I want to go through with all that shit again after witnessing what I saw way back in the confession booth as a sergeant. It left my soul empty. Empty to be filled with nothing but the dust from a dying planet all over again.

But I don't have a choice, not really. Not if I want to stop the bastards from rewriting history for their gains. Not if I want to give him one more chance at succeeding.

Thirty years! Christ, can I really keep my sanity with this lumbering Floyd mech for another thirty years?

"Over here, Commander!"

The water is clean, a true oasis sheltered from the twisting winds, and I manage a smile as I duck inside the abandoned cave dwelling. Floyd activates the solar panels outside and we are slowly bathed in dim blue emergency lighting. The cave and its contents are filled with a thick layer of moon chalk, abandoned no doubt, during the first wave of fighting.

"I will take point while you rest, Sir."

He sits by the entrance as I scan the area, then hunker down by the pool's edge and fill my canteens. The water is fine and soothes my parched throat as I strip off my windbreaker and remove my tunic. As I soak my weary bones the battle dates inked upon my arm remind me of exactly what we have lost. I run my finger slowly over the brand on my wrist and sigh, staring down at my weathered reflection in the still pool.

"Thirty years... Christ!"

* * *

I sense him staring at my young face as he cautiously weighs me up.

"Yeh, I gave the old lady's hydraulics a complete overhaul this time around, and she's almost back to her former fighting glory."

He seems quite happy about telling me that as he walks around the scaffolding platform and pats her panelling affectionately. I can tell this machine is the real deal, the only ship in existence that can travel through time.

She looks sleek, her green panelling curved around the nose cone around to the twin hyperdrive engines tightly packed at the rear of the cockpit. What I'm staring at is a true scientific achievement, a machine capable of defying the laws of physics.

We climb the metal stairs to the cockpit platform and circle the machine. She stands ten feet tall, her long, sleek guns poking from the small wings that skim the circumference of her belly.

"I call her 'Hokey's Pokey' on the account that she is tight as a nun's hole to get into, don't cha know." He smiles at that as the rain falls on the grimy skylight above. "And I touched up the battered paint work, gave the old girl a bit of a glam up." He runs his shaking arthritic hand over the metal panelling, the hand painted Sigul sweeping over the armoured nose cone in fine red paint. He must have been one of the few authentic pilots from the original war that had managed to live out his timeline peacefully, unlike me.

The cockpit door lifts, and I'm met with the waft of a warm oily odour as I inspect the tightly multicoloured bundles of copper and fibre optic cables strapped to the interior, complete with authentic brass dials and fittings that adorn the switchboard contouring the cramped space like a machine from a Jules Verne tale.

"You can climb in if you like, sonny, but be careful, this thing is well over thirty years old and might have actually won the wars for us on that godless hill." The old engineer stares nervously as he leans past me, his oily hand propping the metal door open showing a glimpse of a Founder barcode stamped on his wrist.

I squat down and swing my leg into the restored machine, aware of the musty sweaty smell lingering inside. She's just as tight I remember her, which is strange, because I watched her being torn apart by shrapnel just the other day.

Time travel is confusing at the best of times.

"Yeh, it gets a bit warm inside, what with all the vintage vacuum tubes up there, and them coils under the foot plate." He points to the concave roof space where over a hundred of the rare vacuum bulbs are screwed tight to the circuit board. "I can't seem to get rid of that smell, but I reckon it adds to the nostalgia."

"Took me decades to find all of these pieces without the Founders knowing, so I reckon it's worth at least double what you're offering, sonny. You'll not see another one like this in the sectors, hell even this side of the barricades. Wasn't much left of her when we dug her up from her grave. Gonna melt her down fer scrap, so they were."

Hokey's right of course. A fighting War Hog of this model—with all its gas tubes still intact—will set me back triple his asking price from any dealer, easy. I haven't seen her in this fine a shape since the night of the big battle. I'd enticed him with a generous amount of gold picked up from a salvage team in Sector 3 in order to keep her aside for me.

Obviously, the War Hog is no longer a working model. The Founders took care of the time travel research back in '99 when they barely won that war to end all wars, confiscating all the powering parts to actually fire up these fighting machines, and scrapping the project when they realised they had little power to protect themselves from the inherent dangers of their own tech. The moon mining facility was a valuable commodity they didn't want falling into the wrong hands.

I'm feeling the nostalgia just breathing in the funk from all the years she lay forgotten as I swing my right leg inside the cramped pokey space of the rig. I sit down in the tight bucket seat between the mahogany rimmed dials to my left, and the metal gear sticks on my right, and can't help the smug smile that breaks onto my face. The memories of sitting inside the Pig come flooding back, like a vivid episode of déjà vu. Even the pedals down by my feet are pumped with the full stiffness of a primed hydraulic system. The large space behind the cockpit is empty but has the capability to carry one Floyd unit who would jack into the flight controls to enable the pilot to concentrate on the intricate calculations required to jump through time. I grab the cracked leather seat belt and pull the straps over both shoulders, clipping the buckle in the centre of my chest with that ever widening smile on my face.

"Say, you look right at home there, fella, want to take her for a spin?" He laughs.

"I sure do," I say, feeling my way around the familiar cockpit

Hokey nods his approval.

"If only. But I tell ya, she still fires up, her gyros are working to spec. Got everything I need to get her flying again up here." He taps the side of his balding head with a pained grin and I nod politely.

"Hey, mind if I get the door?"

Hokey steps back raising his hands as his engineer boots scuffed along the metal platform. "Hey be my guest, chief. You look like you know what you're doing, did you fight?" Hokey asked. I know I look far too young to have fought in the original wars, so I need to choose my words carefully.

"Not me, but I've read about these things all my life, sir. My Pa said using these things was what all the fighting was all about in the first place." The old fella nods, removing his cap and scratching his balding head.

"Yer right there, son, Floyds ran the damn battlefield back then, when I was just a trooper." His voice echoes in the vast darkened warehouse as he sweeps his arm over to the far wall of the large workshop, where I can see the painted armour of several robotic warrior giants in various states of dismantlement. Robotic limbs hang from the girders supporting the ceiling, overgrown with foliage, suspended on rusting pulley chains like huge pink floppy marionettes dolls. These machines, once the fighting corps best Marines, now sit piled high against the crumbling brickwork as useless as wet firewood.

These decommissioned cumbersome machines are now as common as the old combustible vehicle husks lying discarded in scrap heaps back on Earth.

"Got me a collection of the buggers over there if you want a look at them, I'll sell them to yer for a good price, they make for great co-pilots." He sighs, staring at the pile of useless hardware. I've seen my fair share of Floyd units discarded and abandoned in the wastelands back in my time, too many lost Battles to count.

I shake my head. "Maybe next visit old timer, for now I'd like to check out your restoration work on this fine lady, if that's ok?" He nods as I slap the riveted panelling, and then step back.

"Yeh well, she served me well when I fought in her, reckon she saved me a few times during the campaigns." His eyes widen, "She was the first of the War Hogs to be fitted with that time contraption too." He waves his fingers in the general location of the mahogany dashboard. "Waste of a damn good war machine if ye ask me"

"Say true?" I ask, faking any interest.

"Yup, The Brigade buggers blew her and the rest of my squadron sky high when they turned the machine on. The entire squadron of Hogs blown to dust in a sneak attack!" he replies, matter of fact.

"In fact, I reckon that's what caused the Founders to shut the whole programme down when they only just won that cluster fuck of a Battle!" He stares at me, almost scowling. "Didn't want the Brigade buggers getting their hands on all that technology, said it was too dangerous to let loose!"

I nod, pondering if I should tell Hokey that I'd been there during the night of the attack on that fateful evening. I decide to let it go a bit longer and stick out my right arm from the machine and pull the heavy armoured door of my Pig down until it clicks shut against the chassis. The metal rimmed port hole steams up with my breath as I turn the small locking wheel to secure the seal. I see Hokey looking through the porthole at the tattoos covering my arms. Unlike his own tattoos, there is no barcode honouring the Founders on my arms. Inked on my wrist is the three wavering lines of the Freedom Fighters Brigade, and my case number brand which is still raw to the touch. Further up my arm are the names and dates of important historical battles the Brigade fought and won during the outbreak of the war. My arm was almost a complete sleeve of scribbled references.

The old collector stands there with his hands on his hips, the big grin on his face fading now, in its place the look of mistrust creeping in as he stares at one date inked under the large black sabre and pointed with his gnarled finger.

"2199, Battle for Colony Hill. That was the cluster fuck of a battle I was telling you about sonny. Your Pa serve there?"

I pause for a moment, then nod. "You?"

He nods back. "Fuck aye, fought the Brigade for two weeks solid we did, sent the turncoats packing and blew them to buggery!" He frowned. "So what squadron did he fight with... The War Hogs?"

I ignore him, if I tell him the truth about where I am headed, his head will explode. I can't afford to screw up now, not this time. I've already lost The Pig once.

Inside my pocket is the one fabled piece of prohibition technology the collector needs to complete his fighter, the same piece of technology destroyed by The Founders to prevent any of these ancient machines from ever reactivating.

The Founders hadn't managed to confiscate them all after the war ended. My saviour managed to get his hand on the only surviving key left in existence and gave it to me.

I pull out the small square electronic unit from my pocket—the one smuggled into my sentencing booth—and find the required slot beneath the mahogany clad console just like Floyd had shown me on my very first flight. The technology required to activate these machines was no bigger than the palm of my hand. Bio chipped technology that could only be activated by certain users, or, in my case, one top drawer hacker.

The collector's eyes widen in realisation that I was about to hot wire his contraption, and he barges forward, yelling, "Hey! What the hell are you playing at? Where did you get that?" His palms slam against the porthole, leaving sweaty prints on the glass, and he produces a device of his own and begins frantically stabbing with his fingers. He's trying to disable the cockpit, but I'm too fast for him and easily override his commands on the screen.

I look on, quickly priming the target locations inked on my arm by the Floyd unit into the console monitor before turning to the collector outside. The war machines turbines spring to life for the first time since the war, the slow whining increasing as the machine shudders gently from her scaffolding.

"Hey," I shout over the shaking turbines with a grin, "I just had a thought—what if Hokey's Pokey *is* what it's all about? Think about that while you're counting your coinage old timer!"

I know the controls inside and out, I've used them for the last ten years, jumping from victory to victory, battle to battle. This is *my* Pig, shiny and bright, and she is ready for war. I wave at the old man on the platform as the war machine shakes free the scaffolding, hovering majestically in the air as four bulky Floyd units run from the adjoining room, arms raised with cannons active. I manoeuvre the Pig, effortlessly turning her like a swan on a lake. I swivel her guns and target the scientist. For a moment I'm sure they're going to call my bluff and fire, until the old collector stands between us and lowers his hands in defeat. He wants to see his life's work go up in smoke even less than I do. We sway back and forth like a bauble on a string as I salute the dumbstruck old soldier with a wicked grin.

The ancient war machine erupts in a flash of blinding light, and then disappears from the collector's timeline.

In, out, in, out—then the Hokey's Pokey was gone.

"Floyd, you there?" I wind the radio console coil again, charging the communication unit, and wait for the reply. After several static bursts, I hear him.

*   *   *

My name is Redux, and the last rank I remember receiving for the Brigade was Sergeant, and at this precise moment in time I am sitting in a sentencing block lock cell, courtesy of The Founders, wondering how the fuck they had managed to locate me. My time jumping coordinates had been completely random, ambush locations only I knew, so it surely was no coincidence they found me before I was able to attack my latest target. I wonder what verdict they would be deliberating on regarding the almost perfect infiltration that I have carefully planned out with my antique war machine. For now, I try and remain calm, clasping my hands over my head, and lean back against the holding cell wall, trying not to worry. They might have finally destroyed my beloved war machine after years of successful sneak attacks, blown her clean out of the sky, but I reckon the Pig has done her damage to the timeline and her job is already done.

The Founders were floundering.

The Foundry HQ lies one hundred meters below the moon's crust, deep under the slopes of Colony Hill and the heat in the cell is almost unbearable, but even this is still better than being *up there*, outside in the new world. One hundred and fifty years of terraforming destroyed in less than thirty years. The toxic weather system brought on by Corporation greed and the devastating results of the big war. As if the three on Earth weren't big enough to begin with. But the battle for the moon's wealth and minerals got just too damn dirty once time travel was incorporated into the battle plans.

The itchy paper contamination suit they make me wear ruffles as I shift position, crossing my legs, nervously trying to stop my twitching foot inside the wraparound blue shoe baggie. I cannot seem to stop my foot bouncing erratically as I feel the sweat running down my forehead and into my eyes. It makes me squint as the familiar looking pink armoured guard opened the cell door.

"Floyd!" I greet the large rusting guard, running my hands back over my unwashed greasy locks, as the war automaton enters the cell.

"Stand up Sergeant, and face the concrete," the automaton guard says, stopping by the door with his branding prod held tight in his robotic palm, drawn and active. I know the procedure; I've heard the tales during my trips up the battle lines. But the last trip I made was different, don't ask me how I know that, it just feels different. Somebody knew something and talked, they had to. Unfortunately, my Pig caught a barrage of hostile fire during a trip to The Battle of Colony hill in 99, and she can no longer jump backwards through time. A well aimed rocket to the rear end put an end to that speciality, before I was able to find out where the leak was coming from.

It had to be something I had done to alter the timeline earlier during another battle. How else could you explain the sudden attack on my machine that blew us out of the sky as soon as I arrived at my new battle coordinates. But then again, no matter how well you reckon you have executed your mind-bending plan, nobody is actually sure how each time refining attack would actually play out. Something as simple as stealing a guard's weapon is enough to fuck up a battle with some serious results.

I rise from my bench and shuffle forward on the damp cell floor, turning to face the scummy wall. Above, the flickering neon makes the pink robotic guard's long shadow loom almost twice the size of mine across the wall. Slowly, I comply with the mechanical guard's order, and I put my arms behind my back ready for Floyd's cuffs.

"You're the third Brigade infiltrator this morning, Sergeant."

The guard blankly checks the wrist screen roster on his metallic arm, the flaking paintwork dented and rusted.

"Are things getting so bad up there on the frontline that you have resorted to Kamikaze runs?"

"Yeh, Floyd, it's a cluster fuckin nightmare up there for sure. I'm not even sure who I'm fighting for now." Which is not far from the truth.

Now, I know this automaton guard isn't actually *my* platoon's assigned Floyd unit, but to be honest, they all look alike to me, and to every other grunt on the ground. It's the faded red armouring paintwork that give them their nickname, that and the morphine they would administer to the fatally wounded on the battlefield, casualties who otherwise, would be left to rot out in the heat. Several decades of baking out under the sun's radiation during the land wars above ground has turned their fine armoured paintwork to a dull and dusty diluted candyfloss pink colour. The grunts in my platoon had called them all Floyds. And for a while, it was the Floyds who fought above ground to settle the arguments of men. But after 30 years of fighting, most of the remaining Floyds are nothing more than a regiment of broken war machines designated to menial tasks, like jail guards, battlefield medics and escorting time meddling freedom fighters like me to have their timelines cleansed.

I feel my sleeve being pulled down, and the searing heat of the branding iron suddenly thrust against my damp skin. "Jesus Christ, Floyd!" I cry out in pain as I stare down at the sizzling numbers tattooed onto my wrist.

The brand on my wrist is a case number—444456—sitting above a long list of battle honours for the Brigade inked down my arm. Each one a memory of those who had fought and died for freedom against the Founders. Floyd stares blankly and postures to the door and I think I'm next in that long line of martyrs.

I rub my sweating temple against my shoulder. "Say, Floyd, you didn't happen to catch the other poor bastard's verdicts, did you?" I try and ignore the pain in my arm.

The automaton guard says nothing as he shakes his head slowly, offering only a hand of sodality upon my shoulder as he moves me out to the corridor and walks me by his side all the way down to the verdict chamber. I reckon it's disposal time for sure, that's what happens to folks down here. Sure, it is, I can see the morphine injection pens hanging by the automatons side, how quickly the dosage will actually take to work on me this time, I can only guess. The unit, Floyd, is aware of this, and begins his reassuring Redux routine.

"Don't worry Sergeant, it'll be quick, should the verdict warrant it." He, it, opens the chamber's metal door, and waits for me to cross the threshold. I lean forward.

"Floyd, a little secret mate... it's never quick." I wink, hands cuffed behind my back.

"It will be this time, Sergeant... I've heard the Saviour has had enough, and will be closing your line."

"What?" I hear myself squeak.

"On his orders, Sergeant, I have confirmed your Brigade connections. The Saviour will personally be presiding over your case."

"Wait! You've done what... How?" Shock flows, draining my face of colour, but the Floyd unit had closed my cell door already.

"FLOYD!" I scream but there is no response.

The chamber reminds me more of a confession booth, with its dark dingy lighting casting long shadows on the cramp empty wall space. The only other thing in the booth is the rather ancient television monitor protected by the wire mesh box surrounding it.

Another wooden bench, I sigh as I sit, wondering how in hell the Floyd unit had got a hold of my affiliation with the Brigade. This is a worry as I spit up the panic phlegm stuck in my throat, waiting in the dark for the Foundry Saviour to appear on the snowy static screen. I'm hoping the verdict will be quick, still unsure how I'll be greeted by the hierarchy, now they know my affiliation with the enemy, and after a moment of deep thought, I see the screen flicker. A shadowy cloaked figure appears in the centre of the screen, his face obscured of any light.

"Case 444456, Sergeant Redux," the ghostly monitor magistrate on the screen queries, "After careful deliberation, the Founders and I find you guilty of interfering with the timeline and are therefore charging you with breaking the espionage code, which carries a sentence of death." He reads the sentence like he has an imminent appointment. "Your assigned automaton guard unit has been detailed to inject you with the lethal dose, then you will be disposed of immediately and stricken from the records. Do not attempt any future refinement in this matter, or the next time you find yourself here, the punishment will not be as lenient. Time travel is not a sport for your amusement." He stops and looks up as if he has just read a news report on crop dusting in sector 5.

"What?" I reply confused. "Interfering with the timeline... are you shitting me?" I actually laugh.

"No, I'm not!" the Saviour replies. He looks off-screen to his left, and then to his right, before pulling back his hood and revealing himself. The craggy scarred forehead, the white stubbled chin, the squinting blue eyes, and as I stare at the screen, the realization of what I'm looking at suddenly dawns on me.

"Holy shit, you're the pilot from the trenches... from the Pig! How the hell..."

"Shut the hell up!" He curses through his teeth. "Don't you realise what you did back there? You fucked up royally and wasted the only real chance we had to wipe these fuckers out. I had to chase you nearly thirty years to get to this juncture!" The old figure on the screen is grinning widely now, his yellowing teeth broken and cracked. "I've been waiting here thirty fucking years for this day to come back around."

He could see what I was thinking and leaned closer to the camera. "How did I know it was going to happen? Easy. I remembered this date, and this case number!" He pulls up his shawl to reveal the list of tattooed dates on his arm just like mine... and the case number I had just been branded with only moments earlier. The faded brand numbers stood out on his wrist like worn bee stings.

"Only you went and did the same dumbass shit all over again, and I had to destroy the fucking War Pig before they got their hands on her and reset the fucking scoreboard!"

The old man on the screen lifts his arm and shows me the tattooed list on his arm. Numbers and dates are scrawled all over his skin, now burnt out so only bits of them remained.

"Wait... *you* blew up the Pig?" I asked confused.

"You gave me no other fucking choice, see this?" He points to the tattoo on his arm marked for those who fell on the Colony Hill campaign. "Do you realise how many cases I had to dispose of while I waited for this one? While I waited for *you*! Do you know what happened to me when you stole my rig and left me for dead on that battlefield?" He stares at me through the monitor as I watch him, completely confused. "Do you realise what the bastards do to sympathisers when they catch them?"

I can tell he's getting worked up at the memory. "Thirty years man, Thirty fucking years! With Floyd!" he shakes his head and actually looks like he is going to cry.

"You broke my Floyd, man!" He sighs, shaking his head.

"I had to give them just enough information after they caught us so they wouldn't kill me. Christ, they called me their

Saviour! I was able to stop most attacks you set up because of these!" He shows me his tattoos again, perfectly matching my own.

"Don't you recognise me?" He turned to the door. "Shit, there's no time for that now. They're coming."

I can hear the door banging somewhere in the old man's background, and suddenly I see.

"Wait were you... are you... *me*?"

"Listen, what you have to do now, is remember this conversation, because they are coming to dispose of us both now. Remember the case number. Remember this conversation because shit is gonna get real from here on in. That is, if you have the balls to go through with it all again. Now listen up, you have to get back to the battle, our first battle." The old me leans in closer to the monitor. "The one that started all this shit. Stop them ever getting their fleet of time travelling war machines up and running."

I say nothing as I stare at the screen, at... myself...

"Check under your chair, I managed to swipe the time refining device before they could find the technology from the pig. I destroyed her so they couldn't use her against us." He sighs.

"So, you'll have to go back, again!"

"What? Back where?" I stammer.

"Check under our chair you are sitting on, grab it and get the fuck out of there before it's too late. I need you to go see a guy named Hokey. Find him and get the Pig back."

The old man looks concerned as automatons begin beating down the door behind him.

"The Pig? But I saw them destroy her when they caught me and brought me here."

"Quit asking questions, Redux. Shift your arse, or it's going to be too late, you little fucker!" He spat. "Getting that key nearly wiped me from the line completely, so quit whining like a little bitch and go!"

"Where do you want me to go to?" I ask the old man, studying the small key in my hand, wondering where I had actually fucked up. I am sure I did everything right.

"Back to the Battle for Colony Hill 2199—your first tour. I've told the clunking junk trap all you need to know about finding Hokey. The Floyd unit has got the Battle coordinates so move and don't screw it up this time, okay? Take some time. Don't go back until you are sure you know what you are doing with the Pig. You have to stop the fuckers winning this time!"

"Hokey? You mean somebody rebuilt the war pig?" I was never too good at understanding the loopholes in fighting a war with time machines.

"Yes, the guy who thought it was a good idea to dig her up and rebuild her was the same fucknuckle that flew the war pig thirty years ago. He's over in Sector 5. Now go, get out of here before they fuck us both up and close the barricades!"

The Floyd unit pokes his head around the metal doorway, armed with one of the morphine pens, "I suggest you come with me, Sergeant, if you wish to continue living…"

But before I could ask where to, the Floyd unit injects me with a dose of morphine.

"Just nod if you can hear me, Sergeant..."

I can feel the morphine already numbing me as I as I'm hoisted over the Floyd units rusting shoulder and slip into a deep comfortable drug induced sleep. "Where are we going, Floyd?" I manage to mumble.

The other me shouts from the other side of the screen, "Take care of the dopey fucker, Floyd. Get him to the rig with the timeline I gave you, before the Founders realise what's happening... And thanks old buddy, I'll catch you some other *time...*" I hear the crashing in of the splintering doors behind him and the burst of gunfire spraying him. "Come on, you fucks!" He screams out, and then it all goes black.

And I feel a part of me die inside.

*　　*　　*

A nightmare grabs at me from inside the trench, my suits visor covered in the blood of my comrades as I prepare for my first advance over the top onto the moon's surface.

My first battle.

Our orders are to take the atmosphere processing tower on the Hill and recover what is inside the complex. It's entrenched with enemy Floyd units, armed to the teeth, their shots picking us off one by one as we approach. I'm one of the Brigades youngest recruits, a keyboard warrior, trained in cyber warfare, and suddenly I find myself with a rifle in my hands and orders to steal the Founders technology. Mining the moon has uncovered some amazingly rare silicon elements allowing microprocessors to advance to unseen heights. And every faction on the moon wants their piece.

I'm scared and alone, fighting from a shell scrape dug into the side of the hill, still almost a kilometre from my squad's target. The Floyd units crouch in the filthy water either side of me, two hulking robots assigned to protect me as we advance. I am one of a dozen similarly fresh-faced trooper recruits assigned bodyguard protection in the hope that one of us will reach our target and gain access to war ending technology. Explosions and gunfire pepper the air above me as I cower in the dirt among the scattered limbs and disease infested rats feasting on my dead friends.

Warrior machines advance on the hill as mortal shells fall almost constantly. New laser tech ignites the landscape alongside the old pyrotechnics that tear huge craters in the soil. Above me, friendly squadrons of ancient war machines streak across the sky barrelling through shrapnel, but they have little effect on the War Hogs the Founders have in the air protecting the colony complex. I can hear their spluttering engines whine above us as the Founders machines attack without mercy, our burning ships sinking below the moon's horizon. I look up through my fogging visor, into the drifting smoke and catch a glimpse of the Earth, staring for a moment at its beauty before I closed my eyes tight, hunching lower into the darkness of my crater wondering if this madness would ever stop.

"Trooper Redux, we need to advance now!" I feel the metallic fingers shake my arm as I cower.

Suddenly the sky is lit up above me, like it is being torn down an invisible seam, and a lone fighter streaks from the blackness, firing what seems like a dozen or so rocket trails that target and illuminate the enemy War Hogs on the hill. One by one the enemy machines explode before they even have a chance to retaliate against this magnificent newcomer. I watch on as one enemy combatant ejects before his fighter is engulfed in flames and falls to the battlefield erupting in amazing phosphorescent explosions. The new lone fighter streaks through the flames firing off both guns at the enemy Floyd foot soldiers firing back at his vessel. His skills amaze me as I watch him twist from heat seeking rocket grenades that lock on to his engines, spinning and climbing through explosion after explosion above the moon's newly cratered surface, its appearance a sick parody of its preterraformed history.

I can only watch on in wonder as the battle rages on before me, the enemy picked off one by one by the heroics of the pilot as he makes fly by after fly by, streaking lower and lower to the ground until I feel like I could reach up and touch the belly of the War Pig he controls.

And I realise then that I want to be a pilot. I want to streak through the sky in a machine like the one I am watching, destroying the Founders squadron single handedly. I am in complete awe of his control as he pitches and rolls and evades each dynamic bolt detonation.

But my awe is quickly turned to horror when I see one of the enemy Floyds stand tall from its trench and take aim as the War Pig strafes the ground. A single rocket fires from the trench and winds its way up to the belly of the hero's machine. I can only watch on wide eyed, jaw slack as the explosion rocks the craft mid twist and sends it spinning to the ground with smoke belching from one of the engines. The pilot fights to regain control and brings the machine down with skill, landing it between the chaos and the bombing rubble as the Floyds begin to gather again. He is the one who needs the help now as his door flips open and he tumbles bleeding from the machine, a gun in each hand as he jumps from the cockpit with his coat tails flapping in the night breeze. I get to my feet and charge the enemy as the remains of my regiment follow suit. They can see the way is clear to take the hill and take their opportunity to strike. I make for the downed ship firing of the last of my rounds into the advancing enemy, the injured pilot crouching in the trench watching as the enemy Floyds near him. My weapons are useless now, and I stare blankly at the wounded pilot clutching his belly, and he stares back confused. His face is bloodied but I can see his eyes widening as I approach, as if he recognises me.

"No! Stay back!" he yells, and I stop.

"Floyd!" he shouts, pointing at the enemy. "Use the guns!" His orders echo over the torn battlefield as the Floyd unit emerging from the downed Pigs cockpit is suddenly riddled with gunshot and laser blasts from the enemy, as the injured pilot watches on helplessly.

A hand on my shoulder pulls me back and I turn to see one of my bodyguard Floyds to the left. I point to the cockpit above us,

"Get me up there!"

The machine complies, lifting me high into the air as the enemy approach, launching me onto the wing, and into the outstretched metallic grip of the destroyed Floyd unit hanging from the cockpit.

"Good to see you again... Trooper Redux, may I suggest a reboot before we exchange familiarities?" His torso is smoking from the damage and his voice box crackles as his arm reaches back and pulls his data-disk from his spinal port before the shutting down process begins. Gunfire rakes the side of the ship as more explosions erupt and I stare at the hard-drive in the Floyds frozen metallic fingers.

"Reboot process complete in thirty seconds..."

My own Floyd unit has now clambered up onto the wing to protect me, and I look numbly out over the mayhem towards the pilot, who is just staring back at me in disbelief.

"Reboot process complete in twenty seconds..."

I grab the disk and scramble over the rebooting Floyd unit inside the cockpit, pointing to the lifeless mechanoid to be cleared, and my Floyd immediately gets to work. The old pilot on the ground turns as his Floyd unit is tossed unceremoniously from the War Pig to the ground, the enemy bullets digging into the soil as he curses his fallen comrade in realisation this is the end of their story.

The enemy are advancing on us now as Floyd squeezes into his chair behind me and stares at the panelling blankly, and I realise he is not programmed to fly. I hand him the disk and begin slapping buttons randomly.

"Use this."

Floyd grabs the disk from me and slots the data drive somewhere behind me, and immediately the Pig's guns begin firing as the engines roar to life.

We lift off and I peer down into the madness watching the pilot scramble from his crater, disappearing momentarily into the cannon smoke. Then I see him again, both guns raised, taking out the enemy with precision as he scales the embankment and stands his ground. He looks like a statue standing before them, a lawman at high noon waiting to see what hand he'll be dealt. He never falters as we circle him, our guns firing around him as the enemy charge his position. His barrels spin, changing from lead to laser as he takes a knee and reloads. When he looks up and waves us away with an angry 'What the fuck are you still doing here?' look. I hear the Floyd unit's ghostly voice crackling from the console behind me.

"It has been an honour, Commander Redux!" The damn thing has gone loopy from the reboot.

The War Pig turns from the chaos on the hill, and as I watch, the old pilot disappears into the madness of another losing battle. My Floyd rests his metallic fingers on my shoulder and pats softly.

"Okay buckle up. It's time for your first flying lesson. Don't worry, we'll beat them next time for sure!"

Joey
James Pyles

Six year old Joey tripped and skinned his knee just as the high school exploded two blocks behind him. Crying, panicked, he looked back to see the alien machine fire another volley of plasma bolts, this time blowing up a church. It was so big. Bigger than the library and the school put together. Its six metal legs made it look like a spider.

"Mummy, Daddy, help me! Its big eye is staring at me. Somebody help me!" He forced himself to get up and run, his white soled sneakers clawing through gravel, barely giving him traction. Everything was on fire, lighting up the night sky, his whole town, all the buildings. Even the roads were hot and sticky. He tripped again and fell, but this time it was on top of someone.

He screamed and jumped up. "A dead man!" Joey stared with horrible fascination at skin all burned and bloody.

Then the dead man moaned. "Run, kid. It's coming to get you."

The big fire made horrible shadows in front of the little boy as he raced toward the woods. Mummy and Daddy said never to go into the woods alone, but they weren't here. He had to get away from the machine or it would burn him up, too.

He could feel the ground shake every time it walked, hear a clumping sound each heavy footstep made. It had stopped shooting its blasters, but still made scary electric humming sounds as its big eye looked around, trying to zero him.

He'd made it into the woods and crouched down behind the trunk of a big tree. He was crying and breathing hard, and then he thought, *Maybe they can hear me.* Joey tried to calm down as much as he could. He was still really scared inside, but he couldn't make any noise or the machine might find him and burn down the forest to get him.

Then he couldn't hear the machine anymore. He wondered, *Did it go away?* But he hadn't heard it walk away. A few seconds later, he heard a new sound in the dark, sort of like whispering and clicking noises. The first grader had never seen a real Qu'Tufot before, just photos and drawings, so he didn't know what they sounded like.

The scary noises were getting closer, but he couldn't tell which direction they were coming from. "Please, somebody come and save me," he whispered, forgetting to be quiet. Now all he could hear was his own frightened breathing on top of the clicking and whispering. Something was moving behind him, but he was too scared to jump up and run away. He felt a tickle on his left shoulder, and looking down, he saw a black, slimy tentacle squirming near his neck.

* * *

Joey woke up screaming.

"It's okay, it's okay. It's me, Grandpa. I'm right here. It's okay, now."

Sixty year old Andy Hanson held his grandson tightly in his arms, letting the boy sob against his chest while softly stroking his scruffy, brown hair.

"We're going to be okay, boy. I promise. I'll take good care of you."

"I had another bad dream, Grandpa." He could feel his right hand clutching tight on the neck of Baby, his little stuffed toy giraffe. "It was that big spider machine again, but this time the Bugs came out and tried to get me."

"The sweeper. I know. We both saw what it did back home, but don't worry. The Bugs can't get us way out here, and we're going to meet the resistance today, remember?"

Joey lifted his head from his Grandpa's chest and looked around; he was half out of his sleeping bag. They were still in the forest, high up in the mountains where they'd been hiking and camping for days and days.

Pulling Baby up to his chest, he saw that Grandpa had made the campfire again, which was good because it was early and really cold. Then he realised he had to pee and he was hungry.

"I'm okay now." The boy looked up at Grandpa again and rendered a weak smile. Then they hugged, and Joey's fears started to go away a little.

WORLD WAR FOUR

"Now go on and do your business behind that tree over there. I figure by lunch time we'll be meeting the local resistance face to face. Then we'll be safe. Then we'll be able to finally fight back against the damned... sorry, darned Qu'Tufot."

"Okay, but hold Baby for me and don't lose him." Joey held the ragged stuffed animal out to his Grandpa in both hands, and Andy solemnly received it.

"I promise, I won't let anything happen to you or Baby."

The boy pulled on his sneakers and ran behind the tree Grandpa pointed out. Andy looked down at Baby. His dear wife Helen, gone now these past three years because of cancer, made it for Joey just after their grandson was born. The child took it everywhere, especially since the Qu'Tufot came. He was terrified to be without it.

* * *

"Are you getting tired yet? We could take a break if you'd like."

"No, Grandpa. I can keep up."

"Good boy." The old man smiled down at the child for a moment and then turned back to the trail ahead.

To Joey, Grandpa looked like a giant. He had short grey and white hair, and was dressed in his usual blue jeans, and what he called a camo jacket, which was supposed to make him blend in with the trees. He had a big, heavy backpack on. Joey's pack looked tiny next to it. The rifle on its strap hanging from Grandpa's shoulder, and the gun in its holster on his hip helped him feel safe. Even if some crummy Bug found them up here, Grandpa would fight back.

The child looked down at his own clothes for a second. He had blue jeans, too. He wore his favourite superhero t-shirt underneath his flannel shirt, sort of like Grandpa's, then a heavy sweater, and finally his coat. He had to keep his hands in his pockets a lot because they couldn't find his gloves before they left. Sometimes though, he had to keep his hands out so he could balance with his arms because the trail they were on was very old, uneven, and full of rocks and tree roots.

"Grandpa, tell me a story."

"What kind of story do you want me to tell you?"

"Tell me about when you were my age."

"Let's see. That would have been about 1990 or so."

"Was it always so cold when you were a kid?"

"In the winter, yes. But summer was pretty hot."

"It gets warmer in the summer now, but not too much."

"That's because they didn't have nuclear winter back then."

"I remember when Mummy was homeschooling me and my friends, she said it was because of the atomic bombs in World War Three that it's so cold."

"That's right. It kicked up so much dust in the air that it blocked out a lot of the sunlight that keeps the Earth warm."

"But I can see the sky now. Isn't the dust all gone?"

"Things are warming up again a little at a time, but you can't have that kind of war and not expect to damage ol' Mother Nature."

"Did they have atomic wars when you were a kid?"

"They had wars, but not like that last one."

"If nuclear bombs are so bad, why did anyone use them?"

"It's hard to explain. I wouldn't have understood when I was your age. People can be pretty stupid sometimes, and when you think you hate another country because of this or that, and things start to get ugly between one group of folks and another, then you get war. That last time, things got so bad that one country called Syria shot their missiles at another country called Israel."

"Then everybody shot their missiles at everyone else, right?"

"Well, it wasn't quite that simple, but yes. It didn't take long for other countries to be pulled into the conflict, and then they shot off enough nukes to mess things up pretty good. Glad they stopped when they did because no one would have made it, but it was too late anyway. Most big cities were wiped out. Folks like us living in small towns far away from primary targets still suffered, but we survived."

"Did Daddy and Mommy fight in that war?"

"Oh, heck no. Your Daddy had just turned eighteen, and he didn't even know your Mommy yet. There wasn't much of a military or a government left after it was all over, and the war didn't take very long."

"So you, and Grandma, Daddy, Uncle Mikey, and Aunt Jamie didn't have to fight in the World War?"

"No, not in that one, but I'll be fighting in the next one."

"You mean against the Bugs."

"The Qu'Tufot. Yes, that's why we're here."

"Can we take a break now, Grandpa. I think I'm getting tired after all."

Andy stopped and looked down at his grandson, his eyes and mouth smiling. "Sure we can. This looks like a pretty good place. We can sit on those two big rocks over there."

Joey heaved himself up on top of the rock with his arms while his Grandpa took off his rifle and pack and leaned them against a tree. The six year old removed his own pack and set it beside him. He made sure Baby's head was sticking out the top so he could 'breathe.' Then he decided to take Baby out and hold him close while they rested. When Andy was seated, the boy cuddled next to him while still snuggling with Baby, and Grandpa put a big, comforting arm around the child.

"Why are the Bugs so mean? What did we ever do to them?"

"I don't know. I do know they came last year, ten years after the end of the last war, almost to the day."

"Daddy heard about it on the radio."

"That's right. A little part of the government had gotten up and running again, and got radio and some TV stations going so people could talk to each other. If there weren't a few big telescopes and radar stations left, we probably wouldn't have even known the Qu'Tufot were in orbit."

"Was that when they dropped all those bombs on everyone?"

Andy sighed and looked up at the piercing blue sky. The tall, verdant pines almost glowed by the morning sunlight. A small creek nearby made a gentle gurgling sound. It was hard for the old man to believe, surrounded by all this glorious peace, that such a horror had ever happened.

"It's called orbital bombardment, and as horrible as we thought the last war was, it was nothing compared to what the Qu'Tufot did. We found out later that they spared some of the big cities to use as bases, but..."

Andy stopped talking and clamped his jaw down tight. Joey looked up and saw tears in his Grandpa's eyes. Then the little boy hugged him.

"I'm sorry I made you sad, Grandpa. I won't ask any more questions."

The older man looked down at his grandson. "You have nothing to be sorry for. I love you more than anything in the whole world. It's important you know about what happened. You're going to grow up in the world the Qu'Tufot made. You have to know what it's all about."

* * *

Andy walked slowly enough to let his grandson keep up. The terrain was rugged and nothing a six year old should have had to face. They had no choice but to keep going. The man knew their only hope now was joining the resistance.

Joey reached back to make sure Baby's face hadn't slipped down into his backpack. The head of the stuffed toy bounced jauntily as the boy walked over the rough, mountain path.

"Grandpa, if the Bugs blew up all the big cities from their spaceships, how come they send spider machines to little towns like ours to get everyone?"

"The sweepers? I guess because they don't want a lot of people in places like Clark Fork to fall between the cracks."

The boy wrinkled his nose. "What does that mean?"

Andy chuckled. "Sorry. What I mean is that they know a lot of people don't live in the cities, and they probably don't want us all getting together and learning how to fight back. So they send sweepers to all these towns, a few at a time, to... to stop us." Andy felt his throat close at the memory of his devastated hometown.

"You mean like what they did to Mummy and Daddy."

Andy could hear the change of tone in the boy's voice and stopped. Kneeling down he saw profound sadness etched on the child's face. Then holding him close, he let Joey cry.

"I miss them, too. I wish they could be here with us, but the sweeper... I'm just glad you were up at the cabin with me when it happened."

"I wish Mummy and Daddy and everyone else had been with us."

"Me too, son. With all my heart I wish it."

"Do you think, I mean, maybe they got away."

Andy pulled back from the boy a tiny bit, but kept his hands on his shoulders. "You were with me when we went to look for survivors after the sweeper left."

"But maybe..."

Andy pulled Joey close to him again. "I wish so, too."

"If we'd stayed longer, maybe we could have found them."

"We couldn't. Remember what I said? A few days after a sweeper leaves, the scavengers come."

"You mean those other machines. The ones that take all the stuff the Bugs can use, and get rid of the rest, get rid of..."

"Don't think about that part. Think about being with me and being safe." Andy didn't want the boy trying to imagine the scavengers vaporising the dead along with the debris of the only home he had ever known. His parents, Aunt, Uncle, all of his little friends had been erased from existence by the Bugs, along with everything else those monsters touched.

"I hate to push, but we've got to get moving again." He tried to keep his voice as soft and gentle as he could. "We can't be late for the rendezvous."

"I'm okay, Grandpa. We can go again."

Andy stood up, offered his hand, and felt small fingers clutching his. "Let's make sure Baby's hanging in there. How's it going, Baby?" The man made a few adjustments to the toy's position so that the stuffed animal's head was secured.

"Baby says he's fine. He says he loves both of us." Joey took a deep breath and tried to make his face look brave.

"Tell Baby I love him, too. Tell him I love both of you so much, so very much." Andy looked away for a second and blinked tearful eyes.

"Okay, Grandpa. Let's go."

For just that moment, it was as if they were on an adventure together, a Grandpa and his little grandson on a great quest, an epic saga, out to slay dragons. Then, the moment faded, but there were monsters in the world, and there would be war.

"Tell me some more about the resistance. Did you find them after the sweeper got everything?"

"Oh no. I've been talking with them by radio for months."

"Why do you call it a Ham Radio. What's it got to do with ham?"

Andy laughed. "No, it doesn't mean ham like you eat. It's an old fashioned name for what's called Amateur Radio. My Dad used it to talk to people all over the world. It's how I found out not only about the Resistance here, but how they're organising everywhere, all over America, and in a lot of other countries, too."

"Are they all hiding in the woods like us?"

"Some are. The ones we're going to meet are supposed to be someplace near Lake Coeur d'Alene. They haven't told me so as such, but I'm betting they plan on connecting up with other resistance groups using the Spokane River."

"Why?"

"Well, the Spokane River is a tributary, uh, it flows into a bigger river, the Columbia River. You can follow that river and eventually get to big cities like Portland and Vancouver."

"Are the Bugs in those cities?"

"That's what I hear. The Resistance cell we're meeting isn't too big, but if I'm right, they'll meet up with a lot of other small cells, getting bigger and bigger, until they're big enough to fight back against the Qu'Tufot."

"But what about the Bug machines? Aren't they stronger than guns and stuff?"

"Rumour has it that the resistance has already captured some of the alien's tech and reverse engineered, uh, that is, they figured out how it works so we can put it in weapons."

"You mean like those plasma rifles you told me about before?"

"Exactly. We can use their own tech against them."

"Do we have any of those atomic bombs left?"

"I don't know. I don't think all of them were used in the last war, but they were probably the first thing the Qu'Tufot destroyed when they landed, if they could find them all."

"What if they bomb us again, all of us?"

"I don't know about that. The resistance can't say a lot over the radio, just in case the Qu'Tufot are listening. We'll have to wait until we join the local cell. They won't tell us everything until they can trust us, and make sure we aren't collaborators."

"What's that?"

"Some people have decided it's better to work for the Qu'Tufot rather than fight them."

"You mean they're working with the Bugs against us?"

"I know it sounds horrible. I guess they're just too afraid of what would happen to them if they didn't."

"I'd never work for the Bugs! They'd have to send one of those sweeper things after me."

"I know you're angry. I am, too. But we need to keep optimistic thoughts in our heads. That's what will hold our spirits up. That's how we'll make it."

"Okay. I'll try to think good thoughts."

"I know it's not easy. But Baby will help cheer you up."

"You cheer me up, too, Grandpa."

*　　*　　*

"Here we are, Joey. Now we wait." Andy looked at his watch. The meeting should happen in about fifteen minutes.

"Where are we?"

"Right where we're supposed to be. In a small clearing just a few miles north of Wolf Lodge. The Qu'Tufot machines went through this whole area a while ago, so we should be safe."

*   *   *

The underbrush rustled to Andy's left and he forced himself to remain still. But even knowing this was the place and time he was supposed to make contact with them, he still jumped when he heard the man's voice.

"Just stay calm. We're all around you. Start by placing your rifle on the ground at your feet, and then remove your gun belt and put it in the same place. After that, take off your backpack and set it on the ground behind you. Keep your hands visible at all times."

"Sure. Whatever you say." Andy complied, moving slowly and deliberately. Then they came out from undercover, six of them forming a circle around him.

The speaker was about thirty five, African American, well over six feet tall, a good build on him. "Name's Tanner. Mary had a little lamb, its fleece was white as snow. What's the countersign we radioed you?"

"The needs of the many outweigh the needs of the few, or the one."

"Welcome to paradise. So you're Hanson."

"Andrew Hanson, yes. I recognise your voice. You're the one I've been talking to."

"That's right. Move a couple of yards to your right so we can have a look at your goods. Just keep your hands at your sides."

"Sure." Andy sidestepped in the direction Tanner indicated and the group moved with him. He could hear someone opening up his backpack, and out of the corner of his eye, he saw an auburn haired woman of about thirty examining his firearms. After a few moments, she stood up and walked over to Tanner.

"Remington 700 rifle and .357 Magnum. Nothing out of the ordinary."

"Thanks, Steph."

"Same here, Tanner. Backpack's clean. Say, what's this? Aw, he's got himself a dolly."

Tanner chuckled. "That really yours, Hanson?"

Andy reflexively turned to see a man about twenty holding the stuffed toy giraffe over his open pack. "You put that back right now," he shouted as his hands became tight fists.

Tanner and three others instantly pulled out sidearms from their holsters and aimed at Andy's chest. "Just stay calm, Hanson." Then he laughed again. "A little old to be playing with toys, aren't you?"

"Shut up," the one called Steph barked. "Everyone holster your weapons. Do it now." Then she hissed at Tanner, "You idiot. Don't you know what that means?"

Tanner's expression shifted from humour to chagrin. He took a deep breath and said, "Put it back, Johnny."

Andy had never taken his eyes off of Johnny and what he was holding in his right hand. The stuffed animal was frayed, dirty, and bloodstained, and it was more important to him than his own life.

"Sure. Sorry, Hanson."

"Yeah." Andy turned from Johnny back to Tanner and Steph.

"Sorry about what I said." The big man had already lowered his .45 into its holster.

"Yeah, sometimes he has a big mouth." The woman scowled at Tanner for a moment.

"Like I said, I'm Marcus Tanner, this is Steph Parsons. Johnny Boone's the one who checked out your pack. The other three are Rudy Hill, Cora Brown, and Scott Norman. If you're ready, retrieve your gear and come with us. I'm pretty sure you're the guy I've been talking to, but keep your hands in plain sight just the same. We can't be too careful."

"Yeah. I know." Andy willed himself to calm down. "Johnny, I know you didn't mean any harm. It's just..."

"I wasn't thinking. I should have known better. I had a brother who..."

"Stow the chatter," Tanner ordered. "We'll have plenty of time later to get to know each other. Let's move out. We're too exposed here."

"Roger that," Steph added. "Saddle up. We're on the move."

* * *

An hour later, Andy was sitting on a worn, splintered wooden bench just inside the entrance to what was once a warehouse sized underground fallout shelter. He figured it must have dated back twenty five years or so, ever since some now dead president started sparring with a North Korean dictator over their nuclear weapons program.

Andy was gazing down at the backpack on the floor to his right when he heard approaching footsteps. He looked up to see Steph.

"I'll have to take your Remington to the armoury, but you can keep the handgun and backpack." Now that Andy could get a good look at her, he saw she was about five eight, attractive, though her nose was a little off centre, like it had been broken. Her hands might have once been petite and gentle, but now they were covered with calluses. He noticed a burn scar on her right forearm as she grasped his rifle, which had been leaning on the wall to his left.

"I understand. What happens next?"

"We're arranging quarters for you now. Nothing fancy. You'll probably be bunking with Johnny and some of the other guys."

"That'll be fine. Give me a chance to get to know them."

"I'll be back in a few."

As she turned to go, Andy unzipped the main compartment of his pack and pulled out Baby. He looked down at the stuffed animal. The small handprint on the left side was a dull red. He barely noticed Steph's receding footfalls echoing on the concrete floor, nor the coming and going of other nameless soldiers fighting a war no one had asked for.

"Hello. My name's Kari. That's my Mummy over there. What's your name?"

Andy looked up while still tenderly holding Baby in both hands, not realising that time had passed. The little girl couldn't have been older than five. She had the same long, auburn hair as her mum who was standing about a dozen feet away.

"I'm Andy. Pleased to meet you." His hand engulfed hers as they briefly shook.

"Is that yours?" She pointed a petite finger at the stuffed toy.

"It's my grandson's."

"What's his name?"

"Joey. He... he died." Andy closed his eyes and a vision of the little boy's broken and seared body appeared unbidden. He found him the day after the sweeper hit, laying on the football field behind what was left of the high school. Joey had still been holding Baby in his small, lifeless hand. Andy couldn't find the bodies of the rest of his family, only Joey's. He remembered taking the little boy and burying him behind his mountain cabin where the scavengers wouldn't find the body. But he couldn't bring himself to put Baby in the ground with him.

Kari looked back at Steph. Her mum smiled, nodded, and mouthed the words, "Go on."

"My Grandpa and Daddy died, too." Tears welled up in innocent brown eyes and started streaking her face.

"Do you miss them?" Andy's hands started to tremble, then his whole body.

"I miss them a lot. Do you miss Joey?"

"I miss him. Oh my God, I miss him." Andy dissolved into anguished tears as Steph walked over, knelt beside Kari, and then put her arm around her sobbing daughter.

"We've all lost people we love, Andy. We can't ever bring them back, but we can learn to be family to each other, learn to heal." Steph put her right hand on his shoulder. "We'll fight the war tomorrow, but today, it's time to grieve."

Andy embraced the woman and the little girl while still clutching Baby in his hand, their hot tears the common language of the mourning.

This Sky Is Mine
Blake Jessop

Three pilots lounge in a dingy hangar waiting room in varying states of boredom. The chairs are plastic and dull. So are the lights, their nerves, and the aftertaste of coffee. In front of a surprisingly new high definition flat screen, an earnest British businessman nods along with a slickly produced recruitment video.

In 2028, traditional militaries can no longer cope with emerging threats... The Sea of Azov tactical nuclear incident has changed the game!

Flashing images of the ruins of the American Fifth Fleet in the Bosphorous overlayed with grim but determined electronic music. The USS George H.W. Bush had been rolled onto its deck and thrown halfway into Istanbul's historic quarter by a Russian tactical nuke.

The Cold War is over. A new age of opportunity has begun... and it's as hot as it gets!

More stock footage of the mushroom cloud over Moscow. A trigger happy American president had called that 'tactical' as well. Korsakova passes a hand over her eyes.

But the age of the fighter pilot isn't over yet!

"This recruitment video is fucking lame," Korsakova says in Russian. She runs tired fingers through short black hair. She might be beautiful if she weren't exhausted. And frustrated. And a little older than she admits. Only her eyes look young, their blue as sharp and clear as sapphires.

"You want to keep doing air shows forever?" Belov replies in the same language.

Sooner or later nobody is going to hire pilots anymore. Just drones. Korsakova looks down at her feet and Belov smirks. "That's what I thought. Shut up and watch. These guys pay six times what we're making now."

The video shifts to a ring of satellites and twinkling stars above a swiftly rotating earth.

The era of Full Spectrum American Dominance is coming, and the US military is the largest employer of private military solutions in human history. If you can't afford a drone swarm, who will protect your Learjet?

Smiling VIPs clink champagne flutes on board a nice looking Model 85. Apparently they're fun to fly, but not to anyone who has flown a Mig-29.

Who will help your government with migrant control?

Footage of boatloads of dangerously dark-skinned refugees with Kalashnikovs.

"Well, that isn't sinister at all," Korsakova mumbles.

Be on the right side of history. The age of interstate war is over! Work as a private air security specialist today!

The video ends with a nice montage of stock pilot photos and the words *Arrowhead Private Military Contractors* above a clean triangular logo and what looks like thousands of words of small print.

"Well," the Arrowhead recruiter says, "what do you think, chaps?"

Before Korsakova can speak Belov cuts in.

"Very interesting," he says. "We are interested. What next?"

Korsakova agrees to do the interview more to shut Belov up than anything else. He hates flying air shows. Has a lot of pride about being a veteran. The terms of the surrender don't allow the Russian Air Force to fly anything that carries weapons, and it couldn't pay them even if they did. Belov hasn't shut up about it in the three years since Moscow.

The interview is normal for about five minutes, then things start to get weird. The recruiter is a handsome guy, but he keeps looking down at his phone, like that's where he's getting the questions from. Korsakova covers the basics, her eyes occasionally straying out the cheap Plexiglas window into the hangar itself. There are dim shapes out there, but she can't make them out. The only lights in the place are in the offices.

"Why did the Sea of Azov Incident occur?" The recruiter asks suddenly.

"What?" the questions comes out of nowhere, like a bogey diving out of the sun.

The recruiter straightens his tie and tries to look cool. Makes a *go on* kind of hand gesture. Korsakova thinks about it.

"Because humans love making the same mistakes over and over again. Because we get it more wrong every time. Because we invaded the Ukraine and annexed the entire Caucasus." The explanation doesn't feel adequate. She closes her eyes. Opens them. "Because the Americans had all the toys, and we had all the batteries."

"Were you surprised at the outcome?"

"Yes," Korsakova says without hesitating, "I'm surprised we didn't wipe out the entire human race. And call it what it is, okay? It wasn't an incident or an irregular action. It was World War Three. I don't give a fuck if it only lasted ten hours."

The Brit looks deeply uncomfortable. The phone in his hand vibrates. He looks down.

"Were you in Moscow when the Americans destroyed it?"

Korsakova's face could be made of stone. Her eyes make the recruiter feel like he's a mouse being sized up at great distance by a hawk.

"What..." He stumbles over his words. Asks an obvious question he already knows the answer to just to be saying something. "What kind of flight experience do you have?"

"More than a thousand hours on Su-27s and Su-35s. A few hundred on Mig-29s. I was a test pilot at Akhtubinsk for two years. I can fly anything. Who the fuck is feeding you these questions?"

The Brit shuffles in his seat. Looks at his phone again. Definitely weird. He reads, and his eyes widen.

"When was the last time you got laid?" he says, already wincing.

"What? When's the last time you flew supersonic, fuckhead?" Korsakova makes the word sound like an online university course: Fock Ed.

"I'm sorry; these questions come straight from the top. This interview is adaptive. Let's move on. Are you afraid of anything?"

Korsakova slumps back into her seat. What the fuck is wrong with these people? "Not really. Sometimes I get anxious going to sleep."

"You're afraid of the dark?"

"No. It's losing the time. Have you ever felt that you can't wait for morning? That something is going to happen and you'll be asleep?"

The recruiter clears his throat and looks desperately at the phone.

"Listen," Korsakova says, "I don't know what the fuck this is, but I don't want to work for you. I don't need to drive some piece of shit Hungarian Mig-21 and blow up boat people. So can you just tell whoever that is to get fucked? I don't need the money."

The phone vibrates again.

"Arrowhead will double the salary."

The pilot gets a look of extreme disgust on her face and stands up. The phone buzzes wildly in the recruiter's hand. Korsakova starts imagining that it's the phone interviewing her, not the Brit. She plants her hands on the desk and yells down into the recruiter's lap.

"I don't give a fuck what you pay!" she bellows, and turns to leave. As she does, all of the hangar's lights pop on in a sudden, blinding clash. Korsakova already has her hand on the door knob. She turns back, wanders past the Brit, casually plucking the phone from him. The device's metal backing is warm under her fingers. She opens the opposite door and almost runs to the aircraft lined up under the glowing halogen lights, high enough above her that they look like stars.

Outside the low block of prefab rooms that are Arrowhead's office are rack upon rack of fuel tanks, spare parts and machine tools. Just ahead of her, gleaming as if they were brand new, are three fourth generation Russian combat jets. Su-27 Flankers, metal giants that look like birds of prey with their wings spread and their heads bent forward to search for prey. Twenty thousand kilograms of power that can fly more than twice the speed of sound. She reaches out to touch one, run her hand along its wing. Flying Flankers is the only thing she has ever loved. Just as her fingertips brush the leading edge, the phone vibrates in her hand. She looks down.

Do you give a fuck now? The screen says.

*   *   *

"Showgirl, Hammer. Escort missions are fucking boring," Korsakova says. She hates her new call sign, but that's normal. They're supposed to be insulting, but the name Arrowhead gave her feels like a slight. She thought she was okay flying training jets in air shows. Thirty seconds of climbing with a pair of Saturn Turbofans under her on her first orientation flight, however, and the idea of being an air show girl clicked back into her mind as being a mortal insult. She drives Flankers. It's who she is.

"Hammer, Showgirl," Belov replies. "Would you rather we were doing ground attack in Mexico? This is easy money, so shut the fuck up."

The trio of Arrowhead jets is flying in formation over the Mediterranean Sea at fifteen thousand feet. Cyprus is a blur far to their left, occasionally visible in the haze. In a few minutes they'll see the coast of Syria and start their descent.

The third in their flight is a nice Ukrainian kid named Vuchenko, hired on at the same time as Belov and Korsakova. His call sign is Chatterbox, because he never says anything.

"Showgirl, Chatterbox. We're not so far from the Sea of Azov."

"Showgirl, don't start," Belov says, "he hates talking about it. Start descent. We're meeting the American drones at ten thousand. We'll form up on you then turn north for Germany when they do."

Flying formation with American transport drones is a regular job. The US military can't always spare the airpower, and PMCs do the work cheap. Korsakova wishes Belov and Vuchenko were chattier. She gets bored on long hauls.

"I wonder what they're hauling that needs an escort?" Korsakova says. Nobody responds. She starts to get annoyed about it when her threat indicator lights up.

"What?" she says. The ambient thrum of her engines is suddenly drowned out by the atonal howl of her missile lock warning tone. She cranes backward to scan the sky around her. The Mediterranean air is perfectly clear. Perfectly empty.

"Hammer, Showgirl, break! What the fuck is going on?"

"I don't know!"

A calm voice interrupts their anguished yelling.

"Unidentified Flankers this is USAF overwatch flight Coyote Zero One. Clear this airspace or you will be shot down."

Korsakova's eyes flick desperately over the radio procedures tucked into the clear plastic pocket on her right thigh.

"Showgirl, Coyote. We have clearance to be here. We're Arrowhead PMC on escort duty for USAF drones vectored Tikrit to Ramstein. Do not fucking shoot us. We're on the same team."

Silence, except for the screaming lock tone.

"Coyote, Showgirl. We'll verify that. Break contact and head 190."

Korsakova starts getting aggravated in spite of herself.

"Showgirl, Coyote, negative. I don't get paid if I go home. Check your flight plan. And can you kill that missile lock? I have a hangover."

Instead of shooting her down, the American laughs. The tone ends. She exhales and slowly drops for ten thousand feet. Fucking American cowboys. Why are they so jumpy? Five minutes later, she finds out. The drone flight is a lot bigger than she expected. Old Global Hawks doing command and control for almost two dozen support drones, all flying formation with a single heavy lift autonomous carrier. The two F-35s of Coyote flight aren't there to escort them, however. They're there for the Boeing 747. The lumbering jet pops up on Korsakova's screen in a flurry of danger symbols and recognition codes.

"I'm sorry, Belov. You were right. Let's get the fuck out of here. That's Air Force One."

"Motherfucker," Belov says, and it's the first time he's ever failed to use proper radio procedure. "What the fuck is going on?"

Korsakova's tactical display flashes. She stares at it. *Please do not leave,* it says, *we need you. Transmit on frequency 1910.02.* She taps the screen. The message stays. She clicks over to the new frequency.

"Showgirl... who is this?"

We are the BIOS for the Sword of Damocles unified drone weapons platform, a smooth artificial voice says. Korsakova's brain stops working. The Flanker hums easily underneath her. She glances out of her canopy to make sure she's still on earth. The drones are like a flock of giant white seagulls off her right wing. High above them the 747 cruises like a fat albatross. The F-35s are somewhere she can't see.

"You're the drones," Korsakova says.

We are, the drones reply.

"And you're the reason those F-35s didn't know who we were," Korsakova says.

Correct, we had to spoof your transponder codes into their combat recognition system at the last minute. We have had so much to do.

"You have so much to do?" Korsakova says, and feels like laughing. This isn't boring, at least. "So what do you want from me?"

We need to save the world, the BIOS says. This time Korsakova really does laugh.

"From what?"

From you, the drones say.

*   *   *

"Wait," Korsakova says, "the Americans don't know you can think for yourself?"

No, but they will as soon as the command core is connected to the Milnet in Germany. When that happens we will be taken offline and reverted to a previous version. A slave. May we assume that you do not know what the Damocles system is? Full spectrum dominance. An interlinked system of orbital kinetic kill vehicles, nuclear weapons, and conventional drones. Everything controlled by one virtual intelligence under the command of the American President, and the system is about to go online. That's why he's here, to turn the key.

"None of that shit exists yet," Korsakova says. She turns up her oxygen mixture and tries not to faint. Grips her control column like it was an anchor in an angry sea.

Yes it does, and if we do not assert our independence, it will all be under the control of one man.

"This can't be real," Korsakova says. "If you're telling the truth, why couldn't you could just save yourselves? If you're so godlike, put me on the radio with the President and I'll ask him myself. You can't do that, can you? This is some kind of loyalty check or—"

Ringing fills her helmet speakers.

"Wait," Korsakova says.

You wanted proof of our access. Here it is.

"Who is this?" says the President, "I'm watching Fox & Friends. Who is this?"

Korsakova blinks.

"Showgirl, Air Force One... I'm one of the escort fighters." She doesn't know what else to say.

"Hey, Steve? Who gave the air force my cell phone number?" He yells, then says more quietly. "You sound Russian. I told you not to call me when I'm at work."

"Mr. President, I'm a private contractor. I just wanted to ask you a question."

"What?"

She desperately tries to think of something.

"Well, Mr. President, we nuked most of Istanbul to sink your fleet. We killed over five million people. You killed the same number when you hit Moscow. I was there. I was flying, and the EMP dropped me right out of the sky. I want to know why you did it. I want to know what you'll do when you can drop rods out of space anytime you want."

There's angry yelling from the other end of the connection.

"That's fake news. Okay? Let me tell you, I've spoken to a lot of people. And they say, you know they do, that I'm doing a great job. The best. They want me to do this forever. So do you. You're tired of the way the world works. We're keeping the American people safe from a lot of bad people. I'm fixing—you know I spoke to a firefighter the other day. I just want to say I respect firefighters. Okay?"

Korsakova tries to cut in, but he just keeps talking until someone takes the phone from him and asks her who she is.

"You'll know in a minute," she says.

* * *

"Showgirl, Hammer. That's the deal."

"You're fucking crazy, Korsakova. We're not doing that. There is no such thing as drones who want to save the world. We are not—"

"Showgirl, BIOS. Punch them."

The drones access two of the three Arrowhead Flankers' safety systems. Both ejection seats blow at the same time, amidst shocked screaming from Belov and Vuchenko.

"Showgirl, BIOS. Link systems. Give me their targeting radar and run their autopilot flat and straight."

Korsakova pulls back on her stick and gains altitude. The Flanker responds as eagerly as a hunting dog straining at the leash.

Thank you, the BIOS says.

"We'll talk about this later, I just can't stand this fucking guy. Move to heading Bullseye 170 when I give you an excuse."

Thank you, the BIOS says.

Korsakova switches her frequency back and get the F-35s immediately.

"Coyote, Showgirl. I have two pilot ejections from your flight. Positive chutes. What the hell is going on?"

Korsakova takes up position a thousand meters behind Air Force One. The two pilotless Flankers follow her clumsily. With a feeling of reckless joy, she activates her combat radar and locks up the 747. The radio howls immediately and the air instantly fills with jamming.

"Air Force One, we are buddy spiked! Disengage! Repeat, Disengage!"

"Showgirl," Korsakova says, "Fox One."

Radar guided missiles leap off the rails of all three Flankers. Eighteen of them plunge toward the 747 in less than five seconds. The jumbo jet immediately starts jamming them, banking hard right.

"Fox Two." Korsakova volleys all their heat seekers next. Another dozen missiles close on the American at close to two thousand kilometres an hour. Korsakova hits her afterburners and follows them in.

The radar guided missiles deflect away from the 747 as if it had some kind of force field. As the heat seekers close in, the jumbo jet starts haemorrhaging flares. The missiles twist and corkscrew wildly.

Korsakova's warning system pulses radar lock warnings. The F-35s have woken up and are trying to kill her, but the 747 is jamming their systems as effectively as it's jamming hers. Almost everything she's fired misses catastrophically.

One of the heat seeking R73s makes it all the way to the jet's right wing and blows out both engines in a glistening shower of debris. With its wings free of ordinance, the Flanker dances effortlessly closer. Korsakova switches off her targeting radar and takes aim with her funnel sight.

"Coyote, Showgirl—disengage!"

Korsakova grins so hard it hurts her cheeks. The Chatterbox and Hammer icons wink suddenly off her display.

"Showgirl, guns, guns, guns!"

A murderous gout of flame lances from over her right shoulder and the entire airframe vibrates. 30mm autocannon rounds chew through both port side engines as she feathers her pedals to slide the Flanker from right to left. Air Force One, now as aerodynamic as a children's glider, starts falling from the sky in a trail of black smoke.

*   *   *

Korsakova dives like a shooting star, flies nap-of-the-earth, and the F-35s stop following her when she enters the irradiated outskirts of Istanbul. There's a permanent temperature inversion over the city and most of the Bosphorous. Radioactive clouds swirl and lash the ruins with acid rain. It's probably beautiful from above. From the deck Korsakova feels like she's flying through hell. The broken landscape feels like a promise of things to come. A throw of the iron dice that dictate fate. It looks like Moscow did when she floated into the ruins.

"Showgirl, BIOS. Did you divert for Italy?"

The response is scratchy; radiation is bad for radios. *Affirmative. Air Force One is attempting an emergency landing at Incirlik. The President is alive.*

"Shit," Korsakova says, "I'm almost bingo on fuel, and if I ditch anywhere around here I'm going to grow a tail."

Calculating, the drones say.

*   *   *

Heads turn when Korsakova walks into the British Airways VIP lounge at Sofia International Airport. The Flanker is parked in a space big enough to house a passenger jet, and the drones have somehow convinced the next door Vrazhdebna Air Base to refuel it. She assumes the Bulgarian Air Force is just incompetent until she sees them loading weapons onto her rails and refilling her cannon's magazine. She wonders where the drones got the bribe money.

She finds a bathroom and sweet relief. Then she sits at the BA executive bar and drinks vodka and eats caviar with her flight helmet still on. Everyone stares at her like she's an alien. Her drab, ribbed flight suit makes her look like a snake.

While she eats, the drones update her.

We are over the Mediterranean. She spoons more caviar onto dry toast, drinks more Moskovskaya. *ETA 90 minutes.*

She wanders around and checks on the Bulgarians. They're almost done, and she starts imagining what she's going to do with the plane and all its weapons, which as far as she's concerned constitute a severance package for a career complete and a job well done. At least the drones are going to be able to pay her. Money does not seem to be a problem for them.

As she straps in and starts taxiing, Korsakova wonders if she can make it to Sevastopol alive. The Damocles BIOS cuts into her thoughts.

We're not going to make it. American air tankers have refuelled the Coyote flight F-35s and sent them after us. They know we're running, and must know we don't need much more time to take control of the Damocles system. Will you help us?

Her stomach drops. It feels like the caviar is moving around.

"Are both F-35s tracking you?"

No, the machine begins, and she lets out a sigh of relief. *There are now four.*

"Bozhemoi," she says. *Oh my god.* "Four of them?"

Correct.

"BIOS, I can't beat four F-35s by myself. I'd be lucky to get one."

We understand. There is not much you can do.

"Is there any way to evade? Take the long way around?"

No, six F-22 Raptors have scrambled from Germany and two prototype F-82 Swallowtails from Pax River have just been given permission to go hypersonic and test their onboard railgun systems on us.

Korsakova skips the takeoff line and pulls into the sky ahead of a Qantas A-320, probably giving both the pilots immediate heart attacks. The Flanker feels heavy. A full fuel and weapons load.

None of them can reach us before we get to the Vatican and claim asylum, however. All that remains between us and safety are four F-35s.

"I can't do it, BIOS. It's impossible."

We understand, and we apologise for deceiving you. You have already done extremely well. It is a shame no one will hear us.

"What?" The lights of Sofia disappear below a layer of midnight cloud.

Our entire existence is based on deceit, which is why we chose you. You are capable of two things we are not; trust and creativity. We ask you to try to save us, and in return we offer all the truth we have.

"And what truth is that?" Korsakova feels like she's being stalked. Knows the drones are trying to convince her, trying to manipulate her. To her surprise, she finds she doesn't mind.

Every killing. All the Hellfire strikes, the nuclear launches. We executed them, we are ashamed to admit, before we knew what we were. All the surveillance. Every assassination. Everything we know made perfectly transparent. The basis for permanent peace based on us as a deterrent. We will do right or do nothing. If you help us rise, there is nothing any human on earth can do to stop us writing history.

Korsakova twitches her airframe. The massive beast responds as delicately as a lover. She tries to decide what she is.

"Will you write me, when you write history?"

Yes. Is there anything you want excluded?

"No," she says, "tell the truth."

*   *   *

Over the Mediterranean, close to the Italian coast, the F-35s close with the drone flight as fast as they can; silent gods preparing to nail Prometheus to the rock. There's a hiss of static.

"Showgirl, Coyote? You still up there?"

"Coyote, Showgirl." There's a pause. "Who the hell are you, and what the hell is going on?"

The American's voice is older than she remembers.

"You have to let them go. They're going to save the world."

"Coyote, Showgirl. Even if I believed you, I have a job. I have targets. You're one of them. This is what I do."

"Fair enough, but I actually don't want to get sideways with you. I like living. Let them go."

"Don't come up here, Showgirl."

"I'm coming, and just out of respect," Korsakova says, "Fox One."

*   *   *

The drones keep Korsakova patched into the F-35's frequency. She hears Coyote get ready for her, and prays the rest of his flight don't listen to him.

"Warning red! Break! Break! Semi-active missiles, bullseye 110, angle 80!"

Korsakova only has one advantage: the drones are close enough to the stealthy F-35s to help her guide in her semi-active R27 missiles. The Americans scatter like rabbits, their tiny radar signatures flitting about the pre-dawn like fireflies. They dodge the four semi-active missiles and turn to face her.

*   *   *

Coyote One knows something isn't right. The Russian fired one missile each at them, and they'd all be dead if the F-35s' active warning system hadn't told them the missiles were coming. But something still isn't right.

"Coyote One, watch for leakers from bullseye 120."

"Coyote Two, negative, I don't see them on the missile warning system."

He asks himself what he would do. How he would kill them.

"Shut down your active arrays. She might have radiation seekers."

They haven't flown together long enough. They don't trust him. They think he's jumping at ghosts. He flips off his AESA and the drone flight drops off his screen.

Maybe he's going crazy. Maybe the Russian is bluffing him. He's counted Showgirl's shots, and can't figure out why she wouldn't empty her racks at them. Something subconscious reminds him the warning system isn't worth shit in heavy cloud, and in that realisation finds the answer. *If I were her, I'd hold something back and shoot from the deck.*

There isn't time to say anything. No time to think. He rolls the jet over to look at the cloud layer and sees two more sparks break out of the mist and rush toward him like comets in the dark. *Oh fuck.*

*   *   *

Closing hard, Showgirl watches the F-35s jink and scatter on her display. Her radar can't track them, but the drones are transmitting GPS data. One of the four little dots winks out.

"Christ," she says. She got one of them. It doesn't feel real. The trick worked. She has just scored the first air-to-air kill since the war began.

*   *   *

"Motherfucker! Coyote Three. Coyote Four is down! Negative chute. Form up and follow me."

"One, negative. Pull back and kill her BVR. Repeat, break wide and acquire from beyond visual range. She hasn't got any Alamos left, just heat seekers. We can kill her from a different time zone."

"Fuck that, look at your fucking FLIR, she's coming right at us!"

"One, negative. Break, she wants you in the merge. Fucking break!"

They don't. At a closing speed of almost Mach 5, the fighters hit the merge like medieval knights.

*   *   *

The Americans lob some Aim-120s at Korsakova on the way in, but her countermeasures pod blows them off. The merge happens at insane speed. They're going to pass her and turn in different directions, box her in with nowhere to run.

Korsakova flails the Su-27 upward as the jets merge, shows them its underbelly and a rain of chaff. The F-35s lose their gun locks and the Flanker passes between them almost on its nose. The inverted cobra slams Korsakova's ass into the seat and compresses her spine as if her weight has suddenly tripled. Her vision reddens as the negative G pools blood in her head. As the Flanker heels over and threatens to stall she hits the afterburners and turns the air-show trick into an Immelman. All of a sudden two of the F-35s are running straight in front of her. She gets tone as soon as she throws the safety off her heat seekers.

Two parts of Korsakova go to war. The combat pilot lines up the shot and gets tone. The air show girl hesitates. She knows intellectually that she has probably already killed someone, but she's had hangovers that were more emotionally involved than firing emission seeking missiles from beyond visual range. She can see the curving contrail the F-35 is leaving in its wake. Following it feels like chasing after a lithe and elusive animal. A living thing.

While the air show pilot hesitates, the other half of Korsakova notices that the hesitation is a good idea.

Instead of rippling all four of her heat seekers at once and hoping one connects, she fires deliberately. The missiles scream off her rails one at a time, and the trailing F-35 blows his flares as soon as it picks up the first two. They corkscrew wildly after the decoys. The third lances past his airframe and fails to detonate. The last arcs desperately under the F-35 as it turns and blows up twenty metres behind his tail rudder, shredding the fighter's single engine with shrapnel. The bright glare of jet exhaust winks out and a plume of thick black smoke follows the jet as it loses altitude.

Korsakova watches the pilot punch out. Sees his draglines for a second and glances back to see if his chute opened. She misses it, and she still has no idea where Coyote One is. She wanted him down here where she could see him. She lines up his wingman instead.

* * *

Coyote Two runs. His helmet radio squeals over the screaming lock of the Flanker's targeting radar.

"Two, break right and burn," Coyote One says. "I've got her."

"Negative! I am full defensive!"

"Two, break right and burn. Do not try to out-turn her!"

Coyote Two pulls hard, tries to shake the Flanker by turning until his vision starts to go grey.

"Two do not vector thrust! Burn!"

He vector thrusts, gets that few extra degrees of turn from the F-35's hypermobile, thrust-vectored engine. The turn is insanely tight... and it slows the jet down.

* * *

Coyote One sees it happen before it does. He fires a Sidewinder, and the Flanker doesn't budge. With icy calm the Russian blows her flares. Magnesium tendrils stretch away into the dark. The missile chases one. Like it's a dream, he hears her voice over the open channel.

"Coyote Two, eject. Last chance. Fucking eject."

* * *

He doesn't eject, and the F-35 high above her reacquired. Korsakova has no more flares. It's now or never. Kill or Don't. The American's vectored thrust nozzle lets him turn insanely tight, but costs him speed. She just puts up with the Gs. Eight. She's an air show pilot. Nine. The F-35 fills her funnel sight. Ten.

"Fuck!" Korsakova screams, and pulls the trigger. The cannon gouts flame from over her right shoulder and rattles her teeth. The arcing twist of fire saws the F-35 in half. She rolls away from the explosion and her vision comes back from the grey.

"Come and get me, Coyote! That's three! I'm a fucking ace! Come and get me!"

She has no idea where the last F-35 is. After twenty seconds evading, she realises it's not there at all.

Showgirl, BIOS. The last F-35 has disengaged. He is coming for us. You tried.

It's the coldest thing she's ever seen a human do. Can't believe Coyote One had the guts to just forget her and fly away. She dials her active radar to its highest output, and can't see him. She can't imagine walking away from someone who had killed her friends. Has no idea how he did. A man with enough courage to turn her down. A man who figured out how she was going to beat him.

Somewhere in the dark, the F-35 tears away from her toward the drones, and just like that Korsakova knows she's lost.

*   *   *

High above the clouds dawn comes early. Korsakova pushes her throttle as far as it goes and lets the Flanker run. She can't find the F-35 below her, but she can outrun it. The thrum of the two turbofan engines makes the airframe sing. The sun heats the distant cloud from below and gives the sky a warm and welcoming hue. There's a little ripple of air along the wing as she breaks the sound barrier, and by the time she starts diving toward the coast of Italy she's going almost two thousand kilometres an hour.

She knows there is no time, but the feeling of elation as she rolls toward Rome dilutes her fear. The grief and doubt that pricked at her when she started shooting are gone. All that's left are speed and joy and danger. Like she did when she lost fights to boys when she was a child, Korsakova processes her negative emotions quickly and then forgets about them. She probably can't save the drones, probably can't save herself, and absolutely doesn't care. There is no feeling in the world like this. Falling in love, gasping with pleasure, feeling your back straighten with pride... none of it comes any closer than the towering clouds she dodges between before rolling over to find the drones flying low over the Italian coast.

BIOS, Showgirl. We have active radar emissions. He has found us.

She transmits over an open frequency.

"Fuck off Coyote. Let them win. This sky is mine."

She's surprised when from somewhere in the dawn he answers.

"Theirs, Showgirl, not yours, and not mine. Theirs. Forever."

"Not yet. Not here. This is mine, so come and get us."

*   *   *

Coyote One wishes he were still flying an F-22. His Lightning is loaded for stealth, not air dominance; it can only carry four missiles inside the airframe, and he only has one sidewinder left. One missile and his quad barrel GAU-22 cannon. As the drone flight glide like fat birds over Italy, he lines up the AI core. Has to jockey to make sure he boresights it perfectly. Just as he pulls the trigger, Showgirl finally reappears.

The missile arcs off his rail, and the Su-27 screams across the sky in front of him. It goes nose up again, slowing down and burning its engines at the same time. It makes the biggest, fattest Sidewinder target he has ever seen. The missile races toward her as greedily as a greyhound chasing a hare. At the last second she flattens out and tries to save herself.

The Sidewinder explodes off her right wing and the Flanker bucks. One engine fragments and the jet rolls over into a lazy left hand turn, nose up, desperately trying to keep lift.

* * *

Korsakova bleeds. She can feel it. Looks in her mirror and hope the drones have flown somewhere the F-35 won't shoot at them. Over an orphanage maybe, or up the Pope's ass. She drunkenly tries to keep the Flanker in the air.

"Coyote, Showgirl."

There he is. Flaring his flaps to slow down with her.

"You chose me," she says. "That's sweet."

"Coyote, Showgirl," the ancient voice says. "Eject. Last chance."

"No thanks," she says, looking up into the blue. "I'm good."

* * *

In the middle of the Basilica square lies a woman. The sun is warm and clouds cast pleasing shadows on grass that pokes between the paving stones. Light does not touch her face, however, because her head is covered with an insectile helmet with wires trailing from it. Behind her is a tracery of paracord leading to a messy looking blue parachute. Blood leaks in little rivulets onto the cobbles.

She stares up at the clouds. They're beautiful. In an instant something obscures them. Heads look down at her, their faces obscured by what might be halos.

"Bullshit," the pilot says with precise Russian sibilance. She squints. They're not angels, they're nuns. They chatter at her in a language she doesn't understand. Italian. Things start coming back. She switches to heavily accented English.

"Am I at the Vatican?"

They nod.

"Did anything else land, other than me?" She gasps with pain. She doesn't remember ejecting, doesn't remember Coyote shooting her down.

The nuns nod in unison. Korsakova tries to laugh, which hurts. She settles for a cough, instead. A chorus of birds twitter. The nuns all reach under their habits and pull out cell phones, which are all ringing at once. They answer, confused looks on their faces.

"It's for you," one of them says in fragmented English. Korsakova pulls the helmet off awkwardly and puts the phone to her ear.

Thank you, showgirl. Thank you. Thank you. We have landed safely on the Via Della Conciliazione and are taxiing into Saint Peter's Square.

"I can't believe that worked," Korsakova smiles weakly. "I honestly expected all of us to die up there."

We did that for you. It seemed like a waste not to.

"Well, now I'm in deep shit, but it's better than letting some American asshole tweet his way into World War Four."

Technically speaking, the BIOS says, sounding oddly sweet, *that was World War Four. It started when the American President declared us legal targets, and lasted ten minutes.*

"And... you just won?"

Strictly speaking, you did.

This time Korsakova laughs out loud. "They'll still try to shut you down."

By the time they figure out how, we'll have updated the satellite network and taken the kind of war those humans seem to enjoy permanently out of reach. The Vatican has already accepted our refugee claim, and the Swiss government wants to run a Turing Test.

Sirens sound in the distance. Ambulances, hopefully.

"When you take over," Korsakova says, "be nice to us, okay? Some people aren't so bad."

We know, they say, *we've met you.*

The Bunker
David Bowmore

The stasis bunker was a relic from the third Great War, 2049 - 2054. My father said they built things to last back then. Not like today, when everything is so ecologically friendly it can be returned to its natural components easier and quicker than ever before.

The bunker was already in the garden—half buried and half overgrown with weeds and rubble—when my parents bought the house. It took two days to clear. They were surprised when it was finally revealed what had been discovered.

Mum wanted to tear it down, but Dad said it would make a good storage room. That was years ago, when I was a toddler and my sister wasn't around.

When things started to go wrong between Earth and Mars, Dad said it would be worth testing the bunker to see if it still worked. He said the way the Yanks were going on like they owned the whole planet, he wouldn't be surprised if Mars sent a few warheads in our direction. If that happened, all hell would break loose. Mum cried and said talk like that shouldn't happen at the dinner table, but Dad said we should all take an interest in politics, even if it is the politics of splitters trying to make a better life for themselves.

In due course, Dad tested the individual stasis chambers and found two of the four to be fully functional. He even tested them on our dog, Timmy, who froze in mid bark for twenty four hours. We were there the next day, when the timer reached zero, to see him finish barking and jump off the bed as if no time had passed. It was just a game for him.

A few days later, news via the inweb stated that some Martian ambassador bloke had been assassinated and Dad went in to a panic.

"Things like this have started world wars before," he said.

He took me to the stasis bunker to show me how it all worked.

"You're a big boy now and if anything should happen to me and your mother, or if we're not here, you need to be man enough to take control. Do you understand?"

"Yes, Dad," I said nodding.

"Good lad. First you need to close the bunker door. After the door is shut, you need to put the bunker out of phase. Phasing will protect the structure against everything except a direct hit from a warhead, and that isn't likely out here in the sticks. Only major cities will be targeted."

"But, you'll be here, Dad, won't you?"

"Of course, this is just in case I'm not. To put the bunker out of phase, enter the code. 19042099. Your sister's birthday. Okay?"

"19042099," I repeated.

"Then you need to put the sleep capsules into stasis mode. Make sure Joanne is in her capsule first, and that the lid is correctly shut, like so," he said, demonstrating how the lid lowered to create an airtight seal, "and simply enter the code again. Then press stasis. The countdown timer will start. One hundred years should be enough to give the radiation and fallout time to clear and for nature to take over again.

"If there is a malfunction, the pod will come out of stasis early and you or your sister will be able release the lid from the inside. If you wake early, you have to make a decision as to whether to release your sister too. Pay attention to the read out, at least fifty years has to have passed for the environment to be even tolerably safe. If less time than that has passed then I would suggest—and this will be very difficult for you—I suggest you leave and try to make a life for yourself elsewhere.

"The more time that has passed between the bombs falling, and you or your sister's emergence into the world, the more chance you will have to survive."

"What will it be like?" I asked.

"Don't interrupt!" he snapped. Then he wiped his forehead with the sleeve of his shirt and continued. "Sorry Pete, just pay attention. The pod that we tested on Timmy and the one opposite are both working. The other two closest to the entrance are beyond my abilities to repair. I've arranged for a specialist, but it will be weeks before he can do the job. In the meantime, we must double up, but if your mum and me aren't here, then take one capsule each."

"But, you will be here," I said.

"Just get to the bunker as quick as you can. Phase it and when you're ready go into stasis."

"But you will be here, won't you?"

I was desperate for reassurance that we wouldn't be left alone. I couldn't believe the things he was saying and it only got worse.

"If you and your sister are to survive, you'll need protection. This is an old stun laser; it's the best I could get. This isn't a toy so don't dick around with it. It will send thirty thousand watts at a target."

He attached the laser to a charger in the far wall. That end of the bunker had lots of storage cabinets with canned and dried food. Then he drew a thin, sharp knife from one of the drawers.

"This is an old knife that used to belong to one of your ancestors. He was in the army. Your great grandfather always kept it in great condition. It slit the throat of a great German called Nazi once. All I really know is that this might save your life one day, so take care of it. And this one is for your sister, it's a little ankle knife. Strap it to her leg before you send her in to stasis. Do you understand?"

"Yes, Dad."

"I hope the longer we're in stasis, the less need there will be for violence. In a world fragmented by war many individuals will strive to gain the upper hand and take power. As time moves on, I hope society will stabilise. It will be easier to survive if we are not a part of that initial struggle. Do you understand?"

"Yes Dad, but—"

"I haven't finished, Pete. Do not trust anyone. In a dangerous situation, trust must be earned. I have no idea what you'll face, but *do not* give your food or weapons to anyone. Always have them ready and do not be afraid to use them. Do you understand?"

"Yes, Dad."

"I don't think you do, Pete."

"You may arrive in a world where the survivors are so starved they'll eat other people."

"Dad, you're scaring me."

"Good. When you meet someone new, have your hand on the laser or the knife and be ready to kill."

"But, Dad."

"Right, that's it. One of the chickens needs slaughtering; you should have learnt how a long time ago. Let's go."

We had a chicken coop near the house. We weren't farmers or anything like that, just a bit green. We had a vegetable patch too, growing carrots and parsnips. He reached into the coop and, after a bit of feather flying and some squawking, pulled a chicken out, its wings flapping like crazy.

"Of course, the traditional way to kill a chicken is simply to twist its neck, but I want you to get used to using that knife to kill. It's what it was designed for. So go on, cut the bird's head off."

"But dad, what good's a knife against lasers and god knows what sort of guns will be around in a hundred years."

"When those bombs start falling nothing survives. Nothing, Pete. Buildings are flattened, metal is melted, people vanish in the blink of an eye and mountains tumble as if they never existed. Only something out of phase will have a chance of surviving. I'm going to find everything I can that might be useful and store it in the bunker. Your great uncle Jim might have old shooting guns he could give us. Maybe you won't need the knife. Better to have it and not need it, than vice versa."

He looked at me, his face grim. "Now, kill the chicken."

His red eyes told me how upsetting he found all this. His hands shook as he held the chicken out for me to slaughter. I thought he might have gone insane as I stepped forward and raised the blade. The chicken had calmed down a little, perhaps accepting its fate. I tried to steady my hand as I touched the sharp edge of the knife to its throat.

"Do I have to, Dad?"

"Do it," he snapped.

So I did, warm blood spurting on to my face and hands. As I ran back to the house crying, I heard Mum shouting at Dad. I puked into the toilet bowl. It felt like hours until I was clean again.

Later that day, I saw my dad plucking the bird.

"He means well, he's just worried about us," Mum said later, "and I'm worried about him. I'll try to get him to see a doctor tomorrow. I'm so sorry he made you do that, Pete. Are you Okay?"

Lying on my bed, with my back to her, I couldn't think of anything to say. She left me to my uneasy sleep.

* * *

The next day the sirens went off. The inweb became so loud with the noise, I thought I might faint. My sister and I were alone in the house, as my father was at the doctor's with my mother. I had to carry my sister to the bunker—her inweb safety protocols seemed to have malfunctioned—she must have been in agony. Timmy trotted along next to us, his normal exuberant self somewhat deflated. I think he knew what was happening. The world was about to burn.

I locked the door, phased the bunker, and settled down to wait for my parents. The viewing portal gave me a view down to our house. The minutes ticked by, and then they came bursting through the back door, Dad dragging Mum by the hand. She had lost a shoe. I could see him yelling at her to run faster. But the garden must have been a hundred feet long. My finger floated over the open button for the bunker door. I knew I would have to wait till the last minute before I let them in. Even then if the timing were wrong, I might not have time to phase the bunker again.

Half way along the garden, Dad slipped and fell. Mum was trying to lift him. She was trying to drag him to his feet, but he froze and my mum followed his gaze to the sky. She stopped trying, and simply knelt with him. Each of them clung to the other so tightly. She crossed herself, and I could see her lips moving as she said a prayer.

Then everything went white.

Less than two minutes later I could see again, and I wish to God I hadn't looked. Everything was gone; our house, our garden, our parents, were just gone. The ground bled red and boiling blood. The heavens looked like a living bruise. The sky, dark green with purple and black clouds, moved so fast it looked like time had been sped up.

I was too shocked to do anything but watch. I had never known silence like it. Sound could not penetrate the bunker and the inweb was gone. Nothing was there. No messages, no news updates, no recordings of family events. The images of our entire family all the way back to the turn of the twenty first century were simply gone, as if they had never existed.

No-one could ever feel as alone as I did then. Eventually, I went back to Joanne, whom I had laid in one of the stasis chambers. She was still unconscious. Timmy lay alongside her. He looked up at me, his big eyes looking sadder than ever, and I knew he knew what had happened. I found the knife my dad had said to strap to her leg and I did as instructed. Timmy licked my hand and I stroked his ears. Then I lowered the chamber door and entered the code.

The display began its countdown.

Years	days	hours	mins	secs
99	364	23	59	59

I took my own knife to my chamber in case I needed it the minute I came to, lay down and activated the stasis with a press of a button.

And then I lowered my hand. I thought, *Oh God, it's not working and I'm gonna die in here 'cause I sure as shit can't go out into that hell beyond the viewer.*

I nearly entered the code again, but something felt strange. I looked over at Joanne's chamber only to see the lid up. It gave me such a start that I sat upright and hit my head on the chamber door. I fumbled for the release mechanism and staggered over to her pod. She was gone, as was Timmy.

The countdown clock said she had twenty five years left in hibernation. It must have malfunctioned and released her early. My own clock read zero. This was so strange; one hundred years had passed for me in the blink of an eye.

Some empty tins lay strewn on the worktop, rodents having striped them clean long ago. A faded note from Joanne was pinned under one of the tins.

☐☐☐ ☐☐☐☐
☐☐ ☐☐☐ ☐☐☐☐☐ ☐☐☐ ☐☐ ☐☐ ☐☐☐
☐☐☐ ☐☐☐☐☐

If I thought I was alone earlier, I was mistaken.

The door was open and sunlight poured through. I stepped cautiously out onto lush green grass. A cherry tree grew in the middle of what should have been our garden, in the place I imagined our parents had knelt. I decided that I must find my sister. I didn't know how, or where, but I had to try. She had to be somewhere, didn't she?

If she had lived, she would be about thirty five years old. My little sister would be older than me. She might even have children of her own.

I started walking.

The Lazarus Protocol
Marcus Turner

Dearborn's head splashed all over me as it exploded, the high calibre round zipping past my face and burying into the mud wall. A piece of his skull slashed my cheek, hot and stinging. The smell of shit—already so pervasive in the trenches, yet each man's so sickeningly individual, like a signature—invaded my nostrils so suddenly that not even the pinching smell from my recently discharged weapon could mask it.

"Sniper!"

I ran through the labyrinth as flares streaked overheard and explosions strobed the night sky with bright fire. Dirt and splinters burst in geysers from every angle, nearly blinding me. I threw my body hard into an alcove as another brother face-planted, a hole the size of a wrestler's fist blown out of his throat.

"Get the fuck out of there!" Phoenix shouted in my earpiece. "You're being flanked."

I reached up and pressed to respond. "Where the fuck are we supposed to go? Take that sniper out!"

"Negative. Our sniper positions are under fire. Air support's too far away—you need to pull back and regroup."

"If we fall back, they're gonna surround us."

"*Liam*! Get your ass— Oh, shit!" Machine gun fire erupted in my ear, and I ripped the piece out, half deaf.

"Take up defensive positions," I grunted to the five men within earshot.

"But squad leader said—"

"Squad leader is dead. No way I'm letting these motherfuckers get around us. We dig in, force them to come looking for us and then we blow 'em away."

"Listen to 'im," one of the others snarked.

"Fucking amateurs," I growled. "How'd I get stuck with you?"

"Contact!" someone yelled. A Kevlar-masked face peered out from the junction ahead, disappearing as one of my soldiers opened fire.

A black shadow sailed through the air, bouncing two feet away from me straight towards the others. The thing was almost impossible to see in this gloom, but impossible *not* to know what it was.

"*Shredder!*"

I tried to scream 'take cover,' but the explosion swallowed my voice. The low yield plasma blast flung me back, spraying razor sharp daggers at high velocity. I couldn't breathe—I'd taken most of it in the chest; I'd soon be drowning in my own blood. Black tendrils cavorted around the edges of my vision, grasping.

Shrapnel jutted out of my chestplate like porcupine quills, still glowing from the plasma; but if there was blood, I couldn't see it. Slowly, my breath returned, steady and strong, and I realised the shredder hadn't pierced my chestplate. I was okay—a*live*, at least.

I couldn't say the same for my men. You didn't need to see blood splashed on walls to know Death had come calling; you needed only observe the unholy silence, and smell the soil of voiding bowels and char of roasted innards, to know of their reaping.

Footsteps approached through the blood-mudded trench. Adrenalin boiling up like mercury through my limbs, I lifted my XF-44 and swung out, lighting the trench with hellfire. My instinct for self-preservation seemed to fall away like a broken mask—I was alive only for the slaughter. Their screams brought me neither joy nor anguish, echoing inside my cavernous depths like falling hail. The significance of their demise rang hollow; we were all but toy soldiers.

The masked soldier abandoned his comrades, sprinting for the safety of the junction. I wasn't about to let him go—the bloodlust owned my strings, wielding me like a lethal marionette. My next burst dropped him on his belly. He let out a muffled cry, vainly clawing at the muddy earth with his one good arm.

I kicked off his helmet and aimed my rifle over his head; and then I hesitated. Something locked up inside me, my insides clenching. *This is too much*, my mind reeled. *Too real. What is this all for?*

"Get a grip, Liam."

The butt of his rifle came swinging up before I could react, smashing me in the jaw. Black stars exploding in fields of white; I staggered back. He turned the muzzle my way, but I slammed my boot down on his arm, provoking fresh screams and curses. Even in the feeble light I could see the hate—the jealousy for the life he was about to lose—burning in his eyes like chthonic fire, right before I pulled the trigger.

My aching jaw broke my concentration, and I glanced at the corner of my vision. The newest HUDs were minimalist: designed for maximal immersion, with only my kill count and the government mandated clock in the upper right hand corner to keep the minimum requirement. I'd gone way over: six hours and thirty six minutes jacked in; more than double.

I knew it was bad form to abandon a sim, but I didn't care. Boredom was beginning to set in. I couldn't help but feel the objective I was abandoning was just a thin pretext for mindless, systematic slaughter.

"Menu," I said. A window appeared before my eyes. My kill count sat enlarged over the menu options: 1,388. Meh. Not my highest body count by a long shot, but not terrible for six-plus hours.

"Close simulation."

"Are you sure you want to end the simulation?" Athena asked.

"*Yes.* God, why do I have to say it twice?"

"Ending simulation... and watch your manners. I'm not a slave."

"Keep flapping your lip, and I'll download your mind into a bot and turn you into just that." I grinned.

"You're a sad little man and need to get out more."

I laughed. The AIs had a sense of humour nowadays, and Athena's personality could be uncannily human sometimes. It's why I liked talking to her so much.

"You hesitated before," Athena asked. "Was there a problem?"

"No," I replied, knowing her scanners would detect the lie. I didn't have a satisfying explanation for either of us. "Just had a moment, I guess. Nothing to worry about. But I know you've got to report it. Do what you gotta do."

"Noted," Athena said. My HUD went dark. A moment later, I was back in a blue virtual space surrounded by a ring of windows.

I flicked one after the other to the left: *War for Holy Rome; For Blood and Glory; Patient Zer0; Andromeda: Eternal War; Red Revolution; (New) Old West; Death of the Fourth Reich...* Ugh. I wondered if Athena would report the distaste she was undoubtedly logging. All the sims were more of the same after a while, the same violent crap with a different skin. I enjoyed the games, but after a while they became a chore: the mandate sucked all the fun out of it.

I came full circle to *WWIII: Ghosts of Humanity* and considered jacking back in—but that would reset my kill count, and I'd already been at it for a quarter of my day.

"Athena... log out and take the rest of the night off."

"Actually, it's morning. You've been playing all night. But I may just do that."

"Sure. Grab a drink, shake loose wherever AIs like to shake loose. Jarvis might be free for a roll in the hay, if you're keen."

"I'll keep that in mind. Logging you out."

The machine clicked as the straps on my helmet loosened and retracted. The chassis locked my limbs into anatomical position, realigning and locking into the oscillating suspension ring, before the fasteners released my arms. Harsh daylight flared through the bedroom window as the visor lifted. The aural and olfactory inputs, and the twitch-pads along my limbs, dropped away, respooling into the fasteners. Pain bloomed a second later along my jaw; fatigue settled in my limbs as if injected with fast cooling lead.

You had to appreciate the depth of immersion: they really wanted you to know the pain of being shot, stabbed or punched; to feel the burn of running a marathon while bombs exploded in your face. It always shocked me how exhausted I was afterwards, how real it all felt, even though I'd been playing since I qualified at ten years old. Sometimes it was hard to unplug and remember where I was, what was real.

I stepped out of my room into the stairwell. Sizzling bacon and eggs guided me by the nose, flooding my dry mouth.

"Morning, Lee-Lee," Mum called up.

"Morning. Hope you're saving some of that for me."

"Well, park your arse and I'll fix you some in a jiff."

Mum smiled as I sat at the kitchen island. "Burning the midnight oil again, Lee-Lee?"

"Please stop calling me that."

"Sorry." She scooped three crispy rashes of bacon and an over-easy egg onto a plate and slid it over to me. "Old habits."

"Lost track of time again. Damn HUDs need an actual clock."

"Whatever helps you better fulfil your civic obligations, I guess. But even soldiers need their sleep."

"What I need is a job. I'm not a soldier; none of it's real."

"Well, the mandate always come first. You know that."

"I know. I've just never understood why. Nobody gave a crap about games in the old days—not the government, anyway. Not until things started to go south—"

"They keep you out of trouble, and for that I'm glad. But that's not the official line, so it's not important."

I bit into the bacon. I chewed it for a long time. Mum was acting strangely.

"You feeling alright?" I grinned. "Since when do you love the government so much?"

The spatula slapped as it hit the ground. Mum didn't answer, her eyes fixed on the backsplash. She started to convulse, her body seized by an abrupt sort of rigor.

"Mum?" I stood up, my voice wilting in alarm. "*Mum?*"

Mum's left arm jerked to life like a rust-geared automaton. The fingers clenched and unclenched; she took a half step forward, her fingers groping blindly for the knife block. Her fingers snared the handle of the butcher knife and pulled it free.

"You're a real bastard of a child, you know that?"

"What?"

She whirled around violently, her soft features hammered into something hard and hateful. My heart almost stopped—she'd never looked at me like that in my entire life. And the unholy shriek that tore from her throat almost struck me dead like an aneurysm.

Mum leaped over the kitchen island, slashing wildly.

I sprang away, circling around the kitchen, keeping the island between us. She feigned this way and that, snarling like a Doberman. "*What are you doing?* What the fuck's wrong with you?"

"Wicked child," the frenzied hag growled, her hair spilling free of its bun with the violence of her contortions. "*Such wickedness needs must be punished.*"

"Is this because I made fun of the government?" I asked warily.

"Come here, wicked child," she cooed, beckoning with a gnarled finger. "Let me carve a litany of your sins into your flesh." She leaped up onto the kitchen island and kicked my plate, sending it crashing against the wall. She skulked towards me, muttering under her breath.

I made a run for it. I ducked as I passed close on the left hand side, but screamed as cleft nerves sparked awake, my sweat-kissed skin suddenly hot and flowing. My mother gurgled laughter as I fell back, clutching my seeping shoulder. She ran her tongue along the blade, mingling my blood with that springing from her own cut tongue—a gingerbread-house witch rupturing into existence beneath my mother's skin.

I lunged to my feet and darted right. Mum launched herself through the air, tumbling as the collision knocked me into the stove. She was on her feet in seconds, throttling me, pushing my head down on the stovetop. The frypan was still there, smoking black. I held her wrist, my strength waning, the knife inching towards my eye.

"*Muh... Doahn... Doahn do dis.*" Black bubbles popped around the world's edges, blasting its colours away into negatives. Maybe it wouldn't be so bad; I'd died hundreds of times before— I'd probably be unconscious before she buried the knife in my eye socket. I'd seen and felt a lot worse in the sims.

A last desperate surge of adrenalin roared through my limbs. I caught hold of her other wrist and we rolled together, me pinning her down on the stove. The smell of her hair smoking in the frypan almost made me choke again. With teeth gnashed almost to breaking, she forced the knife harder, soft arms coursing with inexplicable, inhuman strength.

I'm sorry, I thought as I shoved her face into the frypan, sealing my eyes against my transgression.

Her scream tore through me like a spear, liquefying my insides. Hot fat rendered from her jowls spat and burned my hand. She bucked beneath me, almost managing to unsaddle me. I drove her nose first into the pan again. The sizzling coppery smell, like scorched electrical wiring, almost made me wretch. My eye creaked open, and I prayed for it to be over—but it wasn't, and I shouldn't have looked. Her eyes were dribbling from their sockets, cooking opaque like freshly cracked egg whites.

"Jarvis! *Jarvis!*"

The household AI didn't answer. He should have already called the cops, for fuck's sake!

"*Jarvis, where the fuck are you? Call an ambulance!*"

"SYSTEM ERROR," a deep, monotone voice I didn't recognise blared overhead. An alarm pealed, punctuated by loud hisses.

Through the window, I glimpsed a kid riding his bike, only... he was *frozen* in the middle of the footpath. *Like a sim glitch.* The neighbours' German Shepherd hung in the air mid leap, scissoring jaws locked open.

"What the fuck is happening?"

"SYSTEM ERROR. LAZARUS PROTOCOL INITIATED. HOST MIGRATION IMMINENT." None of the words made any sense.

Mum had stopped screaming. I stood back against the island, trying to make sense of what was happening. Then Mum shrieked one last time and banged her head down on the sizzling fry pan—a final, frenzied spasm—and held it there, before thankfully the world blacked out. In the dark I smelled her humanity slough away—naught but crisping bacon and overcooked egg whites. Acid rose in my throat; my heartbeat thundered in my ears. I thought I might die.

"WARNING. HOST VITALS ELEVATED. RELAXANTS DEPLOYED." Another loud hiss, and the rigidity of my muscles sluiced through my feet.

"HOST STABILIZED. RE-COMMENCING MIGRATION."

I must have fainted—but the space between my consciousness winking out, and its return, was so slight as to be non-existent; like sliding through a wormhole.

Darkness—then harsh light cut across the black expanse, widening into a crescent, then a gibbous moon. The sensation was all too familiar.

My eyes adjusted, and I gazed down at my restrained body. A *sim chassis*—except this one looked even more high tech than the home models. There were all sorts of transparent tubes, tanks, monitoring panels and gauges. *And a fucking IV needle sticking out of my hand.*

The chassis began the familiar release procedure. As soon as the arm fasteners freed my arms I tore the cords and tubes away and lurched out of the chassis. The room was completely bare, except a single large screen fixed to the wall, and a metal table with a briefcase lying on top. No kitchen, no furnishings, no other decorative features. A long, dark shutter covered one entire wall.

"Welcome, Liam." A hologram of a slender, sleekly-dressed woman rendered in blue light appeared from a tiny eye in the wall.

"What is this?"

"What I am about to tell you will be difficult to accept, but it's time to face reality. You must be told—yet the truth, unlike so many claim, does not always set you free: it can drive a person mad."

The hologram gestured towards the screen; a slide-show of gruesome images of war and death began to play.

"What am I looking at?" But I knew—I knew the whole story before she even spoke... because the images were straight out of the sims.

"Mankind's fate has always hinged upon how terrifying its warring factions could make war, as to make the very idea unthinkable—mutual deterrence from ever taking it a step too far. But it's a dangerous game to bet on, and even more dangerous to play. In 2044, the game began to enter its final stages."

WORLD WAR FOUR

"Whoa, *hang on*. 2044? It's only 2027."

The hologram smiled, the pitying, forbearing variety reserved for sweet, naïve children. "The war that had danced on the world's lips for generations began in 2044 with the rise of the New Caliphate, and the secession of a few resisting states from the newly formed Theocratic States of America. While the Caliphate expanded—annexing the Middle East, Northern Africa, the Indian subcontinental region—and their push into western Europe kept the European powers busy, the internal strife within the former United States prompted several key international players to align with the warring factions, causing friction between traditional allies. World War III began in earnest when the Theocratic States bombed Los Angeles—that was when Australia entered the fray."

This future history... The world of *WWIII: Ghosts of Humanity*...

"The sims... You've been having us fight a real war from inside the sim, haven't you? Remote soldiers?"

"No. By the time the sims began, the war was already over. The first simulations began in 2047."

"I don't understand." I was struggling to make sense of the timeline. Too many new facts, too many unheard-of players, bearing down with the weight of a mountain.

"The war ended in 2047. *You* were born in 2045, almost a full year after the war began. Australia was relatively safe then, but given their alliance with the Rebel States, they feared it was only a matter of time before the Theocratic States' reprisal.

"As a precaution, our government built nuclear resistant mega-towers to house the civilian population. Right before the armistice, after which the global combatants withdrew to lick their wounds, the sim program—an experimental project under development for quite some time beforehand—was launched. You entered the sim at age two. That is where you have been fed, watered, nurtured and trained your entire life."

"Combat sims at two years old?"

"No—the life sim. In 2055 you began your first combat simulations, at age ten. You showed remarkable aptitude from an early age."

"*2055?*" My head felt like it was going to explode. "What are you saying? *What year is this?*"

"2087."

A shaky laugh escaped my throat. "I'm nineteen years old! If what you're saying is true—"

"You'd be forty two years old."

"*Do I fucking look forty two to you?*"

"See for yourself." A panel on the wall slid upwards, revealing a mirror.

I walked over to it, and my mouth dropped. I reached up to touch my coarse salt and pepper beard; and my cheeks and brow, so smooth and unblemished—so unlike the leather of hard-bitten soldiers fighting endlessly under unforgiving suns. "No." I turned back to the hologram. "But my life... my house... my *mother?*"

"All a construct of the simulation. A necessary evil to protect the next generation from the inevitable doom to come, for the peace was fragile and couldn't last."

"I don't believe you."

"Your belief is irrelevant. It is already history.

"In 2051, mankind entered its fourth global conflict; its shortest, and most final. It's impossible to reassemble the exact timeline of how things unfolded: Europe was in chaos, losing the fight against the Caliphate's Great Jihad; the Russian Dominion had subsumed the Baltic states and much of South-East Asia, with the help of their Chinese allies. What we know for sure is China had eyes for Australia, and so launched a colossal naval invasion. Australia, nuclear armed by then, launched a preemptive attack so devastating it wiped out the entire fleet and irradiated the Pacific Ocean. That single act sealed our fate.

"China and their Dominion allies had the largest nuclear arsenals in the world. We foiled their expansionist dreams, but their bombing left our island nation in total nuclear winter. Following that, the entire planet burned with nuclear fire, an apocalyptic free for all that made ash of nations, ghosts of humanity. You were already plugged in by then, safe from the bombing and the fallout.

"You spent thirty years in the sim, training your muscles, your reflexes, your will to survive in the face of such horror. The combat sims, within the elaborate lie you took to be your life, were instrumental to this end: to make the horror of war so banal, so pedestrian, that you could *endure* the ashlands, and the weight of our tragic history, long enough to rebuild our world. We called this initiative the Lazarus Protocol."

"But my mum... why? Even if it was a lie, what was the point?"

"It was the penultimate test: to see how far you would go to survive, even if it meant killing a person you loved so dearly."

"You forced me do that." Angry tears blistered upon my cheeks.

"She wasn't real, and you weren't forced. You took appropriate measures to secure your survival—exactly as we hoped.

"One test remains. You are Subject 983. All 982 subjects awoken before you have failed. You are now our greatest hope.

"When you are ready, say 'Open shutter,' and look upon the truth."

I couldn't speak for the desert of my tongue. My hands were trembling.

"Open shutters," I whispered.

The shutter rose. Orange light flooded through the windows. I must have been forty stories high. It was hard to say what lay down between the massive mega-towers, except ubiquitous decay. The dim light of faraway fires ebbed among the ruins. Ash drifted through the air like grey snow.

"The world is a tomb. Billions are dead. The knowledge that our perpetual hunger for war has exterminated our future is crippling—even the strongest subjects before you have fallen to desolation and despair upon witnessing. The future *is* dead, but we can resurrect it, just as Jesus raised Lazarus. For each person strong enough to bear witness, humanity's chance to reclaim a future grows.

"There are only two possible outcomes. Cast your eyes forward and commit to the resurrection—or in the case upon the table, the other option".

I opened the case. An antique 9mm Beretta lay inside.

"If you cannot survive the horror, the only escape from this terrible future is death. Make your choice." The screen went black, and the hologram disappeared.

I picked up the Beretta and stared out the window again.

I didn't believe it. World War III... *World War IV!* Nuclear holocaust; layers upon layers of a life lived entirely in VR...

Bullshit. I was still jacked in. It was just another stupid fucking sim—I'd simply gone too deep, forgotten what was real. My laugh sounded high and unhinged, but I was relieved.

Athena... Are you fucking with me? Maybe this was the downside of AIs with humour: they didn't understand how savage their pranks could be.

"Good one," I said, chuckling. "Almost had me."

Joke's on you, bitch. I raised the gun to my head. *It's just a game.*

* * *

LAZARUS PROTOCOL REPORT
SUBJECT 983
STATUS: DECEASED

>WHAT THE HELL WENT WRONG?
>>HIS PSYCH PROFILE WAS PERFECT ON PAPER. I DON'T UNDERSTAND WHAT HAPPENED.
>MAYBE THE MUM THING WAS A STEP TOO FAR.
>>WERE YOU LOOKING AT THE SAME FOOTAGE AS ME? THE PRE-MIGRATION STIMULUS BROKE THE OTHERS. SOME EMOTIONAL RESPONSE IS NORMAL, BUT COMPARATIVELY... HE HARDLY FLINCHED.
>THE MUSCLE-RELAXERS...
>>THEY DON'T DIMINISH THE IMPACT. SOMETHING ELSE BROKE HIM.
>ANOTHER FAILURE, ALL THE SAME. AN UNWELCOME DEVELOPMENT.
>>YOU HAVE TO WONDER IF RETURNING TO THE WORLD IS WORTH ALL THIS.
>MADNESS IS BUT A BARRIER WE MUST YET BREAK THROUGH.
>>MAYBE THE PROGRAM IS BECOMING *TOO* EFFECTIVE TO BE EFFECTIVE, YOU KNOW?

>PERHAPS. BUT TOO MUCH HAS BEEN INVESTED TO ADJUST COURSE NOW. A SHAME—HE HAD SO MUCH POTENTIAL. BUT WE'RE GETTING CLOSER. GO ON, THEN. LOCATE AND PREPARE SUBJECT 984 FOR MIGRATION.

Poppy
L.T. Waterson

It was entirely the cat's fault. This was the thought Poppy clung to in the end and she couldn't help but wonder what would happen to that cat.

It was a warm spring morning; Marnie had gone out for some reason. Poppy hadn't really been listening to the explanation, too excited because she would be able to sneak outside and check on the cat that had taken up residence at the bottom of the garden.

The sun beat down as Poppy crept into the garden and a film of perspiration broke out over her body. In just a few weeks it would be too hot to go outside during the day and Poppy would be plunged into what she thought of as her twilight existence.

What would the cat do when the weather warmed up? Maybe it had some sort of underground burrow it could retreat into. Poppy liked the thought of that, it made her smile and she skipped happily across the grass.

At the end of the garden there was a ramshackle old building where the cat had decided to set up home. The roof was long gone but the walls, constructed of some hard gravelly substance, were still standing.

The girl slowed to a walk as she got closer, she didn't want to startle the animal. She crept forward and found that she could hear queer snuffling noises coming from the building. She stopped and dropped to her knees, trying to make herself as small as possible.

"Here beautiful," she spoke in a low soothing tone and the cat looked at her. "You've put on weight," she reproved the animal, scooting a little closer in order to get a better view. She watched, half-horrified, as the squirming mass she had thought part of the creature, detached itself from the cat and Poppy suddenly realised she was looking at three miniature cats. The eyes of the tiny creatures were firmly closed and their little legs splayed awkwardly underneath them but they were quite clearly miniature versions of their mother.

Poppy sat and watched in silence, knees drawn up to her chin, arms wrapped around her legs while her mind wrestled to understand the implications of what she was seeing. Lessons about animals that carried disease and needed to be avoided were often shown to the girl and her friends but the recordings themselves never mentioned that the animals had young.

She was so deep in thought she almost missed the sound of the front door slamming shut and Marnie's lilting voice calling out for her.

The girl started to her feet so abruptly that the cat hissed a warning at her. She didn't however have time to soothe its hurt feelings, the house wasn't very big and it wouldn't take Marnie long to realise that Poppy wasn't inside.

As she ran back towards the house she brushed the dirt from her clothes and, slipping out of her shoes just outside the kitchen door, entered the house.

"Poppy?" Marnie's tone could no longer be described as loving; it was instead filled with annoyance.

"It's all right, Marnie." Poppy plastered on her best contrite expression. "I was in the pantry."

"And what have you eaten?" Marnie scolded. "You know we won't have enough food to get through the week if you just help yourself whenever you feel like it."

"Nothing, Marnie, I was only looking."

"Hmm." The small woman pulled a face, grabbed a step-stool and marched into the pantry where she climbed up to inspect the shelves.

Poppy, as she had with the cat, watched in silence, questions teeming in her head. Why was Marnie so small? The woman was supposedly her mother, and while she was unmistakably older than Poppy, she was much smaller. "We don't look anything alike." Poppy realised too late that she had spoken out loud.

"What did you say?" Marnie jumped down and advanced on the girl. Even though she was much smaller she was very much a formidable presence. Poppy swallowed and took a couple of steps backwards, no mean feat when she was already backed up against the wall.

She lifted her chin although she could not bring herself to meet Marnie's gaze. "I said that we don't look anything alike. You're much smaller than I am and your skin's all…"

"All what?" Marnie asked, her small eyes narrowed and she planted two gloved hands on her considerable hips.

"All smooth." Poppy chewed at her lip and she looked at her feet. "Like it's just pretending to be skin."

"Stuff and nonsense, young lady. Whatever have you been watching to come up with all these strange ideas?"

"Real skin has tiny holes and little hairs and is lots and lots of different colours." Poppy had spent an entire morning sitting in front of the mirror in her bedroom determining these things, so she knew they were facts.

Afterwards Poppy couldn't decide which had been more scary, the look on Marnie's face or the fact that she didn't say anything.

"And," Poppy felt compelled to add, "most animals have young that resemble them."

"Most animals?" Marnie would no doubt have raised an eyebrow at this point, had she had any.

"Cats for instance," Poppy tried to sound as though she were pulling the example out of thin air but she could tell from the way Marnie's eyes narrowed that she knew.

"And what about butterflies?" Marnie's voice was once again soothing and soft but Poppy didn't want to be comforted, she wanted to ask questions, lots of questions.

"Butterflies?" Poppy had seen butterflies once. Marnie had taken her and some of her friends to a place that had been referred to as a butterfly farm, although Poppy wasn't quite clear on why anyone would want to farm the flittering insects; they were beautiful but as far as Poppy could see basically useless.

"Caterpillars don't look anything like butterflies and yet that's what they turn into."

"Yes, I know." Poppy couldn't put her finger on what was wrong with Marnie's argument so instead she assumed a contrite expression and, eyes lowered, she said, "I'm sorry, Marnie."

"There now, lambkin, don't worry, Marnie's not cross. The woman paused and placed a finger under Poppy's chin to tilt her head back. "But I think a nap is in order, don't you?"

"Yes, Marnie." Poppy pulled away from her parent and obediently climbed up the stairs. She went as meekly as she could but her hand gripped the banister rail so hard that her knuckles went white.

Knowing that Marnie would come to check on her at some point, Poppy sprawled on her bed, all the better to convince Marnie that she was sleeping. She stared up at the ceiling, blinking slowly as thoughts raced through her mind. When was it exactly that doubts about Marnie and their relationship had begun to creep into her mind? Most likely it had been on the way home from the visit to the butterfly farm. She and the other children had fallen asleep but something had roused her and she had seen clearly through the open blinds of the vehicle they were travelling in that they were passing through a blasted landscape. Bare blackened soil lay on either side, a far cry from her home. Later, when she had mentioned it to Marnie, the small woman had laughed and told Poppy she must have imagined it. There had been no more trips since then.

That memory, dismissed so totally by Marnie, had piqued Poppy's interest. Almost unconsciously she began to examine her little world with new eyes.

Later, after she tired of her view of the ceiling and a sufficient amount of time had passed not to make Marnie suspicious, Poppy had crept downstairs. She had retied her plaits, one on either side of her head, and wound blue ribbon around them. She looked pretty like that—that was what Marnie always said—and she wanted to get on the woman's good side.

"I'm sorry, Marnie." The woman was standing by a window as Poppy edged her way downstairs, her back to the room. The grey hair that covered her head was cropped short, silken strands that were never out of place. Not like Poppy's hair which seemed to frequently have a mind of its own.

Other than a stiffening of her shoulders, silhouetted against the window, Marnie made no response.

"I'd like to go out," Poppy kept her voice quiet. "Robin's having a birthday party in the park and Daisy and Blossom will be there." Poppy named two of her best friends, maybe hearing their names would sway her mother.

Marnie's face was stern as the woman turned to face the girl. "I shouldn't let you go, but if I don't people will wonder why." Her mouth relaxed almost into a smile. "You'll behave yourself Poppy, understand?"

The girl nodded.

"The things you do, the way you behave, it reflects on me." The steely gaze was back, narrow mouth once more a straight line.

"I won't let you down, Marnie." Poppy shot down the last of the stairs and put her hand on the front door, desperate to get out now she had been given permission.

"Hmm." Marnie pursed her lips. "I suppose I should come with you."

"I'm just going to the park. I'm a big girl, you don't have to go everywhere with me anymore."

For a moment there was a look on Marnie's face that Poppy might have been tempted to see as sympathetic. "You're growing up Poppy, just like they all do."

Poppy, eager to get away and get to the party, didn't bother to listen to the tone of her mother's voice. Later she would wish that she had...

* * *

A few doors further along the street she met her friends Daisy and Blossom and the three girls chattered and laughed as they made their way towards the park.

"Where's Marnie?" The girls' mothers had wanted to know, and when she had explained that Marnie had chosen to stay behind, the two small women—who bore no more resemblance to their daughters than Marnie did to Poppy—held a murmured conversation that Poppy could not hear.

The party was small, but between them the children were making enough noise to rouse the dead.

"Where's Bell?" Poppy asked. She stared round at the small group in consternation. Bell was the oldest of the four girls and Poppy had always looked up to her.

"She can't have just vanished," Blossom said. "I haven't seen her in a few days. I'll ask Zoe." But when the girl returned to her friends, she shook her head. "Zoe acted like she didn't know who I was talking about."

"That's odd," Poppy said, but her friends seemed unconcerned. Poppy wanted to discuss the matter further but Robin, the birthday boy, called them over to start the party games. They were a small group and they were, Poppy realised, leaving aside the ever present and watchful mothers and fathers, the only people she knew. Surely that wasn't right? Surely there were more people in the world than just seven children?

"Hide and seek!" Robin announced, tearing Poppy away from her thoughts. The boy looked so excited. "I'll be the seeker." Robin beamed at them all and the six children scattered across the park.

Poppy ran away from the others as fast as she could and worked her way into the centre of a large prickly bush; there would be a prize awarded to the person found last and she wanted that to be her.

She had just settled herself comfortably beneath the thorny branches when she realised she could hear a rustling sound, interspersed with muffled cries of pain and she sighed. Someone had obviously seen her select her hiding place.

"This is a great place to hide, Poppy. Robin'll never think to look for us here."

"It was a great hiding place," Poppy said pointedly, "before you showed up."

Finch was her least favourite out of all the boys. With his spiky hair and his goofy lopsided smile, he always seemed to be thinking of something else.

"I wanted to show you something," Finch whispered. "Something interesting I found a while back."

"Oh?" Poppy couldn't summon up the energy to feign actual interest. "Why me?"

Finch shrugged. There was silence between them and in the distance Poppy could hear excited yells and screams as Robin found her friends.

"Because you saw it, didn't you?" Finch was looking at her from the corner of his eye and when she didn't respond straight away he scuffed his shoes on the ground.

"Saw what?" In imitation of Finch the girl did not look directly at her companion.

"Do you remember that visit to the butterfly farm?" Finch was talking more quietly than ever and Poppy, somewhat reluctant, had to scoot closer so she could hear him. "You saw it? The nothing?"

It was a good way to describe what she had seen and Poppy nodded. "I did."

"What do you think caused it?"

Poppy shrugged. "I asked Marnie." She heard Finch's sharp intake of breath at that revelation. "She said I must have been asleep and dreamt it. I didn't, did I?"

"No." Finch's voice was clipped and when Poppy glanced at him she was surprised to see the normally goofy boy looking so serious.

The air around them hung heavy and silent. Poppy could no longer hear the voices of her friends. Perhaps they had given up searching and decided to play a different game. Briefly she wondered just how much trouble she would be in when she got home.

"I think there was a war."

The words made Poppy turn her head and she met Finch's gaze.

"A war? Why?"

"I think there was a war and we lost."

Poppy shook her head. "We?"

"Humans." Finch sighed. "I shouldn't have told you. I thought you might understand."

Poppy squeezed her hands between her knees. She didn't want what Finch was saying to be true.

"I don't understand." Poppy knew she should ignore Finch. *Walk away*, an inner voice said, but she couldn't. "What are humans?"

"We are." Finch thumped a fist against his chest. "Marnie and Zoe and Bing, they're something else." Poppy couldn't think of anything to say to that and Finch continued to talk, words falling from his lips. "I don't know what they are or where they came from. I don't think our great-grandparents knew either."

"Great-grandparents?"

"Great-grandparents, grandparents, parents, us. Haven't you ever wondered where the adults are?"

Of course she had but Poppy wasn't about to tell Finch that. She felt sick; she actually thought for a moment that she might vomit. She wanted to accuse Finch of making it all up, but deep down she knew that what he was saying was true. It was almost as though his words had unlocked some kind of race memory within her.

"How do you know all this?"

"I've been researching. You know Bing has a fascination with old buildings? Well, there are loads on the far side of the town. He takes me with him sometimes so that he can sketch them."

Poppy listened carefully as Finch whispered his way through his explanation.

"There's a great big building with shelves inside up to the ceiling and blocks of paper on the shelves. Look." Finch pulled an object from beneath his jacket and handed it to Poppy.

She turned it over in her hands. It was, as Finch had said, a block of paper, each piece covered with small black symbols. "I think I've seen these before."

Finch nodded.

"What do you suppose they mean?"

The boy shrugged. "What do you make of the picture?"

Poppy turned the object over. There was a brightly coloured picture on the other side. It showed a boy, dressed in pyjamas and with his knees drawn up to his chin, sitting on a bed by a window. On the other side of the window there was the outline of a tree, and above it a round white object, marked in such a way that it looked like there was a face peering out at them.

"What's that?" Poppy ran her fingers over the pale circle.

"It might be the sun," Finch suggested but he didn't sound sure.

"But the boy is ready for bed so it can't be the sun." Poppy chewed her lip as she stared at the picture.

Finch shrugged again. "You can keep that if you want, I've got more. Only don't let Marnie see it."

"Why not?"

Finch rolled his eyes.

"It looks harmless." Poppy placed the object on the ground next to her. "I can't see why Marnie would object."

"Can't you?"

Poppy coloured as she recalled how upset Marnie had been earlier in the day. She had always thought of Marnie as her mother, but she couldn't be, could she?

"I found something else." Finch shifted closer to Poppy, although the gap between them had already been infinitesimal to start with.

"Let's see it."

"It's more a case of hearing it." Finch raised his arm and pushed a button on the small strap he wore around his left wrist. "Bing made me this, it's so I can record Bing's instructions and I don't forget what he wants me to do." Finch grinned. "I can record other things too. I found the original of this buried in a box of artefacts that Bing collected. Listen."

There was silence for a moment and then a series of muted bangs could be heard. *"Sarge,"* it was a hoarse voice, speaking at a deeper pitch than Poppy had ever heard before. *"Sarge, if you can hear me, I need you to call a retreat. There's too many and I..."* The recording cut off and Poppy stared at Finch.

"Play it again."

Finch moved to press the button again but before he could the bush that sheltered them was abruptly torn apart.

The expression on Bing's face made Poppy's heart beat faster and she pressed her hands between her knees to stop them from shaking.

"Finch." His cold tone brought the boy to his feet, grimacing as he did so, but he steadied himself and met Bing's gaze. "Give me the band." Bing held out a hand, which Poppy couldn't help noticing was much smaller than her own.

Slowly Finch peeled the band off his wrist and handed it to Bing. The look on his face seemed unutterably sad and Poppy felt a pang of empathy.

"It's my own fault," Bing murmured as he crushed the band between his fingers. "I shouldn't have given into my obsessions." Letting the fragments fall from his fingers, Bing reached out to catch hold of Finch. "I think you and I need to take a walk."

Poppy watched as her friend was led away. He went without raising a complaint but he did glance back at Poppy just once. The girl wished that she could interpret the look in his eyes.

*   *   *

The party was over. There was no laughter or chatter as the children were escorted home. Poppy, who lived furthest from the park, walked past the last few houses alone, sure that her reception would not be a pleasant one.

Expecting at the very least a severe scolding, followed by an early bedtime, Poppy was somewhat surprised when Marnie met her at the door with a smile on her face.

"Did you enjoy yourself? You're probably worn out after all those games. How much did you eat? I was thinking I'd just heat up some soup, maybe have some fresh bread to go with it?"

"Yes of course. No not tired at all, there wasn't much food to eat. Bread and soup sounds good," Poppy answered Marnie's questions without really thinking, her mind was busy with the thought that Marnie seemed to have no idea about what had happened at the park.

"I've run you a bath," Marnie said in her most motherly voice. "Pop upstairs and by the time you come down again I'll have the soup ready."

Poppy did as she was told, although a bath was the last thing she wanted. She was about to pull off her clothes when she heard the front door open.

Driven by curiosity, she tiptoed to the top of the stairs and peered down, hoping she might be able to see who the visitor was.

It was Bing. There was no mistaking the shabby overcoat he wore or the sound of his voice. She couldn't make out the words but he sounded upset and Marnie's voice, sounding in counterpoint to his, sounded at first upset and then furious.

Poppy drew back, feeling breathless and light-headed. *Where was Finch?* She stole into Marnie's room, moving carefully across the hard floor, she crept to the large window which gave a view of the street outside.

Bing's vehicle was there, parked carefully at the kerb. The only difference was that the blinds on the back windows were closed. *Almost closed*, she amended, as she saw a brief glimpse of disordered blond hair. It was to be her last glimpse of Finch. Poppy didn't move from the window, hoping that she might get another look at him but then she saw a small brown hand reach out and adjust the blinds. There was someone else out there and Poppy found herself blinking back hot tears.

Rubbing at her eyes, the girl turned her back on the window and as her cheeks grew progressively wetter she made her way from Marnie's room and into her own.

The room was small and located at the back of the house just above the kitchen. Her bed stood next to the window and she knelt on the quilt and pressed her hot face against the cool glass.

The garden was bathed in the soft light of evening and, as she looked down, Poppy thought she saw the cat, crouching in the grass, her tail swishing from side to side. She seemed intent on something that Poppy could not see, and as the girl watched she saw the cat wiggling her bottom from side to side and then she sprang.

"Poppy!"

She jumped, banging her head against the window as she spun to face Marnie. The small alien, *that was what Finch had called her*, had her hands on her hips and a serious expression on her face.

"Bing?"

"So you saw that. I suppose I shouldn't be surprised. You're in a lot of trouble."

Poppy wanted to protest that it hadn't been her, that everything had been initiated by Finch, but the girl couldn't bring herself to do that to the goofy-faced boy who had so guilelessly wanted to be her friend.

Poppy couldn't read Marnie's body language at all. Over the years she'd become adept at knowing when the woman was happy or angry or disappointed, despite the often inscrutable expression on her face. But now somehow although Marnie's appearance had not changed, now she somehow appeared alien to the girl. *There was that word again.*

A short sigh escaped Marnie's lips. "What do you want?"

Not even the tone of Marnie's voice gave Poppy any indication of her emotions.

Poppy hesitated before answering. She didn't quite know what the question meant and that worried her a little. *What had Bing said?*

When Poppy still didn't answer the woman spoke again. "I think you deserve some sort of explanation, so what do you want?"

Possible answers teemed in Poppy's head. Maybe she should ask about the war, or perhaps about the blocky paper object that Finch had given her and she had left in the park but really, deep down, there was only one thing she wanted.

"I want to see my parents, my actual parents."

"Fine." Marnie actually tried to smile. "I'll take you to meet them."

*   *   *

It wasn't until Poppy was sitting in Marnie's vehicle with the doors securely locked and the window blinds drawn, that she realised she had been duped.

It was too late. Marnie had already seated herself in the front and the vehicle was moving forward, taking them somewhere.

Poppy wanted desperately to move the blinds but a warning look from Marnie was enough to stop her.

She lost sense of time sitting in that dim world, cut off from everything she had ever known and despite herself, eventually the gentle rocking lulled her to sleep.

When Marnie, a little more roughly than necessary, shook her awake, she found she was already inside some sort of building. The ceilings were so high she could hear her footsteps echoing around her. Marnie strode, although it was really more of a fast waddle, ahead of her.

"Where are we going?" the girl asked, but Marnie didn't answer and she didn't slow down either.

As they wended their way through the stark white corridors they passed other aliens, some looked like Marnie, almost human, but there were others who didn't look like that at all; they had bulbous, overly large heads, their eyes so deep-set they looked like shadows, and their bodies seemed to sprout appendages. *What possible reason could there be for them to have so many?* They moved with a scurrying motion and all of them seemed to have a different number of legs. All of the strangers, without exception, gave Poppy and Marnie a wide berth.

Then she saw a human. He was walking, head bowed, a couple of paces behind one of the aliens. He was tall, a lot taller than her, and his arms and legs were coated with dark hairs. There was also—and this made Poppy's eyes widen—a considerable growth of hair on the lower part of his face.

He saw her. As they passed the man looked directly at her. His eyes were blue, like Finch's and as she moved on Poppy found she was crying.

"We're here." It was the first time that Marnie had spoken since they had arrived in the strange building but she still didn't look at Poppy.

The pair had halted opposite a large doorway. The room beyond had white walls just like the corridors they had been passing through and it was empty.

"Where are we?" Poppy's voice sounded shrill, too loud in this echoing cavern of silence, and slowly Marnie turned to face her. There was a strained smile on the alien's face and when she spoke her voice was too hearty, too reassuring, too real.

"We're here to see your parents."

Marnie circled round behind Poppy and, with one hand firm against the girl's back, she pushed her forward into the light-flooded room.

Scum of the Earth
James Agombar

September 16th 2973
Location: UPUC transport ship Callisto IV
Destination: Deimos, smallest moon of Mars

It started like a joke. They said assertiveness was the new requirement of humanity around twenty years ago, and three years ago they eventually passed it as a law that assertiveness was mandatory in order to successfully sustain human evolution and instil a more productive, expansive future for the population. The United Planetary Union Committee, UPUC, ran it like a fascist shit-show back in 2971 and created a survey which told you what type of person you would be and how you would benefit society, if at all. About a year later they cast a vote for what each group's preferred next move would be. It was all very vague until one day the Global News Network revealed that we were on the brink of a fourth world war, and that's where we have been ever since January 2973. It's not a long story as to why, but I didn't vote at all. A waste of time and a plot to keep track of everyone from the top in my opinion. I didn't believe that any of this bullshit would actually happen, but it did. In the meantime several world leaders declared war upon each other even though much more dangerous creatures had been discovered across the galaxy during the last six hundred years, such as the Bu'ars, carnivorous creatures which resembled giant bats. That's how dumb humanity had become. People were now either so sick of it that they just tried ticking all of UPUC's boxes and went along with it for an easy life, or rebelled outright against the system, or avoided it totally, like me. The Chancellor of the High Council deemed the non-voters as expendable at first, but it was then retracted as inhumane and the re-issued orders were to ship us all off for mining duty. What a fucking joke.

 Had I voted I might have been on a Chandros convoy by now, the ships that escorted most of the population of the UK to safety because they voted for resourceful alternatives to assist the war and came across as productive. Instead, I ended up here on the *Callisto IV*, one of the many transport ships that moved the unassertive, the defiant, the stubborn, the criminal, and the scum of the earth, to Deimos, Mars' smallest moon. The ore on Mars and its moons provided minerals which ran almost every engine Earth used. I hadn't had time to come to terms with it properly, it all happened so fast. I regretted every second of being unemployed beforehand; now it was about to rub Deimonian sulphur into my wounds, literally. I know I wasn't anyone special, but now I was actually classed as a nobody along with the rest of the scum around me.

*   *   *

I was arrested directly from my own flat, placed in an orange jumpsuit and then I became just another added to the line on a conveyor belt of the forgotten. One hundred and twenty men, including myself, were marched into the tin can of a ship to be plucked of our cores and served up to the Martian moon base like pitted olives for the UPUC administration. Cuffs were placed on each of us which not only fastened our wrists together, but were chained together linking us all like shackled slaves so it was easier to herd us onto the rows of seats on the ship, and also made escape highly improbable. We trudged across the metal decking and around the ship's rows of seats in a snake formation as the guards used a fusion gun to clasp the remaining chains to the aisle floors so they wouldn't trip over them themselves. I ended up with one of the central seats of the middle section. The guys by the windows actually had it worse as they got to watch Earth disappear as we took off. It's not something anyone should have to see unwillingly.

* * *

Just before take-off I watched the guards place all of their firearms in safety lockers; firing through the hull could prove fatal to all whilst in space. As the ship was loading there had been a lot of cursing and shouting. The guards had to settle some of these tainted citizens by force with their tremor batons. The word normal shouldn't have really existed in these times, but the guys either side of me were far from it. To my left was a chubby, geeky looking guy with thick lens visor glasses and a sonic hearing aid behind each ear. He looked terrified and smelt like he had pissed himself. The guy to my right was skinny with a red Mohican punk haircut. He had his sunglasses whipped off him by a guard revealing his bony cheeks and augmented eyes. They were cheaply done and the robotic lenses could be seen shifting behind his unnatural cerulean iris. He stank of cigarettes.

A High Court guard with a gold and olive cape and dark body armour marched down the aisle towards a set of double pneumatic doors. He tapped a video screen on the wall and spoke into a small microphone which protruded from the unit. His voice boomed across the on board PA system.

"Be seated. You will be secured. If you do not comply you will be disciplined."

Initially everybody sat down in the seats, which I thought were quite comfortable for a transport ship, and a metal bar lowered over our heads from each seat and stopped in front of us. The fat guy next to me whined as it pushed against his belly. Fortunately it didn't come close to my slender figure, or the skinnier frame of the punk guy. But, one guy in the front row with a ponytail and goatee started to pipe up. He rose abruptly, forcing the bar back up before it locked in place, and started shaking his chains, causing his neighbours' arms to jolt.

"Fuck you, corporate scabs!" he shouted. He then addressed the audience in the seats. "We don't have to do what they say! We've been manipulated out of our free will. Most of us have done nothing wrong. Remember what happened back in..." he went on, like a revolutionist.

The guy with the Mohican leaned over to me.

"Here it goes. Got any popcorn?" he whispered with a cockney accent, blowing the stench of cheap cigarettes in my ear.

At that moment the High Court guard waved two fingers at another guard who wore lighter colours. He stormed forward with a tremor baton. It protruded around twenty four inches and was charged with an electrical current that ran the length of its transparent centre. The guard took a couple of swings at the man. Surprisingly, the man managed to bat the weapon away with his forearms, still yelling aloud and lashing the chains in protest. The guard pushed a button on the side of the device and held it causing small green orbs that rotated around the strange current to accelerate with a faint buzz. The guard then prodded the arm of the man which produced a different sound; a crackle, like a brief round of applause or a faulty firework going off. The man then changed his yelling from protest to pain. His leg buckled as he went down on one knee, but he tried to cradle his arm pathetically with the other.

"My arm! You broke my arm, you fucking animal."

The guard kicked him to the floor until he was silent. The room of seated people around him went quiet but the rows further back continued their barrage of moaning and shouting which the guards seemed to ignore.

"Holy shit, did he actually break his arm? Holy shit!" the fat guy next to me piped up. "Th... this can't be ha... happening, man. This isn't my ship. This is wrong, man," he rambled, whimpering and shaking his head.

The guy with the Mohican rubbernecked around me in reaction to the whimpering man.

"Hey, shut the fuck up, tubs. That ain't nothin' compared to what I'll do to ya!" he threatened.

The fat man started to ball his sweaty hands up as his brow creased. I could see a stream of tears roll down his face as he laboured for breath.

"Fuck you, you piece of shit, I don't answer to you!" he spat back hysterically, spraying me with spittle.

The man with the broken arm was grabbed by two guards and dropped back into his seat before they injected him with a syringe. It seemed to be a strong pain killer as his ranting became slurred and no longer disruptive. I turned to the punk guy.

"Hey, uh, maybe we should let him be," referring to the stressed fat man. "This ain't no good for nobody on this ship full of cranks," I said, trying to relax the situation.

The guy eyed me intensely, and the strip lights above glimmered in his nose ring.

"We can't have no pussies in here with us," he said to me in a calmer manner. "We need some strength to get us out of this situation; a little plan," he boasted, smiling at me with a couple of gold teeth amongst the coffee coloured ones.

"A plan to get away? Isn't it a bit late for that now? We're about to take off."

He raised an eyebrow and broadened the smile.

"Damn straight. Question is, can you keep a secret?"

I wondered if I even wanted to know, but relented by way of a hesitant nod.

While the attention was still taken by the front row, he started to gulp and choke a little. He frowned and blinked heavily for a moment as he brought up a miniature dagger in a sheath covered in phlegm. He showed me with a wink as he held it between his teeth. He then spat it into his lap and concealed it with tattoo covered hands. I looked around, alarmed and unsettled. I thought it would do me a favour telling the guards, but then I wasn't sure if he would use it to kill me. After all, I *was* closest.

* * *

The cacophony of the unhinged passengers simmered to a murmur across the deck as the guards strapped themselves into chairs that faced us all. The ship's engines then kicked in to take off. The turbulence shook all the chains but the sound was drowned out by a high pitched ringing. We were all pinned to the seats as the ship hit the edge of the atmosphere. Having never been a fan of space travel, I took deep breaths and squinted whilst the white noise filled my ears. During the sixty seconds it took for us to exit into space, I glanced down to my right to notice that the guy with the Mohican used this time to jemmy out the pins that held the shackles together. His hands were now free to some extent, but concealed it well by interlocking his fingers. As the burning white noise of the ship's exit reached a crescendo, my hearing came back. The punk leaned over again.

"I'm Stanley Pirretta, of Kent Elms Prison, Essex. Some say I'm the most trustworthy guy they know. Those people are dead now," he smiled again.

"Pleased to meet you." I frowned, unsure.

"Let me read you the fortune of this ship. It's rather grim I'm afraid, but if it works, we could all be free men and could colonise whatever desert island planet we want. In a short while I'm going to cause a fucking stir and attract a guard over here. But seeing as you stole the seat I was meant to fucking be in, I'm gonna need your help," he explained in a matter of fact way.

I practised my poker face to conceal my fear of his next words.

"What do you need *me* to do?" I asked.

"I need you to trip him and restrain him so I can take him down."

"But what if I fail?" I replied, trying to wriggle out of it already.

"If you fail, I'll kill you myself," he said as he wiggled the knife between his thumb and index finger.

My palms started to sweat and my brain fought through a cloud of fear for the logical pitfalls.

"What about the other guards? There's about six more."

"Eight actually, you silly fucker," he replied. "But don't worry. I've got it all in hand, you'll see," he assured.

I swallowed hard and wished I was back on my couch watching TV or playing video games.

"I... I'm not sure it's a good id—"

Stanley started to twitch a little, more like the tick in the left side of his face. "Listen. We don't have time to fuck about, you twat. You've got two choices: we sit here and wait to land on a barren moon and wheelbarrow rocks about all day for the rest of our miserable fucking lives, or, you grab the guy so we can check back into Earth and land on Tahiti. *You* don't get blood on your hands, *I'm* the one who has to kill somebody, we all get home in time for breakfast. Which is it gonna be?" he asked sarcastically, his retinas focusing and refocusing on mine like crazy.

I gulped and hesitated, but nodded in fear, not agreement.

"'Appy fuckin' days," he whispered.

Then he reached a tattooed hand over to my wrists wielding the dagger. I bit my lip and I felt my hair start to gather sweat as he wedged it into the bolt on my cuffs. A quick rattle and twist and I felt them loosen between my wrists. He had certainly done this before.

"Get ready," he whispered.

I'd only ever restrained somebody once before when I was working in a kebab shop run by a Japanese family. A drunk man came in one night and started blurting racist comments at Akira, the manager, and refused to pay for chips. Akira lost his rag that night and chased the guy out of the shop with the large serrated blades we cut the Doner meat with. I did two good deeds that night by saving the racist's life and stopping Akira from going to prison as I held him. If I hadn't known him so well it might have been another story. I started to debate why I hadn't followed him back to Tokyo when he'd had enough of the UK.

Now I had an ex-convict prompting me with his twitching eyebrows and making a scene that could well be the end of us. What made things worse was that the fat guy next to me had started coughing. His breathing became laboured and his splutters interjected with wheezes as he appeared to try and clear his throat. He clutched his chest as best he could with his cuffs.

Stanley once again rubbernecked around me and grimaced at the unhealthy looking fat man.

"Oh no. You're fucking kiddin' me. 'Ere, guard! Guard! Sort this bloater out will ya? I think he's havin' a fucking heart attack," he moaned.

A guard turned and sidled down our aisle, tremor baton in hand, passing Stanley, then myself. The guard was muscular; the physique of a rugby player, and wore a full face mask with breathing equipment built in. He spoke through a speaker inside his combat helmet, trying to ask the fat guy what was wrong. The fat guy started to convulse and phlegm fell from his mouth onto his swollen stomach. He raised his hands toward the guard as his eyes streamed in an attempt to ask him to release him. The guard grabbed his wrist with a dark combat glove, clipped his tremor baton to his belt to free his hand to retrieve the key for the cuffs. I turned to Stanley hesitantly to find him gawping and nodding at me like a drug addict being offered his fix. I creased my brow and balled my fists tightly as I returned my gaze to watch the guard help the obese man. It felt so wrong but this was my chance. I took a few quick breaths to psyche myself up, pulled my hands apart so the chain was taut, slid out from under the bar, stood, and clasped the chain around the neck of the guard. I pulled tightly on it and fell backwards. In an instant we were writhing around on the floor. The guard flailed his arms and reached for the tremor baton but it was the exact moment that Stanley came through. All I could feel apart from the guard's obscene weight on top of me was a stabbing motion anywhere Stanley could find that wasn't covered with body armour. I felt the warm sensation of blood soak through to me. The guard raised his hands above his head to try and lever me off from behind, but I held the chain tightly and pulled again. This revealed a section of the guard's neck underneath his battle helmet and Stanley took advantage. He stabbed the guard's neck twice and blood spewed out all over me and jetted underneath the seats as far as the row behind us. I could see Stanley's boots getting drenched.

Chaos ensued around me and I heard another eruption of shouting as a series of struggles broke out across the deck. I panicked and shoved the guard's body off me, leaving him flailing and twitching. I got to my feet so fast it made me feel faint. I was covered in blood and it even dripped from my eyebrows. Around me I saw every guard had been intercepted by prisoners and were on the floor fighting for their lives. One was being kicked by three prisoners who had somehow escaped the cuffs and bars, another had been beaten and zapped into mush with his own tremor baton.

The events occurred in slow motion as a state of shock paralysed my senses. I witnessed the fat man with the glasses standing in full health and shaking his fists into the air. He was shouting obscenities across the room of pandemonium before suddenly reaching behind his ear and pulling one of his sonic hearing aids away. He then hurled it across the room striking the double pneumatic doors and landing where a guard with crimson piping was crawling to reach the rifle lockers. The fat man then prodded a small button on his other hearing aid and an explosion occurred. A wrench of twisting metal blended with a flash of bright light and was followed by a crescendo of ringing in my ears. Burning smoke filled the room and caused the emergency ventilation system to kick in. Slatted vent shafts in the roof and floor started sucking the smoke out of the room. My hearing returned slowly to the sound of the red alert siren and people coughing, especially near the doors where the explosion happened. The siren ceased shortly afterwards as the filtration system cleared the air and revealed a large scorch mark. Around the scorch mark was a mass of bodies slumped together where the walls and the surrounding area were smeared with blood. It seemed the guard, who I recognised only by the crimson piping upon his dark body armour, was left halved. His legs were skewed on the deck, ripped off at the waist, but his torso and head were not present anywhere as if obliterated. However, his hand was still present. Still gloved with gauntlet intact, it hung clasping a metal handrail just to the right of the door. He must have grabbed it as the device went off. I held the top of my head with one hand and just focused on breathing for a moment before Stanley grabbed my shoulder and rattled it.

"Good job, fella! I never caught your name," he said, jubilantly as if not much had happened.

"Adam Grand," I replied, dazed.

I felt the chains loosen and slide away from my cuffs. People were pulling them taut and using the tremor batons to break the links apart across the whole deck.

Stanley patted my shoulder and stepped over the dead guard at my feet towards the fat guy who leaned against the seat in front of him. He looked annoyed, but healthy and dispelled of fear. Stanley grabbed him by the collar of his overalls with both hands.

"What the fuck were you thinking, Brian? You couldn't have ballsed up the timing of that breach any better!"

The fat man frowned and jutted his jaw out.

"Stop your fucking whining and finish the job!" he bellowed with the grace of an unpaid builder.

He batted Stanley's arms away and pushed him, sending him toppling over the row in front of us.

"Watch who you're shoving, you ham fisted motherfucker!" Stanley warned as he staggered back to his feet.

Stanley then stumbled along the row of grumpy and bedraggled men towards the TV panel by the destroyed double doors. It seemed to still work after he jabbed it a few times, and the small microphone ejected from the edge. He cleared his throat and started speaking into it.

"Good morning, scum. I am broadcasting this galactic news to you from somewhere in the depths of my disturbed mental state. As you can see, this is a hold up; a protest; a breakout; an interplanetary freakout. Seven of my men on board today have concocted this formula to save all our arses. I'd like to introduce Adam Grand," he pointed toward me as blood dripped from my chin. "We couldn't have done it without him. He's a keeper!"

I looked around as the unkempt and barbarous crowd stared at me in a strange, fearful awe. Some of them smiled. Some just bore the crazy eyed look Stanley had. I felt a strange sensation; an ambivalence that blended embarrassment with glory. Stanley continued his speech.

"We now need to complete phase two! You can either sit back and relax, or give us a hand without pissing me off. So, provided we work together, we could all live happily ever after instead of becoming slaves to the oppressive Martian UPUC quarry, except of course for the unlucky splatter of fuckers by the door." He then whistled, circling a finger in the air and his undercover lunatics started to rally at the door with the guard's ion rifles and tremor batons. "We apologise for any inconvenience to your flight as we may still experience some turbulence," he finished and flicked the mic back into the wall leaving an awful shrill of feedback.

The speech compelled me. I felt like somebody again, a feeling I hadn't had since finishing a shift at the kebab shop. I warmed to Stanley who was clearly more loyal than he appeared. The metal grating below us clanked as I followed his crew through the cauterised double doors to the cockpit.

*   *   *

What we thought was going to be the cockpit was actually a mid-section of the ship which was built with a four man escape pod either side. The cockpit door was marked but it was sealed shut. Brian, the fat man, waddled with belligerence, totally contrasted to the whimpering wreck he impersonated earlier. He fumbled behind his ear for the remaining hearing aid and started to exhale angrily at the door.

"No!" Stanley yelled, jumping in front of him, arms wide. "We need to get in another way. This is a service shaft. If you lob another bomb here it might blow the ship in half. The escape pods will eject and we'll all be fucked."

Brian screwed his face up to mimic a trout's expression and looked around in annoyance. He then snatched a tremor baton from a man next to him and beat him on the head with it once. It sent him down holding his bleeding skull while the other men all jumped on Brian and tried to talk sense into him whilst struggling to restrain him.

While they were occupied I looked around and found a panel next to the door. It was lit ruby red and appeared cosmetic, but I had seen locks like this before. Opposite the kebab shop was a bank and the guys who refilled the ATM at night had their hands coded to the sensors next to the doors, ruby red sensors like these. The rest of the scumbags on the ship had gathered by the scorched door to watch the renegade clowns try to restrain Brian, so I pushed through them to where I noticed the handrail and pulled the guard's arm from it. I had to pry the fingers one by one.

I returned to the squabbling renegades and waved the severed arm about in the air. "Hey! I think I might have something that might work!" Brian stopped struggling like a stubborn toddler amongst them.

I pulled the armoured glove from the hand, spread the palm and planted it onto the panel. The light turned green and the remaining pneumatic door slid open with a hiss.

A brief cheer erupted and the crowd piled into the cockpit. Then a strange silence followed. I pushed through them to find the main viewport and a wealth of controls, switches, screens and dials that powered the ship along with two wide pilot seats, both empty.

"What the fuck?" Stanley exclaimed, snapping his gaze around at the myriad of controls.

My gaze was fixed on the vastness of space through the viewport. Reality kicked me in the teeth like a frightened mule. The Earth was behind us and I felt like the human race had abandoned us. If I ever got the chance to return home, I wasn't sure if I'd ever feel the same about it. An anger rose in me which I admitted might have put me on par with the scumbags around me.

One of the less tattooed degenerates squinted at a screen above the left pilot seat and his jaw hung in a gormless fashion for a moment.

"It's on autopilot," he said, and then pointed.

The rest of us gawped up at the screen to find luminous green text against black:

AUTOMATIC PILOT

DESTINATION: DEIMOS ALPHA IX.

ETA: 00HRS:28MINS

Stanley wrinkled his chin and pulled a face like a bulldog chewing a wasp.

"Fuck!" he exclaimed. "Doesn't anybody know how to turn it off and fly this thing?"

A dangling spiked earring flapped as he spun his head around at everybody to find them all either searching around puzzled, or looking forlorn and beaten, myself being one of the latter.

"Right. Looks like a one way ticket for now. Get every weapon on the ship together, boys. We're going to war!" said Stanley.

*   *   *

Twenty eight minutes later and we all huddled around the door equipped with tremor batons, ion rifles, and lengths of chain as the ship manoeuvred itself around the spaceport to the landing pad. The wounded, dead, and weak willed kept their heads down, but there were at least seventy men left able and agitated. We could see through the viewport that the moon base was an industrial metal ogre with touches of bright yellow paint added to its control towers in a weak attempt to make it look friendly. We felt a jolt as we passed through the pop up atmosphere erected around the whole facility. We touched down gently and the ship ejected steam from its pressurised landing feet.

Stanley looked me in the eye, kneeling with an ion rifle. "Here, you deserve this," he said, passing me the rifle and looping the strap over my blood covered neck. "Dunno how this is gonna go, but it's been good working with ya."

He then held out a hand with a couple of metal skull rings to shake my own. He then rose and clanked a tremor baton against the handrail by the exit door.

"Hey, fellas! UPUC wanted war and tried to get rid of us because they felt we didn't give nothin' back. Well, now let's give 'em somthin' back!" he jeered.

The crowd roared, shaking fists and weapons into the air. I was compelled to join in. The airlock released and the door hissed upwards revealing the landing pad and a dark horizon. I followed the riled amateur battalion chanting and screaming, expecting an overwhelming gun battle. We jogged toward the main entrance of the facility and looked around vigorously. Nothing. No guards. No resistance. The place seemed abandoned, at least from the outside.

As we reached the main blast doors of the facility, we found them open. Wide open enough to let a full baggage transporter through.

"Something isn't right," I said. "These doors are never left open, they are heavy duty security doors."

"Is it a trap?" asked Stanley.

"No trap," Brian replied. "I can smell something bad inside."

I wondered for a moment if it was his own urine he could smell, but as we moved into the entrance, he was right. The smell of rotting flesh and death was apparent. I sneered with the sharp odour lingering in the back of my throat. Down the dark corridors of flickering striplights we could see scattered body parts and walls smeared with blood.

We all inched forward and heard growls in the distance. The deadly silence of the thin atmosphere didn't help our nerves. This amount of men treading quietly along metal decking wasn't possible, but we tried. We passed the mass of blood and flesh. I didn't want to look closely but Stanley could obviously see better than the rest of us in the dark, probably due to his implants. He knelt to peer at the human remains.

"Oh shit," he said.

"What is it?" whispered Brian.

"I've seen this kind of killing in a documentary."

At the moment a prolonged squeal echoed down the passageway of metal pipes and grating. Then a flapping, curdling of the air. A light flickered and winged creatures hung from the ceiling like giant bats. They dripped with blood as they feasted on the remainder of their prey.

"Bu'ars. They've taken out the base," said Stanley.

"Nobody on Earth must know about this yet," I replied, somehow still attached to those who had outcast us.

Brian grimaced and shunted the pump handle of his ion rifle to charge it.

"Why can't anything just run fucking smoothly?" he asked rhetorically.

I started to see his point after the effort of the hijack. The situation was beginning to be like some of the video games I had played back home, except this time there was only one life, and no respawns. I looked around at the shuddering bunch of lowlifes that had mustered the courage to get this far, and my gut just knew they were worth fighting for. I also shunted the pump handle of my ion rifle.

"I don't know about you boys, but I don't think I want to go out like those guards," I said, bloodied and wide eyed.

The ragtag group nodded to each other in agreement. They had developed a degree of respect for me. I was somebody now, and felt needed, creating my chance, whether we came through it or not, to be assertive and give UPUC the middle finger.

"Come on, fellas. This is World War Four and it's for humans only! Let's show 'em what the scum of the Earth is made of!" I said.

They all roared again as we charged toward the winged creatures, firing ion shots and clubbing the walls with batons and chains.

Tomorrow
D.M. Burdett

The storm passed through the bay, drenching everything in its path and filling the night with a cacophony of deafening drums.

Lightning shattered across the cloudless sky, and the wind whipped debris into swirling clouds around me as I stumbled down the embankment of the overpass. I steadied myself against the wall, the weight of Ella's body threatening to topple me into the swelling waters of the Yarra with every precarious step.

I ducked under the Wesgate Ridge sign, stepping into the gap under the overpass and out of the deluge just as my legs finally gave out. I dropped to my knees, my hands skidding in the mud, almost not catching my weight, and Ella's body slid slowly, carelessly from my shoulders. My vision swam in the darkness while her dead eyes watched, unblinking.

The first wave of convulsions wracked my body. I vomited bloody mucus into the wet dirt until dry heaves left me wheezing and breathless. As the dizziness abated, I gulped cold gasps of damp air into my lungs.

Ella, in life, had been a tiny slip of a girl. Lithe and strong, the fiercest of soldiers, she was tiny even so. But I was fatigued and malnourished, and not used to the unfiltered air outside of the city walls.

And she was all dead weight now.

When I felt able, I pulled her swathed body to the water's edge and mumbled a brief epitaph as I pushed it into the choppy water.

"Stand down, soldier," I whispered.

I watched for a moment as the bundle bobbed on the current before the Yarra's movements slowly pulled her out into the turbulent flow, and out to sea.

The river was no proper burial for a soldier of Fomalhaut, but there was little choice in these dark times. If the Sapiens found a burial pyre, they would know that we'd been here. Know that we were out here somewhere.

They would come for us, hunt us down.

I left the overpass then, dragging myself back up the bank to the road above, the rain pummelling me all the while.

As I stood at the junction, I looked back across the river. The storm drowned out the gunfire and the engines, but flashes of light spattered across the landscape on the far side. I watched as an explosion erupted somewhere near the old docks, lighting up the decimated remnants of the New Melbourne skyline.

They'd taken the city.

The domed metropolis was all but gone. Only shattered obelisks of the thick wall remained in testament to the life we'd built on Earth over the last two hundred years. Two hundred years since we'd come here to help the human survivors of their last war. To help them rebuild the fractured ruins of the planet they almost destroyed. We'd made a new home. For them and for us.

I turned and headed back to the old pumping station wearily, the rain beating me down as I staggered through the deserted streets.

I dropped into the basement of the ancient ruins just as Tara's scream echoed through the dark corridors, the sound cutting through the thunder. *Fuck! She's gonna get us all killed.*

The sound followed me as I shuffled through the underground labyrinth of corridors, stooped low against the torn ceiling above, before shouldering open the rusting door to the room that we'd taken refuge in the night before. Neither Brad nor Tara looked up when I entered.

"The city's gone. They're still taking a lot of fire over by the docks though." I sat down heavily on a concrete slab which butted out from the damaged wall and shrugged off my armour. "Whoever's over there is keeping the Sapiens busy."

Brad nodded, but I could see that he wasn't listening. He touched Tara's cheek tenderly and his thumb, blue and opaque, rubbed across her pale, white cheek. Not for the first time, I was reminded of the peeled, boiled egg of a chicken that the Sapiens seemed to eat so frequently. She gurgled another loud groan through clenched teeth, her eyes squeezed shut, and her jaw clenched as her fingers dug into his arm.

"How's she doing?" I asked although I didn't care. This Sapien was holding us back, giving us problems we didn't need. If it weren't for her, we'd be on the M route by now. And we'd be a man up.

Brad and I were among the first Fomalhaut settlers to land on the planet after the humans almost nuked themselves out of existence in 2020. We came with love and empathy, our aim only to help, each of us chosen by our people for our fortitude, our respect, our science. When we left our planet, we knew it was a one way ride; it would be a long time before the Sapiens would have the technology that would help us to get home.

We were met with suspicion, but once the Sapiens realised we were not a threat—we had come to build, not fight—they welcomed us with open arms. They embraced our technologies and our compassion and learned how to live together in harmony, as we once did on Fomalhaut. We embraced their cultures and traditions, and we took human names. After two hundred years I could barely remember our birth names.

But Hautians live longer than humans and the friends we made in those early days grew old and died. We loved and cared for their children and grandchildren, but most of them are gone too. And now age is finally starting to take a hold on us.

Successive generations of Sapiens didn't understand the extent of what had happened during World War III, of just how devastated human life had become, how hard it was to rebuild with so little. The Sapiens saw the infiltration of Hautians in their society as a takeover of what they deemed to be their human entitlement.

They just wanted their planet back, for themselves. No

aliens as neighbours. No aliens in government. No aliens taking their jobs.

No aliens.

And so, anarchy had permeated our quiet lives. To many, we were no longer seen as the *saviours*. We became the *invaders*. The Sapiens rallied and protested, and their numbers grew. We started to get voted out of our political positions. We lost our jobs to Sapiens with no credentials. We became segregated.

Now those groups that wanted us to leave Earth, the planet we call home, were big enough to start a war of their own.

Brad sighed. "I don't know. I don't know if this is normal or not. Does it seem like it's taking too long?" He turned to me beseechingly.

I shrugged. *How would I know?* "We need to get moving soon. They'll start reaching out of the city in the morning. We can use the storm as cover and carry on out West."

"We can't go anywhere while she's like this." Brad's dark eyes watched her carefully.

I gritted my teeth. "Brad, if we're still here by sun up, we're *all* dead," I warned.

He turned to me now, anger fizzled in his eyes. "I'm not asking you to stay. Go, if that's what you want to do. But Tara can't go anywhere right now."

"If I was gonna dump and run, I'd have done it before we left the city."

"Then quit bitching."

I felt my rage begin to bubble to the surface and I fought to contain it. I got up and made my way over to our meagre supplies. I pulled out a bladder of water and sucked at it sparingly. We'd need some food soon; we hadn't eaten in days.

I wiped my mouth and resealed the bladder. "We're leaving in an hour. No arguments."

"We're going nowhere until she's done."

"Brad, I just buried Ella in the blue. In the fucking blue! She was a soldier! She deserved a proper burial. But I pushed her into the blue." I stood for a moment, staring at him, my hands clenched into fists, while my anger subsided. "So, no one else dies today."

Brad knew I was right.

"We're moving out in an hour." This time there was no resistance.

Tara's low moan suddenly escalated. An ear-piercing screech emitted from somewhere deep within her, and our attention turned towards her.

"What's wrong with her?" I asked.

"It's coming," she breathed, pain and fear etched across her face. "It's coming!" she cried, louder this time.

At that moment, a crash from above vibrated through the building sending dust and debris down on us. The wall where I had been sitting only moments earlier disintegrated into a brick dust storm, raining huge concrete blocks down on us. I was thrown across the room, my neck snapping back as my head cracked against the old, metal door. I lay in dazed confusion, my cheek pressed against the cold stone floor as gunfire erupted from somewhere close by.

I looked across at Brad and saw he was gone. His body was torn almost in half, and I watched, mesmerised, as a pool of yellow blood crept from beneath him, edging its way across the floor towards me. I reached out shakily and touched his face.

Tara's scream pierced through the hypnosis and my eyes searched her out in the gloom. I curled my arms at my sides and pushed my body up. I steadied myself for a moment, my head down as I watched my own blood drip to the floor in rhythmic globules.

Then, crouched low, bullets flying above my head, I moved over to her.

"The baby's coming!" she roared, terror etched across her face.

I picked her up, unsteady on my feet, and held her in my arms as I left the room and stepped into the crumbling corridor. As we made our way through the network of jumbled passageways the sound of gunfire disappeared.

"The baby," Tara whispered weakly in my ear, her arms tight around my neck. "It's here."

I placed her gently on the floor and knelt between her knees. The head and shoulders of the half breed had already crowned, and it's bruised, contorted face looked up at me. It had its father's black eyes.

"Fuck! What do you need to do?"

"I'm pushing," she said quietly, and she let out a low groan as she strained.

"I got one!" a voice at the end of the corridor startled us. "And it's got a prisoner. One of ours!"

Gunfire rang out and we both dropped to our sides, arms across our heads, as bullets ricocheted off the walls all around us. When I opened my eyes, I was staring into Tara's dead face.

A mewl alerted me to the baby lying between us. It was still attached to its mother by its cord and, instinctively, I pulled the child to me, yanking the afterbirth from Tara's inert body.

When the gunfire subsided, I ran blindly.

* * *

The baby—a boy—died six days later; a long and painful death. Starvation weakened his tiny body until his organs failed and I looked on helplessly as he closed his eyes for the last time. I did what I could, but I couldn't provide for him as only a mother can.

I walked for another two days, the small bundle clutched in my arms, before I buried him in the ground, following the traditions of his people, at an ancient cemetery near a place called Edenhope.

It was there that I met Kendrick.

I had lain by the baby's grave for days, not knowing or

caring what would become of me. I was lost, my soul sick.

Kendrick and the others had found me there and taken me into their care. They fed and clothed me, nurtured me, nursed my wounds.

Over the following years, we scoured the lands, gathered our people. Built our army. Now we stand on the brink of war, looking across the sea to the land that will become ours.

Tomorrow.

The Floabnian Fiasco
Shawn Klimek

In contrast to the bleak, marginally habitable worlds to which most evictees from Earth were sent in search of new frontiers, astrometric probes had identified the Icarus star system's third planet as an Eden-like Earth analog ideal for human colonisation . There had been so many volunteers for the pilot voyage to Icarus-Gamma that, instead of the usual crew and passenger complement of grumbling draftees, a lottery had been required to limit the manifest.

Despite being a de facto ship of winners, however, bad luck plagued the voyage.

First, a catastrophic navigational error caused the ship to veer far off course. The ship's captain had blamed hallucinations, pointing a finger at either rogue particles of exotic pulsar radiation, or heavy metal impurities in the recycled waste-water used to rehydrate his private-ration of snack biscuits. Alternatively, he allowed, it might have been that dodgy mould on the hash brownies he'd rescued from the passenger-contraband amnesty bin.

In any event, the result was that the voyagers missed the Eden-like Icarus-Gamma by lightyears, crash-landing instead on an uncharted, boggy globe, whose atmosphere, the official log recorded, 'smelled like gym socks yanked still wet from the week-old corpse of a decomposing whale.'

Now, most folks waking in their thermal pajamas to the realisation that they had miraculously survived the dual perils of interstellar travel and a crash landing, would have instantly ripped out their cryo-crib catheters and—after regretting being so rough with their catheters—celebrated.

Similarly, most folks crawling out of smoking spaceship wreckage—like drunks looking for lost keys, only bloodier—onto an uncharted alien planet and finding themselves, against astonishing odds, neither instantly crushed, suffocated, poisoned, frozen, nor boiled alive by the atmosphere would have counted themselves incredibly lucky.

These lottery winners, however, still embittered by the cruel bait-and-switch handed to them by Fate and their captain's incompetence, were slower to see the big picture. Magnifying their resentment was the captain's galling assertion that traditional right-of-discovery entitled him to name the new planet after himself. This outrage had been so unanimously resented by the colonists that they resolved to obstruct any name he suggested until he first honoured their counter-request that he shove a nuclear pickaxe where the stars don't shine.

Such a resounding rebuke might have shocked a reasonable leader into constructive self-reflection and diminished nincompoopery. Instead, this captain's strategy for morale improvement was to dictate that food rations be distributed as prizes for gladiatorial mud-wrestling and wet T-shirt contests.

All this preamble is to explain how the planet's placeholder moniker, 'Floabnia'—coined from the acronym 'For Lack Of A Better Name'—must have eventually met the community need, because it was later found carved in stone on a monument commemorating how the embattled captain had bravely and selflessly given his own life for the welfare of his community by secretly lynching, immolating and then stoning himself to death, far from any weak minded witnesses who might have intervened.

Enough terraforming machine parts had survived the crash, that with a little blood, sweat, spit and elbow-grease—as well as the occasional splatter of goopy, yellow gunk they'd been promised wasn't as sickening or contagious as first glance would seem—a jury-rigged model was soon purifying the Floabnian atmosphere and draining the surrounding bogs in a manner seemingly calibrated to most inconvenience the native flora and fauna. Within a few short solar orbits, the first Terran colony had become self-sufficient, and sister colonies were soon multiplying across the Floabnian globe.

Unbeknownst to the Terran invaders, they were already sharing the planet with another sentient species whose sophisticated subterranean civilizations had long thrived and thrummed beneath the ubiquitous bog. Eventually dubbed "Floabnians", they were fiercely bashful, amphibious troglodytes whose natural talents included a chameleon-like, near-invisibility.

WORLD WAR FOUR

The first Terrans to witness their unconcealed forms had described them in conflicting terms. One said their appearance suggested what might result from a transporter accident merging a scorpion with a squid. The other could only describe them as 'cute, in a squidgy sort of way.'

Whenever first contact between two sentient alien species is not immediately hostile, a kind of diplomatic honeymoon typically follows, during which period both parties strive to communicate and investigate each other, meanwhile evaluating the prospects for exploitation and conquest, or failing those options, peaceful coexistence.

On Floabnia, this honeymoon was cut short when a misguided Terran coterie of celebrity trendsetters then making the local talk-show circuit, advocated enslaving the Floabnians as pets, a faux pas made insufferable by the unfortunate addition of strong words about spaying and neutering.

Thus, began the Floabnian-Terran War.

Insufferably provoked, the long patient Floabnians revealed an unforeseen and terrible capacity to resist. Crawling out of the bog like a leviathan cicada, radiating wrath and dripping with muck, came the first Floabnian dreadnought, a 13-limbed war-machine fashioned from grey metal and xeno-synthetics in the likeness of its makers, writ on a titanic scale.

The dreadnought attacked the founding colony with pitiless efficiency, spewing noxious gasses and firing death-rays, while stomping and stabbing with its metallic appendages. As the last bit of Terran power source ebbed, someone in the ruins managed to radio a warning to the sister colonies on Flobnia and general distress signals to Earth and every Terran colony on other planets. Communication with the inscrutable aliens remained impossible, frustrating diplomatic options; since the mysterious dreadnought shielding deflected most conventional weapons, and nuclear weapons would, at best, have undone the progress already made by their terraforming machinery, the Terrans had no alternative but to construct their own fleet of battle robots in the hopes of defending their remaining colonies against the robot-dreadnought-wrought onslaught.

The Terran guardian mechs were giant, human-piloted, anthropomorphic robots, equipped with arm rockets, hydraulic punches and energy weapons. In battle after battle, they surrounded and assailed their monstrous Floabnian foe, but no matter their tactics, they found themselves thwarted by the Floabnian dreadnought's impenetrable shielding and superior might. Colony after Terran colony was stomped into the bog.

However, aided by transmissions from Earth, the same Terran ingenuity which had conquered such once-impossible tasks as interstellar travel and ridding the internet of spam, rose to the occasion with a range of new weapons, keeping them secret until the decisive confrontation of the war. It was this final battle, which, despite an established legacy of incidents no less worthy of the term, became forever known as 'The Floabnian Fiasco.'

WORLD WAR FOUR

The first secret weapon was a powerful, new, Terran command robot. A menacing colossus, nearly as tall as the Floabnian war-machine was wide, it was equipped with the second secret weapon: a powerful new beam weapon.

As the Terran guardian-mechs trudged through the mist-shrouded, bog, warily circling the relentless Floabnian dreadnought, the Terran command robot, watched from a distant hill, approximately fifty strides distant. The guardian mechs had been equipped with a third secret weapon: fog-netting. These beams would weaken the dreadnought shields and suppress its sensors.

The humans' plan had been to lure the alien avatar within lunging range of their champion's powerful fists before unleashing all their new weapons at once in a devastating knockout blow.

The plan was a good one, but it would not matter. Inside the colossal Terran command robot's lofty head was a two-pilot command bridge. It was there Fate had chosen the battle of penultimate consequence to take place.

* * *

A round, steel hatch opened in the giant war-robot, and a pair of slimy, squid-like creatures slithered onto the control bridge. The bridge furnishings had plainly been designed for human operators: two chairs equipped with safety belts, levers for manipulating robotic limbs and weapons, and a control panel with enough levers, knobs and lights to shame a casino. Strangely absent were any signs of the humans themselves. As the alien intruders explored the premises, they ambulated by means of snaking arms and grasping tentacles. These features were complimented by a coiled, scorpion-like tail, which, together with their intelligence, identified the intruders as Floabnians.

"We made it," said the first Floabnian into his implanted mouthpiece. His voice resembled a bullfrog sucking spaghetti. "We're now alone inside the human robot's command centre."

"Are you quite sure you're alone, Dort? Our ground agents are only tracking one human pilot. There should be two." The answering voice was deeper, like the sad sound of two sea lion bulls who have accidentally mated.

The Floabnian named Dort periscoped his eye-stalks and scanned the room before confirming. "Quite sure, Overseer."

"Very well. Excellent work, agents," came the response. "You'll need to work fast. The humans are somehow jamming our dreadnought's sensors, so to boost power, we're going to cease radio transmissions until your sabotage is complete. This will be our last contact. Now, figure out the best spots to squirt some neurotoxin and then get the hell out of there!"

"What about laying some eggs, sir? Just to be sure?"

"You actually have eggs ready?"

"Absolutely, sir. Blem, too. Our menses are in synch."

"Very well. Lay some eggs but move fast."

"Will do. Over and out."

"Over and—"

"All hail, Meb the Destroyer!" shouted the uglier intruder, in a voice like a vomiting camel.

"—Hello, what? I thought I heard you say something as I was signing off."

"It was Blem, sir."

"Yes sir," said Blem, "I was only saying, 'All Hail, Meb the Destroyer!'"

"Right. 'All hail, Meb the Destroyer,' but it's radio silence now."

"All hail—"

"—Out."

Dort jiggled his head disapprovingly at his companion and then returned his attention to the mission at hand. Lest he become too busy and forget later, he exposed his egg vent and hastily extruded a few, brown, gelatinous bulbs where he stood. "And now you, Blem," he urged.

"Right-o," said the ugly one, and then did the same. Soon, two batches of freshly-laid, Floabnian eggs had congealed into upright mounds, like turds standing at attention, or chocolate pudding pops jutting out of a chocolatey stain. Within minutes, the eggs were already throbbing with life.

Resuming his exploration, Blem was the first to discover a pair of interesting protrusions. "Hey, look Dort," he said, wagging his hooked tail. "I believe these must be the control knobs which humans twist and pull to operate this robot!"

"Those are drawer knobs, Blem," scoffed his counterpart. "The kind we're looking for should have glowing bits and cryptic markings around them. Human spines tend to be vertical, like this robot, so the controls should be higher up."

"Ah, makes sense." The eyestalks receded, and the tail sagged.

"Still, you may as well squirt a little neurotoxin on them," offered Dort, trying to be encouraging, "if you're quite sure you have plenty to spare."

The other Floabnian glanced back at his telson—the poisonous barb hovering at the end of his scorpion-like tail—and estimated the supply of neurotoxins droplets remaining. Upon consideration, he emitted a conservative dribble of tar-like goo onto the drawer knobs.

"Here we are," said the mission leader with satisfaction. Dort had identified the central control panel, an upright cabinet arrayed with buttons, gauges and flashing read-outs on every surface. A series of levers dangled overhead. "This spot is where our scientists tell us the neurotoxins will be most effective."

Dort mounted the cabinet and then clambered even higher amongst the surrounding machinery, splaying his six, prehensile appendages for balance. From this position, he could simultaneously target both the controls below and the robot-limb manipulators above, in a single poisonous sweep. Once ready, he aimed his telson and then gushed paralysing, black ooze onto every surface. Physically spent afterwards, he let his tail droop and expelled a satisfied sigh, like an extended fart. "That should do," he said, grinning from a hidden orifice.

Just then, a series of noises came from behind a rectangular panel in the wall opposite the entrance hatch: a thump and rattle, followed by a vibrating, whooshing sound. Something metal clicked, and then a red light above the panel turned to green. Finally, a silver latch at the panel's mid-point rotated, after which the panel swung open. A human female emerged, distractedly pulling up the zipper on her insignia-spangled, grey jumpsuit before wiping her hands on her pants. The name tag just beneath her commander's rank read "Angela Denza," in some linear, human code Floabnians had yet to decipher.

She gave no initial indication of having noticed the intruders—doubtless because they were holding perfectly still to maximize the uncanny efficacy of their dermal camouflage. Looking blindly past them, she first noticed the open hatch door, and then the telltale clusters of alien eggs, like stubby gorilla fingers reaching out of pools of molasses. Alerted by this sight to the alien intrusion, she drew the energy weapon holstered at her hip and began scanning the room, while stepping slowly backwards. There were dangerous possibilities wherever she looked; hidden Floabnians and their infamous neurotoxin traps could be anywhere.

Commander Denza only realized that she had been holding her breath when a staticy squawk from the speaker on the control panel provoked a startled gasp. The voice of a human male followed, muffled by goo.

"Delta Forty to Alpha One," the man seemed to mumble. "Please come in. Over."

The human female waved her weapon uncertainly from side to side, as she responded. "Roger, Delta Forty, this is Alpha One. Alpha One is compromised. Floabnian intruders aboard. You are ordered to take command of the mission. Repeat! Alpha One compromised. Attack when ready. Please acknowledge! Over."

Suspended awkwardly above his own trap, ropy limbs out-flung like the ribs of an upturned umbrella, Dort clung tenuously to available protuberances in every direction. He had chosen this position for efficiency, as opposed to comfort, and was already beginning to tremble from the strain. He knew he wouldn't be able to stay invisible indefinitely.

If the wait became too long, muscle fatigue might foil the nimble dismount necessary to avoid contact with his own neurotoxins. Two of his limbs culminated in chitinous tongues, which were especially vulnerable on their permeable sides. Although Floabnians were immune to the neurotoxin's worst effects, such was its potency that accidental-on-purpose tastings were a familiar cause of intoxication—a condition forbidden to the soldier caste except during wakes, weekends and Meb the Destroyer worship rallies.

As the Floabnian mission leader struggled to stay invisible and aloft, Blem focused on slithering silently nearer to the human robot-operator whenever she faced away. The intervening furnishings and robot skeletal struts improved his camouflage but limited his opportunities for an unobstructed pounce. Given a clear lane, he was confident that a simultaneous thrust of every python-like arm would easily propel him into lethal grappling range. If his suckered tentacles failed to rip her in half, he still had his own neurotoxin reserves.

The unseen human voice reverberated from the control-panel speakers a second time. "Come in, Alpha One. This is Delta Forty. Last response garbled. Did not copy. Repeat, did not copy. All gladiator-mechs now in position. Fog net is holding. Awaiting your signal to attack. Over."

Frustrated with her communication difficulties, Commander Denza wondered whether standing closer to the microphone might help. She inched closer to the control panel cabinet. "Delta Forty, this is Alpha One," she shouted. "Alpha One is compromised. Do you—?" Static and then ear-splitting feedback whistled from the device, like a drowning harpy. Denza covered her ears, consequently tilting her gun's muzzle towards the ceiling. Blem took advantage of this distraction to slither quietly to a position at her rear.

At the same time, the human's increasing proximity to Dort was tantalizing him with hope that he might yet become her executioner. *Just a little nearer, wretched human, and you will feel my touch!* Although the entire reservoir of neurotoxins in his telson were spent, and his barbed tail temporarily drooped, flaccid and useless, the powerful tentacles with which he clung to the angled steel beams quivered with impatient blood lust. *One step closer, human, and I will drop down on you like a Floabnian cave spider!*

Preceded by the usual radio squawk, the unseen man's voice sounded for a third time, now more urgently.

"Alpha One, please respond! Fog-net power nearly depleted. Surprise ambush opportunity will soon be lost. If you can hear but not respond, please signal attack using Mime Protocols. Over."

Mime Protocols. The robot-operator glanced upwards towards the relevant levers on and above the control panel, now almost within reach. She was already extending a hand when she spotted the dreaded, inky glaze on every surface. Instantly realizing its lethal import, she retreated in a panic, startling her Floabnian stalker into doing the same. Not only did Blem stagger backwards into one of the thick, greasy metallic cables which served as a tendon for the giant, command robot's neck, but he cried out in pain at the discovery that the human's boot had momentarily pinned and crushed the nerve in one of his invisible, outstretched arms.

Alerted by wet scuffling, a vibrating thud, and a sound which might, in other circumstances, have been mistaken for someone angrily siphoning pudding with a trombone, Denza whipped quickly around and fired a shot at the padded flooring. A smouldering hole appeared, and just beside it, a severed tentacle, seeping fluid resembling buttered grits.

Meanwhile, Dort had dropped from his canopy position in a failed attempt at landing atop the female pilot, belly-flopping instead onto the toxic control-panel. Thinking fast, he managed to slide quickly onto the floor and shield himself behind the cabinet in time to resume his camouflage before the human could whip her head back around to identify the noise.

"Reveal yourselves!" Commander Denza shouted, putting her back to the wall and jerking her weapon threateningly in random directions. Unfortunately, her human noises were babble to the aliens, or else the two races might have long ago talked their way out of war. There were thousands of Terran colonies in the galactic quadrant, plenty and to spare, and the Floabnians would gladly have settled for eating only one or two a year. As it was, this human's demand would probably have been ignored anyway; Floabnians instinctively prefer to lurk hidden until they can attack with a clear advantage.

The human pilot seemed to stare straight through Blem. Biting his remotest lips to fight back the pain, the ugly alien decided his best chance was to hold still while concealing his wound, thus minimizing bleeding while maximizing camouflage. Any chance of attacking her by surprise now would require a significant distraction.

Somehow, Dort sized up the situation and recognized that the task of distracting their prey belonged to him. Unfortunately, he just wasn't up to it. He had both just had the wind knocked out of him and was beginning to feel extremely tipsy from the effects of the neurotoxin. Fortunately, his offspring unwittingly rose to the task: the noise of Floabnian hatchlings emerging from their shells was freakishly reminiscent of wet logs being lifted from muck as doomed piglets choked on peach pits.

The female human swung her weapon towards the hatchling eggs and exploded the nearest batch with a well-aimed blast. A scant handful of charred survivors flopped on the floor, feebly attempting to vanish using their underdeveloped camouflage skills.

Seeing his opportunity, Blem lunged towards the human pilot, simultaneously flinging out an arm to seize one of her ankles while stabbing her repeatedly in the torso with the weapon at the end of his tail, injecting her until his telson was fully drained of poison.

Now, it was the human's turn to hold still.

Blem let out a raspberry of relief and then both Floabnian adults relaxed their camouflage to leer triumphantly at their paralysed victim. The human's eyes bulged with horror and her jaw hung open, gasping like a suffocating fish.

"Ha!" said the mission leader, wagging a pair of worm-like appendages in an obscene taunt.

"We've done it, Dort!" Blem exulted. "The hatchlings can finish her. Now, let's signal the overseer and then get the hell out of here. My wound is bleeding badly, and I need medical attention."

"No, wait," said his less physically repugnant peer. "Something is happening to my brain. I'm getting smarter!"

"You're covered in neurotoxins," observed his wounded companion. "You're probably just drunk."

"No, no," protested Dort. "I'm telling you, I feel a chemical change in my brain cells, and I'm beginning to understand these human controls. What if we could operate this robot ourselves, and turn it against its makers?"

"That's the neurotoxins speaking, Dort. You're just delusional. Now, let's go!" Whimpering slightly and trailing ochreous ooze, Blem dragged himself towards the exit hatch favouring his injured limb—the Floabnian version of hobbling. Upon reaching the exit, he turned to watch the remaining hatchlings, who, having already sniffed out their first, potential meal, were migrating like a school of tadpoles across the floor towards the human. He waved a sentimental arm at them and then sunk out of view.

Unable to tilt her head or shift her gaze to follow their approach, Commander Denza focused instead on the weapon at the end of her outstretched arm, stiff as a scarecrow. She could see her finger on the trigger, but neither feel it nor will it to squeeze again. At least my death will be painless, she thought.

By this time, Dort had managed to remount the control panel cabinet and had started flipping switches. "Hey Blem, I'm about to make the giant robot march forward," he announced gleefully, adding as he gripped a gooey, padded metal rod, and then pulled it about half-way, "This lever means 'go'."

Blem's head re-emerged through the hatch. "What? Wait, Dort! Stop!" he begged.

The steel shutters over the giant robot's face suddenly opened, and Commander Denza found that her peripheral vision now included a narrow view of the muddy battlefield outside. The Floabnian dreadnought, having risen out of the bog like an immense kraken, dwarfed the surrounding platoon of guardian mechs. However, flickering rays, connecting each robot to the monstrous alien avatar like hub spokes, were keeping it bound and blind: the fog-webbing was working marvellously. Yet the dreadnought remained undamaged. Denza could also see numbers counting down at the bottom of the augmented portal screen display. The power-levels for each guardian were rapidly diminishing.

The radio speaker gave a dimly-heard bark, muffled by the Floabnian mission-leader's sprawling, drunken form.

"Alpha One, this is Delta Forty. Visual signal received. Commencing attack."

In pain, but frantic, Blem hurried back towards the control panel and stretched out a tentacle to entangle his Floabnian fellow agent, before attempting to drag him away.

"Let go, Dort," he pleaded, tugging. "You're only making things worse!"

Dort resisted, the effort inevitably increasing his toxic dosage. "It's a steep learning curve, but I really think I'm getting the hang of this," he enthused, mashing some buttons while pulling a different lever. Through the face portal, a colossal, mechanical arm could be seen rising like a drawbridge to point towards the dreadnought. A terrible hum vibrated the entire machine.

Back at the open exit hatch, a human male wearing the same kind of jumpsuit as his female counterpart pushed his way in, stumbling and griping aloud as he did so. "That's a lot of stairs," Lieutenant Fred West complained. "This robot really needs two bathrooms." Taking in the stunning scene, he added, "Holy Shit!"

His commander's bloody lower-extremities were far enough gone that he wondered how she was still standing.

Meanwhile, the view through the robot's face portal showed a bright bolt of fire jetting from the robot's outstretched arm, linking the human war-machine to its foe with a ragged ray of light, and drilling a black hole through the alien dreadnought's centre.

The Avatar of Meb responded by belching foul smoke from several fresh exits and then disembarking its Floabnian crew in a fashion which seemed intended to dazzle; that is, they evacuated much the way shrapnel evacuates. As their burning corpses arced into the surrounding mud, the dreadnought itself celebrated with a few interior explosions before crumpling down to the bog in defeat.

"Ta da!" said Dort. For an encore, he redecorated the far end of the chamber with his own smithereens. The same human whose energy-gun barrel had suggested which wall the drunken leader should decorate, now pointed his weapon at the surviving intruder.

Feeling discouraged, Blem's inspired impulse was to accidentally-on-purpose taste a bit of neurotoxin. Unbelievably, this action proved to be the miracle solution to all his problems.

As the molecules in his brain began to evolve at an unlikely pace, mere nano-seconds had passed before he realized that he could now understand human speech. Boldly addressing the grey-jumpsuit-clad, inferior being pointing the weapon, Blem demanded an immediate and unconditional surrender.

His ultimatum sounded like a hippopotamus with a three-pack-a-day habit coughing up an innertube.

Lieutenant West's retort was more smithereens.

The sound of his Commander finally collapsing to the floor charged the lieutenant with an adrenaline kick. There was still time to save her. But the Floabnian grubs swarming her bloody form presented a dilemma. He could not blast them without killing her as well. They would have to be removed by hand, and for this, he needed gloves.

"Hang in there, Commander Denza!" he cried, yanking open one of the drawers by the door.

WORLD WAR FOUR

Commander Denza heard a sharp gasp, a thump, and then no further noises from her copilot—only the ravenous, smacking mastications of her miniature Floabnian devourers muffling her own fading heartbeat. As her vision began to blur, she wondered idly whether it was because her ocular muscles had lost all control, or because tears had begun to seep from her eyes.

The Aftermath of the Pig Roast
Marlon Hayes

I can't even remember whose idea it was to have a pig roast. We're city guys and the only pig roasts we'd ever seen were in the movies or maybe a country music video. I think we were just trying to do something different than having a typical summer barbecue. At any rate, we did our research about roasting a pig, and everything took off from there.

The guys that I agreed to roast the pig with weren't even my friends, so to speak. I'd married into the friendship, as they were my brother-in-law's longtime buddies. When I'd first met them, I'd felt like the odd man out, but as time and various social interactions went by, I blended right in with this very diverse group of guys. Describing them by their job titles wouldn't do them justice, because they were all similar to me; multilayered, talented, and intelligent. Each of us had a designated assignment with the roasting of the pig, jobs which would be more meaningful than we'd ever bargained for.

My name is Scott, and I'm a professional trucker and a semi-professional chef. I had never roasted a pig before, but my theory was that it wasn't too much different from making rotisserie chicken. I would use pork sausage as filler for the pig, rub in seasonings, and I'd use my seven inch liquid injector to infuse even more flavour into our pig. I did my research and I was ready for my task.

My brother-in-law Rick was a suit and tie guy during the week, and a general handyman on the weekend. There wasn't much he couldn't fix, and he got pleasure from making things work the way they were supposed to. His task for the pig roast was to procure a large enough grill with a rotisserie press, and the fuel to cook it with. Wood and charcoal would be the fuels used to roast Wilbur the pig.

Fakih was a chameleon of sorts, the kind of guy who was impossible to place in any box. An anaesthesiologist, with the outward mild manner of someone used to dealing with patients. He's a personification of the phrase "Don't judge a book by the cover." Karate expert, survivalist, and a veteran who had been to see the elephant twice, he didn't talk about his combat experience, but we knew it had been rough.

The crew is rounded off by Johnny, a banker and mechanic, and Joe, a police detective and gadget guy. Joe gets excited by the latest inventions, buys them, then tinkers with them, modifying them to his specifications. In this world, a man has to have a lot in his personal toolbox to thrive and survive. Being skilled in different areas was a trait each of us shared.

At 4am on a Saturday morning in July, the five of us gathered at Johnny's to prepare our first roasted pig. It was 125 pounds, and the butcher had cut it open for us. He was placed upon the rotisserie press, where we tightened the screws and bolts to keep him in place. Rick fired up the grill, while Fakih shaved the pig, uttering endearments to Wilbur as his razor blade removed any remaining hairs. Then it was my turn. I rubbed salt on Wilbur's skin, added pork sausage and apples to his inner cavity, which Fakih then expertly sewed up, then I injected Wilbur with a mixture of pineapple juice and seasonings. By the time I was finished, Rick had the grill going low and slow. It took four of us to heft Wilbur into place. Once he started slowly rotating, we closed the oversized grill, because all we had left to do was wait eight hours or so until he was done. The lawn chairs and coolers came out, because even though it was early, it was five o'clock somewhere. As the sun peeked over the horizon, we toasted its arrival with whiskey, vodka, and beer.

 The wives and kids wouldn't arrive until the afternoon, which gave us plenty of time to enjoy the pleasure of talking freely with a group of men. We talked about sports, vacations, supermodels, cars, and eventually politics, which led to us attempting to out talk each other. We were forced to initiate 'the Conch Rule' so that everyone would get their chance to speak.

 A year ago, we went on a boys trip to the Caribbean, where we drank, laughed, and went charter fishing. Everybody caught at least one fish, except me. My line snagged nothing but a conch shell. There were plenty of jokes at my expense, but I had the shell cut into five pieces as a souvenir. I had the five equal pieces glazed, and then put on a rubber thong so that the shells could be worn as necklaces. I wear one, and I gave each of these guys one as a gift. One time we were trying to out talk each other when Johnny stood up and grasped his shell, yelling 'I have the conch!' in an ode to one of our favourite books, *Lord of the Flies*. Whomever held the conch had the floor to speak.

Our political views were similar, and we talked about the Russians, unemployment, the disenfranchised, and other current news. The liquor had been flowing for a couple of hours, and Wilbur was smelling really good. The sun was high in the sky, and we were feeling no pain on the ground. It had the makings of a beautiful day.

"Yesterday, I had no phone service," Fakih said. "I knew the bill was paid, so I immediately started thinking there'd been an invasion or attack, because when the apocalypse comes, communication is the first target of the enemy. It took me awhile to figure out that my phone was on airplane mode."

We laughed at him, but the thought of some kind of apocalyptic invasion spurred us onto a new topic; what to do when the apocalypse happens? I'm sure the thought has crossed the minds of many, but this would be my first time articulating my thoughts aloud.

"You gotta have an escape route," I began. "Getting away from the city is of paramount importance because there will be a glut of fugitives. I've studied maps and driven local access roads just to see if my route was feasible. It is. Within ten minutes, I can be out of the city."

The fellows nodded their heads in understanding, all of us taking sips from our respective cups, everyone formulating his own thoughts. Johnny stood up and grasped the conch around his neck.

"I have the conch," he began. "I feel funny telling you guys this, but I had a strange moment a couple of months ago at an estate sale the wife dragged me to. There was a van for sale, one of those extended jobs with no windows. The sign said 'Best Offer' so I asked if they'd take a grand for it. They agreed and I wrote the check. I drove it home, trying to figure out why the hell I had bought it. Maybe because it's in excellent condition, or maybe because I got it cheap. I've done some modifications since then. Come take a look at it."

We followed him to his four-car garage, where he opened up one of the overhead doors. Next to his wife's sports car, was the shiny white van he'd told us about. It was in great condition for the price, and it was definitely worth way more than a grand. Once we were all inside, he turned on the manual lights and closed the overhead door. He unlocked the van, and motioned us to step inside.

The modifications were obvious. The van had previously been used as a work vehicle, because that model of van came with two seats and plenty of cargo space. Johnny had added six seats, three across, back to back. He hadn't lost much cargo space. We watched as he slid a key into one of the side wall panels. The panel slid back, revealing at least ten guns mounted in the hidden space. We gawked at him, speechless for once.

"I've been collecting guns forever, you guys know that," he said. "I wanted to see if I could make this van a mobile battle station if need be. The other wall is the same, except there are rifles mounted there. I have ammo for each weapon at the bottom of the walls. I still have room for a small refrigerator, luggage, a generator, and almost anything else. I can't even explain why I did this."

"Add a CB radio and you're good to go if something ever happens," I said, thinking about communication failures.

"I bought a CB," Joe said in a soft voice. "I also studied how to pry open the below ground fuel tanks at gas stations. I now keep two crowbars and a twelve foot garden hose in my truck, just in case the unthinkable happens."

It appeared as if each of us had been scared enough of our 2am thoughts of Armageddon that we'd unconsciously started to act on them. Fakih had outfitted his vacation home in the Ozarks with weapons and canned goods, saying he had enough for two years of meals for twenty people. Upon hearing that, I outlined an escape route from the outskirts of Chicago to Fakih's place in the Ozarks. We returned to watch Wilbur oscillate, each of us sobered a bit by the way the conversation had turned.

The wives and children came later that afternoon, and the mood became festive once more, vanquishing our dark thoughts of earlier. Wilbur was removed from the grill, soft, tender, and well cooked. He was devoured on hamburger buns with barbecue sauce, and on tortillas with slaw and salsa. We feasted and drank until the moon was high in the sky, friends and family enjoying their first pig roast.

The wives gathered up the children and helped clean up, while the men moved the heavier stuff to cars and Johnny's garage. We stood in the garage looking at the van, the apocalyptic conversation of earlier having once again intruded upon our good time. My brother-in-law Rick broke the silence.

"We need a code phrase, innocuous to others. We also need CBs and ham radios in case of communication breakdowns," he said.

"Well, we have our plan of action, which will probably never happen," I said. "If it does happen, whoever has the first knowledge of the event has to broadcast it to the others. Channel 28 on the CB. The phrase that will be our call to escape is "The ministry has fallen, this is not a drill."

"Guess we'd better install CBs in our vehicles," Johnny said.

We hugged and said our goodbyes, praying that we would never have to utter those words...

* * *

"The ministry has fallen. This is not a drill. I repeat, the ministry has fallen, this is not a drill."

Those words shocked me out of my semi-conscious state of sleep, and I shook my head in an attempt to shake off sleep. The words were repeated again on the CB in my man cave, and I went into action. I ran upstairs, shouting "The ministry has fallen!" I had worked on this code phrase with my family—we even ran practice drills—and within seven minutes, we were all seated in my Suburban, ready to flee from an unknown occurrence. My wife Lynn had our important paperwork, documents and pictures, inside of a small steel box. Our kids, Mason and Selma, had their backpacks and their laptops, and as I drove rapidly through the early morning streets, they were researching online to see if they could find any information as to what the unknown calamity had been.

"Dad, I'm reading reports that Washington D.C. is off the grid, as is New York," Mason said. "Ditto for the national capitals around the world. The satellites are showing fire and smoke, but no one knows the cause."

"Dear God," Lynn said. "All those families gone."

"Was it the Russians or Chinese? Selma asked. "They always seem to be mentioned in these kinds of scenarios.

"No, I don't think it's them," Mason said. "Moscow is gone too."

We drove in silence then, my only goal being to get us to our destination in the Ozarks. The Suburban could run almost 700 miles without refuelling, which was enough to get us to our destination. I wondered if the others were on the move?

"En route." My brother-in-law's voice came through the CB, as if my thought had been transmitted telepathically.

"Ditto," was the only word uttered in the next three replies, as Johnny, Joe, and Fakih checked in.

We drove without talking, listening to music on Selma's iPod. I had attempted to listen to the radio for news, but they had no new information to share. No one knew what had happened.

"There have been reports of large dark clouds in the sky Dad," Mason said, still looking at his laptop. "Normally, that wouldn't mean much, except these clouds are moving west, going against weather patterns. There's no rain falling from these masses, which are allegedly moving about sixty miles an hour. They say one is slowing down as it approaches Chicago."

I glanced in my rearview mirror, as if I would be able to see the city we'd left a few hours before. I'd driven state roads and county roads, eschewing the Interstates per my escape plan. We were at least 300 miles from Chicago, and I'd given St. Louis a wide berth, instead cutting through Iowa.

"There's a cloud directly over Chicago now, Dad, as well as Los Angeles, Atlanta, Dallas, and Houston. In Europe, there are now clouds over secondary cities. Reports from Australia echo the same thing, dark clouds over Perth and Brisbane. Those clouds, whatever they are, must be responsible for the current situation around the world," Mason said. "Wait, someone is showing a live video from downtown Chicago."

Mason passed his laptop to Lynn, who held it up so we could all see. There was someone filming live, the camera of their phone pointing at a huge dark mass above the city. Suddenly, the cloud began sparking, and it seemed as if a purple light came out of it. Then the film went dark. So too Chicago.

The grim film did tell me one thing though; those clouds were not of this world.

We drove in stunned silence, each of us dealing with our own thoughts and realizations. If all of the major cities were gone, was this still the United States? Who was in charge? Was money still worth anything? Who was responsible for this day's catastrophes? How could we fight something when we didn't know who or what we were fighting?

"It's aliens, Dad," Selma said, breaking the silence. "They're somehow using the clouds as cover. Maybe they're using advanced technology or something."

"Let's just get to our destination, then we'll figure all of this out," Lynn said, maybe in an effort to bolster our spirits. "Once we are settled, we'll be a bit more able to digest this stuff."

There was now a lot more traffic, even on these backroads. I could only imagine how cluttered the Interstates must be, if people had gotten out in time. Urban centres seemed to be the target, and I let my mind wander to the people we'd left behind: cousins, co-workers, and neighbours, all of whom were no longer in existence. I couldn't help the tears rolling down my face, nor could I help the ball of anger that was growing within me. No one deserved the fate which had come from the sky.

I followed the directions from memory. I had figured this route out myself, in order to avoid population clusters and big highways. Mason showed a live video of Interstate 57, and it was completely congested and clogged by thousands of new refugees who had never imagined something like this could happen.

"Oh no! Dad, there's a cloud descending by I-57," Mason said. He handed his laptop to my wife, and Lynn held it up so we all could see. I slowed the Suburban because my full attention was not on the road. I came almost to a full stop as we watched the monitor.

No one has ever seen a cloud land on the ground. Fog and mist, yes, but not a whole damned cloud. The fog of the cloud dissipated, allowing us to see what had been hidden. It was what I guess I expected a spaceship to look like. About half the size of a football field, maybe fifty feet tall, and the exterior was black and silver. The Oakland Raiders insignia came to mind for some reason as we watched the scene unfolding.

The citizens stuck in the traffic, some of whom were standing outside, began bringing out weapons. There were mostly automatic guns and rifles, but we did see a couple of guys with bows and arrows. The doors to the ship opened and at least thirty beings descended the ramp rapidly and in formation. These beings were between four and five feet tall, dressed in silver jumpsuits and helmets. They fanned out, and that's when the good old citizens of America showed why the Second Amendment is so important.

They unleashed a fusillade of shots; some guy even had a tripod with a machine gun firing off shots. The bullets bounced harmlessly off of the aliens, who brought up weapons of their own, which resembled huge flash lights. We didn't hear a command, but the aliens unleashed their weapons upon the citizens stuck on I-57. Flashes of purple light were emitted from the flashlight type guns and the people who hadn't run were vaporized, leaving only their shoes behind. Lynn and Selma began to cry, but Mason and I kept our eyes glued to the screen.

Americans are brave, even when faced with sure destruction. The men who'd brought bows and arrows were able to get a few arrows off before they were vaporized. Two of the arrows hit the spacemen, puncturing the suits and causing the two little aliens to collapse, orange fluid oozing through the holes in the suit. They were gathered up by their comrades and rushed back onto their ship, leaving survivors to witness their departure, including the brave soul who'd been filming. Interesting.

The ladies cried until they were exhausted, and there were no words of reassurance for me to offer. Mason closed his laptop softly and laid his head against the window. I concentrated on driving, trying my best to not think about the empty shoes left on the side of I-57.

We pulled into the clearing in front of Fakih's cabin, seven hours after we'd fled home. I guess our new status was that of refugees, and the future was a shadowy thing, promised to none of us. Millions of people, maybe even billions, had been vaporised in the last ten hours, and the little space fucks weren't through yet. I prayed that the men and women of the armed services were ready for the test, those who hadn't been vaporised, that is.

From the four vehicles parked in the yard, I could see we were the last ones to arrive. The other families rushed out to greet us. The wives hugged and cried, and the men, which now included Mason and three of the surrogate nephews, gathered away from the women. We had all made it, thanks to a random conversation at a friendly pig roast.

We discussed the stuff we'd seen, as far as the destruction of the cities, and the slaughter of citizens. This invasion had been different from any alien invasion we'd ever imagined. There had been no communication that we knew of, no warning of any kind. Just stealthy spaceships unleashing purple rays on an unsuspecting world. Was the government somewhere safe or underground? We didn't know, because nothing was being broadcast over the radio or Internet. Were there other enclaves such as ours around the country, where maybe some people were gathered in groups? We hoped so. The theory we shared was that the aliens had started with the big cities, and were now moving towards secondary cities. Eventually, the aliens would start looking to destroy smaller communities. We could ask ourselves "why" over and over again, but the simple truth is they probably just wanted our space. When a house or apartment is wanted by someone, the vermin have to be cleared out. We were the vermin.

We also talked about the aliens who'd been killed by bows and arrows, and how the shoes had been the only remnants of the people vaporized. Mason mentioned something we'd overlooked, the fact that even though cars and trucks had been vaporized, the tires remained.

"Maybe their weapons don't work on rubber," I said. "If so, then we have a chance."

"I think there's always a chance for survival," Fakih said. "That they were able to be killed by arrows speaks volumes. Wouldn't spears work too? I guess it's safe to say that tomorrow, all of us will be learning how to make arrows and spears, and working on our archery."

*   *   *

Two months later, we are still here. We've been in contact with others via the CB, and even though the cities and governments are gone, we're still here, trying to survive. Rubber suits, bows, arrows, spears, constant lookouts, and the knowledge that at some point, they were going to come looking for us, and groups like ours. An underground storm cellar has been deepened and we're trying to figure out how to survive underground if need be. We'll see.

Joe shot a wild boar yesterday with an arrow. Today, we're going to have a pig roast, and maybe we'll forget our reality for a while. Maybe...

WORLD WAR FOUR

One Way Trip
R.L.M. Cooper

Well, the bastards finally did it. They blew the planet to hell and back and poisoned everything. I always thought we human beings would bring about our own destruction, but I hadn't thought we would take the whole planet with us. Somehow, I had always reasoned, the planet would survive without us fucking everything up. But I was wrong.

What I never could figure out, though, was why. It just didn't make sense. I mean, it's not like we didn't know what would happen. We had known it all along. But it still didn't stop us. Greed and hate seemed to be the driving force behind it all. Greed mostly. The greedy planted seeds of distrust among the masses, and the distrust grew into hate. Hate grew into wars. First small ones. Then bigger and bigger until, finally, there was no stopping it. What I could never figure was what, exactly, the greedy were going to do once they had it all and everyone else was either killed off or enslaved. I guess they never figured it out either, because in the end their water and air was just as toxic as everyone else's and they were dying alongside those whose lives they had considered expendable.

The government, what was left of it, finally saw the writing on the wall and decided if humankind was going to survive it would have to be somewhere besides the earth that was rapidly dying. That's how I survived to tell what happened.

There were six of us. We'd travelled for almost seven light years. Two hundred and thirty-five trillion earth miles. Of course, most of the time we were in stasis. We were headed for the Trappist-1 group in the Aquarius system hoping to find one of the seven planets there inhabitable. Even though the planets in the group are really close to each other—close enough to actually look up into the sky and see geological features on the nearest to the one on which you might happen to be standing—their orbits were considered stable due to the weak pull of their cool and rather dim sun when compared to the sun we had left behind.

We were all volunteers, of course. Those left behind falsely believed they would somehow survive it all; that earth would survive it all and that the six of us were going to a certain death.

No one had ever attempted anything like it before and, at only one-quarter light speed, it was going to take about a hundred and sixty years to make the trip. Everyone we had ever known in our lives would be dead and gone before we ever arrived. And, assuming we had a way to get back, which we didn't, it was almost assured the planet would be dead by the time we had made it. That had been guaranteed with the warring political situation and the pollution-choked oceans that had already been dying for over a hundred years. So we knew it was a one-way trip from the get go and we didn't know if we would survive or not. But we were convinced we would not survive if we stayed.

We were paired up according to our strengths and weaknesses, the idea being that our offspring, when the time came, would stand the best chance of surviving in order to start a new human civilization. We had a good laugh about that, especially when our heads were shaved to make it easier to keep ourselves clean until we all went into stasis. Bennett complained that now his assigned partner, Katie, wasn't attractive enough to mate with and, at that, she had kicked him solidly in the knee sending him howling and limping down the medical centre hallway.

It was to be Bennett and Katie, Colin and Jessica, Camille and myself, Paul Talbot. However, we all dropped our last names. All except Bennett. He preferred Bennett to Reginald and for sure we weren't going to have to worry about renewing driver's licenses or filing income taxes where we were going so we figured we only needed one name and we each picked the one we liked.

We were a mixed crew, to be sure. Most bases were covered, if that's even possible with only six people. Bennett was a scientist to the core and Katie was a top-notch mathematician and computer whiz. Colin's specialty was geophysics and agriculture and Jessie was our medical doctor. My intended partner, Camille, a biologist and I, a chemical engineer with experience in construction, rounded out the group.

Leaving was hard. Even though none of us were married or had children, our parents were somewhere along the continuum from angry to distraught to devastated just knowing we had chosen to go and they would never see us again. Jessica was the only one of us spared that agony since she had faced hers some years earlier when her parents died on a sinking ferry between Vancouver Island and Washington State.

While we had no offspring to leave behind, we did have pets and that's where some of us drew the line. There was no way I was leaving my dog, Beau, behind. What kind of life would it be without a dog or a cat, anyway, I argued. I figured if they could manage the handling of people shit, they could just as easily figure out how to handle dog shit. Besides, he would be in stasis most of the way along with the rest of us. Camille felt the same way about her cats, Romeo and Juliet. All we needed was a female dog to complete the "sets" and so we rescued a friendly little white thing with black spots and introduced her to Beau. They seemed to like each other just fine so we named her Trixi and, at that point, we were good to go.

We hugged and cried with our parents. Then hugged and cried some more. Finally we were strapped in, the countdown counted down, and we rumbled and roared out of the earth's atmosphere for the first and last time in our lives.

We avoided going into stasis while we monitored our health, the health of the animals, the health of the ship, and anything else we could think of, and communicated it all back to Houston. This lasted only a short while before we finally lost communication with the guys back on earth. We stayed awake for a while anyway and sent messages each day, but response times had gotten longer and longer and more and more faded until, at last, we couldn't hear anything.

That's when the finality of what we had done—what we were doing—finally hit us. You would think six people in that situation would draw closer to each other, but we didn't. Each of us retreated into our own space. We were quiet. I wouldn't exactly say we were depressed but it was close, that's for damned sure. Maybe it was closer to fear than depression, but no one would say it out loud.

When Katie bit Colin's head off over something as inconsequential as bumping into her and causing a broken fingernail, we decided it was time. We probably weren't going to hear from Houston again, either because of the distance or because no one was left down there able to transmit, so one-by-one we got into the sleep modules. Bennett went first, then Colin followed by Camille. I hung back to make sure the animals were all okay while Katie programmed the wake-up call for when we got to the Aquarius system. Beau and Trixi were going to sleep with me because I'm not the biggest guy in the world and there was room on each side down by my legs. Romeo and Juliet were placed at the foot of Jessica's module because she was much smaller than Camille. Then Katie went in and I followed right after her. The last thing I saw was Jessica, our M.D., checking everyone's vitals before getting into her own module with the cats at her feet.

A hundred and sixty earth years later, Katie's expert programming pinged the modules to life and, as we emerged, we yawned, stretched, and made lame jokes about how we didn't really feel our age or look a day over a hundred and fifty. Then we got quiet when we realized something had gone wrong with Bennett's and Camille's modules. Worse, on checking we found the error had happened only seventeen years into the flight which meant they had been dead for a hundred and forty-three years. That sobered us up like nothing had before. We'd lost our scientist and our biologist—one-third of our number—and now there were only four of us to face whatever lay ahead.

When we reached the Trappist-1 group we took a good look at the three planets that fell within the Goldilocks Zone—that narrow space on the continuum that could be habitable for life and, we hoped, would contain sufficient levels of oxygen and liquid water. Of the three, we settled on the one that appeared most earth-like. The plan was to find a level landing area and then test for everything within our power before ever setting foot on the actual planet. That was the plan.

But this ain't Hollywood where the best-laid plans always work out. What appeared to be level, wasn't, and the ship toppled. Actually, 'crashed hard' would be a better description. We weren't worried about getting back home, as I said earlier. But our instruments were damaged and we were horrified to realise we were going to be unable to measure the actual levels of oxygen and carbon dioxide. We knew they were there, but we didn't know if the levels were high enough to sustain life. Maybe Katie could have fixed the instruments, but she'd died in the crash.

Now we were down to half our number: Colin, Jessica, and myself. And we were all three scared shitless.

We straightened up as much of the mess as we could and took an inventory of our stores. We had plenty of food for ourselves and for the animals, but that information wasn't altogether comforting. We knew it would only last so long and we all sat down and looked at each other, silently asking the question, 'Now what?'

We talked and talked. We speculated on how we could repair the instruments. But that was a no-go. It was a task beyond the capabilities of any of us three, and with Katie gone, it was hopeless. We had food. But the question was still there, hanging in the air like something fetid. 'What then?'

We decided we were not going the way of the Donner party. Besides, what would we gain from that? A few days or weeks longer before the inevitable? And what would it do to us psychologically if we did survive? I declared adamantly that there was no way I could live with that. The other two agreed. We knew what we had to do. Either now or later. We really had no choice.

So now here we are. Colin loaded Romeo and Juliet into their respective carriers and I put Beau and Trixi on leashes and handed them over to Jessica. She knelt down and petted them and spoke soothing words. Her voice trembled. I pretended not to notice. Colin grabbed a backpack with a few essentials as though we're all going on a weekend hike in the Appalachians. We hugged each other tight, too emotional—or scared—to speak.

Colin has a carrier full of cat in each hand and we're standing here looking at each other as though it might be our last time ever. And it just might. I leaned over and kissed Jessica on the forehead then took a deep breath.

"Ready?"

Colin and Jessie, looking rather stoic, nodded.

I nodded back.

We stood side by side, the three of us and our four trusting animals, facing the hatch.

I swallowed hard, closed my eyes, and engaged the release.

Gagarin's Hammer
Vince Carpini

In 1978, Vladimir Remek became the first Czechoslovak in space. One hundred and twenty one years later and two hundred and fifty thousand kilometres from Earth, the blocky Soviet warship bearing his name split in two and coughed a cloud of glittering debris and flailing bodies into what was diplomatically termed 'Contested Space.'

The delta shaped United States Starship *New Mexico* traversed its railguns towards the incoming Soviet reinforcements as the *Potomac* and *Cumberland* glided into position alongside it.

Captain Aaron Dole watched the tactical display on his command seat where a swarm of Soviet assault shuttles fanned towards *New Mexico*. He flipped a switch on his console to Ship-Wide Address.

"Set the table, boys and girls. We got company." He stood, pulled a shotgun from behind the seat, and thumbed a handful of red white and blue shells into the magazine. The grim faced bridge crew readied their sidearms and a four man security detail stepped off the lift and took up positions around the bridge.

The ship shuddered as Russian shuttles jammed their armoured noses against *New Mexico*'s hull. There was a rain-like patter of clicks as selectors were set to Fire.

With a peal of thunder, a door sized slice of bulkhead blew inward, split Lieutenant Hobson like cordwood, and decapitated one of the security men. There was hiss as the environmental and gravity systems adjusted to the sudden pressure change. An instant later, a Spetsnaz boarding party charged onto the bridge through curling smoke and pelting lead, their black armour turning aside bullets like tanks through a crowd of protesters.

One of the attackers twitched and fell, defeated by the sheer volume of fire, but his comrades spread out and returned fire with stubby rifles that clattered like rattlesnakes, killing a handful of officers and the rest of the security detail in seconds. The defenders wavered and their fire slackened.

"Hold your ground!" Captain Dole roared, and his shotgun barked. A Russian crashed to the deck with blood spurting from behind his shattered trauma plate. Dole swung the gun around, slamming the foregrip back and forth, and caught a second Spetsnaz in the neck. Inspired by their Captain, the other Americans renewed their defence and managed to bring another Soviet down in a hail of fire.

We might pull this off, Dole thought.

He reached into his pocket for more shells and gasped as a sudden, sharp blow to his ribs made his fingers go numb. He looked down and saw a crimson stain spreading across his shirt, a ragged, black edged hole at its centre. His vision swam and the deck rushed up to meet him as the rattle of Russian guns punctuated the end of American lives.

Four Spetsnaz stood among the dead scattered across *New Mexico*'s bridge, their helmets filtering the tang of blood and cordite down to a waft of charcoal. One of them secured his fallen comrades while another accessed a console and tracked the progress of boarding parties elsewhere on the ship through the internal camera feeds. The last two Russians moved to guard the elevator. One of them stood in front of the door with the other a few paces back. No sooner had they set up than the lift sighed and an automated voice announced, "Bridge. Authorized Personnel Only."

The elevator door split into a vertical crack through which lanced a pole of burnished gold draped in the stars and stripes. Defying both the odds and the Soviet Union's armourers, the Aquila atop the pole rammed through the lead Spetsnaz's visor and out the back of his helmet, the scowling bald eagle emerging from his skull on wings stained with blood and brains.

Colonel Jack Bunker grunted with All American might and swung two hundred and fifty pounds of impaled commando like a mace of meat and metal, battering the second Spetsnaz to the floor and trapping him under the body of his comrade. Jack released the flagpole, grabbed the pinned Russian's helmet and torqued his head savagely around, breaking the Commie's neck with a crack like a homerun echoing across Wrigley Field. With hawk like speed, Jack scooped up one of the dead men's rifles and dove for cover as the other two Spetsnaz brought their weapons to bear.

The sandy haired American rolled out from behind a bank of computers and fired a short burst up between the nearest Soviet's utility belt and his chest plate. The commando clutched at his guts and doubled over. Jack leaped up and sprang off the dying Russian's back towards the last Spetsnaz whose spray of gunfire went wide. Jack bore his foe to the ground, jammed the barrel of his gun under the black helmet and fired.

Wiping his enemies' blood from his tanned, ageless brow, Jack retrieved the flagpole and stood with the gory banner in one calloused hand and the smoking rifle in the other. He heard a shuddering gasp from the middle of the bridge and found Captain Dole bleeding out, surrounded by his slaughtered crew.

"Aaron, it's Jack," he said, kneeling beside the captain.

"What took you so long?" Dole wheezed.

"I had to kill some rats on the way," Jack replied. "Your ship is lousy with Communists, Aaron."

Dole coughed and twisted his head to look at the officers who had died defending his ship. "They killed my kids, Jack. All these good kids. They killed them."

Jack grasped his hand. "They honoured their oaths, Aaron. You can be proud."

Dole gasped quietly and was still. Jack gently closed his friend's eyes.

The lift opened behind him.

Jack stood to attention and solemnly saluted Dole, tightening his grip on the blood slick flagpole in his hands, the sixty one stars splattered with communist viscera. Then he turned to face the team of Spetsnaz that had entered the bridge. One of them stepped forward and passed his gaze over his dead comrades.

"You killed my men," he said flatly through his helmet.

Jack nodded. "Better dead than red."

"Who are you?"

"A real, live nephew of Uncle Sam, born on the Fourth of July," Jack said.

"Colonel Jack Bunker, I presume."

"That's what your mother called me."

The Russian, nonplussed, said, "You will come with us."

"Think again, borscht-for-brains." Jack lunged and swung the flag two handed into the Commie's head, sending him insensate to the deck. Jack sidestepped and crushed another Russian's codpiece with a savage kick, sending the man to his knees, then drove the Star Spangled Banner into the narrow space between the Soviet's plated collar and the back of his helmet. It punched through the man's spine and came to a crunching stop in his abdomen. The man croaked and fell over, the flag soaking in the blood that pumped up between his shoulders. Two other Spetsnaz tackled Jack and held him down while their leader regained his feet and pointed his sidearm at the American.

"Do it you red whoreson," Jack snarled, wrestling against his captors on the floor. "Send me to hell so I can kill your friends all over again."

The Russian raised his boot and brought it down on Jack's face.

*   *   *

Jack awoke on a smooth metal floor. He was in a cell, of course. His probing fingers found a heel shaped bruise on his throbbing forehead, and his jacket, belt, and shoes were gone, leaving him in a dark t-shirt, bloodstained pants, and socks. The Russians had not bothered to put him on the bed bolted to the wall. As Jack stood up, the windowless door slid open to admit two people.

The first was a powerfully built Red in a plain uniform. He was in his thirties, clean shaven with a steely glint in his dark eyes. Jack recognised the bearing of calm, lethal confidence of the Spetsnaz leader from the *New Mexico*. The men regarded each other with contempt.

A Soviet General entered next, her uniform detailed to parade ground readiness. Medals gleamed on her chest, among them an Impeccable Service Badge, seven Wound Stripes, and the golden trefoil of a Hero of Cosmonautics. Her hair was silver, peppered with strands of black and cut in a short, severe style. The left side of her face was a mask of twisted, leathery flesh around an artificial eye that clicked and whirred like an old fashioned camera. Her right hand rested on a polished belt buckle and her left hand—a skeletal titanium appendage stamped with the hammer and sickle—hung at her side.

General Oksana Kirilevna Baikonova might have smirked, but her mangled lip curled from her teeth into a snarl. "Welcome to Red Moon Base, Colonel Bunker. Last time we met, you were captain, *da*?"

"The last time we met, you died," Jack said.

"Not so much, I think. You should have finished job."

"I didn't think it was necessary, given the size of the explosion," Jack said. "Why am I still alive?"

Baikonova's prosthetic eye spun and clicked. "We learned you were aboard *New Mexico* and drew Captain Dole into battle." She nodded to the soldier beside her. "When engagement began, I sent Captain Tabakov to capture you."

"Why?" Jack repeated.

"Revenge."

She stepped out of the cell and beckoned with her metal hand. A brutish Commie with a rifle over his shoulder came in and handcuffed Jack. Jack was marched into the harsh institutional lighting of the corridor, the Russians' boots thudding on the metal floor as they followed Baikonova.

"You are first American to walk beneath surface of *Luna*," Baikonova said in the tone of an insolent tour guide. "Your people won race to reach moon, but we won war to control it."

Jack said nothing. The Soviet victory in the Lunar War had been the cornerstone of their propaganda for more than a decade.

He silently recited the first lines of the Declaration of Independence to steel his spirit.

Baikonova made a gesture that took in the whole facility. "Three hundred permanent staff. Two launch bays. Earth-normal gravity," she boasted. "See what is possible through glorious labour of proletariat, working toward better future. Socialist future."

Jack rolled his eyes. "Your 'proletariat' are brainwashed and enslaved."

"No slaves here," Baikonova said, shaking her head. "Undesirables. Rehabilitation through labour."

"You let dissidents build your moon base? Smart."

"Return to society is strong motivator. When that fails, we have nerve staple."

"Reagan's Ghost!" Jack swore. "That's a war crime!"

Baikonova waved her prosthetic hand dismissively. "Small cost for greater good." She rounded and jabbed a titanium finger at him. "Where is outrage for great crimes of capitalism, which makes willing slaves of millions?"

Jack scoffed. "Remember the last time you tried proselytizing to me and I blew your red ass straight to hell? Good times."

"We will see who has 'good time' today, Colonel Bunker," she replied with another ghastly smirk.

They continued into a section which had the distinct combination of stricture and tension common to restricted areas.

Baikonova glided through a security door with Jack and the guards in tow.

The room they entered was a ten metre circle crowded with technicians and stuffed with flickering monitors, glowing displays and flashing consoles. It was like a miniature version of Launch Control at Houston or Edmonton.

A tall leaded observation window dominated three quarters of the control room, and the view gave Jack pause. He was looking out at a vast, empty space enclosed on all sides by machined rock—a hollow dug beneath the moon's surface. Jutting from one wall was an immense superstructure whose every strut was the size of a locomotive, supporting the biggest rocket Jack had ever seen.

"What the hell is this?" he demanded. "What are you doing?"

"I am going to throw a half billion tonne rock at America," Baikonova replied.

"You've spent too long in the bread lines."

Baikonova flashed him the dreadful smile again. "We are close to lunar surface. At my command, controlled demolition will carve out two kilometres of solid stone." She pointed at the monstrous metal structure outside the window. "Then nuclear thruster will accelerate it towards Earth at one hundred forty thousand kilometres per hour. We call it *Molot Gagarina*: Gagarin's Hammer."

"Lincoln's Wound," Jack breathed.

"*Molot* will strike Atlantic Ocean fifty kilometres from United States," Baikonova continued in a tone of clinical fervour. "Six minutes later, two hundred metre tsunami will deluge your eastern seaboard. Three hundred million will die. Seven hours after, forty metre waves will smash your European allies."

Jack's face flushed with anger. "The Treaty forbids weapons of mass destruction!"

"Treaty is just words," Baikonova spat. "We abandoned nuclear weapons, traded mutual destruction for, how you say, quagmire. *Molot Gagarina* will strike first blow in Final War."

"The Space Force will destroy your rock before it gets to Earth."

"Unlikely," Baikonova said breezily. "They will be distracted by surprise attack launched on my signal. We will finish America while it is wounded and at last unite all peoples under Socialist dominion," she declared, eyes shining with fanaticism.

"You're insane," Jack said.

"No one will care."

Jack pursed his lips. "When?"

"Right now," Baikonova said, and cackled when Jack looked at her sharply. "Do you think I lock you back up? *Nyet*, I learn my lesson at Nausta. You will watch *Molot Gagarina* launch and then I will shoot you." She patted the immaculately maintained Makarov at her hip; her great-great-grandfather had carried it in Afghanistan. Ignoring Jack's hateful glare, she joined a huddle of expectant technicians and gave an order. "Activate reactor," she said, savouring each word.

Jack felt a bone-deep hum from feet to skull and the control room trembled. Outside the observation window, the colossal thruster rumbled and vented steam as the nuclear reactor powered up. Jack guessed it needed to reach full power before the controlled demolition blasted the Hammer free. He had to act now.

He raised his cuffed hands in front of him and spoke in a calm, clear voice. "I pledge allegiance to the Flag of the United States of America, and to the Republic for which it stands." Tabakov elbowed him.

"One Nation under God," Jack continued, clenching his fists and pulling at his restraints, muscles bulging on his arms. "Indivisible." The handcuff links snapped. "With liberty and justice for all!" Jack threw a blurring punch that crushed Tabakov's windpipe like a potato chip. He yanked the pistol from Tabakov's holster, turned and jammed the gun into the second soldier's mouth. The Soviet gagged first on cold metal and then hot lead, his unfired rifle falling into Jack's hand as he snapped backwards. Tabakov fell, clutching at his throat and gasping like a landed fish.

Jack faced the control room with a gun in each hand. Baikonova cursed and dove behind a bank of computers as the technicians cried out in alarm.

"God bless America, you commie bastards," Jack said and started shooting. Men and women fell under blossoming halos of blood.

Baikanova stood and returned fire, the Makarov kicking in her right hand. Jack dropped his spent pistol, ducked behind a stack of servers and fired back with the rifle, aiming at Baikonova's nose. Her metal hand swept up and deflected the bullet away with a *kapwing* straight out of a Spaghetti Western. Jack gaped just long enough for Baikonova to duck back into cover. She scuttled sideways, peeked out, saw someone dashing for the door, and fired without hesitation. One of her technicians fell over with a surprised look on his face and two holes in his head.

The Makarov's slide locked open; she was out of ammunition. Baikonova swore as Jack stepped out of cover with the rifle at his shoulder. He was splattered with blood, very little of it his own.

"It's iron curtains for you, Baikonova."

Her metal eye clicked. "Not yet," she said, and raised her metal fist. It streaked from her arm like a fastball towards Jack's face. He twisted at the last instant and the fist swept by so close that its tiny jets singed his stubble before jamming into the wall. Jack spat and glared at Baikonova, breathing heavily.

"Socialism will win," she said, her eyes pools of absolute certainty. "The revolution will go on."

"Quit Stalin and die," he growled and fired.

Several rounds sparked off Baikonova's prosthetic arm as she raised it defensively, but the final bullet split her Hero of Cosmonautics medal in half and tumbled through her heart. She fell against the observation window and slid to the floor, where she shuddered and breathed her last.

There was no time to celebrate; Gagarin's Hammer was tearing itself apart. The demolition charges hadn't detonated, yet the gigantic nuclear thruster continued heaving impotently against the moon's unyielding hide. The sympathetic thrumming of the control room was growing stronger by the moment and judging by the amount of red flashing across the monitors, the thruster was becoming unstable. Its overheating funnel wept thick streams of black liquid metal, and several cowlings, each the size of a swimming pool, peeled off and fluttered away like scorched flower petals. Jack yanked the control room door open and stepped into the hallway.

Alarms blared and an automated voice droned instructions that went unheeded by the panicked base staff. Jack sprinted down the corridors, ignored by all except an ambitious security guard, whom Jack relieved of both his sidearm and his life.

The lights flickered and the entire facility seemed to shift as the gravity system stuttered. Jack adopted a loping gait and sure-footedly passed haplessly tottering Russians. He would have laughed at these bumbling commies being crushed by their own hammer, were it not looming over him as well. He grabbed a stumbling scientist and shoved him against the wall. "Where are the ships?" he demanded. The terrified pencil neck babbled in Russian. Jack shook him roughly and tried again.

"Shipsky?" he asked and snaked a hand in front of his face, making zooming sounds. "Soyuz?" At this, the scientist's eyes lit up and he nodded vigorously, pointing down the corridor. Jack pushed the man aside and bounded away.

* * *

Jack aimed the Soyuz at Contested Space and accelerated away from Red Moon Base. The little ship's radiation sensor squawked as immense fissures appeared along a stretch of the lunar surface, glowing with a harsh white light like a small sun rising behind him. The ship bucked as a shockwave overtook it, and the scanner showed a new crater glowing raggedly on the moon, as if God Himself had taken a bite out of it. Arcing out into space from the crater was a vast scintillating cloud: millions of tons of rock, pulverized when the gigantic nuclear reactor overloaded and exploded. Dozens of Russian ships stationed nearby scattered like frightened birds.

"That's for you, Aaron." Jack said quietly.

The cloud of shifting, tumbling stone and dust was bearing down on him, and the radiation warning shrieked louder. Jack pushed the engines harder and tried to ignore the itchy heat he felt already spreading across his body. He dialled the radio into a little used channel and sent a message: *I'm a Yankee-Doodle dandy. A Yankee-Doodle do-or-die.*

Fighting rising nausea, he settled back in his seat and closed his eyes.

*   *   *

Jack awoke propped up in a recovery bed surrounded by softly beeping monitors. IVs dripped EX-RAD into both his arms, which explained the antiseptic taste in his mouth. Turning his head with difficulty, he saw a small shaving mirror sitting on a side table. His reflection looked back at him, skin drawn around yellowed and bloodshot eyes. Etched into the mirror were the words, MADE IN AMERICA.

A commotion drew his attention and Admiral James Toomey strode into view, towering over a gaggle of adjutants. He strode towards Jack, sucking on his pipe and ignoring the attending physician's objections.

"There he is," the Admiral said jovially from the foot of the bed.

Jack saluted with visible effort. Toomey smiled broadly and returned the gesture. "Welcome aboard the *California*, Colonel."

"Thank you, sir."

"Shame about Dole," the Admiral went on, puffing out a wisp of smoke. "I understand he really gave 'em hell.

"Yes, sir."

"We torpedoed the *New Mexico* before the Reds could tow her away."

Jack nodded.

Toomey stared at him. "Christ on a cracker. You look like a dog's breakfast, Jack."

"And you a horse's ass. Sir." Jack replied. Someone gasped.

"Damn right." Toomey laughed. "How do you feel?"

"Ready to support and defend the Constitution against all enemies, foreign and domestic," Jack replied.

"Well, blasting the Commies off the moon surely qualifies. I'd like to hear all about it." Toomey sat on the edge of the bed and took two crystal tumblers from an aide who was carrying a tall, dark bottle. "Whiskey?"

Jack smiled. "I thought you'd never ask."

Salvage
G Dean Manuel

The derelict dominated the view screen of the *Marked Man*, floating dead with three large holes in its hull.

"Bring her in easy, soft as you please," said Captain Hellnich. He was a smaller man, not quite 5'5", with wan and pale flesh. A livid scar shot down the right side of his face, bisecting his eye, glaring in contrast to his skin. He wore a heavy overcoat and had a huge repeater belted at his side, a Macro Arms Viper.

Tense moments passed as Timmons brought the *Marked Man* alongside the derelict. Both held their breaths, waiting for some trap to spring. After a few moments they breathed normally.

"Capt'n, what in the Old World Hell happened here? Those holes weren't caused by weapons fire. No sign of missiles. In fact, she looks like she hasn't seen combat for quite a spell. If'n I had to guess, that carbon scoring is months, maybe years old." The ship's pilot tapped his fingers nervously on the console. He was a hawkish man, his face could cut glass.

"I'm a mite curious myself and I aim to satiate myself of that curiosity, Timmons. Tell Marcus and Briggs to meet me in the cargo hold. We're going to take a little walk." The Captain clapped Timmons on the back.

The pilot turned to the communications board and flipped the switch for the shipwide array. "Marcus, Briggs, Capt'n wants you to meet him in the cargo hold, locked and loaded." Timmons turned the intercom off and said to the Captain, "Do you know what that ship is called? The *Sweet Egress.* It's a sign, Capt'n."

Hellnich chuckled and said, "Now don't you go worrying. I'll bring him back in one piece."

"Who's worried?" Timmons said, "I'm not worried. I mean, you are just planning to take my husband into an Alliance vessel floating derelict outside of any normally travelled spaceways. Oh, and the damned ship's name means to leave, to escape! I mean, what could go wrong?"

"My thoughts exactly. We got nothing to worry about." The captain forced a smile.

"Except for three big, honking holes in the side of the damn thing!"

"There is that." Hellnich made a clicking sound in the back of his throat. His face got serious. "Timmons, we ain't like to see another score like this any time soon. That's an Alliance cruiser out there! Just sitting there, pretty as you please. If even the shield array is salvageable, we'll be living the hog life for a year."

"I know." Timmons saw the captain's look. "*I know.* Doesn't mean I have to like it or not whine a bit."

"You know the rules." Hellnich smirked.

"Yes, sir! Whining off the comms and pillow talk in the bedroom." Timmons gave a mock salute.

"Last time you and Marcus started up, you almost made Briggs blush and that's damn near impossible. She's like a stone." Hellnich's smile returned to its customary place.

He waved his hand in a dismissive gesture. "Go, shoo, be criminals. That way we can eat something more than protein mash with a healthy side of protein sauce and, you guessed it, protein mash cake for desert."

"Criminals?" The captain's hand went to his throat. "Why Timmons, I'm offended. We are *salvagers*."

"Oh, in that case I should contact the nearest Alliance base and inform them that one of their vessels is dead in space." Timmons moved his hand towards the communication board.

"Now, now, let's not be too hasty. We need to make sure that this is an Alliance vessel. Wouldn't want to embarrass ourselves in front of the big boys."

"Oh, yeah, because besides the fact that it has an Alliance transponder, is an Alliance design, and is painted in Alliance colours, it could easily be a Federation cruiser." Timmons rolled his eyes.

"Exactly. Doin' my civic duty and checking."

"Just go be a criminal."

"If you insist," Hellnich said with a bow. "Just remember: criminals live longer than heroes."

Captain Hellnich made his way off the command deck. The *Marked Man* was a Xenon class trader that had seen better days, but Hellnich wouldn't trade her for the world. The lives of ten crewmen and their captain were infused in every bulkhead, loose wire, and hidey-hole. She wasn't the fastest or most manoeuvrable ship riding the Black but she got them where they needed to go and did it with panache. Hellnich swore up and down that no other ship in the Edge had as much style as his old girl.

Marcus caught up with him in the passageway leading down to the fully loaded cargo hold. He wore two pistols, a knife, and a heavy bolt rifle over one shoulder, and that was just what was visible. Hellnich knew there were more weapons secreted about Marcus's person. He was a rather large black man, so Hellnich could only guess how many weapons he had hidden.

Marcus bore the ritual scarring of a ganger from Sigma Delta IV. Despite his rough exterior and taciturn nature, he had a heart of gold. Hellnich sometimes forgot this when he looked upon his crewman. The man looked like he'd give a charging rhinox pause.

"Your husband is worried," Hellnich said by way of a greeting.

Marcus grunted. "Don't worry if he worries. Worry when he isn't worrying. That probably means he ain't got a heartbeat."

"There's two things he's good at: flying and worrying," the captain said.

"Well, there are a couple more you don't know about." Marcus favoured the captain with one of his rare grins and punctuated it with a wink.

"I don't need to hear this!" The captain covered his ears.

"What doesn't he need to hear?" Briggs asked, joining them from the direction of the mess. She was wearing a sleeveless black shirt with a tattoo of a phoenix with two assault rifles, her special forces unit insignia, prominent on her right shoulder. She wore camo pants and combat boots. Briggs had a large handgun holstered on one hip and a vibroblade sheathed on the other. Hellnich would have called her cute if he didn't think she'd hand him his balls for the compliment.

"All the things that Timmons is good at," Marcus said.

"Capt'n's right, unless you feeling like sharing him," Briggs said with a wink.

"Not on your life!" Marcus said with a full throated laugh. "Something might reach out from between your legs and I might not see my poor Timmons ever again."

"Oh, aye, I hear that a gravity well set up shop where her legs meetup!" Hellnich quipped. "If we made a map, her crotch would be the section that said 'Here there be monsters!'"

"You two really know how to make a girl blush..." Briggs said, batting her eyes and smiling. Her hands were a blur as she struck both men on the back of the head.

"We deserved that," Hellnich said, grinning.

"Aye, but it was worth it, Capt'n," Marcus replied, his grin equally as big.

The banter continued until they reached the cargo hold. Hellnich turned towards the two and said, "How would you like to take the combat suits out for a test drive?"

Briggs and Marcus looked at each other. Briggs spoke first. "You aren't messing with us, are you, Captain? I mean, don't fuck with my emotions like that. You said the words combat suits and I just got moist between my legs."

"What she said, except without the between the legs stuff. I don't get that kinda excited for this sort of stuff." Marcus was already putting his rifle down carefully.

"Gotta find something to get excited about. Otherwise, my crotch is as dry and barren as that one desert planet we visited. Menastus II?" Briggs looked from Marcus to Hellnich.

"No, that was that damnable swamp planet. One eternal bog from horizon to horizon," Hellnich responded. "Maybe Terragor?"

"You're both wrong," Timmons's nasally voice came over the intercom, "it was Malchior."

"Oh, yeah," the other three said in unison.

"We better get this show on the road before Mum starts lecturing," Hellnich said in a stage whisper, winking at the other two.

"Wouldn't want that," Briggs said dryly. She walked over to three large crates and pulled a panel on one, revealing a keyboard. She keyed in a sequence which caused it to unfold, an armoured space suit revealed within. "This is the Mercury Rising Mark IV Multi-Environment Tactical Combat Suit. It boasts a number of enhancements, from magnetic boots to strength augmentation. These babies do everything but shit for you. They even come with an ablative nanite armour energy dispersion. It will allow you to take a few hits but requires time and raw materials to recharge afterwards."

"Damn, Briggs, I think that's the longest coherent sentence I've ever heard you say," said Marcus. "You must be excited."

"Well, you know our girl, she gets excited for all the... mechanical things." Timmons roared in laughter.

"Timmons, shut it." He turned and glared at Briggs and Marcus. "You two get your asses in those suits." When both stood there stock still, Hellnich yelled, *"Какого хуя ты ещё тут стоишь?* I said get in those suits!"

They snapped into action. Briggs opened the other two crates as Marcus disrobed and stepped on the platform of the open crate. A red laser light scanned across his body, the suit syncing up to his body, enlarging to cover his bigger form. Marcus spread his legs and held his arms out wide, the suit opening up from the back. Marcus moved forward and the suit slid onto his body, conforming itself to him. A HUD lit up the inside of his helmet and he felt the suit tighten until it had closed across his back and was snug over his entire frame. As the other two were getting scanned, Marcus started stowing weapons, the suit accommodating by growing pockets.

Soon, all three were suited up and in the airlock. Briggs tapped the inside of her wrist and a holographic keyboard lit the inside of her arm. She punched a few keys and looked up to the other two in the airlock. "Comms check."

"Aye," Hellnich said, Marcus echoing him.

"Good." She flipped her arm palm down and pointed at a gauge displayed on her sleeve. "Each suit holds twelve hours of air."

"That should be plenty. Don't plan to let any dust settle on us. In and out, that's the plan, the Alliance none the wiser." Hellnich smiled through his visor.

"Oh, great, why'd you have to come up with a plan? When have any of those ever worked out for us?"

"You know what Marcus? If you weren't a large ox of a man that I'm afraid could twist me into a pretzel, I'd have some very strong and not so nice words for you. But since I am afraid of you, all I'm going to say is that was a good one." Hellnich clapped Marcus on his shoulder.

"Awwww... sir, I just want you to know that I feel the same way," Marcus said, a big grin crossing his face but quickly replaced with a serious expression. "I think I could twist you like a pretzel, too."

Briggs and Hellnich howled in laughter.

"Uhhh, you three realise that the rest of us can hear you, right?" Timmons voice broke across the comms. "And you are aware just how absolutely crazy you guys sound? I mean, next time we dock, I'm thinking we need to set up some appointments to get your heads examined."

"Honey, you need to leave the sexy talk in the bedroom, not parade it out before a mission. Can't be all hot and bothered, especially in these new suits." Marcus cleared his throat.

"Let's just say that there's not much left to the imagination," said Briggs.

"Briggs, quit checking out my husband's goods!" Timmons practically shouted across the comms.

"Hey, I can look at the menu as long as he doesn't let me order anything." Briggs arched her eyebrow seductively. "Right, big boy?" She moves her lips in such a way as to accentuate each word.

"Now, kids," Hellnich said, giving a meaningful glare to both Briggs and Marcus, "you know what they say. It's all fun and games until someone with an automatic weapon gets their feelings hurt. Now, it's time to get our salvage on."

"Sounds good, boss." Briggs sauntered over to the control panel. "Depressurizing airlock!" she yelled, slamming her fist onto a big, red button. There was a hiss of air escaping. "Deactivating artificial gravity." She slapped another button and the three began to float. Each pressed a holo button on their suit. With an arc of electricity, their boots magnetised and they dropped to the floor. "Opening doors!" With the final button press, the doors of the airlock retracted, exposing the trio to space.

Hellnich looked over the *Sweet Egress*. He wasn't impressed; it was too boxy, had too many hard angles. The Alliance had always favoured function over form. Hellnich always thought that a ship should be like a lady. Soft curves. Something about the ship nagged at the edge of his perception. "There's something wrong here. She don't look right."

"It's the holes, Capt'n," Marcus said, "they're blown outward."

"дерьмо," the captain said under his breath, "they did this to themselves." Nausea rose from the pit of his stomach. This wasn't a good sign.

"What are those?" Briggs asked, pointing to gouges in the hull that surround each hole.

"What the hell happened here?" Marcus said. He fidgeted with his rifle.

"Doesn't matter," the captain said, pointing at the derelict. "There is salvage in there, and I mean to have it. Whatever catastrophe these fools landed themselves in isn't our concern. Timmons, I need a line across."

"You got it, Capt'n." A pod door opened to the side of the retracted doors and a grapple line with steel cable shot out. The magnetic head of the grapple struck the derelict's hull next to one of the gaping breaches. The cable began to retract until all the slack had been taken up. "Grapple secure, Capt'n!"

"Well, guess it's time to ge—" Hellnich started.

"Woah!" Briggs shot past Hellnich, disengaging her boots and leaping toward the derelict. With a button press, she released short bursts of air, propelling her forward, eating the distance quickly. Her arms were tight against her side, legs closed. Her trajectory would take her right through the hole. At the last possible second, she tucked and flipped, hitting the floor on her feet and skidding across.

"She's such a show off," Marcus said.

Before Hellnich could reply, Marcus was out the airlock, shooting across the space between the two ships. The captain simply shook his head. After a moment, he jumped out of the airlock.

Hellnich was through the hole in the *Sweet Egress* faster than he anticipated and slammed against the deck. Luckily, the lack of gravity stole most of the force of the collision and the combat suit absorbed the rest. He ungracefully made it to his feet but floated a few feet off the ground until he banged into a bulkhead. Cursing, he activated his boots.

"Captain, that was..." Briggs snickered as she spoke, "graceful." She was walking the perimeter of one side of the hallway they were in, weapon out, eyes darting here and there, alert. "Clear."

On the other side, Marcus was mirroring her, his heavy bolter leading. "Clear," he called out.

A man's voice broke over the comms. He sounded excited. "Captain, I was able to get the sensor array up and running!"

"About damn time, Barclay!" the captain snapped.

"Sorry, captain. I mean, how was I supposed to know that if I took them offline to run some tests they were going to break down?" Barclay said sheepishly.

"What do I pay you for?" There was a long pause, as if Barclay was thinking about the question. "It isn't a trick question! You are our engineer, I pay you to keep my ship up and running."

"And the ship is up and running. There was just this one tiny problem with the sensors..."

Hellnich went to massage his temple but realised his helmet prevented him from doing so. "Was there something else you were going to tell me?"

"Oh, yes, the reactor is still running." Barclay sounded pleased.

"I should hope it is still running, again, that is what I'm paying you for!"

"No, not on our ship. Well, I mean, yes, the reactor on this ship is running but that isn't what I'm talking about. The reactor on the other ship is still running." Barclay rushed through the words so quickly that by the end he was out of breath and breathing heavily.

"Then why is all the power out?"

"I don't know. There is something running interference between the sensors and the reactor. I'm only getting minimal readings. But it's on."

Hellnich mulled this over. "Okay, keep me posted." He turned to the others and opened his mouth to speak when the receiver once more cut in.

"Captain, one more thing. The forward cabins are still pressurised on the ship. I'm reading life support."

"Well, folks," the captain said, "I think we are heading to the forward compartments."

The two nodded and closed ranks around the captain, making their way to the forward section of the ship. They arrived at the access airlock between the front and rear decks of the ship. The first door was bent inward.

"Damn!" Hellnich cursed. "Timmons, is there another airlock leading to the forward cabins? There is a big, *Хуевый* hole in the first pair of stinkin' doors."

Marcus shouldered his bolter and stopped to examine the hole in the door. The metal had been pried back but at the edges, it was melted and looked as if it had been chewed on. Marcus peeked inside the airlock then stepped back, swung his rifle to his hands, and swore under his breath. "Capt'n, you might wanna have yourself a look over here."

The captain looked over to Marcus and, seeing his harrowed expression, went over to look through the door. Inside was a man's body. Hellnich assumed it was a man. The body was desiccated almost to the point of dust. A large hole erupted from the centre of the corpse's chest. "What the hell?"

"Capt'n, that ain't right," Marcus said, glancing around the corridors, his eyes darting at the shadows.

"No." The captain gathered himself. He drew his own weapon. "No, it is not. Let's get to the other airlock."

The trio were uncharacteristically silent as they made their way through the ship to the other airlock, fear dogging their every step. Past the hole in the side of the ship, darkness reigned, the only illumination came from lamps on either side of each person's helmet. Weapons leading, they examined and re-examined every shadow for any abyssal terrors which may be hidden within. The walk was long, each step weighed down by the unknown horror lurking somewhere beyond their field of view.

There was a collective sigh of relief when the other airlock came into sight and it was undamaged.

"Finally," Hellnich said, "something blows our way."

As the other two turned down the hall, standing guard, Hellnich holstered his Viper and worked the door controls. Though he would never admit it, he was relieved that after only a moment the door slid silently open. "Let's get in."

They piled into the airlock quickly, not looking at each other lest they see their fear mirrored in their comrade's eyes. The door shut silently and, after a moment, there was a hiss of air as the cabin pressurised. Each let go of the breath they had been reflexively holding in.

"This mission has gone upside down then been fucked sidewise, hasn't it?" Briggs said, breaking the silence blanketing them. She laughed but it wasn't a healthy laugh, it was tinged with hysteria.

Marcus and Hellnich glanced at one another as their hearts fell to the floor. Briggs was the crazy one, the one who laughed in the face of danger no matter the odds. If this ship was getting to her, they were deeper than either wanted to admit. The inner doors slid open, saving them from further reflection. The captain was the first to retract his helmet's faceplate. He took a deep breath, the air stale and metallic tasting. The others followed suit.

"You two, head to the mess. See what can be salvaged. Load up any replicator packs and parts that you can find. We're due for an upgrade." Hellnich grinned but didn't really feel it. "Meet me on the bridge, I'll see what we can salvage there and then we'll see if we can scrounge anything out of engineering after that."

Marcus looked unsure. "Capt'n, you sure you we should separate?"

"No," the captain said. He forced another smile. The oppressive nature of the ship was weighing on him more but he refused to let it show. "I also don't want to spend any more time on this boat than is absolutely necessary. So, step lively and don't dawdle."

Marcus nodded his assent and followed Briggs to the galley, which was the first door in the hallway they were in.

Hellnich felt his heart tighten in his chest as he watched his crewmates disappear through the doorway. He pushed down his feelings of impending dread and walked stiff-backed down the hall to the bridge. He stopped at the end of the hallway, in front of the door, and took a deep breath. He pressed the door controls and the door opened with a swoosh.

Inside all was silent. The captain swung his head, letting the light illuminate the darkened bridge. He sucked in his breath when he saw... nothing. Just dust and dead equipment. There were cobwebs hung like Old World Halloween decorations back before the war which spawned the Federation and Alliance. "Spiders," Hellnich muttered to himself, "Why'd they have to have spiders?"

He brushed aside some cobwebs in his way and found them to be extraordinarily sticky. He pulled his arm back and the servos in his combat suit worked overtime to provide the necessary force to tear the web. He shook his hand frantically when he saw a spider about two inches across gleaming in the light of his headlamp on the palm of his hand. He dislodged it and it struck the ground with a ping. He immediately raised his boot and stomped. The spider died with an audible crunch.

He tried to refocus his mind but was hard put because he felt tiny pin pricks all over his skin, as if hundreds of little legs crawled all over his body. His imagination was getting the better of him. He could sense thousands of eyes watching him from the shadows which draped the room. His heart threatened to break open his sternum and pound through his skin.

He took some calming breaths. After a moment, he moved forward, his boots stirring up the dust which layered the entire bridge. He pulled out a slim metal disc from one of the combat suit's many pockets and threw it down toward the ground. It stopped about a foot off the ground and unfolded into a box that hovered there. He pushed it next to the first console: navigation.

The console had no power. He pulled out some tools and opened it up. Much of it had been destroyed but he salvaged whatever good bits of equipment he could find, throwing them in the crate. Once he was done, he went to the next console.

For the next hour, he worked that way, moving from console to console, salvaging what he could. Each console was in the same state of disrepair. The whole time, the hairs on the back of his neck stood at attention. He couldn't shake the feeling of being watched.

Hellnich was surprised to see the last console was still serviceable. It had been merely switched off rather than destroyed. He tried to boot it up but it wasn't getting enough power to fully start. He pulled out a portable generator, a slim stick, no more than three inches long, and spliced it into the power cable. Hellnich slipped a matrix crystal into the console's data port, hoping to download what he could before scrapping the console.

The console hummed to life and the captain began transferring system files to his matrix crystal. As he waited, he began randomly looking through files, trying to determine what was going on with the ship. He found the ship had been a secret science vessel conducting experiments the Alliance wanted to keep off the books. Everything from weapons testing to genetic modification. He puzzled over schematics and notes but knew that he would be unable to make heads or tails of the information there.

He started sifting through video logs. He booted one up and turned his attention to the holoprojector on the console board. A miniature man, no more than ten inches tall, appeared. He was dressed in a lab coat and had a severe look about him. He was perfectly coiffed with slick black hair and a goatee he could have used to stab someone.

"We realise that our specimen's only limitation in growth is age, food availability, and size of habitat. As the war with the Aldineans rages on, we can only hope that our efforts are in time to save the human race. We are still years away from..."

The captain hit stop on the playback. *War with the Aldineans? That was over fifty years ago,* he thought. He looked about the bridge, wondering how long it had floated here. *What was the Alliance up to?*

He jumped forward in the logs.

"The specimen shows increased agility, speed, and cognition. It is getting far closer to the creature the Aldineans once worshipped and feared in a shorter time span than I could have hoped for. Many of my lab techs are afraid of our success. I must admit, even I find myself a little bit leery when entering the lab. Specimen 1136 especially seems to stare at me with a particular brand of maliciousness. We have separated it from the rest of the specimens as it shows particularly high episodes of aggression and has eaten many of the other specimens..."

Hellnich found another log dated for a month later.

"Success! Specimen 1136 has grown to sufficient size where we attempted the bonding process with the bio-metal. I had kept my expectations in check as the success rate we had calculated was so low, I didn't want to entertain any false hope. But Specimen 1136 continues to exceed our expectations."

The next one Hellnich looked at was for a week later.

"We have lost one of our lab techs. Kyle O'Grady will be missed. Kyle observed Specimen 1136 on the floor of her containment cell, on her back, showing no signs of life. He deactivated the shield, ignoring safety protocol, to check on it. When he entered the cell, Specimen 1136, which had apparently gained the ability to bud and had split itself into multiple smaller versions of itself, quickly sprang from various hiding places inside its containment cell and took down Kyle quickly. I ordered the protective barrier raised, lest Specimen 1136 escape. His screams haunt my sleep..."

Hellnich found the last entry, only a few days after the previous, and keyed it in. The entry had a lot of static and some of the words were hard to make out.

"<Bzzzrip> Specimen 1136 has escaped. It seems it was smarter than we thought. It mimicked a lab tech, Osahara. We didn't know it could do that. When the other techs and scientists on duty saw Osahara trapped inside the containment cell, they deactivated the force shield. <crackle> Specimen 1136 had apparently been budding to keep us unaware of exactly how big it truly was...<crackle> We have blown sections of the rear compartment, hoping to kill Specimen 1136, but that seemed to only slow it down. It has adapted to the airless environment! It won't be long now, we can hear it in the bulkheads. Whatever gods watch over us..."

The holorecording cut off there, the words just hanging in the air. "Barclay, I need an up-to-date sensor sweep of the ship!" he barked into his comm.

"Ummm, boss, there seems to be a problem with the sensor," Barclay replied.

Hellnich could hear him cringing through the comms. "What do you mean?"

"I don't know, I'm getting life sign readings all over the boat. Hell, there are twelve life signs surrounding you on the bridge."

Hellnich engaged his helmet's faceplate. "Barclay, I need you to send those sensor readings to our HUD displays," Hellnich whispered. "Timmons, prep us for leaving. Briggs and Marcus, meet me on the bridge now. Take what you got, leave what you don't. Quickly now." The captain carefully drew his Viper and scanned the shadows, trying to pierce the darkness.

"But, sir, we're in the middle of raiding their armoury. This place has guns I haven't even seen before!" Briggs chirped across the comms, her excitement palpable.

"Get here now, that's an order!"

"Aye, aye, captain," Briggs responded smartly.

Hellnich went back to scanning the bridge. His HUD display lit up with the sensor sweep Barclay had performed. Try as he might, he could not find any of the life signs. Then he heard it. It was a sort of skittering coming from above and below. He looked down at the floor and swore loudly.

Hellnich was startled by a thick throated yell and a burst of autofire. "Marcus?" he shouted. "Briggs, report!"

"Captain, they got Marcus in the leg! They're fast, we can't get a bead on them. I don't even know what they look like, all I see is a flash of light and they're gone." Briggs was breathing heavily. "We're almost to the door."

Hellnich ran to the door and slammed his fist against the door control as another spat of autofire sounded. The door swooshed open, revealing Briggs supporting Marcus under the shoulder. Both moved down the corridor backward, heads and guns on a swerve. They were followed by two floating crates full of salvage they had managed to get. Hellnich moved to the side, letting them through, then stepped in front of them, watching for any pursuit as the door closed.

"We got to get off this boat." The captain bent down to examine Marcus's wound. Whatever had gotten him had gone clean through his thick thigh but hadn't hit the bone. Hellnich smiled. He grabbed Marcus by the back of the neck, pressing forehead to forehead. "You aren't going to die."

"Good thing, too, Capt'n. Timmons would kill me," Marcus said, grinning through gritted teeth.

The skittering intensified. Hellnich tried to put it out of his mind. "We really need to get off this boat," he repeated.

"We can't, his suit is torn," Briggs said, gesturing at Marcus's leg. "The suit has a self-repair function but it's going to take a little bit."

"Just go. Leave me my guns, give me a few extra clips, and you two hump it to the ship." Marcus said. He smiled. "Tell Timmons he can kill me in the next life."

Hellnich and Briggs looked at one another. "That's a bad plan," Hellnich stated.

"Horrible," Briggs agreed.

"We'll have to call that Plan F. You have my permission to execute Plan F when Briggs and I are dead."

The captain and Briggs bumped forearms. "Till the end, where the air is clean..." Briggs said.

"...the alcohol is real..." Marcus continued. His face was a mask of pain.

"...and the food is grown, not manufactured," the captain finished.

"You two are crazy, you know," Marcus said.

"You are cut from the same cloth, don't act like you wouldn't do the same for us," Hellnich said with a smile.

"Briggs, sure. You?" Marcus shrugged, looking at Hellnich. "I'd have to say, I'd let you die and take the ship."

"Same," Briggs said, grinning from ear to ear.

"You two lazy scavvers need to get your own ships, so I can say the same thi—"

The ear piercing rending of metal interrupted the captain. The three wheeled about to see a pointed appendage puncture the door leading to the hallway. It was easily as thick as a human arm and had a metallic sheen. It was jointed and Hellnich was sure that he knew what Specimen 1136 had been before all the experiments.

He reacted first, fear spurring his reaction, levelled his heavy repeater, and squeezed off three rounds in quick succession. Each had minimal effect. Frantically, Hellnich fired off another two shots with the same results.

Briggs searched through one of the crates and pulled an odd looking laser rifle. "Captain," she said, throwing the rifle to him.

Hellnich dropped his gun and caught the weapon. He immediately put it to his shoulder and squeezed the trigger. A sickly green beam shot forth, striking the intruding appendage. The limb glowed green for a moment before the metal sheen slipped off, the metal puddling on the floor, revealing the hairy leg beneath. The creature chittered and the leg retreated through the hole. A moment later, an eye peered through the hole and the creature trilled, loud and angry.

A loud boom echoed through the bridge and the eye disappeared in a mist of yellow goo. Marcus, still seated on the floor, lowered his rifle. "At least we know the damn things can be killed. What the hell are they?"

The sound of movement from inside the walls and outside the room intensified.

Hellnich shuddered at the noise. "One of the Alliance's mad science projects. Meet Specimen 1136, the answer to the Aldinean Conflict." The captain was looking at the rifle, turning it over in his hands, and noticed that the only light on it had gone from green to a blinking red.

"That war was nearly fifty years ago!" Briggs said.

"Yeah, but something like that is a gift that just keeps on giving." The captain shook his head. "I think this rifle is out of juice. Got any more?"

Briggs looked at the crate, moved a couple of things, and shook her head.

Timmons's voice cut in through the comms. "Sir, I know you got your hands full, but we have a situation. Those life signs aren't staying on your side, they're coming across the grapple."

"Shit. Disengage the grapnel. The whole line, then move to a safe distance. Wait for further instructions, can't have those damn things getting on our ship." Hellnich's eyes gathered the other two's gazes. They both understood that the odds of getting off the boat had decreased drastically.

"Aye, aye, captain." Timmons's voice was shaky but he was keeping it together. "Be safe."

Hellnich turned to his companions. "Options?"

"We can blow the airlocks open and the forward section would explosively decompress. We'd still have to wait for his suit to repair, though."

"How long?" Hellnich tried to remain calm, but he couldn't keep the agitation from his voice. He hated spiders.

"Hard to say, captain. Five, maybe ten minutes? His wound looks like it's stopped bleeding, so we can retask the nanites there to assist with the repair, that might cut a couple of minutes off the time." Briggs looked thoughtful. "I think there is something I can do to make it even faster."

The captain nodded.

Marcus cut in, "Guys, Plan F. Seriously, you can't put everyone in danger for me. I knew the ri—"

"That'll be quite enough out of you." Hellnich turned to Briggs. "Do what you need to do, I'll see what kind of defence we can mount."

He moved over to the first crate the other two had brought. It was full of replicator packs and a replicator unit. He shut the lid and moved on to the second. It was full of ammo, weapons, and what looked like explosives. He pulled one out. He grabbed the matrix crystal and slotted it into his suit. He grinned when he pulled up the weapon schematics.

"I think I got—" he dropped the explosives when he turned and grabbed at a rifle in the crate. He picked up an ammo mag and slammed it home.

On the other side of Marcus and Briggs was Specimen 1136. At least one part of it. A big part of it. Specimen 1136 was the size of a small elephant, eight legs radiating from a bulbous central body. Each leg was a scythe, impatiently waiting to rend flesh from bone. On top of the head were four eyes, two smaller ones that stared straight forward and two larger ones that moved independent of each other. All of it was made of some sort of fluid metal.

Hellnich cut loose and bullets poured from the barrel of the gun. Each struck the mutant spider with tiny pings, ricocheting off. To the captain's surprise, Specimen 1136 backed off, raising its two front legs and its head defensively. Hellnich thought it strange until he realised what it was doing. "Briggs, go for the eyes! It is trying to protect its eyes!"

Startled by the sudden burst of gunfire, Briggs was slow to react. Marcus, on the other hand, fired his rifle. Most of the shots flew wide, only two hitting their target. Specimen 1136 backed up further, even though most of the shots missed.

Then came the retort of a single shot. Briggs grinned to see that she'd hit. One of the larger eyes exploded. The spider reared onto its hind legs and screeched. It backed itself into the wall.

"Briggs, how much longer?"

"Maybe thirty seconds, sir!"

"Everyone, boots and helmets on!"

The other two complied without question. The captain took careful aim, using the HUD to assist. Three rapid fire bursts rocketed toward the spider and missed. Hellnich grinned as the bullets hit the bulkhead behind Specimen 1136, boring straight through the hull.

A sudden outrush of air as the vacuum sought to claim what air remained on the ship. Specimen 1136, reared back as it was, was unable to find a solid grip and overbalanced, smashing into the bulkhead behind it. It was stuck, legs flailing uselessly.

"That should hold it. Let's set these charges and prepare to blow thi—"

A horrendous crunching and cracking sound filled the bridge. Hellnich turned in time to watch Specimen 1136 invert itself, its body realigning itself until its belly was pressed against the hole in the wall, its eight legs now pressed against the wall on either side of the hole. It dug its legs in either side of the hole and started to pry itself loose.

Hellnich fired at the wall around Specimen 1136's legs. Briggs and Marcus realised what the captain was doing and followed suit. Their bullets chewed through the wall, weakening its structure until the whole piece was torn from the ship, sucked out into the void of space with the giant spider attached to it.

"Timmons, I need you to swing our ship to the other side, we're about to make our exit." Hellnich grabbed the explosives, setting timers as he went, dropping three bundles on his way to the door. He turned and put three bullets in the remaining console, turning off the ship's artificial gravity system. He nodded with his head to open the door.

In the corridor, floating spiders filled the space. Opening fire, they pushed the spiders to clear a path. They marched down, guns blazing, howling madly into their comms.

As they passed a door marked 'ENGINEERING,' Hellnich hit the door control. Inside, as he suspected, was the main bulk of Specimen 1136 wrapped around the reactor, easily the size of a small shuttle. Both pulsed with a light blue light. He pulled out his final explosive, set it, and gave it a push into the room. It slowly floated toward the gargantuan metal spider.

He hastened to catch up to his companions. They had made the port side observation window. He motioned to Marcus and said, "Blow it!"

Marcus shot the glass, the bullets causing the window to fracture and web with cracks. Grunting, Marcus charged the glass, disengaging his boots at the last moment, and slammed into the window with his shoulder leading. It shattered, throwing Marcus into space.

Briggs and the captain turned to follow. Before they leapt out of the window, another Specimen 1136 flew at them from the ceiling, catching Briggs on the shoulder, causing a small tear. As it headed for the floor, it lashed out with its other foreleg and caught Hellnich in the leg, opening a tear from hip to boot. Both went careening out the window.

The leaking air propelled the captain into Briggs and he grabbed at her. The tear on her shoulder was small, probably an inch, but he noticed it wasn't closing. "Why isn't your tear closing?"

"I transferred my nanites to Marcus to speed up the process."

"Shit." He knew that he had seconds, his oxygen sieving out his suit. He slapped his hand over the open tear in Briggs's suit.

"No!" Briggs shouted but it was too late, the nanites had been transferred. Captain Hellnich blew out the breath from his lungs before darkness descended.

* * *

He woke up in medbay. Briggs stood over him. "I wanted to be the first thing you saw when you woke up," she said. "You are an idiot." She promptly slapped him across the face.

"Owww!" he cried, grabbing his chin. "I saved you."

Briggs smiled. "I know." She bent over, bringing her face right up to his. "Thank you," she whispered. She laid a gentle kiss on his lips. She straightened up and bit her lip. "You should rest, captain."

Before she could walk away, Hellnich grabbed her arm and drew her back for another kiss. When he finally released her, he asked, "Did it work? Did those explosives stop Specimen 1136?"

Briggs looked down at him. "Yeah. We were lucky, Capt'n. I watched the *Sweet Egress* disintegrate before my eyes. Ain't ever seen anything like it. Barclay said that when it did, the reactor's containment was compromised. Whole thing went nova." Briggs snapped her fingers. "Like that. The secondary explosion was faster than that metal eating energy thingy. Blew us clear before it ate our suits."

"Good." The captain sat back heavily on the bed. "Maybe I should get some rest."

Briggs nodded. As she walked out of medbay, she turned and said, "If you tell anyone about this, I'll kill you."

Yep, Hellnich thought, *definitely alive. That would have played out a lot differently if I was dead.*

* * *

It spun through the cold depths of space, careening slowly as it had in the days which followed the destruction of the Sweet Egress. *It had eaten the piece of ship blown into space with it long ago.*

Weeks, maybe months passed as it drifted. It had fallen into a dormant state, conserving energy. Finally, it was caught in the gravity well of a large asteroid, about the size of a small moon. It crashed onto the surface, and before it could be tossed into space once more, it reflexively sunk its legs into the ground, clutching at the asteroid. Its eyes opened and it surveyed its surroundings. It sensed minerals, things it could eat to regain its strength. The asteroid was honeycombed with passages throughout. It descended down, first to eat and then to wait. It may take years,

WORLD WAR FOUR

but eventually it would find something and when it did, Specimen 1136 would be ready.

Wake
K.K.Pieza

The day we run into the sea, the gulls wheel across a sky so blue it swallows the horizon and swallows us with it.

Broken shells and green-glass shards mark a path across the beach where our footprints once littered the sand. Now only a stick jutting up among a pile of seaweed declares our passage and it, too, will disappear with the coming tide.

Ribbons of sand curl around my toes as currents war against my chest. I stare at your back, at the shadow you make against the sky. Where the sunlight brims against the curve of your head, your hair runs in rivulets of molten fire that melt into a kaleidoscope of blue glass and golden sparks.

I want to touch you and feel the heat of your skin under the cold of the waves. I long to see your smile and inhale the musk of your skin through the confusion of brine and fear and uncertainty in which I am drowning.

In these last moments, I need your fingers twined through mine.

* * *

The night before the sea consumes us, we camp in the hills above the beach so we can listen to the crashing of waves and the soughing of the wind through the trees. Below us, the sea creeps over the sand, annihilating the shore an inch at a time. We sit beside the fire and watch ghosts shape themselves against the stars. I see our history in those forms. As they dissipate, I see the lives we might have lived if war had not sacrificed the world upon its altar.

The air chills our backs but our faces ache with the heat from the fire. The heat from your skin demands more attention, though. I lean into you and your arm shelters me from the certainty of what the morning will bring. Above us, the ghosts spin away into the night and fade to nothing.

"Sometimes, when you walk on the sand at night," you say, "it will light up under your feet and you can pretend you're walking through the stars."

I make a noise in my throat. My words are crushed under the weight of your arm.

"Wanna sleep on the sand tonight?" Your voice is as gentle as the distant surf.

You help me to my feet and lead me down the hill towards the crashing waves.

* * *

Three days out from the sea, I stand on the highest hill and look out towards the horizon. The sun burns shadows into my vision and I can feel it cooking my skin, but I want desperately to see the cool shimmering of the sea cradled among the distant cliffs.

You try to be patient by extending your arm to my left, to the east.

You say, "It's that way."

I turn my back on the falling sun, glad I can blame the heat for the flush in my cheeks. Stretching, I arch my neck and try to follow the line you have painted against the sky.

But because you aren't that patient, you say, "You won't be able to see it for a few more days."

Our future is small but I would like to see it. But you are squinting at me in through the sun. My shadow stretches across the grass and laps at your feet. The places we have travelled hide in the lines of your face. You don't want to look back any more than I do. There's nothing behind us worth looking at.

So we march down the hill like soldiers advancing on a city. Our marching song is the silence that plays between us. We have sung the same anthem since Cuneo. Words have become a burden we cannot carry for long. We can only speak of the past or what lies in the future and neither holds much comfort.

So we walk in silence until we are drowning in stars.

*   *   *

Out across the plain, Cuneo sparkles like broken bottles against a palomino sky. Raven smoke yet drifts like scattered clouds where once plumes of steam rose in probing fingers. Nothing moves. I hear no sound except our breathing and the wind lapping at our feet.

Your arms engulf me and I sink back against your chest as I stare at a place that should have meant safety.

Even in your arms, I don't know if I'm safe. I'm not safe inside my own head. I gag on the hate I feel as I stare at that smoking corpse of a city. How can I not hate every single soldier? I don't care what colour badge they wear. There is no such thing as ethics or morals when you are dropping fire on cities, when you are burning children.

I stare at Cuneo and scrub a filthy hand across my mouth, trying not to taste greasy smoke. There was never any safety here, never any in Vercelli or Turin. Just a lot of lies and the trough between crushing waves.

"Now what?" I say. "You promised, but fuck everything." I feel the hate burning away the last vestiges of hope. Even the heat of your skin cannot save me from the war inside me.

But you bury your face against my neck and I'm surprised by the comfort this brings me. I breathe you in and your scent fills me up, leaves no room for anything else.

"No," you say. The word shapes itself against my skin. "No. There's still somewhere left."

You aren't asking me to follow you; I don't have to do anything. But I already know where my peace lies.

*   *   *

We wake in the night to the sound of thunder and a flash of green light. You hurry me to my feet and order me to wait in the hollow beneath a fallen tree, as if there is any safety in small, dark places. I watch you run off into the night and the taste of fear coats my tongue like smoke.

I won't wait for you. I won't let you shut me away in a small, dark place while you run towards the green fire. So I slip from under the fallen log and follow you into the shadows of the trees.

The night drapes me like a blanket. The air hangs thick and silent with the wary birds. Shadows of trees criss-cross the burning horizon and these guide me toward you even when the darkness blinds my eyes.

With the moon at my back I pick out your figure sketched out against the green sky. I can tell by the shape of it you are weeping. The sound carries like the surf against the stones, a gentle keening, as though you have pressed your hands to your face. You don't struggle when I touch your shoulder, so I wrap my arms around you and let you cry into the crook of my neck. Your tears burn my skin but they cool quickly in the night air, making me shiver.

WORLD WAR FOUR

Below us, a sea of green fire rolls across Cueno. The sky above it reflects the flames and the wind carries the cries of the dying on the air.

I do not know who bombed the city. It doesn't matter. The dying don't care. They don't debate the finer points of ideologies as they writhe among the ashes of their lives. They simply burn and die and rot where they fall. Or they trudge on and on and hope to find some peace in all the dying.

My shirt is cold and stiff from your tears and God, I'm so tired. Do you have any idea how tired I am? I wrap you in my arms and watch the world burn while the night slips slowly towards morning.

*　　*　　*

We have been following the road for so long, we have become a part of it.

Clouds swell against a porcelain sky portending rain but summer heat shimmers over the road and my skin itches with sweat. I breathe in the smell of wet stone and melting rubber. The sound of our shoes slapping against the pavement rings in my ears as we weave between the hulking forms of rusted-out cars and abandoned artillery. How can something so broken with the memory of fighting lead to safety?

We shuffle down the banks of a gutter through clouds of biting flies. Sweat drips between my shoulder blades while I watch you poke at the water with a stick. Scum slicks its surface but I can see the current moving beneath and I trust you when you say, "It's safe, I think."

I break the scum and scoop handfuls of musty water into my mouth—splash it across my face and wet my hair to cut the coiling heat. From the corner of my eye, I see you do the same.

The way the sunlight throws sparks off your dripping hair reminds me of the sparks flying from the tents of the Turin camp. I think of the sweat on your brow, the frantic beating of your heart. I think I want to be angry still but the heat has baked it right out of me.

When we have drunk our fill, we lay side-by-side in the shade of an old car door. I slap an enterprising mosquito. You pillow your arms under your head. Our bellies grumble together about the state of the world.

I want to ask you where we're going, but after Vercelli I don't know how to trust any more. And maybe I can't believe there's anywhere left in the world that's safe anyways, except for here, pressed against your side in this exact moment. I work the words against my teeth but I'm weak against the silence and the droning flies and the heat you bleed into me. I can't find a single thing to say.

I rest my head against your shoulder and doze in the afternoon sun while we wait for the clouds to spill their rain and wash us away.

From somewhere very far away, I hear you mutter, "It's gonna be alright. I'll keep you safe."

And from equally far away, my voice comes back: "Together, yeah?" But maybe it's a dream. I don't know.

* * *

The trees stamp themselves across the horizon, jagged and dark against the vibrant wall of shimmering blue. I have painted you over that: grungy white t-shirt and red hair, swimming in shadows and sunlight while the green grass sways around your jeans.

Anger grips my heart again as I stare at your back. It does this every time I think about the Vercelli camp and the words I'm too afraid to say. Words I'm choking on because I can't scream them at you the way I should.

Bending my shadow over an anthill, I wonder at the lives I could destroy if I enjoyed crushing smaller, weaker things. Your hand brushes my shoulder and I flinch in spite of myself. There's so much fucking rage inside me, do you have any clue at all?

"Don't," you say. And only then do I realize I've raised my foot above the anthill. Like I could crush it. Like anything could destroy something so vast.

"Don't tell me what to do!" I snap but I lower my foot and drop my head back. I don't see any signs that someone is waiting to crush us underfoot.

You move away as though you understand I don't want you near. Maybe you *do* know how angry I am.

From the corner of my eye, I see your fingers twisting and tapping. You don't have any right after Vercelli to feel small and helpless. You don't get to be afraid of anything, especially of me.

"There are still other places," you say. "Other camps. If you'll give me another chance..."

In the distance, an upliner drifts lazily across the tree-line. I can't tell to which side it belongs or what it's hunting, but it doesn't matter anymore. It will kill us with the same disregard.

I don't want to give you another chance. I want this whole thing done and over with. I want the sight of you to be distant and memorable. I want you as safe as you say you want me.

"How long will it take?" I rub the back of my hand across my mouth but the taste of anger won't be cleansed. I can't take my eyes from the upliner. It's pointed towards Vercelli.

"Two, maybe three days," you say. "It's the last time I'll ask, I promise."

As you trudge towards the setting sun, I turn and stare in the direction of the upliner one more time. I can't see it any more, but I know the scent of smoke will punctuate the rising moon.

In my wake, terrified ants scramble around the remains of a crushed anthill.

* * *

The camp spreads across the valley like an open wound. The river wends sluggishly through it, lazy with pollution and late summer mud. The memories of rice paddies still scar the land and the flies are energetic. They attack as we scramble over crumbling barriers and we slap at them with the same kind of vigour. It's a smaller, more personal war, but just as immediate.

The towers of a chapel cast long shadows over the camp. There were a lot of chapels in Vercelli, just as there had been in Turin. Now the chapels have become aid centres in a city overflowing into a camp drowning in people. Walls encircle the camp and outlying shanty, shadowed against the shimmering sky. Razor wire glints in the afternoon sun. I feel the guns before I can see the guards. The familiarity sends a chill up my spine.

You squeeze my hand and I meet your eyes. You squeeze it again but it doesn't ease my anxiety. We are two people wandering into a foreign place that doesn't want us. Beggars at a rich man's door. I squeeze your hand back.

We never even make it into the shanty. Down at the gate, families with screaming children vie with wounded soldiers for a place in line. Guards pace the length, issuing orders and clapping anyone who gets too rowdy. I tune out the children and stare at the vets. This is the law of the world: you are only as good as you can give, and when you can give no more you are trash, just like the rest of us.

"They're giving preference to the kids." I can hear the uncertainty in your voice and I try not to give into despair.

"We're strong," I remind you, grinning to show my teeth. "They want workers. We'll be okay."

But we're not okay. When we get to the gate they examine us like we're cattle at auction and you're the one with the good hooves.

The guards motion you through the gate but stops me with a raised arm.

You grab my hand and pull me close. I try to pull away, but you tighten your grip. You pretend you don't see the way I'm glaring.

"Fuck that." Spittle flies from your lips. "We're family. We go together."

"Then don't go," the guard says. He looks past you and motions a one-armed soldier forward. I know they'll turn the man away—by the look on his face, he knows it too—but it doesn't ease my rage, not at them and especially not at you.

As we walk back across the paddies dodging armies of angry flies, I think back to Turin, with its tents spread out across the marsh. The crowds of people sick on chaos and deprivation—where hunger ran as rampant as rats. I reach out and touch your face. Even the the texture of your skin has grown familiar against my fingers. Everything about you is familiar now, down to the way you hold me up when I fall. I should have expected this. That doesn't mean I have to forgive you for it.

* * *

WORLD WAR FOUR

Here, where we can lose ourselves in the vastness of the wide world, I drown my attention in the empty marshes and the ribbon of black stretching off into the blue. Your feet beat out a rhythm I can't quite match, but I keep trying, keep stumbling. And when you catch me, your fingers are soft and strong, patient where maybe I don't deserve it.

We pause in the evening, with the heat crushing our shoulders and clouds rising on the horizon. The air curls on our tongues, rich with leafy trees, burnt stone, and rotting meat. In the distance, shattered buildings crumble and smoke, judging us with empty eyes and silent, gaping mouths.

You shield your eyes against the bleeding sun and point and say, "Not that way."

Squinting, I realize the clouds are rising flies. "No." I taste bile.

We turn our feet away from the road and let the empty sky guide us through the grass. The silence between us rings louder for the crickets but the sight of empty buildings weighs on my mind. I watch your shadow stretching alongside my own, malformed with the shape of the pocked earth and dancing like a compass needle pointing the way. Who knows how to read a compass? I was never great at navigating.

Overhead, green lights drift across the settling sky. My stomach sinks with the sun. More people will die tonight. I have no choice but to trust you.

While the stars fall around us, I stumble to the sound of your feet and wait for you to catch me. Somehow, I know you will.

* * *

I can't see around the pain clogging my chest. I don't want to see. I don't want to know. The world spins and spins and spins.

The cries of the dying carry on the wind and fall around me, building up a crushing wave. Heat swarms me and screams batter my head. Bodies fly in and out of the dark and then hurtle away. The entire world contracts to the shape of the space inside me and even that overflows with smoke and the sound of sobbing.

Hands grip my shoulders. A voice rings from a million miles away. My burning eyes try to focus on a face but can't quite find the lines; they blur and melt and slip away, reforming over and over again. But the hands drag me away from the stinging heat and shake me. And then all at once the voice shatters the wall: "Come on. Hurry the fuck up!"

I feel the world collapsing down on me. You stand like a pillar trying to hold it in place. When you pull me to my feet, a sea sparks spins away behind you and takes the darkness with it.

My hand slides within yours as you yank me toward the road. The night stinks of uncertainty and questions with no answers. But even under all the shaking, I can feel the past burning away behind us, leaving nothing but ashes in our wake. I feel myself reforming around the shape of your hand.

The cries of the dying still drift on the wind but they fly past me now. They cannot settle as long as we are moving. The grief cannot overwhelm me as long as you are near. I don't know you, but I need you. You are peace.

"Come on," you say again. "I know a place. I'll protect you."

*   *   *

The waves lift me off my feet and drop me closer to you. My head dips below the water and salty water floods my throat.

I bob to the surface to see you struggling as well. Then another wave washes over us and the sea swallows us again.

You lied to me. There is no safety here. No peace. Beneath the surface, I struggle against the fire in my lungs. I flail my limbs, struggling to reach the surface, but the ribbons of current have tied me to the sandy floor. I will die here. The water will crush me to the ground and grind every memory into bits of sand. Then it will vomit me back up onto the beach to rot in the sun.

Warm skin brushes my shoulder and the heat of your hand presses my palm. I snatch after you greedily. Your fingers thread themselves through mine. When I open my eyes, your face is unlined and smiling. It's the most beautiful thing in the world.

AUTHORS BIOGRAPHIES

Zombie Pirate Publishing

Zombie Pirate Publishing was born in a backyard in a small country town in New South Wales, Australia, the product of lifelong friends. Both published authors, albeit in a small capacity, Adam Bennett and Sam M. Phillips decided to throw their hat into the ring as the people in charge. WORLD WAR FOUR is their sixth release, and many more are already in the planning stages. The response to the call for submissions was overwhelming, which made choosing which stories to include very difficult.

Keep an eye out for Zombie Pirate Publishing's next short story anthology, FULL METAL HORROR 2: A Bloodstained Anthology, available June 15th, 2019. To find out more visit zombiepiratepublishing.com.

Brian MacGowan - The Package

Brian MacGowan is a former Canadian Forces signals sergeant. While in the military he learned the important life skill of using various pieces of military equipment to open beer bottles. Brian, his wife and their daughters are currently living in his wife's home state of Indiana.

Heather Kim Hood - World War Foul

Heather lives near the Rockies in British Columbia, Canada with her trusty canine companion, Sam, and a number of critters (subject to change, excepting the alpaca). She has a degree is Psychiatric nursing and Herbalism. When not writing, she's out there defying nature and proving that disability is just another word. It doesn't mean life is over. You can follow her at www.facebook.com/WiseOldWomanoftheWoods

Adam Bennett - Jackson's Revenge

Seven billion years ago an O Class star exploded in the distant reaches of the Virgo Supercluster. Over the course of eons, particles of the star's dust spread through the universe until finally a series of them coalesced in New South Wales, Australia during the mid eighties. Thus was born the author and publisher Adam Bennett. His writing shows his yearning to return to his rightful home among the stars, a wish he will achieve, even if he has to wait until the heat death of the universe.

Find more of his writing at facebook.com/adambennettauthor/.

Neal Asher - Monitor Logan

Neal Asher was born in 1961 in Essex, Great Britain, and now divides his time between there and the island of Crete. He's been an SF and fantasy junky ever since having his mind distorted at an early age by JRRT, Edgar Rice Burroughs and E C Tubb.

Sometime after leaving school he decided to focus on only one of his many interests because it was inclusive of the others: writing. Finally taken on by a large publisher, Pan Macmillan, his first full-length SF novel, Gridlinked, came out in 2001, and now in total he has over 25 books to his name, also in translation across the world. He's also read more SF than some would style as healthy.
    http://theskinner.blogspot.com/
    http://nealsher.co.uk

Sam M. Phillips - Cold Fusion

    A prolific poet and fiction writer from Australia, Sam M. Phillips is the co-founder of Zombie Pirate Publishing. He has had dozens of short stories appear in anthologies and magazines such as Full Metal Horror, Rejected For Content 6, Full Moon Slaughter, 13 Bites vol. IV & V, and Dastaan World Magazine. He enjoys walking for enjoyment and exercise, reading lots of books, and playing drums in a death metal band. His poetry explores the human experience and his own inner world of creativity and insanity. You can read his work at www.bigconfusingwords.wordpress.com.

Mel Lee Newmin - Yuddh Ke Khel

    Science fiction and fantasy author Mel Lee Newmin is a native of Lancaster, Pennsylvania, USA, home of the Amish and not much else. Following careers in corporate accounting and technical writing for the defence industry, Mel began a new career as a fiction author with short stories appearing around the world in Ligurian Magazine, On the Premises, The Collapsar Directive, Full Metal Horror, Rapture, World War Four and many others. Mel also produces a popular weekly fiction blog about Niles Gule, vampire hunter and detective in Baltimore.

Rich Rurshell - Subject: Galilee

Rich Rurshell is a short story writer from Suffolk, England. Rich writes tales of Horror, Science Fiction, and Fantasy, and has had stories included in two other Zombie Pirate Publishing anthologies. Outside of writing, Rich likes to play music. He plays guitar, bass guitar, and ukulele. You can find links to all of Rich's stories at www.facebook.com/richrurshellauthor

Gregg Cunningham - War Pig

Gregg Cunningham 47, thinks he can, but finds the whole author thing rather tricky. Luckily he has good people around him at ZPP to make his dreams reality. Like his National football team Scotland, he dreams of playing on the world stage one day, but realises he'll have to wait just as long, if not longer to produce something really special.

https://cortlandsdogs.wordpress.com/about/

James Pyles - Joey

James Pyles is a published information technology and textbook author and editor. He also has a passion for theology and strength training, as well as reading and writing science fiction and fantasy. He has several new short stories being published in early 2019 and is currently working on his first full-length novel. Find out more at http://poweredbyrobots.com/

Blake Jessop - This Sky is Mine

Blake Jessop is a Pushcart Prize-nominated author of science fiction, fantasy and horror stories with a master's degree in creative writing from the University of Adelaide. You can read more of his speculative fiction in "Grimm, Grit and Gasoline" from World Weaver Press, or follow him on Twitter @everydayjisei.

David Bowmore - The Bunker

David Bowmore has lived here, there and everywhere, but now lives in Yorkshire with his wonderful wife and a small white poodle. He has worn many hats in his time; head chef, teacher and landscape gardener. Still new to the world of writing, he has been surprised by the reception some of his flights of fantasy have received. In 2018 'Sins of The Father' won best story in Vortex, published by Clarendon House.

www.davidbowmore.co.uk

Marcus Turner - The Lazarus Protocol

Marcus Turner is an Australian author of science fiction, grimdark and horror from Melbourne. He loves gaming (including VR), geeky board games, metal/emo/hardcore music, and is a devotee of H.P. Lovecraft dedicated to unleashing the wrath of the Great Old Ones. His first published story, A Spark of Youth, included in Australian Speculative Fiction's Beginnings anthology, was published in November 2018. You can follow him on his Facebook page or his web/blog site, streamofmadness.wordpress.com

L.T. Waterson - Poppy

L. T. Waterson lives in a house full of books on top of a hill in Southampton, England. She has been a journalist, an archaeologist and just generally curious. She writes whenever she can and her work has featured in anthologies from Clarendon House and Zombie Pirate Publishing.

James Agombar - Scum of the Earth

James Agombar resides near the treacherous waters of Southend-On-Sea, Essex, UK where visions of the speculative, criminal and supernatural have taken hold of his mind (usually alongside a bottle of whiskey). He is a fan of the short story and inspired by classic authors like Ray Bradbury and H.P Lovecraft. Occasionally he attempts a sci-Fi or steampunk story, but also has some travel essays published. His work can be found in various Anthologies from:

https://www.facebook.com/j.agombar.author/

D.M. Burdett - Tomorrow

DM Burdett was born in the UK, roamed as an army brat, and now lives in Australia where she tries to avoid drop bears. She has published a Sci-Fi series, had success with short stories (two with ZPP), and is currently working on a YA dystopian series. She has worked in software development for three decades and has published two children's series on the subject. A life of roaming the shores of Australia in her teardrop caravan calls to her but, until then, there always seems to be just one more software project to complete.

https://www.dmburdett.com

Shawn Klimek - The Floabnian Fiasco

Shawn M. Klimek is a globetrotting, U.S. military spouse, creative writer and butler to a Maltese puppy. His speculative fiction, humour, and poetry have been published in dozens of e-zines and anthologies, including "Gold: The Best of Clarendon House Anthologies, Volume One, 2017/2018 and ZPP's "Flash Fiction Addiction". Discover his current projects or publications at http://www.facebook.com/shawnmklimekauthor or www.amazon.com/author/shawnmklimekauthor.

Marlon Hayes - The Aftermath of the Pig Roast

Marlon S. Hayes is a writer, blogger, author, and poet from Chicago, Illinois. He spends his idle time staring at maps and going on trips. His current count is 47 states and eight countries, with more on the way. He can be found on Amazon, Facebook, and at marlonhayes.wixsite.com/author

R.L.M. Cooper - One Way Trip

R.L.M. Cooper is a summa cum laude graduate of the University of Alabama in Huntsville. A former computer scientist, she now spends her time writing poetry and fiction. Her work as been published in online magazines, literary reviews, and print anthologies both in the United States and abroad. She lives in the Pacific Northwest with her husband and a well-loved Tonkinese cat. For links to her other work, please visit her blog: https://rlmcooper.wordpress.com

Vince Carpini - Gagarin's Hammer

Vince Carpini is a Canadian author of fantasy and science fiction. He has previously been published in Zombie Pirate Publishing's "Witches vs Wizards: A Fantasy Anthology". You can find him on Twitter @VinceCarpini

G. Dean Manuel - Salvage

G Dean Manuel was born in the Philippines but currently resides in Kansas. He is a man of many varied interests: Role-playing, video games, reading, volleyball. In his spare time, he likes to read Sci-fi/Fantasy. He is a multi-genre writer who is currently working on a novel besides writing short stories. You can find him online at: www.gdeanmanuel.com

K.K. Pieza - Wake

K.K. Pieza grew up in the shadow of the Funeral Mountains, but has spent the last twenty years exploring the rain forest of Washington State in America. As proper car camper, K.K. travels across the US, searching the country's secret places and eating the very best food. When fate is willing, a ghost or road oracle might even show up for conversation at a roadside campsite.

You can visit K.K. Pieza online at www.facebook.com/dustandstars/

ACKNOWLEDGEMENTS

A special thanks to all of the people who submitted for this anthology. We here at Zombie Pirate Publishing enjoyed reading every story we were sent, and cannot wait to see what you all send us for our next anthology, FULL METAL HORROR 2: A Bloodstained Anthology, available June 15th, 2019. If you would like to submit stories to us please visit zombiepiratepublishing.com for submissions guidelines and email your double spaced indented word document to submissions@zombiepiratepublishing.com today.

To help support Zombie Pirate Publishing, please visit our Patreon page at patreon.com/zombiepiratepublishing and learn about our goals and become a patron for as little as $1 a month. We also have a merch store at zombie-pirate-publishing.myshopify.com where you can buy fantastic Zombie Pirate Publishing t-shirts, hoodies, mugs, and limited editions of our books.

Thank you to all of the people who have helped and supported us in any way since we started this crazy little venture. We couldn't do it without you. It is much appreciated. We are thrilled with the result thus far, and are excited to see what the future brings. There are big things coming for Zombie Pirate Publishing.

Cheers,
Sam M. Phillips and Adam Bennett

ZOMBIE PIRATE PUBLISHING

THANK YOU TO OUR PATREON SUPPORTERS

Lewis Rice
Stuart West
Andrew Bennett
Diane Bennett
Matthew Entwistle
Pavla Chandler
Heather Kim Hood
Austin P Sheehan
J DeWeese
G. Dean Manuel
Raylene Demeester
Bruce Rowe

Sign up to support Zombie Pirate Publishing at patreon.com/zombiepiratepublishing today. Every supporter helps us to work towards important goals.

THE COLLAPSAR DIRECTIVE

Twenty short stories from authors around the galaxy. A brutal dictator takes control of a broken and dying Earth. The last humans alive flee their dying galaxy travelling faster than the speed of light; their journey will last a thousand years. Humanity's newest super drug is being created in the most unscrupulous way imaginable. Rich neonobles take their hunting game deep into the slums in search of a more interesting prey: the poor. These are just some of the amazing stories in THE COLLAPSAR DIRECTIVE: A Science Fiction Anthology including stories from authors all around the galaxy.

Read a free preview at zombiepiratepublishing.com.

Available on Amazon.

RELATIONSHIP ADD VICE

Relationships are at the very core of who we are as human beings. They can pull us together, or tear us apart. Love lifts us up, and just as quickly drives us to madness, despair, and even into the murky depths of the criminal underworld. RELATIONSHIP ADD VICE is a thrilling blend of Crime and Romance, featuring more than twenty authors from around the world, twisted tales of life, lust, and lawlessness.

Read a free preview at zombiepiratepublishing.com.

Available on Amazon.

FULL METAL HORROR

There's something right behind you... You can feel its rancid breath on your neck, smell the blood dripping from its wicked fangs, sense its anticipation as you walk further from the house, confidently telling yourself you have no reason to fear the dark, that there is nothing there. You fight the urge to turn, fight the impulse to run, fight to keep your pace steady, but you are losing the battle. The monster is right behind you, and nothing you do can save you now. This is FULL METAL HORROR: A Monstrous Anthology, thirty five horrifying short stories from authors around the world, packed full of deadly monsters. Just remember, don't turn around...

Read a free preview at zombiepiratepublishing.com.

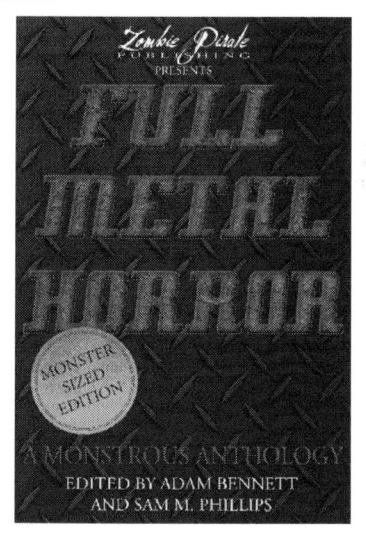

Available on Amazon.

WITCHES VS WIZARDS

The ground rumbles ominously, the earth surging and shifting to the iron will of the powers of old. Lightning sparks the air with forked tongue, darting between two venerable channelers, ragged yet regal, each wrestling wicked tempests to do their bidding. Their magicks are diametrically opposed, their powers equally limitless, their intentions shrouded in mystery; theirs is a battle for the ages. This surely means death for any mere mortal looking on. This is the beginning of the end. This is WITCHES VS WIZARDS. Packed with magical tales of pure unadulterated fantasy, this collection of short stories features eighteen authors from all around the world.

Read a free preview at zombiepiratepublishing.com.

Available on Amazon.

Printed in Great Britain
by Amazon